"Higgins scores again . . . Very few modern writers can grab you with their first paragraph and pull you into, and through, their story almost non-stop. Jack Higgins is one of them, and the old master is at it again in *Thunder Point*. Higgins is probably at his best in *Thunder*, another good read that mines the legends about Germany's Nazi regime of World War II . . . Readers have usually compared all of Higgins's subsequent work to his legendary *The Eagle Has Landed*. Now they've got a new touchstone."

—*Denver Post*

"A master of suspense . . . Jack Higgins weaves an original and imaginative tale that will delight his readers and win him many new ones."

—*United Methodist Reporter*

"A darn good read . . . I can heartily recommend *Thunder Point*."

—*Nashville Banner*

"When it comes to thriller writers, one name stands well above the crowd—Jack Higgins."

—*Associated Press*

"Higgins spins as mean a tale as Ludlum, Forsyth, or any of them."

—*Philadelphia Daily News*

Turn to the back of this book for a sneak preview of Jack Higgins's *SHEBA*—a novel of World War II intrigue, coming in January 1995.

THUNDER POINT

JACK HIGGINS

BERKLEY BOOKS, NEW YORK

THUNDER POINT

A Berkley Book / published by arrangement with
Septembertide Publishing, B.V.

PRINTING HISTORY
G. P. Putnam's Sons edition / June 1993
Berkley edition / September 1994

ISBN: 0-425-14357-0

BERKLEY®
Berkley Books are published by The Berkley Publishing Group,
200 Madison Avenue, New York, New York 10016.
BERKLEY and the "B" design
are trademarks belonging to Berkley Publishing Corporation.

PRINTED IN THE UNITED STATES OF AMERICA

10 9 8 7 6 5 4 3 2 1

For my daughter Hannah

Whether Reichsleiter Martin Bormann, Head of the Nazi Party Chancellery and Secretary to Adolf Hitler, the most powerful man in Germany after the Führer, actually escaped from the Führer Bunker in Berlin in the early hours of May 2, 1945, or died trying to cross the Weidendammer Bridge has always been a matter of conjecture. Josef Stalin believed him to be alive, Jacob Glas, Bormann's chauffeur, swore that he saw him in Munich after the war and Eichmann told the Israelis he was still alive in 1960. Simon Wiesenthal, the greatest Nazi hunter of them all, always insisted he was alive, and then there was a Spaniard who had served in the German SS who insisted that Bormann had left Norway in a U-boat bound for South America at the very end of the war . . .

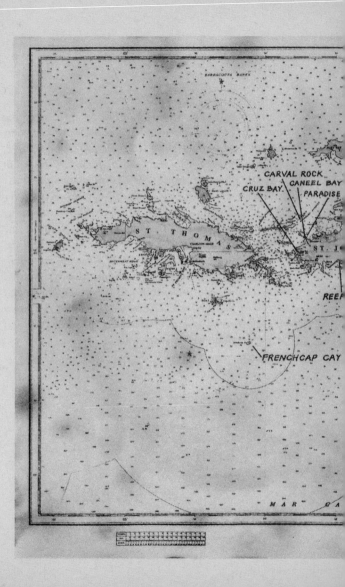

BARRACOUTA BANK

CARVAL ROCK
CANEEL BAY
CRUZ BAY
PARADISE

ST. THOMAS

ST. J

REEF

FRENCHCAP CAY

MAR CA

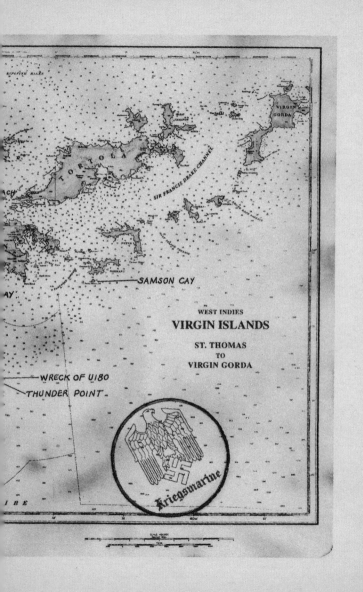

SAMSON CAY

WEST INDIES
VIRGIN ISLANDS

ST. THOMAS
TO
VIRGIN GORDA

WRECK OF U180
THUNDER POINT

VIRGIN
GORDA

TORTOLA

SIR FRANCIS DRAKE CHANNEL

Kriegsmarine

PROLOGUE

The city seemed to be on fire, a kind of hell on earth, the ground shaking as shells exploded, and as dawn came, smoke drifted in a black pall. In the eastern half of Berlin, the Russians were already formally in control, and refugees, carrying what they could of their belongings, moved along Wilhelmstrasse close to the Reich Chancellery in the desperate hope of somehow reaching the West and the Americans.

Berlin was doomed, everyone knew that, and the panic was dreadful to see. Close by the Chancellery, a group of SS was stopping everyone they saw in uniform. Unless such individuals could account for themselves, they were immediately accused of desertion in the face of the enemy and hung from the nearest lamp post or tree. A shell screamed in, fired at random by Russian artillery. There were cries of alarm and people scattered.

The Chancellery itself was battered and defaced by the bombardment, particularly at the rear, but deep in the earth protected by thirty meters of concrete, the Führer and his

1

staff still worked on in a subterranean world that was totally self-supporting, still in touch by radio and radio-telephone with the outside world.

The rear of the Reich Chancellery was also damaged, pock-marked by shell fire, and the once lovely gardens were a wilderness of uprooted trees and the occasional shell hole. One blessing: there was little air activity, low cloud and driving rain having cleared the sky of aircraft for the moment.

The man who walked in that ruined garden on his own seemed curiously indifferent to what was happening, didn't even flinch when another shell landed on the far side of the Chancellery. As the rain increased in force, he simply turned up his collar, lit a cigarette and held it in cupped hand as he continued to walk.

He was not very tall, with heavy shoulders and a coarse face. In a crowd of laborers or dock workers, he would have faded into the background, nothing special, not memorable to the slightest degree. Everything about him was nondescript, from the shabby ankle-length greatcoat to the battered peaked cap.

A nobody of any importance, that would have been the conclusion, and yet this man was Reichsleiter Martin Bormann, Head of the Nazi Party Chancellery and Secretary to the Führer, the most powerful man in Germany after Hitler himself. The vast majority of the German people had never even heard of him, and even fewer would have recognized him if they saw him. But then he had organized his life that way, deliberately choosing to be an anonymous figure wielding his power only from the shadows.

But that was all over, everything was finished, and this was the final end of things. The Russians could be here at any moment. He'd tried to persuade Hitler to leave for Bavaria, but the Führer had refused, had insisted, as he had publicly declared for days, that he would commit suicide.

An SS Corporal came out of the Bunker entrance and hurried toward him. He gave the Nazi salute. "Herr Reichsleiter, the Führer is asking for you."

"Where is he?"

"In his study."

"Good, I'll come at once." As they walked toward the entrance several shells landed on the far side of the Chancellery again, debris lifting into the air. Bormann said, "Tanks?"

"I'm afraid so, Herr Reichsleiter, less than half a mile away now."

The SS Corporal was young and tough, a seasoned veteran. Bormann clapped him on the shoulder. "You know what they say? Everything comes to he who waits."

He started to laugh, and the young corporal laughed with him as they started down the concrete steps.

When Bormann knocked on the study door and went in the Führer was seated behind the desk, examining some maps with a magnifying glass. He glanced up.

"Ah, Bormann, there you are. Come in. We don't have much time."

"I suppose not, my Führer," Bormann said uncertainly, unsure of what was meant.

"They'll be here soon, Bormann, the damned Russians, but they won't find me waiting. Stalin would like nothing better than to exhibit me in a cage."

"That can never be, my Führer."

"Of course not. I shall commit suicide, and my wife will accompany me on that dark journey."

He was referring to his mistress, Eva Braun, whom he had finally married at midnight on the twenty-eighth.

"I had hoped that even now you would reconsider whether or not to make a break for Bavaria," Bormann told him, but more for something to say than anything else.

"No, my mind is made up, but you, my old friend, you have work to do."

Hitler stood up and shuffled round the table, the man who only three years previously had controlled Europe from the Urals in the east to the English Channel. Now, his cheeks were sunken, his jacket appeared too large, and when he took Bormann's hands, his own shook with palsy. And yet the power was there still and Bormann was moved.

"Anything, my Führer."

"I knew I could depend on you. The Kamaradenwerk, Action for Comrades." Hitler shuffled back to his chair. "That is your task, Bormann, to see that the National Socialism survives. We have hundreds of millions in Switzerland and elsewhere in the world in gold in numbered accounts, but you have details of those."

"Yes, my Führer."

Hitler reached under his desk and produced a rather strange-looking briefcase, dull silver in appearance. Bormann noted the Kriegsmarine insignia etched in the top right-hand corner.

Hitler flicked it open. "The keys are inside along with a number of items which will prove useful to you over the years." He held up a buff envelope. "Details of similar accounts in various South American countries and the United States. We have friends in all those places only waiting to hear from you."

"Anything else, my Führer?"

Hitler held up a large file. "I call this the Blue Book. It contains the names of many members of the British establishment, both in the ranks of the aristocracy and Parliament, who are friendly to our cause. A number of our

American friends are there also. And last, but not least," he passed another envelope across. "Open it."

The paper was of such quality that it was almost like parchment. It had been written in English in July 1940, in Estoril in Portugal, and was addressed to the Führer. The signature at the bottom was that of his Royal Highness the Duke of Windsor. It was in English and the content was quite simple. He was agreeing to take over the throne of Great Britain in the event of a successful invasion.

"The Windsor Protocol," Hitler said simply.

"Can this be true?" Bormann asked in astonishment.

"Himmler himself vouched for it. He had the Duke approached by his agents in Portugal at the time."

Or said that he had, Bormann told himself. That devious little animal had always been capable of anything. He replaced the document in its envelope and handed it to the Führer, who replaced it and the other items in the briefcase. "This is standard issue to the U-boat captains at the moment. Completely self-sealing, water- and fireproof." The Führer pushed it across to Bormann. "Yours now." He gazed in space for a moment in reverie. "What a swine Himmler is to try and make a separate peace with the Allies, and now I hear that Mussolini and his girlfriend were murdered by partisans in northern Italy, strung up by their ankles."

"A mad world." Bormann waited for a moment, then said, "One point, my Führer, how do I leave? We are now surrounded here."

Hitler came back to life. "Quite simple. You will fly out using the East-West Avenue. As you know, Field Marshal Ritter von Greim and Hannah Reitsch got away in an Arado just after midnight yesterday. I spoke personally to the Commander of the Luftwaffe Base at Rechlin." He glanced at a paper on his desk. "A young man, a Captain

Neumann, volunteered to fly in a Feiseler Storch during the night. He arrived safely and is now waiting your orders."

"But where, my Führer?" Bormann asked.

"In that huge garage at Goebbels' house near the Brandenburg Gate. From there he will fly you to Rechlin and refuel for the onward flight to Bergen in Norway."

"Bergen?" Bormann asked.

"From where you will proceed by submarine to South America, Venezuela to be precise. You'll be expected. One stop on the way. You'll be expected there too, but all the details are in here." He handed him an envelope. "You'll also find my personal signed authorization in there giving you full powers in my name and several false passports."

"So, I leave tonight?" Bormann asked.

"No, you leave within the next hour," Hitler said calmly. "Because of the driving rain and low clouds there is no air cover at the moment. Captain Neumann thinks he could achieve total surprise, and I agree. I have every confidence you will succeed."

There could be no arguing with that and Bormann nodded. "Of course, my Führer."

"Then there only remains one more thing," Hitler said. "You'll find someone in the bedroom. Bring him in."

The man Bormann found in there wore the uniform of a Lieutenant General in the SS. There was something familiar about him and Bormann felt acutely uncomfortable for some reason.

"My Führer," the man said and gave Hitler a Nazi salute.

"Note the resemblance, Bormann?" Hitler asked.

It was then that Bormann realized why he'd felt so strange. It was true, the General did have a look of him. Not perfect, but it was undeniably there.

"General Strasser will stay here in your place," Hitler said. "When the general breakout occurs he will leave with the others. He can stay out of the way until then. In the confusion and darkness of leaving it's hardly likely anyone will notice. They'll be too concerned with saving their own skins." He turned to Strasser. "You will do this for your Führer?"

"With all my heart," Strasser said.

"Good, then you will now exchange uniforms. You may use my bedroom." He came round the desk and took both of Bormann's hands in his. "I prefer to say goodbye now, old friend. We will not meet again."

Cynical as he was by nature, Bormann felt incredibly moved. "I will succeed, my Führer, my word on it."

"I know you will."

Hitler shuffled out, the door closed behind him and Bormann turned to Strasser. "Right, let's get started."

Precisely half an hour later Bormann left the Bunker by the exit into Hermann Goering Strasse. He wore a heavy leather military overcoat over his SS uniform and carried a military holdall, which held the briefcase and a change of civilian clothes. In one pocket he carried a silenced Mauser pistol, and a Schmeisser machine pistol was slung across his chest. He moved along the edge of the Tiergarten, aware of people everywhere, mainly refugees, crossed by the Brandenburg Gate, and arrived at Goebbels' house quite quickly. Like most properties in the area it had suffered damage, but the vast garage building seemed intact. The sliding doors were closed, but there was a small Judas gate, which Bormann opened cautiously.

It was dark in there and a voice called, "Stay where you are, hands high."

Lights were switched on and Bormann found a young man in the uniform of a Captain in the Luftwaffe and a flying jacket standing by the wall, a pistol in his hand. The small Feiseler Storch spotter plane stood in the center of the empty garage.

"Captain Neumann?"

"General Strasser?" The young man looked relieved and holstered his pistol. "Thank God, I've been expecting Ivans ever since I got here."

"You have orders?"

"Of course. Rechlin to refuel and then Bergen. A distinct pleasure, actually."

"Do you think we stand a chance of getting away?"

"There's nothing up there to shoot us down at the moment. Filthy weather. Only ground fire to worry about." He grinned. "Is your luck good, General?"

"Always."

"Excellent. I'll start up, you get in and we'll taxi across the road to the Brandenburg Gate. From there I'll take off toward the Victory Column. They won't be expecting that because the wind is in the wrong direction."

"Isn't that dangerous?" Bormann asked.

"Absolutely." Neumann climbed up into the cabin and started the engine.

There was broken glass and rubble in the street and the Storch bumped its way along, passing many astonished refugees, moved across the Brandenburg Gate and turned toward the Victory Column in the distance. The rain was driving down.

Neumann said, "Here we go," and boosted power.

The Storch roared down the center of the road, here and there people fleeing before it, and suddenly they were airborne and turning to starboard to avoid the Victory Column. Bormann was not even aware of any ground fire.

"You must live right, Herr Reichsleiter," the young pilot said.

Bormann turned to him sharply. "What did you call me?"

"I'm sorry if I've said the wrong thing," Neumann said. "But I met you at an award ceremony once in Berlin."

Bormann decided to leave it for the moment. "Don't worry about it." He looked down at the flames and smoke below as Berlin burned, the Russian artillery keeping up a constant bombardment. "Truly a scene from hell."

"Twilight of the Gods, Reichsleiter," Neumann said. "All we need is Wagner to provide suitable music," and he took the Storch up into the safety of the dark clouds.

It was the second part of the journey which was particularly arduous, cutting across the east coast of Denmark and then up across the Skagerrak, refueling at a small Luftwaffe base at Kristiansand for the final run. It was pitch-dark when they reached Bergen and cold, very cold, a little sleet mixed with the rain as they landed. Neumann had contacted the base half an hour earlier to notify their arrival. There were lights in the control tower and the buildings, a poor blackout. The German occupying forces in Norway knew that the end was near, that there was no possibility of an Allied invasion. It simply wasn't necessary. An aircraftsman with a torch in each hand guided them to a parking place, then walked away. Bormann could see a Kubelwagen driving toward them. It stopped on the other side of the parked aircraft of which there were several.

Neumann switched off. "So, we made it, Herr Reichsleiter. Rather different from Berlin."

"You did well," Bormann said. "You're a fine pilot."

"Let me get your bag for you."

Bormann got down to the ground and Neumann passed him the bag. Bormann said, "Such a pity you recognized me," and he took the silenced Mauser from his greatcoat pocket and shot him through the head.

• • •

The man standing beside the Kubelwagen was a naval officer and wore the white-topped cap affected by U-boat Commanders. He was smoking a cigarette and he dropped it to the ground and stamped on it as Bormann approached.

"General Strasser?"

"That's right," Bormann told him.

"Korvettenkapitän Paul Friemel." Friemel gave him a half-salute. "Commanding U180."

Bormann tossed his bag into the rear of the Kubelwagen and eased himself into the passenger seat. As the other man got behind the wheel, the Reichsleiter said, "Are you ready for sea?"

"Absolutely, General."

"Good, then we'll leave at once."

"At your orders, General," Friemel said and drove away.

Bormann took a deep breath, he could smell the sea on the wind. Strange, but instead of feeling tired he was full of energy and he lit a cigarette and leaned back, looking up at the stars and remembering Berlin only as a bad dream.

1992

1

Just before midnight it started to rain as Dillon pulled in the Mercedes at the side of the road, switched on the interior light and checked his map. Klagenfurt was twenty miles behind, which meant that the Yugoslavian border must be very close now. There was a road sign a few yards further on and he took a torch from the glove compartment, got out of the car and walked toward it, whistling softly, a small man, no more than five feet four or five with hair so fair that it was almost white. He wore an old black leather flying jacket with a white scarf at his throat and dark blue jeans. The sign showed Fehring to the right and five kilometers further on. He showed no emotion, simply took a cigarette from a silver case, lit it with an old-fashioned Zippo lighter and returned to the car.

It was raining very heavily now, the road badly surfaced, mountains rising to his right, and he switched on the radio and listened to a little night music, occasionally whistling the tune until he came to gates on the left and slowed to read the sign. It badly needed a fresh coat of paint, but the inscription was clear enough. Fehring Aero Club. He turned in through the gates and followed a track, lurching over potholes until he saw the airfield below.

He switched off his lights and paused. It seemed a poor sort of place, a couple of hangars, three huts and a rickety excuse for a control tower, but there was light streaming out from one of the hangars and from the windows of the end hut. He moved into neutral, eased off the brake and let the Mercedes run down the hill silently, coming to a halt on the far side of the runway from the hangars. He sat there thinking about things for a moment, then took a Walther PPK and black leather gloves from the attaché case on the seat next to him. He checked the Walther, slipped it into his waistband at the rear, then pulled on the gloves as he started across the runway in the rain.

The hangar was old and smelled of damp as if not used in years, but the airplane that stood there in the dim light looked well enough, a Cessna 441 Conquest with twin turboprop engines. A mechanic in overalls had the cowling on the port engine open and stood on a ladder working on it. The cabin door was open, the stairs down and two men loaded boxes inside.

As they emerged, one of them called in German, "We're finished, Doctor Wegner."

A bearded man emerged from the small office in one corner of the hangar. He wore a hunting jacket, the fur collar turned up against the cold.

"All right, you can go." As they walked away he said to the mechanic, "Any problems, Tomic?"

"No big deal, Herr Doctor, just fine-tuning."

"Which won't mean a thing unless this damn man Dillon turns up." As Wegner turned, a young man came in, the woollen cap and reefer coat he wore beaded with rain.

"He'll be here," Wegner told him. "I was told he could never resist a challenge, this one."

"A mercenary," the young man said. "That's what we've come down to. The kind of man who kills people for money."

"There are children dying over there," Wegner said, "and they need what's on that plane. To achieve that I'd deal with the Devil himself."

"Which you'll probably have to."

"Not kind," Dillon called in excellent German. "Not kind at all," and he stepped out of the darkness at the end of the hangar.

The young man put a hand in his pocket and Dillon's Walther appeared fast. "Plain view, son, plain view."

Dillon walked forward, swung the young man round and extracted a Mauser from his right-hand pocket. "Would you look at that now? You can't trust a soul these days."

Wegner said in English, "Mr. Dillon? Mr. Sean Dillon?"

"So they tell me." Dillon slipped the Mauser into his hip pocket, took out his silver case one-handed, still holding the Walther, and managed to extract a cigarette. "And who might you be, me old son?" His speech had the hard, distinctive edge to it that was found only in Ulster and not in the Republic of Ireland.

"I am Dr. Hans Wegner of International Drug Relief, and this is Klaus Schmidt from our office in Vienna. He arranged the plane for us."

"Did he now? That's something to be said in his favor." Dillon took the Mauser from his hip pocket and handed it back. "Doing good is all very fine, but playing with guns when you don't know how is a mug's game."

The young man flushed deeply, took the Mauser and put it in his pocket, and Wegner said mildly, "Herr Schmidt has made the run by road twice with medical supplies."

"Then why not this time?" Dillon asked, slipping the Walther back in his waistband.

"Because that part of Croatia is disputed territory now," Schmidt said. "There's heavy fighting between Serbs and Moslems and Croats."

"I see," Dillon said. "So I'm to manage by air what you can't by road?"

"Mr. Dillon, it's a hundred and twenty miles to Sabac from here and the airstrip is still open. Believe it or not, but the phone system still works quite well over there. I'm given to understand that this plane is capable of more than three hundred miles an hour. That means you could be there in twenty minutes or so."

Dillon laughed out loud. "Would you listen to the man? It's plain to see you don't know the first thing about flying a plane." He saw that the mechanic high on his ladder was smiling. "Ah, so you speak English, old son."

"A little."

"Tomic is a Croatian," Dr. Wegner said.

Dillon looked up. "What do you think?"

Tomic said, "I was in the airforce for seven years. I know Sabac. It's an emergency strip, but a sound asphalt runway."

"And the flight?"

"Well, if you're just some private pilot out here to do a bit of good in this wicked world you won't last twenty miles."

Dillon said softly, "Let's just say I've seldom done a good thing in my life and I'm not that kind of pilot. What's the terrain like?"

"Mountainous in parts, heavily forested, and the weather forecast stinks, I checked it myself earlier, but it's not only that, it's the airforce, they still patrol the area regularly."

"Mig fighters?" Dillon asked.

"That's right." Tomic slapped the wing of the Conquest with one hand. "A nice airplane, but no match for a Mig." He shook his head. "But maybe you've got a death wish."

"That's enough, Tomic," Wegner said angrily.

"Oh, it's been said before." Dillon laughed. "But let's get on. I'd better look at the charts."

As they moved toward the office Wegner said, "Our people in Vienna did make it plain. Your services are purely voluntary. We need all the money we can raise for the drugs and medical supplies."

"Understood," Dillon said.

They went into the office where a number of charts were spread across the desk. Dillon started to examine them.

"When would you leave?" Wegner asked.

"Just before dawn," Dillon told him. "Best time of all and least active. I hope the rain keeps up."

Schmidt, genuinely curious, said, "Why would you do this? I don't understand. A man like you." He seemed suddenly awkward. "I mean, we know something of your background."

"Do you now?" Dillon said. "Well, as the good doctor said, I find it hard to resist a challenge."

"And for this you would risk your life?"

"Ah, sure and I was forgetting." Dillon looked up and smiled and an astonishing change came to his face, nothing but warmth and great charm there. "I should also mention that I'm the last of the world's great adventurers. Now leave me be like a good lad and let me see where I'm going."

He leaned over the charts and started to examine them intently.

Just before five the rain was as relentless as ever, the darkness as impenetrable, as Dillon stood in the entrance of the hangar and peered out. Wegner and Schmidt approached him.

The older man said, "Can you really take off in weather like this?"

"The problem is landing, not taking off." Dillon called to Tomic, "How are things?"

Tomic emerged from the cabin, jumped to the ground and came toward them wiping his hands on a rag. "Everything in perfect working order."

Dillon offered him a cigarette and glanced out. "And this?"

Tomic peered up into the darkness. "It'll get worse before it gets better, and you'll find ground mist over there, especially over the forest, mark my words."

"Ah, well, better get on with it as the thief said to the hangman." Dillon crossed to the Conquest.

He went up the steps and examined the interior. All the seats had been removed and it was stacked with long, olive-green boxes. Each one was stenciled in English: Royal Army Medical Corps.

Schmidt, who had joined him, said, "As you can see, we get our supplies from unusual sources."

"You can say that again. What's in these?"

"See for yourself." Schmidt unclipped the nearest one, removed a sheet of oiled paper to reveal box after box of morphine ampoules. "Over there, Mr. Dillon, they sometimes have to hold children down when they operate on them because of the lack of any kind of anesthetic. These prove a highly satisfactory substitute."

"Point taken," Dillon said. "Now close it up and I'll get moving."

Schmidt did as he was told, then jumped to the ground. As Dillon pulled up the steps Wegner said, "God go with you, Mr. Dillon."

"There's always that chance," Dillon said. "It's probably the first time I've done anything he'd approve of," and he closed the door and clamped it in place.

He settled into the left-hand pilot's seat, fired the port engine and after that the starboard. The chart was next to him on the other seat, but he had already pretty well committed it to memory. He paused on the apron outside the hangar, rain streaming from his windscreen, did a thorough cockpit check, then strapped in and taxied to the end of the runway, turning into the wind. He glanced across to the three men standing in the hangar entrance, raised a thumb, then started forward, his engine roar deepening as he boosted power. Within a second or two he had disappeared, the sound of the engines already fading.

Wegner ran a hand over his face. "God, but I'm tired." He turned to Tomic. "Has he a chance?"

Tomic shrugged. "Quite a man, that one. Who knows?"

Schmidt said, "Let's get some coffee. We're going to have a long wait."

Tomic said, "I'll join you in a minute. I just want to clear my tools away."

They crossed toward the end hut. He watched them go, waited until they'd gone inside before turning and swiftly crossing to the office. He picked up the telephone and dialed a lengthy series of numbers. As the good doctor had said, the telephone system still worked surprisingly well over there.

When a voice answered he spoke in Serbo-Croatian. "This is Tomic, get me Major Branko."

There was an instant response. "Branko here."

"Tomic. I'm at the airfield at Fehring and I've got traffic for you. Cessna Conquest just left, destination Sabac. Here is his radio frequency."

"Is the pilot anyone we know?"

"Name of Dillon—Sean Dillon. Irish, I believe. Small man, very fair hair, late thirties I'd say. Doesn't look much. Nice smile, but the eyes tell a different story."

"I'll have him checked out through Central Intelligence, but you've done well, Tomic. We'll give him a warm welcome."

The phone clicked and Tomic replaced the receiver. He took out a packet of the vile Macedonian cigarettes he affected and lit one. Pity about Dillon. He'd rather liked the Irishman, but that was life and he started to put his tools away methodically.

And Dillon was already in trouble, not only thick cloud and the constant driving rain, but even at a thousand feet a swirling mist that gave only an intermittent view of pine forest below.

"And what in the hell are you doing here, old son?" he asked softly. "What are you trying to prove?"

He got a cigarette out of his case, lit it and a voice spoke in his earphones in heavily accented English. "Good morning, Mr. Dillon, welcome to Yugoslavia."

The plane took station to starboard not too far away, the red stars on its fuselage clear enough, a Mig 21, the old Fishbed, probably the Soviet jet most widely distributed to its allies. Outdated now, but not as far as Dillon was concerned.

The Mig pilot spoke again. "Course one-two-four, Mr. Dillon. We'll come to a rather picturesque castle at the edge of the forest, Kivo it's called, intelligence headquarters for this area. There's an airstrip there and they're expecting you. They might even arrange a full English breakfast."

"Irish," Dillon said cheerfully. "A full Irish breakfast, and who am I to refuse an offer like that? One-two-four it is."

He turned onto the new course, climbing to two thousand feet as the weather cleared a little, whistling softly to himself. A Serbian prison did not commend itself, not if the stories reaching Western Europe were even partly true, but in the circumstances, he didn't seem to have any choice and then, a couple of miles away on the edge of the forest beside a river he saw Kivo, a fairytale castle of towers and battlements surrounded by a moat, the airstrip clear beside it.

"What do you think?" the Mig pilot asked. "Nice, isn't it?"

"Straight out of a story by the Brothers Grimm," Dillon answered. "All we need is the ogre."

"Oh, we have that too, Mr. Dillon. Now put down nice and easy and I'll say goodbye."

Dillon looked down into the interior of the castle, noticed soldiers moving toward the edge of the airstrip preceded by a jeep and sighed. He said into his mike, "I'd like to say it's been a good life, but then there are those difficult days, like this morning for instance. I mean, why did I even get out of bed?"

He heaved the control column right back and boosted power, climbing fast, and the Mig pilot reacted angrily. "Dillon, do as you're told or I'll blast you out of the sky."

Dillon ignored him, leveling out at five thousand, searching the sky for any sign, and the Mig, already on his tail, came up behind and fired. The Conquest staggered as cannon shell tore through both wings.

"Dillon—don't be a fool!" the pilot cried.

"Ah, but then I always was."

Dillon went down fast, leveling at two thousand feet over the edge of the forest, aware of vehicles moving from the direction of the castle. The Mig came in again firing his machine guns now and the Conquest's windscreen disintegrated, wind and rain roaring in. Dillon sat there, hands firm on the control column, blood on his face from a glass splinter.

"Now then," he said into his mike. "Let's see how good you are."

He dropped the nose and went straight down, the pine forest waiting for him below, and the Mig went after him, firing again. The Conquest bucked, the port engine dying as Dillon leveled out at four hundred feet, and behind him the Mig, no time to pull out at the speed it was doing, plowed into the forest and fireballed.

Dillon, trimming as best he could for flying on one engine, lost power and dropped lower. There was a clearing up ahead and to his left. He tried to bank toward it, was already losing height as he clipped the tops of the pine trees. He cut power instantly and braced himself for the crash. In the end, it was the pine trees which saved him, retarding his progress so much that by the time he hit the clearing for a belly landing, he wasn't actually going all that fast.

The Conquest bounced twice, and came to a shuddering halt. Dillon released his straps, scrambled out of his seat and had the door open in an instant. He was out headfirst, rolling over in the rain, and on his feet and running, his right ankle twisting so that he fell on his face again. He scrambled up and limped away as fast as he could, but the Conquest didn't burst into flame, it simply crouched there in the rain as if tired.

There was thick black smoke above the trees from the burning Mig and then soldiers appeared on the other side of the clearing. A jeep moved out of the trees behind them, top down, and Dillon could see an officer standing up in it wearing a winter campaign coat, Russian-style, with a fur collar. More soldiers appeared, some of them with

Dobermans, all barking loudly and straining against their leashes.

It was enough. Dillon turned to hobble into the trees and his leg gave out on him. A voice on a loudhailer called in English, "Oh, come now, Mr. Dillon, be sensible, you don't want me to set the dogs on you."

Dillon paused, balanced on one foot, then he turned and hobbled to the nearest tree and leaned against it. He took a cigarette from his silver case, the last one, and lit it. The smoke tasted good as it bit at the back of his throat and he waited for them.

They stood in a semicircle, soldiers in baggy tunics, guns covering him, the dogs howling against being restrained. The jeep rolled to a halt and the officer, a Major from his shoulder boards, stood up and looked down at him, a good-looking man of about thirty with a dark, saturnine face.

"So, Mr. Dillon, you made it in one piece," he said in faultless Public School English. "I congratulate you. My name, by the way, is Branko—John Branko. My mother was English, is, I should say. Lives in Hampstead."

"Is that a fact." Dillon smiled. "A desperate bunch of rascals you've got here, Major, but *Cead míle fáilte* anyway."

"And what would that mean, Mr. Dillon?"

"Oh, that's Irish for a hundred thousand welcomes."

"What a charming sentiment." Branko turned and spoke in Serbo-Croatian to the large, brutal-looking Sergeant who sat behind him clutching an AK assault rifle. The Sergeant smiled, jumped to the ground and advanced on Dillon.

Major Branko said, "Allow me to introduce you to my Sergeant Zekan. I've just told him to offer you a hundred thousand welcomes to Yugoslavia, or Serbia as we prefer to say now."

Dillon knew what was coming, but there wasn't a thing he could do. The butt of the AK caught him in the left side, driving the wind from him as he keeled over. The Sergeant lifted a knee in his face. The last thing Dillon remembered was the dogs barking, the laughter, and then there was only darkness.

When Sergeant Zekan took Dillon along the corridor, someone screamed in the distance and there was the sound of heavy blows. Dillon hesitated but the Sergeant showed no emotion, simply put a hand between the Irishman's shoulder blades and pushed him toward a flight of stone steps and urged him up. There was an oaken door at the top banded with iron. Zekan opened it and pushed him through.

The room inside was oak beamed with granite walls, tapestries hanging here and there. A log fire burned in an open hearth and two of the Dobermans sprawled in front of it. Branko sat behind a large desk reading a file and drinking from a crystal glass, a bottle in an ice bucket beside him. He glanced up and smiled, then took the bottle from the ice bucket and filled another glass.

"Krug champagne, Mr. Dillon, your preferred choice, I understand."

"Is there anything you don't know about me?" Dillon asked.

"Not much." Branko lifted the file, then dropped it on the desk. "The intelligence organizations of most countries have the useful habit of frequently co-operating with each other even when their countries don't. Do sit down and have a drink. You'll feel better."

Dillon took the chair opposite and accepted the glass that Zekan handed him. He emptied it in one go and Branko smiled, took a cigarette from a packet of Rothmans and tossed it across.

"Help yourself." He reached out and refilled Dillon's glass. "I much prefer the non-vintage, don't you?"

"It's the grape mix," Dillon said and lit the cigarette.

"Sorry about that little touch of violence back there," Branko told him. "Just a show for my boys. After all, you did cost us that Mig and it takes two years to train the pilots. I should know, I'm one myself."

"Really?" Dillon said.

"Yes, Cranwell, courtesy of your British Royal Air Force."

"Not mine," Dillon told him.

"But you were born in Ulster, I understand. Belfast, is that not so, and Belfast, as I understand it, is part of Great Britain and not the Republic of Ireland."

"A debatable point," Dillon said. "Let's say I'm Irish and leave it at that." He swallowed some more champagne. "Who dropped me in it? Wegner or Schmidt?" He frowned. "No, of course not. Just a couple of do-gooders. Tomic. It would be Tomic, am I right?"

"A good Serb." Branko poured a little more champagne. "How on earth did you get into this, a man like you?"

"You mean you don't know?"

"I'll be honest, Mr. Dillon. I knew you were coming, but no more than that."

"I was in Vienna for a few days to sample a little opera. I'm partial to Mozart. Bumped into a man I'd had dealings with over the years in the bar during the first interval. Told me he'd been approached by this organization who needed a little help, but were short on money."

"Ah, I see now." Branko nodded. "A good deed in a naughty world as Shakespeare put it? All those poor little children crying out for help? The cruel Serbs."

"God help me, Major, but you have a way with the words."

"A sea change for a man like you I would have thought." Branko opened the file. "Sean Dillon, born Belfast, went to live in London when you were a boy, father a widower. A student of the Royal Academy of Dramatic Art at eighteen, even acted with the National Theatre. Your father returned to Belfast in 1971 and was killed by British paratroopers."

"You *are* well informed."

"You joined the Provisional IRA, trained in Libya courtesy of Colonel Qaddafi and never looked back." Branko turned a page. "You finally broke with the IRA. Some disagreement as to strategy."

"Bunch of old women." Dillon reached across and helped himself to more Krug.

"Beirut, the PLO, even the KGB. You really do believe in spreading your services around." Branko laughed suddenly in a kind of amazement. "The underwater attack on those two Palestinian gunboats in Beirut in 1990. You were responsible for that? But that was for the Israelis."

"I charge very reasonable rates," Dillon said.

"Fluent German, Spanish and French, oh, and Irish."

"We mustn't forget that."

"Reasonable Arabic, Italian and Russian." Branko closed the file. "Is it true you were responsible for the mortar attack on No. 10 Downing Street during the Gulf War when the British Prime Minister, John Major, was meeting with the War Cabinet?"

"Now do I look as if I'd do a thing like that?"

Branko leaned back and looked at him seriously. "How do you see yourself, my friend, gun for hire like one of those old Westerns, riding into town to clean things up single-handed?"

"To be honest, Major, I never think about it."

"And yet you took on a job like this present affair for a bunch of well-meaning amateurs and for no pay?"

"We all make mistakes."

"You certainly did, my friend. Those boxes on the plane. Morphine ampoules on top, Stinger missiles underneath."

"Jesus." Dillon laughed helplessly. "Now who would have thought it."

"They say you have a genius for acting, that you can change yourself totally, become another person with a look, a gesture."

"No, I think that was Laurence Olivier." Dillon smiled.

"And in twenty years, you've never seen the inside of a cell."

"True."

"Not any longer, my friend." Branko opened a drawer, took out a two-hundred pack of Rothmans cigarettes and tossed them across. "You're going to need those." He glanced at Zekan and said in Serbo-Croatian, "Take him to his cell."

Dillon felt the Sergeant's hand on his shoulder pulling him up and propelling him to the door. As Zekan opened it Branko said, "One more thing, Mr. Dillon. The firing squad operates most mornings here. Try not to let it put you off."

"Ah, yes," Dillon said. "Ethnic cleansing, isn't that what you call it?"

"The reason is much simpler than that. We just get short of space. Sleep well."

They went up a flight of stone steps, Zekan pushing Dillon ahead of him. He pulled him to a halt outside an oak door on the passageway at the top, took out a key and unlocked it. He inclined his head and stood to one side and Dillon entered. The room was quite large. There was an army cot in one corner, a table and chair, books on a shelf and, incredibly, an old toilet and in a cubicle in one corner. Dillon went to the window and peered through bars to the courtyard eighty feet below and the pine forest in the near distance.

He turned. "This must be one of your better rooms. What's the catch?" Then realized he was wasting his time, for the Sergeant had no English.

As if perfectly understanding him Zekan smiled, showing bad teeth, took Dillon's silver case and Zippo lighter from a pocket and laid them carefully on the table. He withdrew, closing the door, and the key rattled in the lock.

Dillon went to the window and tried the bars, but they seemed firm. Too far down anyway. He opened one of the packs of Rothmans and lit one. One thing was certain. Branko was being excessively kind and there had to be a reason for that. He went and lay on the bed, smoking his cigarette, staring up at the ceiling and thinking about it.

In 1972, aware of the growing problem of terrorism and its effect on so many aspects of life at both political and national level, the British Prime Minister of the day ordered the setting up of a small elite intelligence unit, known simply by the code name Group Four. It was to handle all matters concerning terrorism and subversion in the British Isles. Known rather bitterly in more conventional intelligence circles as the Prime Minister's private army, it owed allegiance to that office alone.

Brigadier Charles Ferguson had headed Group Four since its inception, had served a number of Prime Ministers, both Conservative and Labour, and had no political allegiance whatsoever. He had an office on the third floor of the Ministry of Defence overlooking Horse Guards Avenue, and was still working at his desk at nine o'clock that night when there was a knock at the door.

"Come in," Ferguson said, stood up and walked to the window, a large, rather untidy-looking man with a double chin and untidy gray hair who wore a baggy suit and a Guards tie.

As he peered out at the rain toward Victoria Embankment and the Thames, the door opened behind him. The man who entered was in his late thirties, wore a tweed suit and glasses. He could have been a clerk, or even a schoolmaster, but Detective Inspector Jack Lane was neither of these things. He was a cop. Not an ordinary one, but a cop all the same, and after some negotiating, Ferguson had succeeded in borrowing him from Special Branch at Scotland Yard to act as his personal assistant.

"Got something for me, Jack?" Ferguson's voice was ever so slightly plummy.

"Mainly routine, Brigadier. The word is that the Director General of the Security Services is still unhappy at the Prime Minister's refusal to do away with Group Four's special status."

"Good God, don't they ever give up, those people? I've agreed to keep them informed on a need-to-know basis and to liaise with Simon Carter, the Deputy Director, and that damned MP, the one with the fancy title. Extra Minister at the Home Office."

"Sir Francis Pamer, sir."

"Yes, well that's all the cooperation they're going to get out of me. Anything else?"

Lane smiled. "Actually, I've saved the best bit till last. Dillon—Sean Dillon?"

Ferguson turned. "What about him?"

"Had a signal from our contacts in Yugoslavia. Dillon crashed in a light plane this morning, supposedly flying in medical supplies only they turned out to be Stinger missiles. They're holding him in that castle at Kivo. It's all here."

He passed a sheet of paper across and Ferguson put on half-moon spectacles and studied it. He nodded in satisfaction. "Twenty years and the bastard never saw the inside of a prison cell."

"Well, he's in one now, sir. I've got his record here if you want to look at it."

"And why would I want to do that? No use to anyone now. You know what the Serbs are like, Jack. Might as well stick it in the dead-letter file. Oh, you can go home now."

"Good night, sir."

Lane went out and Ferguson crossed to his drinks cabinet and poured a large Scotch. "Here's to you, Dillon," he said softly. "And you can chew on that, you bastard."

He swallowed the whisky down, returned to his desk and started to work again.

2

———

East of Puerto Rico in the Caribbean are the Virgin Islands, partly British like Tortola and Virgin Gorda. Across the water are St. Croix, St. Thomas and St. John, proudly American since 1917 when the United States purchased them from the Danish government for twenty-five million dollars.

St. John is reputed to have been discovered by Columbus on his second voyage to the New World in 1493 and without a doubt is probably the most idyllic island in the entire Caribbean, but not that night as a tropical storm, the tail end of Hurricane Able, swept in across the old town of Cruz Bay, stirring the boats at anchor in the harbor, driving rain across the roof tops, the sky exploding into thunder.

To Bob Carney, fast asleep in the house at Chocolate Hole on the other side of Great Cruz Bay, it was the sound of distant guns. He stirred in his sleep, and suddenly it was the same old dream, the mortars landing everywhere, shaking the ground, the screams of the wounded and dying. He'd lost his helmet, flung himself to the ground, arms protecting his head, was not even aware of being hit, only afterwards, as the attack faded and he sat up. There was pain then in both arms and legs from shrapnel wounds, blood on his

31

hands. And then, as the smoke cleared, he became aware of another Marine sitting against a tree, both legs gone above the knees. He was shaking, had a hand outstretched as if begging for help, and Carney cried out in horror and sat bolt upright in bed, awake now.

The same lousy old dream, Vietnam, and that was a long time ago. He switched on the bedside lamp and checked his watch. It was only two-thirty. He sighed and stood up, stretching for a moment, then padded through the dark house to the kitchen, switched on the light and got a beer from the icebox.

He was very tanned, the blond hair faded, both from regular exposure to sea and sun. Around five foot eight, he had an athlete's body, not surprising in a man who had been a ship's captain and was now a master diver by profession. Forty-four years of age, but most people would have taken seven or eight years off that.

He went through the living room and opened a window to the veranda. Rain dripped from the roof and out to sea lightning crackled. He drank a little more of his beer, then put the can down and closed the window. Better to try and get a little more sleep. He was taking a party of recreational scuba divers out from Caneel Bay at nine-thirty, which meant that as usual he needed his wits about him, plus all his considerable expertise.

As he went through the living room he paused to pick up a framed photo of his wife, Karye, and his two young children, the boy Walker and his daughter, little Wallis. They'd departed for Florida only the previous day for a vacation with their grandparents, which left him a bachelor for the next month. He smiled wryly, knowing just how much he'd miss them, and went back to bed.

At the same moment in his house on the edge of Cruz Bay at Gallows Point, Henry Baker sat in his study reading in the light of a single desk lamp. He had the door to the veranda open because he liked the rain and the smell of the sea. It excited him, took him back to the days of his youth and his two years' service in the Navy during the Korean War. He'd made full Lieutenant, had even been decorated with the Bronze Star, could have made a career of it. In fact they'd wanted him to, but there was the family publishing business to consider, responsibilities and the girl he'd promised to marry.

It hadn't been a bad life considering. No children, but he and his wife had been content until cancer took her at fifty. From then on he'd really lost interest in the business, had been happy to accept the right kind of deal for a takeover, which had left him very rich and totally rootless at fifty-eight.

It was a visit to St. John which had been the saving of him. He'd stayed at Caneel Bay, the fabulous Rock Resort on its private peninsula north of Cruz Bay. It was there that he'd been introduced to scuba diving by Bob Carney and it had become an obsession. He'd sold his house in the Hamptons, moved to St. John and bought the present place. His life at sixty-three was totally satisfactory and worthwhile, although Jenny had had something to do with that as well.

He reached for her photo. Jenny Grant, twenty-five, face very calm, wide eyes above high cheekbones, short dark hair, and there was still a wariness in those eyes as if she expected the worst, which was hardly surprising when Baker recalled their first meeting in Miami when she'd tried to proposition him in a car park, her body shaking from the lack of the drugs she'd needed.

When she'd collapsed, he'd taken her to the hospital himself, had personally guaranteed the necessary financing to put her through a drug rehabilitation unit, had held her hand all the way because there was no one else. It was the usual story. She was an orphan raised by an aunt who'd thrown her out at sixteen. A fair voice had enabled her to make some kind of living singing in saloons and cocktail lounges, and then the wrong man, bad company, and the slide had begun.

He'd brought her back to St. John to see what the sea and sun could do. The arrangement had worked perfectly and on a strictly platonic basis. He was the father she had never known, she was the daughter he had been denied. He'd invested in a cafe and bar for her on the Cruz Bay waterfront called Jenny's Place. It had proved a great success. Life couldn't be better and he always waited up for her. It was at that moment he heard the jeep drive up outside, there was the sound of the porch door and she came in laughing, a raincoat over her shoulder. She threw it on a chair and leaned down and kissed his cheek.

"My God, it's like a monsoon out there."

"It'll clear by morning, you'll see." He took her hand. "Good night?"

"Very." She nodded. "A few tourists in from Caneel and the Hyatt. Gosh, but I'm bushed."

"I'd get to bed if I were you, it's almost three o'clock."

"Sure you don't mind?"

"Of course not. I may go diving in the morning, but I should be back before noon. If I miss you, I'll come down to the cafe for lunch."

"I wish you wouldn't dive on your own."

"Jenny, I'm a recreational diver, no decompression needed because I work within the limits exactly as Bob Carney taught me, and I never dive without my Marathon diving computer, you know that."

"I also know that whenever you dive there's always a chance of some kind of decompression sickness."

"True, but very small." He squeezed her hand. "Now stop worrying and go to bed."

She kissed him on the top of his head and went out. He returned to his book, carrying it across to the couch by the window, stretching out comfortably. He didn't seem to need so much sleep these days, one of the penalties of growing old, he imagined, but after a while his eyes started to close and sleep he did, the book sliding to the floor.

He came awake with a start, light beaming in through the venetian blinds. He lay there for a moment, then checked his watch. It was a little after five and he got up and went out on to the veranda. It was already dawn, light breaking on the horizon, but strangely still, and the sea was extraordinarily calm, something to do with the hurricane having passed. Perfect for diving, absolutely perfect.

He felt cheerful and excited at the same time, hurried into the kitchen, put the kettle on and made a stack of cheese sandwiches while it boiled. He filled a thermos with coffee, put it in a holdall with the sandwiches and took his old reefer coat down from behind the door.

He left the jeep for Jenny and walked down to the harbor. It was still very quiet, not too many people about, a dog barking in the distance. He dropped into his inflatable dinghy at the dock, cast off and started the outboard motor, threaded his way out through numerous boats until he came to his own, the *Rhoda,* named after his wife, a thirty-five-foot Sport Fisherman with a flying bridge.

He scrambled aboard, tying the inflatable on a long line, and checked the deck. He had four air tanks standing upright in their holders; he'd put them in the day before himself. He opened the lid of the deck locker and checked his equipment. There was a rubber and nylon diving suit which he seldom used, preferring the lighter, three-quarter-length one in orange and blue. Fins, mask, plus a spare because the lenses were correctional according to his eye prescription, two buoyancy jackets, gloves, air regulators and his Marathon computer.

"Carney training," he said softly, "never leave anything to chance."

He went round to the prow and unhitched from the buoy, then went up the ladder to the flying bridge and started the engines. They roared into life and he took the *Rhoda* out of harbor toward the open sea with conscious pleasure.

There were all his favorite dives to choose from, the Cow & Calf, Carval Rock, Congo, or there was Eagle Shoal if he wanted a longer trip. He'd confronted a lemon shark there only the previous week, but the sea was so calm he just headed straight out. There was always Frenchman's Cap to the south and west and maybe eight or nine miles, a great dive, but he just kept going, heading due south, pushing the *Rhoda* up to fifteen knots, pouring himself some coffee and breaking out the sandwiches. The sun was up now, the sea the most perfect blue, the peaks of the islands all around, a breathtakingly beautiful sight. Nothing could be better.

"My God," he said softly, "it's a damn privilege to be here. What in hell was I doing with my life all those years?"

He lapsed into a kind of reverie, brooding about things, and it was a good thirty minutes later that he suddenly snapped out of it and checked on his position.

"Christ," he said, "I must be twelve miles out."

Which was close to the edge of things and that awesome place where everything simply dropped away and it was two thousand feet to the bottom, except for Thunder Point and that, he knew, was somewhere close. But no one ever dived there, the most dangerous reef in the entire region. Even Carney didn't dive there. Strong currents, a nightmare world of fissures and channels. Carney had told him that years before an old diver had described it to him. A hundred and eighty feet on one side, then the ridge of the reef at around seventy, and two thousand feet on the other. The old boy had hit bad trouble, had only just made it to the surface, had never tried again. Few people even knew where it was anyway, and the sea out there was generally so turbulent that that in itself was enough to keep anyone away, but not today. It was a millpond. Baker had never seen anything like it. A sudden excitement surged in him and he switched on his fathometer, seeking the bottom, throttling back the engines, and then he saw it, the yellow ridged lines on the black screen.

He killed the engine and drifted, checking the depth reading until he was certain he was above the ridge of the reef at seventy feet, then scrambled round to the prow and dropped the anchor. After a while, he felt it bite satisfactorily and worked his way round to the deck. He felt incredibly cheerful as he stripped, pulled on the orange and blue nylon diving suit, then quickly assembled his gear, clamping a tank to his inflatable. He strapped the computer to the line of his air pressure gauge, then eased himself into the jacket, taking the weight of the tank, strapping the Velcro wrappers firmly across his waist and hooking a net diving bag to his weight belt as he always did with a spotlight inside in case he came across anything interesting. He pulled on a pair of diving gloves, then sat with his feet on the platform at the stern and pulled on his fins. He spat on his mask, rinsed it, adjusted it to his face, then simply stood up and stepped into the water.

• • •

It was incredibly clear and blue. He swam round to the anchor rope, paused, then started down, following the line. The sensation of floating in space was, as always, amazing, a silent, private world, sunlight at first, but fading as he descended.

The reef where the anchor was hooked was a forest of coral and sea grass, fish of every conceivable description, and suddenly a barracuda that was at least five feet long swerved across his vision and paused, turning toward him threateningly, which didn't bother Baker in the slightest, because barracuda were seldom a threat to anyone.

He checked his dive computer. It not only indicated the depth he was at, but told him how long he was safe there and constantly altered its reading according to any change in depth he made during the dive. He was at this point at seventy feet and he turned and headed over to the left-hand side, where the reef slid down to a hundred and eighty. He went over the edge, then changed his mind and went up again. It was amazing how much an extra ten or fifteen feet reduced your bottom time.

There was a reasonably strong current; he could feel it pushing him to one side. He imagined what it must be like when conditions were bad, but he was damned if that was going to stop him having a look at the big drop. The edge of the reef over there was very clearly defined. He paused, holding on to a coral head and peered over, looking down the cliff face into a great blue vault that stretched into infinity. He went over, descended to eighty feet and started to work his way along.

It was interesting. He noted a considerable amount of coral damage, large sections having obviously been torn away, recently, presumably the result of the hurricane although they were on a fault line here and earth tremors were also common. Some distance ahead, there was a very obvious section where what looked like an entire overhang had gone revealing a wide ledge below, and there was something there, perched on the ledge yet part of it hanging over. Baker paused for a moment, then approached cautiously.

It was then that he received not only the greatest thrill of his diving career but the greatest shock of a long life. The object which was pressed on the ledge and partly sticking out over two thousand feet of water was a submarine.

During his naval service Baker had done a training course in a submarine when based in the Philippines. No big deal, just part of general training, but he remembered the lectures, the training films they'd had to watch, mainly Second World War stuff, and he recognized what he was looking at instantly. It was a type VII U-boat, by far the most common craft of its kind used by the German Kriegsmarine, the configuration was unmistakable. The conning tower was encrusted with marine growth, but when he approached he could still discern the number on the side—180. The attack and control room periscopes were still intact and there was a snorkel. He recalled having heard that the Germans had gradually introduced that as the war progressed, a device that enabled the boat to proceed under water much faster because it was able to use the power of its diesel engines. Approximately two-thirds of it rested stern first on the ledge and the prow jutted out into space.

He glanced up aware of a school of horse-eyed jacks overhead mixed with silversides, then descended to the top of the conning tower and hung on to the bridge rail. Aft was the high gun platform with its 20mm cannon and forward and below him was the deck gun, encrusted, as was most of the surface, with sponge and coral of many colors.

The boat had become a habitat as with all wrecks, fish everywhere, yellow-tail snappers, angel and parrot fish and sergeant-majors and many others. He checked his computer. On the bridge he was at a depth of seventy-five feet and he had only twenty minutes at the most before the need to surface.

He drifted away a little distance to look the U-boat over. Obviously the overhang, which had recently been dislodged, had provided a kind of canopy for the wreck for years, protecting it from view, and at a site which was seldom visited, it had been enough. That U-boats had worked the area during the Second World War was common knowledge. He'd known one old sailor who'd always insisted that crews would come ashore on St. John by night in search of fresh fruit and water, although Baker had always found that one hard to swallow.

He swung over to the starboard side and saw what the trouble had been instantly, a large, ragged gash about fifteen feet long in the hull below the conning tower. The poor bastards must have gone down like a stone. He descended, holding on to a jagged, coral-encrusted edge, and peered into the control room. It was dark and gloomy in there, silverfish in clouds, and he got the spotlight from his dive bag and shone it inside. The periscope shafts were clearly visible, again encrusted like everything else, but the rest was a confusion of twisted metal, wires and pipes. He checked his computer, saw that he had fifteen minutes, hesitated, then went inside.

Both the aft and forward water-tight doors were closed, but that was standard practice when things got bad. He tried the unlocking wheel on the forward hatch, but it was immovable and hopelessly corroded. There were some oxygen bottles, even a belt of some kind of ammunition, and the most pathetic thing of all, a few human bones in the sediment of the floor. Amazing that there was any trace at all after so many years.

Suddenly he felt cold. It was as if he was an intruder who shouldn't be here. He turned to go and his light picked out a handle in the corner, very like a suitcase handle. He reached for it, the sediment stirred and he found himself clutching a small briefcase in some kind of metal, encrusted like everything else. It was enough and he went out through the gash in the hull, drifted up over the edge of the reef and went for the anchor.

He made it with five minutes to spare. Stupid bastard, he told himself, taking such a chance, and he ascended just by the book, one foot per second, one hand sliding up the line, the briefcase in the other, leaving the line at twenty feet to swim under the boat and surface at the stern.

He pushed the briefcase on board, then wriggled out of his equipment, which was always the worst part. You're getting old, Henry, he told himself as he scrambled up the ladder and turned to heave his buoyancy jacket and tank on board.

He schooled himself to do everything as normal, stowing away the tank and the equipment following his usual routine. He toweled himself dry, changed into jeans and a fresh denim shirt, all the time ignoring the briefcase. He opened his thermos and poured some coffee, then went and sat in one of the swivel chairs in the stern, drinking and staring at the briefcase encrusted with coral.

The encrusting was superficial more than anything else. He got a wire brush from his tool kit and applied it vigorously and realized at once that the case was made of aluminium. As the surface cleared, the Eagle and Swastika of the German Kriegsmarine was revealed etched into the top right-hand corner. It was secured by two clips and there was a lock. The clips came up easily enough, but the lid remained obstinately down, obviously locked, which left him little choice. He found a large screwdriver, forced it in just above the lock and was able to prize open the lid within a few moments. The inside was totally dry, the contents a few photos and several letters bound together by a rubber band. There was also a large diary in red Moroccan leather stamped with a Kriegsmarine insignia in gold.

The photos were of a young woman and two little girls. There was a date on the back of one of them at the start of a handwritten paragraph in German, August 8, 1944. The rest made no sense to him as he didn't speak the language. There was also a faded snap of a man in Kriegsmarine uniform. He looked about thirty and wore a number of medals, including the Knight's Cross at his throat. Someone special, a real ace from the look of him.

The diary was also in German. The first entry was April 30, 1945, and he recognized the name, Bergen, knew that was a port in Norway. On the flyleaf was an entry he did understand. Korvettenkapitän Paul Friemel, U180, obviously the captain and owner of this diary.

Baker flicked through the pages, totally frustrated at being unable to decipher any of it. There were some twenty-seven entries, sometimes a page for each day, sometimes more. On some occasions there was a notation to indicate position, and he had little difficulty in seeing from those entries that the voyage had taken the submarine into the Atlantic and south to the Caribbean.

The strange thing was the fact that the final entry was dated May 28, 1945, and that didn't make too much sense. Henry Baker had been sixteen years of age when the war in Europe had ended, and he recalled the events of those days with surprising clarity. The Russians had reached Berlin and reduced it to hell on earth, and Adolf Hitler, holed up in the Führer Bunker at the Reich Chancellery, had committed suicide on May the 1st at 10:30 P.M. along with his wife of a few hours only, Eva Braun. That was the effective end of the Third Reich and capitulation had soon followed. If that were so, what in the hell was U180 doing in the Virgin Islands with a final log entry dated May 28?

If only he could speak German, and the further frustrating thing was that he didn't know a soul in St. John who did. On the other hand, if he did, would he want to share such a secret? One thing was certain: If news of the submarine and its whereabouts got out, the place would be invaded within days.

He flicked through the pages again, paused suddenly and turned back a page. A name jumped out at him. *Reichsleiter Martin Bormann.* Baker's excitement was intense. Martin Bormann, Head of the Nazi Party Chancellery and Secretary to the Führer. Had he escaped from the Bunker at the end, or had he died trying to escape from Berlin? How many books had been written about that?

He turned the page idly and another name came out at him: the *Duke of Windsor.* Baker sat staring at the page, his throat dry, and then he very carefully closed the diary and put it back in the case with the letter and photos. He closed the lid, put the case in the wheelhouse and started the engines. Then he went and hauled in the anchor.

Whatever it was, it was heavy, had to be. He had a U-boat that had gone down in the Virgin Islands three weeks after the end of the war in Europe, a private diary kept by the captain which mentioned the most powerful man in Nazi Germany after Hitler, and the Duke of Windsor.

"My God, what have I got into?" he murmured.

He could go to the authorities, of course, the Coast

Guard, for example, but it had been his find, that was the trouble, and he was reluctant to relinquish that. But what in the hell to do next, and then it came to him and he laughed out loud.

"Garth Travers, of course," and he pushed up to full throttle and hurried back to St. John.

In 1951 as a Lieutenant in the U.S. Navy, Baker had been assigned as liaison officer to the British Royal Navy destroyer *Persephone,* which was when he had first met Garth Travers, a gunnery officer. Travers was on the fast track, had taken a degree in history at Oxford University, and the two young officers had made a firm friendship, cemented by five hours in the water one dark night off the Korean coast, which they'd spent hanging on to each other after a landing craft on which they'd been making a night drop with Royal Marine Commandos had hit a mine.

And Travers had gone on to great things, had retired a Rear Admiral. Since then he'd written several books on naval aspects of the Second World War, had translated a standard work on the Kriegsmarine from the German which Baker's publishing house had published in the last year he'd been in the business. Travers was the man, no doubt about it.

He was close inshore to St. John now and saw another Sport Fisherman bearing down on him and he recognized the *Sea Raider,* Bob Carney's boat. It slowed, turning toward him, and Baker slowed too. There were four people in the stern dressed for diving, three women and a man. Bob Carney was on the flying bridge.

"Morning, Henry," he called. "Out early. Where you been?"

"French Cap." Baker didn't like lying to a friend but had no choice.

"Conditions good?"

"Excellent, millpond out there."

"Fine." Carney smiled and waved. "Take care, Henry."

The *Sea Raider* moved away and Baker pushed up to full power and headed for Cruz Bay.

When he reached the house, he knew at once that Jenny wasn't there because the jeep had gone. He checked his watch. Ten o'clock. Something must have come up to take her out. He went into the kitchen, got a beer from the icebox and went to his study, carrying the briefcase in one hand. He placed it on the desk, pulled his phone file across and leafed through it one-handed while he drank the beer. He found what he was looking for soon enough and checked his watch again. Ten after ten, which meant ten after three in the afternoon in London. He picked up the telephone and dialed.

In London it was raining, drumming against the windows of the house in Lord North Street where Rear Admiral Garth Travers sat in a chair by the fire in his book-lined study enjoying a cup of tea and reading the *Times*. When the phone rang, he made a face, but got up and went to the desk.

"Who am I talking to?"

"Garth? It's Henry—Henry Baker."

Travers sat down behind the desk. "Good God, Henry, you old sod. Are you in London?"

"No, I'm calling from St. John."

"Sounds as if you're in the next room."

"Garth, I've got a problem, I thought you might be able to help. I've found a U-boat."

"You've what?"

"An honest-to-God U-boat, out here in the Virgins, on a

reef about eighty feet down. One-eighty was the number on the conning tower. It's a type seven."

Travers' own excitement was extreme. "I'm not going to ask you if you've been drinking. But why on earth has no one discovered it before?"

"Garth, there are hundreds of wrecks in these waters; we don't know the half of it. This is in a bad place, very dangerous. No one goes there. It's half on a ledge which was protected by an overhang, or I miss my guess. There's a lot of fresh damage to the cliff face. We've just had a hurricane."

"So what condition is she in?"

"There was a gash in the hull and I managed to get in the control room. I found a briefcase in there, a watertight job in aluminium."

"With a Kriegsmarine insignia engraved in the top right-hand corner?"

"That's right!"

"Standard issue, fireproof and waterproof, all that sort of thing. What did you say the number was, one-eighty? Hang on a minute and I'll look it up. I've got a book on one of my shelves that lists every U-boat commissioned by the Kriegsmarine during the War and what happened to them."

"Okay."

Baker waited patiently until Travers returned. "We've got a problem, old son, you're certain this was a type seven?"

"Absolutely."

"Well the problem is that one-eighty was a type nine, dispatched to Japan from France in August forty-four with technical supplies. She went down in the Bay of Biscay."

"Is that so?" Baker said. "Well how does this grab you? I found the personal diary of a Korvettenkapitän Paul Friemel in that briefcase and the final entry is dated May twenty-eighth, nineteen forty-five."

"But V.E. day in Europe was May the eighth," Travers said.

"Exactly, so what have we got here? A German submarine with a false number that goes down in the Virgins three weeks after the end of the bloody war."

"It certainly is intriguing," Travers said.

"You haven't heard the best bit, old buddy. Remember all those stories about Martin Bormann having escaped from Berlin?"

"Of course I do."

"Well I can't read German, but I sure can read his name and it's right here in the diary, and another little bombshell for you. So is the Duke of Windsor's."

Travers loosened his tie and took a deep breath. "Henry, old son, I must see that diary."

"Yes, that's what I thought," Baker said. "There's the British Airways overnight flight leaving Antigua around eight this evening our time. I should be able to make it. Last time I used it we got into London Gatwick at nine o'clock in the morning. Maybe you could give me a late breakfast."

"I'll be looking forward to that," Travers said and replaced the receiver.

The Professional Association of Diving Instructors, of which Henry was a certificated member, has strict regulations about flying after diving. He checked his book of rules and discovered that he should wait at least four hours after a single no-decompression dive at eighty feet. That gave him plenty of leeway, especially if he didn't fly down to Antigua until the afternoon, which was exactly what he intended.

First he rang British Airways in San Juan. Yes, they

had space in the first-class cabin on BA flight 252 leaving
Antigua at 20.10 hours. He made the booking and gave
them one of his Gold Card numbers. Next he rang Carib
Aviation in Antigua, an air-taxi firm he'd used before. Yes,
they were happy to accept the charter. They'd send up one
of their Partenavias early afternoon to St. Thomas. If they
left for the return trip to Antigua at four-thirty, they'd be
there by six at the latest.

He sat back, thinking about it. He'd book a water taxi
across to Charlotte Amalie, the main town on St. Thomas.
Forty minutes, that's all it would take, fifteen at the most
by taxi to the airport. Plenty of time to pack and get himself
ready, but first he had to see Jenny.

The waterfront was bustling when he walked down into
Cruz Bay this time. It was a picturesque little town, totally
charming and ever so slightly run-down in the way of most
Caribbean ports. Baker had fallen in love with the place the
first time he'd seen it. It was everything you'd hope for.
He used to joke that all it needed was Humphrey Bogart
in a sailor's cap and denims running a boat from the harbor
on mysterious missions.

Jenny's Place was slightly back from the road just before
Mongoose Junction. There were steps up to the veranda, a
neon sign above the door. Inside it was cool and shaded,
two large fans revolving in the low ceiling. There were
several booths against the walls, a scattering of marble-
topped tables across a floor of black and white tiles. There
were high stools at the long mahogany bar, bottles on glass
shelves against the mirrored wall behind. A large, handsome black man with graying hair was polishing glasses,
Billy Jones, the barman. He had the scar tissue around the
eyes and the slightly flattened nose of a professional fighter.
His wife, Mary, was manager.

He grinned. "Hi there, Mr. Henry, you looking for Jenny?"

"That's right."

"Went down the front with Mary to choose the fish for tonight. They shouldn't be too long. Can I get you something?"

"Just a coffee, Billy, I'll have it outside."

He sat in a cane chair on the veranda, drinking the coffee and thinking about things, was so much within himself that he didn't notice the two women approach until the last minute.

"You're back, Henry."

He looked up and found Jenny and Mary Jones coming up the steps. Mary wished him good morning and went inside and Jenny sat on the rail, her figure very slim in tee-shirt and blue jeans.

She frowned. "Is something wrong?"

"I've got to go to London," he told her.

"To London? When?"

"This afternoon."

Her frown deepened and she came and sat beside him. "What is it, Henry?"

"Something happened when I was diving this morning, something extraordinary. I found a wreck about eighty or ninety feet down."

"You damn fool." She was angry now. "Diving at that kind of depth on your own and at your age. Where was this?"

Although not a serious diver, she did go down occasionally and knew most of the sites. He hesitated. It was not only that he knew she would be thoroughly angry to know that he'd dived a place like Thunder Point and it certainly wasn't that he didn't trust her. He just wanted to keep the location of the submarine to himself for the moment, certainly until he'd seen Garth Travers.

"All I can tell you, Jenny, is that I found a German U-boat from nineteen forty-five."

Her eyes widened. "My God!"

"I managed to get inside. There was a briefcase, an aluminum thing. Watertight. I found the Captain's diary inside. It's in German, which I can't read, but there were a couple of names I recognized."

"Such as?"

"Martin Bormann and the Duke of Windsor."

She looked slightly dazed. "Henry, what's going on here?"

"That's what I'd like to know." He took her hand. "Remember that English friend of mine, Rear Admiral Travers?"

"The one you served in the Korean War with? Of course, you introduced me to him the year before last when we were in Miami and he was passing through."

"I phoned him earlier. He's got all sorts of records on the German Kriegsmarine. He checked on the boat for me. One-eighty, that's what's painted on the conning tower, but one-eighty was a different type boat and it went down in the Bay of Biscay in nineteen forty-four."

She shook her head in bewilderment. "But what does it all mean?"

"There were stories for years about Bormann, dozens of books, all saying he didn't die in Berlin at the end of the War, that he survived. People had sightings of him in South America, or so they said."

"And the Duke of Windsor?"

"God knows." He shook his head. "All I know is this could be important and I found the damn boat, Jenny, me, Henry Baker. Christ, I don't know what's in the diary, but maybe it changes history."

He got up and walked to the rail, gripping it with both hands. She had never seen him so excited, got up herself and put a hand on his shoulder. "Want me to come with you?"

"Hell no, there's no need for that."

"Billy and Mary could run things here."

He shook his head. "I'll be back in a few days. Four at the most."

"Fine." She managed a smile. "Then we'd better get back to the house and I'll help you pack."

His flight in the Carib Aviation Partenavia was uneventful except for strong headwinds that held them back a little so that the landing was later than he'd anticipated, around six-thirty. By the time he'd passed through customs, collected his luggage and proceeded to the British Airways desk, it was seven o'clock. He went through security into the departure lounge and the flight was called ten minutes later.

The service in British Airways First Class was as superb as usual. He had carried Korvettenkapitän Friemel's case through with him and he accepted a glass of champagne from the stewardess, opened the case and browsed through it for a while, not just the diary, but the photos and the letters. Strange, because he didn't understand a word. It was the photo of the Kriegsmarine officer that really intrigued him, presumably Friemel himself, the face of the enemy, only Baker didn't feel like that, but then seamen of all nations, even in war, tended to have a high regard for each other. It was the sea, after all, which was the common enemy.

He closed the case and put it in the locker overhead when takeoff was announced and spent his time reading one or two of the London newspapers which were in plentiful supply. The meal was served soon after takeoff, and after it had been cleared away the stewardess reminded him that each seat had its own small video screen and offered him a brochure which included a lengthy list of videos available.

Baker browsed through it. It would at least help pass the time, and then he shivered a little as if someone had passed over his grave. There was a film there he'd heard about, a German film, *Das Boot,* in English, *The Boat,* from all accounts a harrowing story of life in a U-boat at the worst time in the War.

Against his better judgment he ordered it and asked for a large Scotch. The cabin crew went round pulling down the window blinds so that those who wished to might sleep. Baker inserted the video, put on the earphones and sat there, in the semidarkness, watching. He called for another Scotch after twenty minutes and kept watching. It was one of the most disturbing films of its kind he had ever seen.

An hour was enough. He switched off, tilted his seat back and lay there, staring through the darkness thinking about Korvettenkapitän Paul Friemel and U180 and that final ending on Thunder Point, wondering what had gone wrong. After a while, he slept.

3

It was ten o'clock when the doorbell rang at the house in Lord North Street. Garth Travers answered the door himself and found Henry Baker standing there in the rain, the briefcase in one hand, his overnight case in the other. He had no raincoat and the collar of his jacket was turned up.

"My dear chap," Travers said. "For God's sake, come in before you drown." He turned as he closed the door. "You'll stay here of course?"

"If that suits, old buddy."

"It's good to hear that description of me again," Travers told him. "I'll show you to your room later. Let's get you some breakfast. My housekeeper's day off, so you'll get it Navy style."

"Coffee would be fine for the moment," Baker said.

They went to the large, comfortable kitchen and Travers put the kettle on. Baker placed the briefcase on the table. "There it is."

"Fascinating." Travers examined the Kriegsmarine insignia on the case, then glanced up. "May I?"

"That's why I'm here."

Travers opened the case. He examined the letters quickly. "These must be keepsakes, dated at various times in nineteen forty-three and -four. All from his wife from the looks of things." He turned to the photos. "Knight's Cross holder? Must have been quite a boy." He looked at the photos of the woman and the two little girls and read the handwritten paragraph on the back of one of them. "Oh dear."

"What is it?" Baker asked.

"It reads, 'my dear wife Lottie and my daughters, Ilse and Marie, killed in a bombing raid on Hamburg, August the eighth, nineteen forty-four.' "

"Dear God!" Baker said.

"I can check up on him easily enough. I have a book listing all holders of the Knight's Cross. It was the Germans' highest award for valor. You make the coffee and I'll get it."

Travers went out and Baker found cups, a tin of instant milk in the icebox, had just finished when Travers returned with the book in question. He sat down opposite Baker and reached for his coffee.

"Here we are, Paul Friemel, Korvettenkapitän, joined the German Navy as an officer cadet after two years studying medicine at Heidelberg." Travers nodded. "Outstanding record in U-boats. Knight's Cross in July forty-four for sinking an Italian cruiser. They were on our side by then, of course. After that he was assigned to shore duties at Kiel." He made a face. "Oh dear, mystery piles on mystery. It says here he was killed in a bombing raid on Kiel in April, nineteen forty-five."

"Like hell he was," Baker said.

"Exactly." Travers opened the diary and glanced at the first page. "Beautiful handwriting and perfectly legible." He riffled the pages. "Some of the entries are quite short. Can't be more than thirty pages at the most."

"Your German is fluent as I recall," Baker said.

"Like a native, old boy; my maternal grandmother was

from Munich. I'll tell you what I'll do, an instant translation into my word processor. Should take no more than an hour and a half. You get yourself some breakfast. Ham and eggs in the refrigerator, sorry, icebox to you, bread bin over there. Join me in the study when you're ready."

He went out and Baker, relaxed now that everything was in hand, busied himself making breakfast, aware that he was hungry. He sat at the table to eat it, reading Travers' copy of that morning's London *Times* while he did so. It was perhaps an hour later that he cleared everything away and went into the study.

Travers sat at the word processor, watching the screen, his fingers rippling over the keyboard, the diary open and standing on a small lectern on his right-hand side. There was a curiously intent look on his face.

Baker said cheerfully, "How's it going?"

"Not now, old boy, please."

Baker shrugged, sat by the fire and picked up a magazine. It was quiet, only the sound of the word processor except when Travers suddenly said, "My God!" and then a few minutes after that, "No, I can't believe it."

"For heaven's sake, what is it, Garth?" Baker demanded.

"In a minute, old boy, almost through."

Baker sat there on tenterhooks, and after a while Travers sat back with a sigh. "Finished. I'll run it through the copier."

"Does it have anything interesting to say?"

"Interesting?" Travers laughed harshly. "That's putting it mildly. First of all I must make the point that it isn't the official ship's log; it's essentially a private account of the peculiar circumstances surrounding his final voyage. Maybe he was trying to cover himself in some way, who knows, but it's pretty sensational. The thing is, what are we going to do about it?"

"What on earth do you mean?"

"Read it for yourself. I'll go and make some more coffee," Travers said as the copier stopped. He shuffled the sheets together and handed them to Baker, who settled himself in the chair by the fire and started to read.

Bergen, Norway, 30 April 1944. I, Paul Friemel, start this account, more because of the strangeness of the task I am to perform than anything else. We left Kiel two days ago in this present boat designated U180. My command is in fact a craft that was damaged by bombing while under construction at Kiel in nineteen forty-three. We are to my certain knowledge carrying the number of a dead ship. My orders from Grand Admiral Doenitz are explicit. My passenger will arrive this evening from Berlin, although I find this hard to swallow. He will carry a direct order in the Führer's own hand. I will learn our destination from him.

There was a gap here in the diary and then a further entry for the evening of the same day.

I received orders to proceed to the airstrip where a Feiseler Storch landed. After a few minutes an officer in the uniform of an SS General appeared and asked if I was Korvettenkapitän Friemel. He in no way identified himself, although at that stage I felt that I had seen him before. When we reached the dock, he took me to one side before boarding and presented me with a sealed envelope. When I opened it I found it contained the order from the Führer himself, which had been mentioned in Grand Admiral Doenitz's personal order to me. It ran as follows:

From the leader and Chancellor of the State. Reichsleiter Martin Bormann acts with my authority on a matter of the utmost importance and essential to the continuance of the Third Reich. You will place yourself under his direct authority, at all times remembering your solemn oath as an officer of the Kriegsmarine to your Führer, and will accept his command and authority as he sees fit and in all situations.

I recall now, having seen Bormann once at a State function in Berlin in 1942. Few people would recognize the man, for of all our leaders, I would conclude he is the least known. He is smaller than I would have thought, rough featured with overlong arms. Frankly, if seen in working clothes, one would imagine him a docker or laborer. The Reichsleiter enquired as to whether I accepted his authority which, having little option, I have agreed to do. He instructed me that as regards my officers and the crew, he was to be known as General Strasser.

1 May. Although the officers' area is the most spacious on board, it only caters for three with one bunk lashed up. I have taken this for myself and given the Reichsleiter the Commanding Officer's compartment on the port side and aft of what passes for a wardroom in this boat. It is the one private place we have, though only a felt curtain separates his quarters from the wardroom. As we left Bergen on the evening tide, the Reichsleiter joined me on the bridge and informed me that our destination was Venezuela.

2 May 1945. As the boat has been fitted with a snorkel I am able to contemplate a voyage entirely underwater, though I fear this may not be possible in the heavy weather of the North Atlantic. I have laid a course underwater by way of the Iceland-Faroes narrows and once we have broken into the Atlantic will review the situation.

3 May 1945. Have received by radio from Bergen the astonishing news that the Führer has died on the 1st of May fighting valiantly at the head of our forces in Berlin, in an attempt to deny the Russians victory. I conveyed the melancholy news to the Reichsleiter, who accepted it with what I thought to be astonishing calm. He then instructed me to pass the news to the crew, stressing that the war would continue. An hour later we received word over the radio that Grand Admiral Doenitz had set up a provisional government in Schleswig-Holstein. I doubt that it can last long with the Russians in Berlin and the Americans and British across the Rhine.

Baker was more than fascinated by this time and quickly passed through several pages which at that stage were mainly concerned with the ship's progress.

5 May. We received an order from U-boat command that all submarines at sea must observe a cease-fire from this morning at 08.00 hours. The order is to return to harbor. I discussed this with the Reichsleiter in his quarters, who pointed out that he had the Führer's authority to continue still and asked me if I queried it. I found this difficult to answer and he suggested that I consider the situation for a day or two.

8 May 1945. We received this evening by radio the message I have been expecting. Total capitulation to the enemy. Germany has gone down to defeat. I again met with the Reichsleiter in his quarters and while discussing the situation received a ciphered message from Bergen instructing me to return or to continue the voyage as ordered. The Reichsleiter seized upon this and demanded my obedience, insisting on his right to speak to the crew over the intercom. He disclosed his identity and the matter of his authority from the Führer. He pointed out that there was nothing left for any of us in Germany and that there were friends waiting in Venezuela. A new life for those who wanted it, the possibility for a return to Germany for those who wanted that. It was difficult to argue with his reasoning and, on the whole, my crew and officers accepted it.

12 May 1945. Continued south and this day received general signal from Canadian Navy in Nova Scotia to any U-boat still at sea, demanding we report exact situation, surface and proceed under black flag. Failure to do so apparently condemning us to be considered as pirate and liable to immediate attack. The Reichsleiter showed little concern at this news.

15 May 1945. The snorkel device is in essence an air pipe raised above the surface when we run at periscope depth. In this way we may run on our diesel engines underwater without using up our batteries. I have discovered considerable problems with the device, for if the sea is rough, and nothing is rougher than the Atlantic, the ball cock closes. When this happens, the engines still draw in air, which means an instant fall in pressure in the boat and this gives the crew

huge problems. We have had three cases of ruptured
eardrums, but proceeding with the aid of the snorkel does make it difficult for us to be detected from
the air.

17 May 1945. So far into the Atlantic are we now
that I feel our risk of detection from the air to be
minimal and decided from today to proceed on the
surface. We carve through the Atlantic's heavy seas,
continually awash, and our chances of encountering
anyone in these latitudes are slim.

20 May 1945. The Reichsleiter has kept himself to
himself for much of the trip except for eating with the
officers, preferring to remain on his bunk and read.
Today he asked if he could accompany me when I
was taking my watch. He arrived on the bridge in
foul weather gear when we were barreling through
fifteen- and twenty-foot waves and thoroughly enjoyed
the experience.

21 May 1945. An extraordinary night for me. The
Reichsleiter appeared at dinner obviously the worse
for drink. Later he invited me to his quarters where
he produced a bottle of Scotch whisky from one of
his cases and insisted I join him. He drank freely,
talking a great deal about the Führer and the final days
in the Bunker in Berlin. When I asked him how he
had escaped, he told me they had used the East-West
Avenue in the center of Berlin as a runway for light
aircraft. At this stage he had finished the whisky,
pulled out one of his duffel bags from under the bunk
and opened it. He took out an aluminium Kriegsmarine
captain's briefcase like my own and put it on the bunk,

then found a fresh bottle of whisky.

By now he was very drunk and told me of his last meeting with the Führer, who had charged him with a sacred duty to continue the future of the Third Reich. He said an organization called the Odessa Line had been set up years before by the SS to provide an escape line, in the event of temporary defeat, for those officers of SS and other units essential to the continuance of the struggle.

Then he moved on to the Kamaradenwerk, Action for Comrades, an organization set up to continue National Socialist ideas after the war. There were hundreds of millions salted away in Switzerland, South America and other places and friends in every country at the highest level of government. He took his aluminium case from the bunk, opened it and produced a file. He called it the Blue Book. He said it listed many members of the English aristocracy, many members of the English Parliament, who had secretly supported the Führer during the nineteen-thirties and also many Americans. He then took a paper from a buff envelope and unfolded it before me. He told me it was the Windsor Protocol, a secret agreement with the Führer signed by the Duke of Windsor while resident at Estoril in Portugal in 1940 after the fall of France. In it he agreed to ascend the throne of England again after a successful German invasion. I asked him what value such a document could be and how could he be sure it was genuine. He became extremely angry and told me that, in any event, there were those on his Blue Book list who would do anything to avoid exposure and that his own future was taken care of. I asked him at that point if he was certain and he laughed and said you could always trust an English gentleman. At this point he became so drunk that I had to assist him on to the bunk. He fell asleep instantly and I examined the contents of the briefcase. The names in his Blue Book list meant nothing to me, but the Windsor Protocol looked genuine enough. The only other thing in the briefcase was a list of numbered bank accounts and the Führer order and I closed it and placed it under the bunk with his other luggage.

Baker stopped at this point, put the diary down, got up and walked to the window as Garth Travers entered.

Travers said, "Here's the coffee. Thought I'd leave you to get on with it. Have you finished?"

"Just read what Bormann told him on the twenty-first of May."

"The best is yet to come, old boy, I'll be back," and Travers went out again.

25 May 1945. 500 miles north of Puerto Rico. I envisage using the Anegada Passage through the Leeward Islands into the Caribbean Sea with a clear run to the Venezuelan coast from there.

26 May 1945. The Reichsleiter called me to his quarters and informed me that it was necessary to make a stop before reaching our destination and requested to see the chart for the Virgin Islands. The island he indicated is a small one, Samson Cay, south-east of St. John in the American Virgin Islands, but in British sovereign waters being a few miles south of Norman Island in the British Virgin Islands. He gave me no indication of his reason for wishing to stop there.

27 May 1945. Surfaced off the coast of Samson Cay at 21.00 hours. A dark night with a quarter moon. Some lights observed on shore. The Reichsleiter requested that he be put ashore in one of the inflatables, and I arranged for Petty Officer Schroeder to take him. Before leaving he called me to his quarters and told me that he was expecting to meet friends on shore, but as a precaution against something going wrong he was not taking anything of importance with him. He particularly indicated the briefcase which he left on the bunk and gave me a sealed envelope which he said would give me details of my destination in Venezuela if anything went wrong and the name of the man I was to hand the briefcase to. He told me to send Schroeder back for him at 02.00 hours and that if he was not on the beach I was to fear the worst and depart. He wore civilian clothes and left his uniform.

Travers came back in at that moment. "Still at it?"

"I'm on the final entry."

The Admiral went to the drinks cabinet and poured Scotch into two glasses. "Drink that," he said, passing one to Baker. "You're going to need it."

28 May 1945. Midnight. I have just been on the bridge and noticed an incredible stillness to everything, quite unnatural and like nothing I have experienced before. Lightning on the far horizon and distant thunder. The waters here in the lagoon are shallow and give me concern. I write this at the chart table while waiting for the radio officer to check for weather reports.

There was a gap here and then a couple of lines scrawled hurriedly.

Radio report from St. Thomas indicates hurricane approaching fast. We must make for deep water and go down to ride it out. The Reichsleiter must take his chance.

"Only the poor buggers didn't ride it out," Travers said. "The hurricane caught them when they were still vulnerable. Must have ripped her side open on the reef where you found her."

"I'm afraid so," Baker said. "Then I presume the current must have driven her in on that ledge under the overhang."

"Where she remained all these years. Strange no one ever discovered her before."

"Not really," Baker said. "It's a bad place. No one goes there. It's too far out for people who dive for fun and it's very dangerous. Another thing. If the recent hurricane hadn't broken away the overhang, I might well have missed it myself."

"You haven't actually given me the location yet," Travers remonstrated.

"Yes, well, that's my business," Baker said.

Travers smiled. "I understand, old boy, I understand, but I really must point out that this is a very hot potato."

"What on earth are you getting at?"

"Number one, we'd appear to have positive proof after all the rumor and speculation for nearly fifty years, that Martin Bormann escaped from Berlin."

"So?" Baker said.

"More than that! There's the Blue Book list of Hitler's sympathizers here in England, not only the nobility but Members of Parliament plus the names of a few of your fellow countrymen. Worse than that, this Windsor Protocol."

"What do you mean?" Baker asked.

"According to the diary, Bormann kept them in a similar survival case to this." He tapped the aluminium briefcase. "And he left it on the bunk in the Commanding Officer's quarters. Now just consider this. According to Friemel's final entry he was in the control room at the chart table, entering the diary when he got that final radio report about the hurricane. He shoves the diary in his briefcase and locks it, only a second to do that, then gets on with the emergency. That would explain why you found the briefcase in the control room."

"I'll buy that," Baker agreed.

"No, you're missing the real point, which is that the case survived."

"So what are you getting at?"

"These things were built for survival, which means it's almost certain Bormann's is still in the Commanding Officer's quarters with the Blue Book, the Windsor Protocol and Hitler's personal order concerning Bormann. Even after all these years the facts contained in those documents would cause a hell of a stink, Henry, especially the Windsor thing."

"I wouldn't want to cause that kind of trouble," Baker told him.

"I believe you, I know you well enough for that, but what if someone else found that submarine?"

"I told you, no one goes there."

"You also told me you thought an overhang had been torn off revealing it. I mean, somebody *could* dive there, Henry, just like you did."

"The conditions were unusually calm," Baker said. "It's a bad place, Garth, no one goes there, I know, believe me. Another thing, the Commanding Officer's compartment is forward and aft of the wardroom, on the port side, that's what Friemel said in the diary."

"That's right. I was shown over a type VII U-boat. The Navy had one or two they took over after the War. The captain's cabin, so-called, is across from the radio and sound rooms. Quick access to the control room. That was the point."

"Yes, well my point is that you can't get in there. The forward watertight hatch is closed fast."

"Well you'd expect that. If they were in trouble, he'd have ordered every watertight hatch in the boat closed. Standard procedure."

"I tried to move the wheel. Corroded like hell. The door is solid. No way of getting in there."

"There's always a way, Henry, you know that." Travers sat there frowning for a moment, then said, "Look, I'd like to show the diary to a friend of mine."

"Who are we talking about?"

"Brigadier Charles Ferguson. We've known each other for years. He might have some ideas."

"What makes him so special?"

"He works on the intelligence side of things. Runs a highly specialized anti-terrorist unit responsible only to the Prime Minister, and that's privileged information, by the way."

"I wouldn't have thought this was exactly his field," Baker said.

"Just let me show him the diary, old boy," Travers said soothingly. "See what he thinks."

"Okay," Baker said. "But the location stays my little secret."

"Of course. You can come with me if you want."

"No, I think I'll have a bath and maybe go for a walk. I always feel like hell after a long jet flight. I could see this

Brigadier Ferguson later if you think it necessary."

"Just as you like," Travers said. "I'll leave you to it. You know where everything is."

Baker went out and Travers looked up Ferguson's personal phone number at the Ministry of Defence and was speaking to him at once. "Charles, Garth Travers here."

"My dear old boy, haven't seen you in ages."

Travers came directly to the point. "I think you should see me at your soonest moment, Charles. A rather astonishing document has come into my hands."

Ferguson remained as urbane as ever. "Really? Well we must do something about that. You've been to my flat in Cavendish Square?"

"Of course I have."

"I'll see you there in thirty minutes."

Ferguson sat on the sofa beside the fireplace in his elegant drawing room and Travers sat opposite. The door opened and Ferguson's manservant Kim, an ex-Ghurka Corporal, entered, immaculate in snow-white jacket and served tea. He withdrew silently and Ferguson reached for his cup of tea and continued reading. Finally he put the cup down and leaned back.

"Quite bizarre, isn't it?"

"You believe it then?"

"The diary? Good God, yes. I mean you obviously vouch for your friend Baker. He isn't a hoaxer or anything?"

"Certainly not. We were lieutenants together in Korea. Saved my life. He was chairman of a highly respected publishing house in New York until a few years ago. He's also a multi-millionaire."

"And he won't tell you the location?"

"Oh, that's understandable enough. He's like a boy again. He's made this astonishing discovery." Travers smiled.

"He'll tell us eventually. So what do you think? I know it's not really in your line."

"But that's where you're wrong, Garth. I think it's very much in my line, because I work for the Prime Minister and I think he should see this."

"There is one point," Travers said. "If Bormann landed on this Samson Cay place, there had to be a reason. I mean, who in the hell was he meeting?"

"Perhaps he was to be picked up by somebody, a fast boat and a passage by night, you know the sort of thing. I mean, he probably left the briefcase on board as a precaution until he knew everything was all right, but we can find out easily enough. I'll get my assistant, Detective Inspector Lane, on to it. Regular bloodhound." He slipped the papers comprising the diary back into their envelope. "Give me a moment. I'm going to send my driver round with this to Downing Street. Eyes of the Prime Minister only, then I'll see how soon he can see us. I'll be back."

He went out to his study and Travers poured another cup of tea. It was cold and he walked restlessly across to the window and looked outside. It was still raining, a thoroughly miserable day. As he turned, Ferguson came back.

"Can't see us until two o'clock, but I spoke to him personally and he's going to have a quick look when the package arrives. You and I, old son, are going to have an early luncheon at the Garrick. I've told Lane we'll be there in case he gets a quick result on Samson Cay."

"Umbrella weather," Travers said. "How I loathe it."

"Large gin and tonic will work wonders, old boy." Ferguson ushered him out.

They had steak and kidney pie at the Garrick, sitting opposite each other at the long table in the dining room, and coffee in the bar afterwards, which was where Jack Lane found them.

"Ah, there you are, Jack, got anything for me?" Ferguson demanded.

"Nothing very exciting, sir. Samson Cay is owned by an American hotel group called Samson Holdings. They have hotels in Las Vegas, Los Angeles and three in Florida, but Samson Cay would appear to be their flagship. I've got you a brochure. Strictly a millionaire's hideaway!"

He passed it across and they examined it. There were the usual pictures of white beaches, palm trees, cottages in an idyllic setting.

"Garden of Eden according to this," Ferguson said. "They even have a landing strip for light aircraft, I see."

"And a casino, sir."

"Can't be too big as casinos go," Travers pointed out. "They only cater for a hundred people."

"Isn't the numbers that count, old boy," Ferguson said. "It's the amount of cash across the table. What about during the War, Jack?"

"There was always a hotel of some sort. In those days it was owned by an American family called Herbert, who were also in the hotel business. Remember Samson Cay is in the British Virgin Islands, which means it comes under the control of Tortola as regards the law, customs and so forth. I spoke to their public record office. According to their files the hotel stayed empty during the War. The occasional fishermen from Tortola, a couple caretaking the property and that's all."

"Doesn't help but thanks, Jack, you've done a good job."

"It might help if I knew what it was about, sir."

"Later, Jack, later. Off you go and make Britain a safer place to live in." Lane departed with a grin, and Ferguson turned to Travers.

"Right, old boy, Downing Street awaits."

● ● ●

The Prime Minister was sitting behind his desk in his study when an aide showed them in. He stood up and came round the desk to shake hands. "Brigadier."

"Prime Minister," Ferguson said. "May I introduce Rear Admiral Travers?"

"Of course. Do sit down, gentlemen." He went and sat behind his desk again. "An incredible business this."

"An understatement, Prime Minister," Ferguson replied.

"You were quite right to bring it to my attention. The royal aspect is what concerns me most." The phone rang. He picked it up, listened, then said, "Send them up." As he replaced the receiver he said, "I know you've had your problems with the Security Services, Brigadier, but I feel this to be one of those cases where we should honor our agreement to keep them informed about anything of mutual interest. You recall you agreed to liaise with the Deputy Director, Simon Carter, and Sir Francis Pamer?"

"I did indeed, Prime Minister."

"I called both of them in immediately after reading the diary. They've been downstairs having a look at it themselves. They're on their way up."

A moment later the door opened and the aide ushered in the two men. Simon Carter was fifty, a small man with hair already snow-white. Never a field agent, he was an ex-academic, one of the faceless men who controlled Britain's intelligence system. Sir Francis Pamer was forty-seven, tall and elegant in a blue flannel suit. He wore a Guards tie, thanks to three years as a subaltern in the Grenadiers, and had a slight smile permanently fixed to the corner of his mouth in a way that Ferguson found intensely irritating.

They all shook hands and sat down. "Well, gentlemen?" the Prime Minister said.

"Always assuming it isn't a hoax," Pamer said. "A fascinating story."

"It would explain many aspects of the Bormann legend," Simon Carter put in. "Arthur Axmann, the Hitler Youth leader, said he saw Bormann's body lying in the road near the Lehrter Station in Berlin, that was after the breakout from the Bunker."

"It would seem now that what he saw was someone who looked like Bormann," Travers said.

"So it would appear," Carter agreed. "That Bormann was on this U-boat and survived would explain the numerous reports over the years of sightings of him in South America."

"Simon Wiesenthal, the Nazi hunter, always thought him alive," Pamer said. "Before Eichmann was executed, he told the Israelis that Bormann was alive. Why would a man faced with death lie?"

"All well and good, gentlemen," the Prime Minister told them, "but frankly, I think the question of whether Martin Bormann survived the war or not purely of academic interest. It would change history a little and the newspapers would get some mileage out of it."

"And a damn sight more out of this Blue Book list that's mentioned. Members of Parliament and the nobility." Carter shuddered. "The mind boggles."

"My dear Simon," Pamer told him. "There were an awful lot of people around before the War who found aspects of Hitler's message rather attractive. There are also names in that list with a Washington base."

"Yes, well their children and grandchildren wouldn't thank you to have their names mentioned, and what in the hell was Bormann doing at this Samson Cay?"

"There's a resort there now, one of those rich man's hideaways," Ferguson said. "During the War there was a hotel, but it was closed for the duration. We checked with public records in Tortola. Owned by an American family called Herbert."

"What do you think Bormann was after there?" Pamer asked.

"One can only guess, but my theory runs something like this," Ferguson said. "He probably intended to let U180 proceed to Venezuela on its own. I would hazard a guess that he was to be picked up by someone and Samson Cay was the rendezvous. He left the briefcase as a precaution in case anything went wrong. After all, he did give Friemel instructions about its disposal if anything happened to him."

"A pretty scandal, I agree, gentlemen, the whole thing, but imagine the furor it would cause if it became known that the Duke of Windsor had signed an agreement with Hitler," the Prime Minister said.

"Personally I feel it more than likely that this so-called Windsor Protocol would prove fraudulent," Pamer told him.

"That's as may be, but the papers would have a field day, and, frankly, the Royal Family have had more than their share of scandal in this past year or so," the Prime Minister replied.

There was silence and Ferguson said gently, "Are you suggesting that we attempt to recover Bormann's briefcase before anyone else does, Prime Minister?"

"Yes, that would seem the sensible thing to do. Do you think you might handle that, Brigadier?"

It was Simon Carter who protested, "Sir, I must remind you that this U-boat lies in American territorial waters."

"Well I don't think we need to bring our American cousins into this," Ferguson said. "They would have total rights to the wreck and the contents. Imagine what they'd get for the Windsor Protocol at auction."

Carter tried again. "I really must protest, Prime Minister. Group Four's brief is to combat terrorism and subversion."

The Prime Minister raised a hand. "Exactly, and I can think of few things more subversive to the interests of the nation than the publication of this Windsor Protocol. Brigadier, you will devise a plan, do whatever is necessary and as soon as possible. Keep me informed and also the Deputy Director and Sir Francis."

"So the matter is entirely in my hands?" Ferguson asked.

"Total authority. Just do what you have to." The Prime Minister got up. "And now you really must excuse me, gentlemen. I have a tight schedule."

The four men walked down to the security gates where Downing Street met Whitehall and paused at the pavement.

Carter said, "Damn you, Ferguson, you always get your way, but see you keep us informed. Come on, Francis," and he strode away.

Francis Pamer smiled. "Don't take it to heart, Brigadier, it's just that he hates you. Good hunting," and he hurried after Carter.

Travers and Ferguson walked along Whitehall looking for a taxi and Travers said, "Why does Carter dislike you so?"

"Because I succeeded too often where he's failed and because I'm outside the system and only answerable to the Prime Minister and Carter can't stand that."

"Pamer seems a decent enough sort."

"So I've heard."

"He's married, I suppose?"

"As a matter of fact, no. Apparently much in demand by the ladies. One of the oldest baronetcies in England. I believe he's the twelfth or thirteenth. Has a wonderful house in Hampshire. His mother lives there."

"So what is his connection with intelligence matters?"

"The Prime Minister has made him a junior minister at the Home Office. Extra Minister I believe his title is. A kind of roving trouble shooter. As long as he and Carter keep out of my hair I'll be well pleased."

"And Henry Baker—do you think he'll tell you where U180 is lying?"

"Of course he will, he'll have to." Ferguson saw a taxi and waved it down. "Come on, let's get moving and we'll confront him now."

After his bath, Baker had lain on his bed for a moment, a towel about his waist and, tired from the amount of traveling he'd done, fell fast asleep. When he finally awakened and checked his watch it was shortly after two o'clock. He dressed quickly and went downstairs.

There was no sign of Travers and when he opened the front door it was still raining hard. In spite of that, he decided to go for a walk as much to clear his head as anything else. He helped himself to an old trenchcoat from the cloakroom and an umbrella and went down the steps. He felt good, but then rain always made him feel that way and he was still excited about the way things were going. He turned toward Millbank and paused, looking across to Victoria Tower Gardens and the Thames.

In St. John, for obscure reasons, people drive on the left-hand side of the road as in England, and yet on that rainy afternoon in London, Henry Baker did what most Americans would do before crossing the road. He looked left and stepped straight into the path of a London Transport bus coming from the right. Westminster Hospital being close by, an ambulance was there in minutes, not that it mattered, for he was dead by the time they reached the Casualty Department.

4

In St. John it was just after ten o'clock in the morning as Jenny Grant walked along the waterfront to the cafe and went up the steps and entered the bar. Billy was sweeping the floor and he looked up and grinned.

"A fine, soft day, you heard from Mr. Henry yet?"

"Five hours time difference." She glanced at her watch. "Just after three o'clock in the afternoon there, Billy. There's time."

Mary Jones appeared at the end of the bar. "Telephone call for you in the office. London, England."

Jenny smiled instantly. "Henry?"

"No, some woman. You take it, honey, and I'll get you a cup of coffee."

Jenny brushed past her and went into the office, and Mary poured a little water into the coffee percolator. There was a sharp cry from inside the office. Billy and Mary glanced at each other in alarm, then hurried in.

Jenny sat behind the desk looking dazed, clutching the phone in one hand, and Mary said, "What is it, honey? Tell Mary."

"It's a policewoman ringing me from Scotland Yard in London," Jenny whispered. "Henry's dead. He was killed in a road accident."

She started to cry helplessly and Mary took the phone from her. "Hello, are you still there?"

"Yes," a neutral voice replied. "I'm sorry if the other lady was upset. There's no easy way to do this."

"Sure, honey, you got your job to do."

"Could you find out where he was staying in London?"

"Hang on." Mary turned to Jenny. "She wants to know the address he was staying at over there."

So Jenny told her.

It was just before five and Travers, in response to a telephone call from Ferguson asking him to meet him, waited in the foyer of the mortuary in the Cromwell Road. The Brigadier came bustling in a few minutes later.

"Sorry to keep you, Garth, but I want to expedite things. There has to be an autopsy for the coroner's inquest and we can't have that unless he's formally identified."

"I've spoken to the young woman who lives with him, Jenny Grant. She's badly shocked but intends to fly over as soon as possible. Should be here tomorrow."

"Yes, well, I don't want to hang about." Ferguson took a folded paper from his inside breast pocket. "I've got a court order from a Judge in chambers here which authorizes Rear Admiral Garth Travers to make formal identification, so let's get on with it."

A uniformed attendant appeared at that moment. "Is one of you gentlemen Brigadier Ferguson?"

"That's me," Ferguson told him.

"Professor Manning is waiting. This way, sir."

The post-mortem room was lit by fluorescent lighting that bounced off the white-lined walls. There were four stainless-steel operating tables. Baker's body lay on the nearest one, his head on a block. A tall, thin man in surgeon's overalls stood waiting, flanked by two mortuary technicians. Travers noted with distaste that they all wore green rubber boots.

"Hello, Sam, thanks for coming in," Ferguson said. "This is Garth Travers."

Manning shook hands. "Could we get on, Charles? I have tickets for Covent Garden."

"Of course, old boy." Ferguson took out a pen and laid the form on the end of the operating table. "Do you, Rear Admiral Travers, formally identify this man as Henry Baker, an American citizen of St. John in the American Virgin Islands?"

"I do."

"Sign here." Travers did so and Ferguson handed the form to Manning.

"There you go, Sam, we'll leave you to it," and he nodded to Travers and led the way out.

Ferguson closed the glass partition in his Daimler so the driver couldn't hear what was being said.

"A hell of a shock," Travers said. "It hasn't sunk in yet."

"Leaves us in rather an interesting situation," Ferguson commented.

"In what way?"

"The location of U180. Has it died with him?"

"Of course," Travers said. "I was forgetting."

"On the other hand, perhaps the Grant girl knows. I mean she lived with him and all that."

"Not that kind of relationship," Travers told him. "Purely platonic. I met her just the once. I was passing through Miami and they happened to be there. Lovely young woman."

"Well let's hope this paragon of all the virtues has the

answer to our problem," Ferguson said.

"And if not?"

"Then I'll just have to think of something."

"I wonder what Carter will make of all this."

Ferguson groaned. "I suppose I'd better bring him up to date. Keep the sod happy," and he reached for his car phone and dialed Inspector Lane.

At precisely the same time Francis Pamer, having made a very fast trip indeed from London in his Porsche Cabriolet to his country home at Hatherley Court in Hampshire, was mounting the grand staircase to his mother's apartment on the first floor. The house had been in the family for five hundred years and he always visited it with conscious pleasure, but not now. There were more important things on his mind.

When he tapped on the door of the bedroom and entered he found his mother propped up in the magnificent four-poster bed, a uniformed nurse sitting beside her. She was eighty-five and very old and frail and lay there with her eyes closed.

The nurse stood up. "Sir Francis. We weren't expecting you."

"I know. How is she?"

"Not good, sir. Doctor was here earlier. He said it could be next week or three months from now."

He nodded. "You have a break. I want to have a little chat with her." The nurse went out and Pamer sat on the bed and took his mother's hand. She opened her eyes. "How are you, darling?" he asked.

"Why, Francis, what a lovely surprise." Her voice was very faded.

"I had some business not too far away, Mother, so I thought I'd call in."

"That was nice of you, dear."

Pamer got up, lit a cigarette and walked to the fire. "I was talking about Samson Cay today."

"Oh, are you thinking of taking a holiday, dear? If you go and that nice Mr. Santiago is there, do give him my regards."

"Of course. I'm right, aren't I? It was your mother who brought Samson Cay into the family?"

"Yes, dear, her father, George Herbert, gave it to her as a wedding present."

"Tell me about the War again, Mother," he said. "And Samson Cay."

"Well, the hotel was empty for most of the War. It was small then, of course, just a little colonial-style place."

"And when did you go there? You never really talked about that and I was too young to remember."

"March nineteen forty-five. You were born in July, the previous year, and those terrible German rockets kept hitting London, V1s and V2s. Your father was out of the army then and serving in Mr. Churchill's government as a Junior Minister, just like you, dear. He was worried about the attacks on London continuing so he arranged passage on a boat to Puerto Rico for you and me. We carried on to Samson Cay from there. Now I remember. It was the beginning of April when we got there. We went over from Tortola by boat. There was an old man and his wife. Black people. Very nice. Jackson, that was it. May and Joseph."

Her voice faded and he went and sat on the bed and took her hand again. "Did anyone visit, Mother? Can you remember that?"

"Visit?" She opened her eyes. "Only Mr. Strasser. Such a nice man. Your father told me he might be coming. He just appeared one night. He said he'd been dropped off in a fishing boat from Tortola and then the hurricane came. It happened the same night. Terrible. We were in the cellar for two days. I held you all the time, but Mr. Strasser was very good. Such a kind man."

"Then what happened?"

"He stayed with us for quite a while. Until June, I think, and then your father arrived."

"And Strasser?"

"He left after that. He had business in South America, and the war in Europe was over, of course, so we came back to England. Mr. Churchill had lost the election and your father wasn't in Parliament anymore, so we lived down here, darling. The farms were a great disappointment."

She was wandering a little. Pamer said, "You once told me my father served with Sir Oswald Mosley in the First World War in the trenches."

"That's true dear, they were great friends."

"Remember Mosley's black shirts, Mother, the British Fascist Party? Did Father have any connection with that?"

"Good heavens no. Poor Oswald. He often spent the weekend here. They arrested him at the beginning of the War. Said he was pro-German. Ridiculous. He was such a gentleman." The voice trailed away and then strengthened. "Such a difficult time we had. Goodness knows how we managed to keep you at Eton. How lucky we all were when your father met Mr. Santiago. What wonderful things they did together at Samson Cay. Some people say it's the finest resort in the Caribbean now. I'd love to visit again, I really would."

Her eyes closed and Pamer went and put her hands under the cover. "You sleep now, Mother, it will do you good."

He closed the door gently, went downstairs to the library, got himself a Scotch and sat by the fire thinking about it all. The contents of the diary had shocked him beyond measure and it was a miracle that he had managed to keep his composure in front of Carter, but the truth was plain now. His father, a British Member of Parliament, a serving officer, a member of government, had had connections with the Nazi Party, one of those who had eagerly looked forward to a German invasion in 1940. The involvement must have been considerable. The whole business with Martin Bormann and Samson Cay proved that.

Francis Pamer's blood ran cold and he went and got another Scotch and wandered around the room looking at the portraits of his ancestors. Five hundred years, one of the oldest families in England, and he was a Junior Minister now, had every prospect of further advancement, but if Ferguson managed to arrange the recovery of Bormann's briefcase from the U-boat he was finished. No reason to doubt that his father's name would be on the Blue Book list of Nazi sympathizers. The scandal would finish him. Not only would he have to say goodbye to any chance of a high position in government, he would have to resign his Parliamentary seat at the very least. Then there would be the clubs. He shuddered. It didn't bear thinking about, but what to do?

The answer was astonishingly simple. Max—Max Santiago. Max would know. He hurried to the study, looked up the number of the Samson Cay resort, phoned through and asked for Carlos Prieto, the general manager.

"Carlos? Francis Pamer here."

"Sir Francis. What a pleasure. What can I do for you? Are you coming to see us soon?"

"I hope so, Carlos. Listen, I need to speak to Señor Santiago urgently. Would you know where he is?"

"Certainly. Staying at the Ritz in Paris. Business, I understand, then he returns to Puerto Rico in three days."

"Bless you, Carlos." Pamer had never felt such relief.

He asked the operator to get him the Ritz in Paris and checked his watch. Five-thirty. He waited impatiently until he heard the receptionist at the Ritz in his ear and asked for Santiago at once.

"Be there, Max, be there," he murmured.

A voice said in French, "Santiago here. Who is this?"

"Thank God. Max, this is Francis. I must see you. Something's happened, something bad. I need your help."

"Calm yourself, Francis, calm yourself. Where are you?"

"Hatherley Court."

"You could be at Gatwick by six-thirty your time?"

"I think so."

"Good. I'll have a charter waiting for you. We can have dinner and you can tell me all about it."

The phone clicked and he was gone. Pamer got his passport from the desk and a wad of traveler's checks, then he went upstairs, opened his mother's door and peered in. She was sleeping. He closed the door gently and went downstairs.

The phone sounded in his study. He hurried in to answer it and found Simon Carter on the line. "There you are. Been chasing you all over the place. Baker's dead. Just heard from Ferguson."

"Good God," Pamer said and then had a thought. "Doesn't that mean the location of U180 died with him?"

"Well he certainly didn't tell Travers, but apparently his girlfriend is flying over tomorrow, a Jenny Grant. Ferguson is hoping that she knows. Anyway, I'll keep you in touch."

Pamer went out, frowning, and the nurse entered the hall from the kitchen area. "Leaving, Sir Francis?"

"Urgent Government business, Nellie, give her my love."

He let himself out, got in the Porsche and drove away.

At Garth Travers' in Lord North Street the Admiral and Ferguson finished searching Baker's suitcase. "You didn't really expect to find the location of that damned reef hidden amongst his clothes, did you?" Travers asked.

"Stranger things have happened," Ferguson said, "believe me." They went into the study. The aluminium briefcase was on the desk. "This is it, is it?"

"Yes," Travers told him.

"Let's have a look."

The Admiral opened it. Ferguson examined the letter, the photos and glanced through the diary. "You copied this on your word processor here I presume?"

"Oh, yes, I typed the translation straight out of the top of my head."

"So the disk is still in the machine?"

"Yes."

"Get it out, there's a good chap, and stick it in the case, also any copy you have."

"I say, Charles, that's a bit thick after all I've done and anyway, it was Baker's property in the legal sense of the word."

"Not any more it isn't."

Grumbling, Travers did as he was told. "Now what happens?"

"Nothing much. I'll see this young woman tomorrow and see what she has to say."

"And then?"

"I don't really know, but frankly, it won't concern you from here on in."

"I thought you'd say that."

Ferguson slapped him on the shoulder. "Never mind, meet me in the Piano Bar at the Dorchester at eight. We'll have a drink."

He let himself out of the front door, turned down the steps and got into the rear of the waiting Daimler.

● ● ●

As the Citation jet lifted off the runway at Gatwick, Francis Pamer got himself a Scotch from the bar box thinking about Max Santiago. Cuban, he knew that, one of the landed families chased out by Castro in nineteen fifty-nine. The Max bit came from his mother, who was German. That he had money was obvious, because when he had struck the deal with old Joseph Pamer to develop Samson Cay Resort in nineteen seventy, he already controlled a number of hotels. How old would he be now, sixty-seven or -eight? All Francis Pamer knew for sure was that he had always been a little afraid of him, but that didn't matter. Santiago would know what to do and that was all that was important. He finished his Scotch and settled back to read the *Financial Times* until the Citation landed at Le Bourget Airport in Paris half an hour later.

Santiago was standing on the terrace of his magnificent suite at the Ritz, an impressively tall man in a dark suit and tie, his hair still quite black in spite of his age. He had a calm, imperious face, the look of a man who was used to getting his own way, and dark, watchful eyes.

He turned as the room waiter showed Pamer in. "My dear Francis, what a joy to see you." He held out a hand. "A glass of champagne, you need it, I can tell." His English was faultless.

"You can say that again," Pamer said and accepted the crystal glass gratefully.

"Now come and sit down and tell me what the trouble is."

They sat on either side of the fire. Pamer said, "I don't know where to begin."

"Why, at the beginning, naturally."

So Pamer did just that.

• • •

When he was finished, Santiago sat there for a while without saying a word. Pamer said, "What do you think?"

"Unfortunate to say the least."

"I know. I mean, if this business ever got out, Bormann on the island, my mother, my father."

"Oh, your mother didn't have the slightest idea who Bormann was," Santiago said. "Your father did, of course."

"I beg your pardon?" Pamer was stunned.

"Your father, dear old Joseph, was a Fascist all his life, Francis, and so was my father, and a great friend of General Franco. People like that were, how shall I put it, connected? Your father had very heavy links with Nazi Germany before the War, but then so did many members of the English establishment, and why not? What sensible person wanted to see a bunch of Communists take over? Look what they have done to my own Cuba."

"Are you saying you knew my father had this connection with Martin Bormann?"

"Of course. My own father, in Cuba at that time, was also involved. Let me explain, Francis. The Kamaradenwerk, Action for Comrades, the organization set up to take care of the movement in the event of defeat in Europe, was, still is, a worldwide network. Your father and my father were just two cogs in the machine."

"I don't believe it."

"Francis, how do you think your father was able to hang on to Hatherley Court? Your education at Eton, your three years in the Grenadier Guards, where did the money come from? Your father didn't even have his salary as an M.P. after he lost his seat."

"To the bloody Labour Party," Pamer said bitterly.

"Of course, but over the years he was allowed to, shall we say, assist with certain business dealings. When my own family left Cuba because of that animal Castro, there were funds made available to us in the United States. I built up the hotel chain, was able to indulge in certain illegal but lucrative forms of traffic."

Pamer had always suspected some kind of drug involvement and his blood ran cold. "Look, I don't want to know about that."

"You do like spending the money though, Francis." Santiago smiled for the first time. "The development of Samson Cay suited us very well. A wonderful cover, a playground for the very rich, and behind that facade, perfect for the conducting of certain kinds of business."

"And what if someone investigated it?"

"Why should they? Samson Holdings is, as the name implies, a holding company. It's like a Russian doll, Francis, one company inside another, and the name of Pamer appears on none of the boards and you'd have to go some way back to find the name of Santiago."

"But it was my grandmother's family who originally owned it."

"The Herbert people? That was a long time ago, Francis. Look, your mother's name was Vail, her mother's maiden name was Herbert I admit, but I doubt that any connection would be made. You mentioned that Ferguson had checked with Public Records in Tortola, who told him the hotel was unoccupied during the War."

"Yes, I wonder how they made the mistake?"

"Quite simple. A clerk nearly forty years later looks in the file and sees a notation that the hotel was unoccupied for the duration, which it was, Francis. Your mother didn't turn up with you until April forty-five, only four or five weeks before the end of the War. In any case it's of no consequence. I'll have my people check the Records Office in Tortola. If there's anything there we'll remove it."

"You can do that?" Pamer said aghast.

"I can do anything, Francis. Now, this Rear Admiral Travers, what's his address?"

"Lord North Street."

"Good. I'll get someone to pay him a call, although I shouldn't imagine he has the diary in his possession any longer or the translation from the sound of Ferguson."

"They'll be careful, your people," Pamer said. "I mean we don't want a scandal."

"That's exactly what you will have if we don't get in first on this thing. I'll get one of my people to check out this young woman, what was her name?"

"Jenny Grant."

"I'll have flights checked to see when she's arriving. Simple enough. She'll be on either the Puerto Rico or Antigua flight."

"And then what?"

Santiago smiled. "Why, we'll have to hope that she'll be able to tell us something, won't we?"

Pamer felt sick. "Look, Max, they won't hurt her or anything?"

"Poor old Francis, what a thoroughly spineless creature you are." Santiago propelled him to the door and opened it. "Wait for me in the bar. I have telephone calls to make, then we'll have dinner."

He pushed him out into the corridor and closed the door.

The Piano Bar at the Dorchester was busy when Garth Travers went in and there was no sign of Ferguson. He was greeted warmly by one of the waiters, for it was one of his favorite watering holes. A corner table was found and he ordered a gin and tonic and relaxed. Ferguson arrived fifteen minutes later and joined him.

"Got to do better than that," the Brigadier told him and ordered two glasses of champagne. "I love this place." He looked up at the mirrored ceiling. "Quite extraordinary, and that chap at the piano plays our kind of music, doesn't he?"

"Which is another way of saying we're getting on," Travers said. "You're in a good mood. Anything happened?"

"Yes, Lane did a check through British Airways at Gatwick. She's on Flight 252 departing Antigua at twenty-ten hours their time, arriving at Gatwick at five past nine in the morning."

"Poor girl," Travers said.

"Will you ask her to stay with you?"

"Of course."

"I thought you might." Ferguson nodded. "Under the circumstances I think it would be better if you picked her up. My driver will have the Daimler at your place at seven-thirty. I know it's early, but you know what the traffic is like."

"That's fine by me. Do you want me to bring her straight to you?"

"Oh, no, give her a chance to settle. She'll be tired after her flight. I can see her later." Ferguson hesitated. "There's a strong possibility that she'll want to see the body."

"Is it still at the mortuary?"

"No, at a firm of undertakers we use on department matters. Cox and Son, in the Cromwell Road. If she asks to go, take her there, there's a good chap."

He waved to a waiter and ordered two more glasses of champagne, and Travers said, "What about the U-boat, the diary, all that stuff? Do I say anything to her?"

"No, leave that to me." Ferguson smiled. "Now drink up and I'll buy you dinner."

And in Antigua, when she went up the steps to the first-class compartment, Jenny Grant felt as if she were moving in slow motion. The stewardess who greeted her cheerfully had the instinct that comes from training and experience that told her something was wrong. She took her to her seat and helped her get settled.

"Would you like a drink? Champagne, coffee?"

"Actually I could do with a brandy. A large one," Jenny told her.

The stewardess was back with it in a moment. There was concern on her face now. "Look, is there something wrong? Can I help?"

"Not really," Jenny said. "I've just lost the best friend I ever had to a road accident in London, that's why I'm going over."

The young woman nodded sympathetically. "There's no one sitting next to you, only six in the cabin this trip, nobody to bother you." She squeezed Jenny's shoulder. "Anything you need, just let me know."

"I'll probably try to sleep through the whole trip."

"Probably the best thing for you."

The stewardess went away and Jenny leaned back, drinking her brandy and thinking about Henry, all the kindness, all the support. He'd saved her life, that was the truth of it, and the strange thing was that try as she might, for some reason she couldn't remember his face clearly and tears welled up in her eyes, slow and bitter.

The Daimler arrived just before seven-thirty. Travers left a note for his housekeeper, Mrs. Mishra, an Indian lady whose husband kept a corner store not too far away, explaining the situation, hurried down the steps to Ferguson's limousine and was driven away, passing a British Telecom van parked at the end of the street. The van started up, moved along the street and parked outside Travers' house.

A telephone engineer in official overalls got out with a toolbox in one hand. He had the name Smith printed on his left-hand breast pocket. He went along the flagged path leading to the back of the house and the rear courtyard. He went up the steps to the kitchen door, punched a gloved hand through the glass pane, reached in and opened it. A moment later he was also opening the front door and another Telecom engineer got out of the van and joined him. The name on his overalls pocket was Johnson.

Once inside they worked their way methodically through the Admiral's study, searching every drawer, pulling the books from the shelves, checking for signs of a safe and finding none.

Finally, Smith said, "Waste of time. It isn't here. Go and get the van open."

He unplugged the Admiral's word processor and followed Johnson out, putting it in the back of the van. They went back inside and Johnson said, "What else?"

"See if there's a television or video in the living room, then take this typewriter."

Johnson did as he was told. When he returned to the living room Smith was screwing the head of the telephone back into place.

"You're tapping the phone?"

"Why not? We might hear something to our advantage."

"Is that smart? I mean, the kind of people we're dealing with, Intelligence people, they're not rubbish."

"Look, to all intents and purposes this is just another hit-and-run burglary," Smith told him. "Anyway, Mr. Santiago wants a result on this one and you don't screw around with him, believe me. Now let's get moving."

Mrs. Mishra, the Admiral's housekeeper, didn't normally arrive until nine o'clock, but the fact that she'd had the previous day off meant there was laundry to take care of so she had decided to make an early start. As she turned the corner of Lord North Street and walked toward the house, an overcoat over her sari against the early morning chill, she saw the two men come out of the house.

She hurried forward. "Is there a problem?"

They turned toward her. Smith said urbanely, "Not that I know of. Who are you, love?"

"Mrs. Mishra, the housekeeper."

"Problem with one of the telephones. We've taken care of it. You'll find everything's fine now."

They got in the van, Johnson behind the wheel, and drove away. Johnson said, "Unfortunate that."

"No big deal. She's Indian, isn't she? We're just another couple of white faces to her."

Smith lit a cigarette and leaned back, enjoying the view of the river as they turned into Millbank.

Mrs. Mishra didn't notice anything was amiss because the study door was half-closed. She went into the kitchen, put her bag on the table and saw the Admiral's note. As she was reading it she became aware of a draft, turned and saw the broken pane in the door.

"Oh my God!" she said in horror.

She quickly went back along the passage and checked the living room, noticed the absence of the television and video at once. The state of the study confirmed her worst fears and she immediately picked up the phone and dialed 999 for the police emergency service.

• • •

Travers recognized Jenny Grant at once as she emerged into the arrival hall at Gatwick pushing her suitcase on a trolley. She wore a three-quarter-length tweed coat over a white blouse and jeans and she looked tired and strained, dark circles under her eyes.

"Jenny?" he said as he approached. "Do you remember me? Garth Travers?"

"Of course I do, Admiral." She tried a smile and failed miserably.

He put his hands lightly on her shoulders. "You look bushed, my dear. Come on, let's get out of here. I've got a car waiting. Let me take your case."

The driver put the case in the boot of the Daimler and Travers joined her in the rear. As they drove away he said, "I expect you to stay with me, naturally, if that's all right?"

"You're very kind. Will you do something for me?" She was almost pleading. "Will you tell me exactly what happened?"

"From what witnesses have told the police he simply looked the wrong way and stepped in front of a bus."

"What a bloody stupid way to go." There was a kind of anger in her voice now. "I mean, here we had a sixty-three-year-old man who insisted on diving every day, sometimes to a hundred and thirty feet in hazardous conditions, and he has to die in such a stupid and trivial way."

"I know. Life's a bit of a bad joke sometimes. Would you care for a cigarette?"

"As a matter of fact, I would. I gave up six months ago, started again on the plane coming over last night." She took one from the packet he offered and accepted a light. "There's something else I'd like, and before we do anything else."

"What's that?"

"To see him," she said simply.

"I thought you might," Garth Travers said. "That's where we're going now."

The undertaker's was a pleasant enough place, considering what it was. The waiting room was panelled and banked with flowers. An old man in black suit and a tie entered. "May I help you?"

"Mr. Cox? I'm Admiral Travers and this is Miss Grant. You were expecting us, I believe?"

"Of course." His voice was a whisper. "If you would come this way."

There were several rooms off a rear corridor with sliding doors open revealing coffins standing on trestles and flowers everywhere, the smell quite overpowering. Mr. Cox led the way into the end one. The coffin was quite simple, made of mahogany.

"As I had no instructions I had to do the best I could," Cox said. "The fittings are gold plastic as I assumed cremation would be the intention."

He slid back the lid and eased the gauze from the face. Henry Baker looked very calm in death, eyes closed, face pale. Jenny put a hand to his face, slightly dislodging the gauze.

Cox carefully rearranged the gauze. "I wouldn't, miss."

She was bewildered for a moment and Travers said, "There was an autopsy, my dear, had to be, it's a court requirement. They'll be holding a coroner's inquest, you see. Day after tomorrow."

She nodded. "It doesn't matter, he's gone now. Can we leave, please?"

In the car he gave her another cigarette. "Are you all right?"

"Absolutely." She smiled suddenly. "He was a smashing fella, Admiral, isn't that what they say in England? The dearest, kindest man I ever knew." She took a deep breath. "Where to now?"

"My house in Lord North Street. You'd probably like a bath, rest up a little and so on."

"Yes, that would be nice."

She leaned back and closed her eyes.

The surprise at Lord North Street was the police car. The front door stood open and Travers hurried up the steps, Jenny behind him. He went into the hall and found the chaos in his study instantly, followed the sounds of voices and found Mrs. Mishra and a young policewoman in the kitchen.

"Oh, Admiral," Mrs. Mishra said as he entered. "Such a terrible thing. They have stolen many things. The television, your word processor and typewriter. The study is such a mess, but I saw their names on their overalls."

"Admiral Travers?" the policewoman said. "Typical daytime robbery, I'm afraid, sir. They gained access through that door."

She indicated the hole in the glass. Travers said, "The bloody swine."

"They were in a Telecom van," Mrs. Mishra said. "Telephone engineers. I saw them leave. Imagine such a thing."

"That's a common ploy during the day, sir," the policewoman said, "to pass themselves off as some kind of workmen."

"I don't suppose there's much chance of catching them either?" Travers inquired.

"I doubt it, sir, I really do. Now if I could have full details about what's missing."

"Yes, of course, just give me a moment." He turned to Jenny. "Sorry about this. Mrs. Mishra, this is Miss Grant.

She'll be staying for a while. Tell the driver to take her case up and show her to her room."

"Of course, Admiral."

Mrs. Mishra ushered Jenny out and Travers said to the policewoman, "There's a chance there could be more to this than meets the eye, officer. I'll just make a phone call and I'll be with you directly."

"Smith and Johnson," Ferguson said. "That's a good one."

"Seems like a run-of-the-mill daytime robbery, sir," Lane said. "All the usual hallmarks. They only took the kind of portable items that convert to quick cash. The television, video and the rest."

"Rather sophisticated, I would have thought, having their very own Telecom van."

"Probably stolen, sir. We'll run a check."

"Rather fortunate I relieved Travers of the diary and the translation software he'd made from it if they were looking for something more important than television sets."

"You really think it could have been that, sir?"

"All I know is that I learned a long time ago to suspect coincidence, Jack. I mean, how often does Garth Travers leave the house at seven-thirty in the morning? They must have seen him go."

"And you think taking the run-of-the-mill kind of stuff was just a blind?"

"Perhaps."

"But how would they know about the existence of the diary, sir?"

"Yes, well that is the interesting point." Ferguson frowned. "I've had a thought, Jack. Go to Lord North Street. Get one of your old friends from Special Branch, someone who specializes in bugging devices, to do a sweep."

"You really think . . . ?"

"I don't think anything, Jack, I'm merely considering all the options. Now on your way."

Lane went out and Ferguson picked up the phone and rang Lord North Street and spoke to Travers. "How's your guest?"

"Fine. Bearing up remarkably well."

Ferguson looked at his watch. "Bring her to my place in Cavendish Square at about twelve-thirty. We might as well get on with it, but don't say a word. Leave it all to me."

"You can rely on me."

Travers put the phone down and went into the living room, where Jenny sat by the fire drinking coffee. "Sorry about all this," he said, "a hell of an introduction."

"Not your fault."

He sat down. "We'll go out soon for a spot of lunch, but I'd like to introduce you to an old friend of mine, Brigadier Charles Ferguson."

She was an astute young woman and sensed something at once. "Did he know Henry?"

"Not directly."

"But this is something to do with Henry?"

He reached across and patted her hand. "All in good time, my dear, just trust me."

Santiago was still at his suite at the Ritz when the man who called himself Smith phoned through from London. "Not a thing, guv, certainly nothing like you described."

"Hardly surprising, but it was worth checking," Santiago said. "A nice clean job, I trust."

"Sure, guv, just made it look run-of-the-mill. I tapped the phone, just in case you wanted to listen in."

"You did what?" Santiago was coldly angry. "I told you, these are Intelligence people involved in this one, the kind of people who check everything."

"Sorry, guv, I thought I was doing the right thing."

"Never mind, it's too late now. Just drop any other commissions you have at the moment and wait to hear from me," and Santiago put the phone down.

In the living room at Cavendish Square Jenny sat beside the fire opposite Ferguson and Travers stood by the window.

"So you see, Miss Grant," Ferguson said, "there will have to be a coroner's inquest, which is set for the day after tomorrow."

"And I can have the body then?"

"Well that is really a matter for the next of kin."

She opened her handbag and took out a paper, which she unfolded and passed to him. "Henry took up serious diving a year or so ago."

"Rather old for that, I should have thought," Ferguson said.

"Yes, well he had a near-miss one day. Ran out of air at fifty feet. Oh, he made it to the surface okay, but he immediately went to his lawyer and had him draw up a power of attorney in my name."

Ferguson looked it over. "That seems straightforward enough. I'll see that it's passed to the coroner." He reached down at the side of the sofa and produced Friemel's aluminium briefcase. "Have you seen this before?"

She looked puzzled. "No."

"Or this?" He opened it and took out the diary.

"No, never." She frowned. "What is this?"

Ferguson said, "Did Mr. Baker tell you why he was coming to London?"

She looked at him, then turned to glance at Travers, then she turned back. "Why do you think he came here, Brigadier?"

"Because he discovered the wreck of a German submarine somewhere off St. John, Miss Grant. Did he tell you about that?"

Jenny Grant took a deep breath. "Yes, Brigadier, he did tell me. He said he'd been diving and that he'd discovered a submarine and a briefcase."

"This case," he said, "with this diary inside. What else did he tell you?"

"Well, it was in German, which he didn't understand, but he did recognize the name Martin Bormann and . . . " Here she paused.

Ferguson said gently, "And . . . ?"

"The Duke of Windsor," she said lamely. "Look, I know it sounds crazy but . . . "

"Not crazy at all, my dear. And where did Mr. Baker find this U-boat?"

"I've no idea. He wouldn't tell me."

There was a pause while Ferguson glanced at Travers. He sighed. "You are absolutely certain of that, Miss Grant?"

"Of course I am. He said he didn't want to tell me for the time being. He was very excited about his find." She paused, frowning. "Look, what are you trying to tell me, Brigadier? What's going on here? Does this have something to do with Henry's death?"

"No, not at all," he said soothingly and nodded to Travers.

The Admiral said, "Jenny, poor old Henry's death was a complete accident. We have plenty of witnesses. He stepped into the path of a London Transport bus. The driver was a sixty-year-old Cockney who won the Military Medal for Gallantry in the Korean War in nineteen fifty-two as an infantry private. Just an accident, Jenny."

"So, you've no idea where the U-boat lies?" Ferguson asked again.

"Is it important?"

"Yes, it could be."

She shrugged. "I honestly don't know. If you want my opinion, it would have to be somewhere far out."

"Far out? What do you mean?"

"Most of the dive sites that tourists use from St. Thomas and St. John are within reasonable distance. There are plenty of wrecks around, but the idea that a German U-boat had remained undiscovered since the end of the war," she shook her head, "that's nonsense. It could only happen if it was somewhere remote and far out."

"Further out to sea."

"That's right."

"And you've no idea where?"

"No, I'm not much of a diver, I'm afraid. You'd need to go to an expert."

"And is there such a person?"

"Oh, sure, Bob Carney."

Ferguson picked up his pen and made a note. "Bob Carney? And who might he be?"

"He has the watersports concession at Caneel Bay Resort. I mean, he spends most of his time teaching tourists to dive, but he's a real diver and quite famous. He was in the oil fields in the Gulf of Mexico, salvage work, all that stuff. They've done magazine articles about him."

"Really?" Ferguson said. "He's the best diver in the Virgin Islands then?"

"In the whole Caribbean, Brigadier," she said.

"Really." Ferguson glanced at Travers and stood up. "Good. Many thanks for your cooperation, Miss Grant. I appreciate this is not a good time, but you must eat. Perhaps you'll allow me to take you and Admiral Travers out for a meal tonight."

She hesitated and then said, "That's kind of you."

"Not at all. I'll send my car to pick you up at seven-thirty." He ushered them to the outside door. "Take care." He nodded to the Admiral. "I'll be in touch, Garth."

He was having a cup of tea and thinking about things half an hour later when Lane arrived. The Inspector dropped a hard, black metal bug on the coffee table. "You were right, sir, this little bastard was in the living room telephone."

"So," Ferguson said, picking it up. "The plot thickens."

"Look, sir, Baker knew about the diary because he found it, the girl knew because he told her, the Admiral knew, you know, the P.M. had a copy, the Deputy Director of the Intelligence Services knew, Sir Francis Pamer knew." He paused.

"You're missing yourself out, Jack."

"Yes, sir, but who the hell was it who knew who would go to the trouble of knocking off Admiral Travers' pad?"

"There you go again, Jack, police jargon." Ferguson sighed. "It's like a spider's web. There are lots of lines of communication between all those people you mention. God knows how many."

"So what are you going to do, sir? I mean, we don't even know where the bloody U-boat is. On top of that, we've all sorts of dirty work going on underneath things. Burglary, illegal phone-tapping."

"You're right, Jack, the whole thing assumes a totally new dimension."

"It might be better to bring Intelligence in on it, sir."

"Hardly, although when you get back to the office, you may phone Simon Carter and Sir Francis and tell them the girl says she doesn't know the site."

"But then what, sir?"

"I'm not sure. We'll have to send someone out there to find out for us."

"Someone who knows about diving, sir?"

"That's a thought, but if there is skulduggery afoot, someone who's just as big a villain as the opposition." Ferguson paused. "Correction, someone who is worse."

"Sir?" Lane looked bewildered.

Ferguson suddenly started to laugh helplessly. "My dear Jack, isn't life delicious on occasions? I spend simply ages getting someone I positively detest banged up, the cell door locked tight, and suddenly discover he's exactly what I need in the present situation."

"I don't understand, sir."

"You will, Jack. Ever been to Yugoslavia?"

"No, sir."

"Good, a new experience for you. We'll leave at dawn. Have them get the Learjet ready. Tell Admiral Travers I'll have to postpone dinner with him and the young lady."

"And the destination, sir?"

"The air strip at Kivo Castle, Jack. Tell them to clear it with the Serbian High Command. I don't think they'll have a problem."

5

Dillon was dozing on his bed at Kivo when the sound of a plane circling overhead awoke him. He lay there for a moment listening, aware of the change in the engine note that indicated a landing was being made. A jet by the sound of it. He went to the barred window and peered out. It was raining hard and as he looked out across the walls he saw a Learjet come in out of low cloud and make an approach to the airstrip. It landed perfectly, then taxied forward so that he could see there were no markings. It disappeared from view and he went and got a cigarette, wondering who it could be.

A shouted command drifted up and there was a crackle of rifle fire. He went back to the window, but he could only see part of the courtyard below. One or two soldiers appeared and laughter drifted up, presumably the General clearing out the cells again, and he wondered how many poor bastards had ended up against the wall this time. There was more laughter and then an army truck crossed his line of vision and disappeared.

"You're in a mess this time, my old son," he murmured softly. "A hell of a bloody mess," and he went and lay on the bed, finishing his cigarette and thinking about it.

• • •

In Paris, Santiago was about to leave his suite for a lunch appointment when the phone rang. It was Francis Pamer. "I tried to catch you earlier, but you were out," Pamer told him.

"Business, Francis, that's why I'm here. What have you got for me?"

"Carter had a word with me. He spoke to Ferguson. He said the girl doesn't know the location of the U-boat. He said that she knew about it, that Baker had told her about his discovery before he left, but that he hadn't told her where the damned thing is."

"Does Ferguson believe her?"

"Apparently," Pamer told him. "At least that was the impression Carter got."

"And what's Ferguson up to now?"

"I don't know. He just told Carter that he'd keep him posted."

"What about the girl? Where is she staying?" Santiago asked him.

"With Admiral Travers at Lord North Street. There's the coroner's inquest tomorrow. Once that's over Ferguson's agreed she can have the body."

"I see," Santiago said.

"What do you think, Max?"

"About the girl, you mean? I don't know. She could be telling the truth. On the other hand, she could be lying and there's only one way to find that out."

"What do you mean?"

"Why, by asking her, Francis, in the proper way, of course. A little persuasion, gentle or otherwise, works wonders."

"For God's sake, Max," Pamer began and Santiago cut him off.

"Just do what's necessary, keep me posted as regards Ferguson's plans and I'll have the girl taken care of. I had intended to return to Puerto Rico tomorrow, but I'll hang on for another day or two here. In the meantime, I'll speak to my people in San Juan, tell them to get the *Maria Blanco* ready for sea. The moment we know for definite that Ferguson intends some sort of operation in the Virgins, I'll sail down to Samson Cay and use it as a base."

Pamer said, "Christ, Max, I don't know whether I'm coming or going with this thing. If it comes out, I'm finished."

"But it won't, Francis, because I'll see that it doesn't. I've always anticipated seeing you in the Cabinet. Very useful to have a friend who's a British Cabinet Minister. I've no intention of allowing that not to happen, so don't worry."

Santiago put the phone down, thought about it for a moment, then picked it up again and rang his house in San Juan on the island of Puerto Rico.

Dillon was reading a book, head propped up against the pillow, when the key rattled in the lock, the door opened and Major Branko entered. "Ah, there you are," he said.

Dillon didn't bother getting up. "And where else would I be?"

"That sounds a trifle bitter," Branko told him. "After all, you're still with us. Cause for a certain amount of gratitude, I should have thought."

"What do you want?" Dillon asked.

"I've brought someone to see you, hardly an old friend, but I'd listen to what he has to say if I were you."

He stood to one side. Dillon swung his legs to the floor, was starting to get up and Ferguson entered the room followed by Jack Lane.

"Holy Mother of God!" Dillon said and Branko went out and closed the door behind him.

"Dear me, Dillon, but you are up the creek without a paddle, aren't you?" Ferguson dusted the only chair with his hat and sat. "We've never actually made it face to face before, but I imagine you know who I am?"

"Brigadier Charles bloody Ferguson," Dillon said. "Head of Group Four."

"And this is Detective Inspector Jack Lane, my assistant, on loan from Special Branch at Scotland Yard so he doesn't like you."

Lane's face was like stone. He leaned against the wall, arms folded, and Dillon said, "Is that a fact?"

"Look at him, Jack," Ferguson said. "The great Sean Dillon, soldier of the IRA in his day, master assassin, better than Carlos the Jackal, some say."

"I am looking at him, sir, and all I see is just another killer."

"Ah, but this one is special, Jack, the man of a thousand faces. Could have been another Olivier if he hadn't taken to the gun. He can change before your very eyes. Mind you, he cocked up his attempt to blow up the Prime Minister and the War Cabinet at Number Ten during the Gulf War as nobody knows better than you, Jack. By God, you gave us a hard time on that one, Dillon."

"A pleasure."

"But you're behind walls now," Lane said.

Ferguson nodded. "Twenty years, Jack, twenty years without getting his collar felt once and where does he end up?" He looked around the room. "You must have been out of your mind, Dillon. Medical supplies for the sick and the dying? You?"

"We all have our off days."

"Stinger missiles as well so you didn't even check your cargo properly. You must be losing your touch."

"All right, the show's over," Dillon told him. "What do you want?"

Ferguson got up and went to the window. "They've been shooting Croatians down there in the courtyard. We heard them as we drove over from the airstrip. They were clearing the bodies away in a truck as we drove in." He turned. "It'll be your turn one of these fine mornings, Dillon. Unless you're sensible, of course."

Dillon got a cigarette from one of the Rothmans packets and lit it with his Zippo. "You mean I have a choice?" he asked calmly.

"You could say that." Ferguson sat down again. "You shoot guns rather well, Dillon, fly a plane, speak a number of languages, but the thing I'm interested in at the moment was that underwater job you did for the Israelis. It was you, wasn't it, who blew up those PLO boats off Beirut?"

"Do you tell me?" Dillon said, sounding very Irish.

"Oh, for God's sake, sir, let's leave the bastard to rot," Lane said.

"Come on, man, don't be stupid. Was it you, or wasn't it?" Ferguson demanded.

"As ever was," Dillon told him.

"Good. Now here's the situation. I have a job that requires a man of your peculiar talents."

"A crook he means," Lane put in.

Ferguson ignored him. "I'm not sure exactly what's going on at the moment, but it could demand a man who can handle himself if things get rough. What I am certain of is that it would require, at the right moment, considerable diving skills."

"And where would all this take place?"

"The American Virgin Islands." Ferguson stood up. "The

choice is yours, Dillon. You can stay here and be shot or you can leave now and fly back to London in the Learjet we have at the airstrip with the Inspector and me."

"And what will Major Branko have to say about it?"

"No problem there. Nice boy. His mother lives in Hampstead. He's had enough of this Yugoslavian mess, and who can blame him. I'm going to arrange political asylum for him in England."

Dillon said, "Is there nothing you can't do?"

"Not that I can think of."

Dillon hesitated. "I'm a wanted man over there in the UK, you know that."

"Slate wiped clean, my word on it, which disgusts Inspector Lane here, but that's the way it is. Of course it also means you'll have to do exactly as you're told."

"Of course." Dillon picked up his flying jacket and pulled it on. "Yours to command."

"I thought you'd see sense. Now let's get out of this disgusting place," and Ferguson rapped on the door with his Malacca cane.

Dillon finished the diary and closed it. Lane was dozing, his head on a pillow, and the Irishman passed the diary to Ferguson, who sat on the other side of the aisle, but facing him.

"Very interesting," Dillon said.

"Is that all you've got to say?"

The Irishman reached for the bar box, found a miniature of Scotch, poured it into one of the plastic cups provided and added water. "What do you expect me to say? All right, Henry Baker's death was unfortunate, but he died happy, by God. Finding U180 must have been the biggest thing that ever happened to him."

"You think so?"

"Every diver's dream, Brigadier, to find a wreck that's never been discovered before, preferably stuffed with Spanish doubloons, but if you can't have that, the wreck on its own will do."

"Really."

"You've never dived?" Dillon laughed. "A silly question. It's another world down there, a special feeling, nothing quite like it." He swallowed some of his whisky. "So this woman you mentioned, this Jenny Grant, she says he didn't tell her where the U-boat is located?"

"That's right."

"Do you believe her?"

Ferguson sighed. "I'm afraid I do. Normally I don't believe in anyone, but there's something about her, something special."

"Falling for a pretty face in your old age," Dillon said. "Always a mistake that."

"Don't be stupid, Dillon," the Brigadier replied sharply. "She's a nice girl and there's something about her, that's all I mean. You can judge for yourself. We'll have dinner with Garth Travers and her this evening."

"All right." Dillon nodded. "So if she doesn't know where the damn thing is, what do you expect me to do?"

"Go to the Virgin Islands and find it, that's what I expect you to do, Dillon. It's no great hardship, I assure you. I visited St. John a few years back. Lovely spot."

"For a holiday?"

"You won't be on holiday, only pretending. You'll earn your keep."

"Brigadier," Dillon said patiently, "the sea is a hell of a big place. Have you any idea how difficult it is to locate a ship down there on the bottom? Even in Caribbean waters with good visibility, you could miss seeing it at a hundred yards."

"You'll think of something, you always do, Dillon, isn't that your special talent?"

"Jesus, but you have the most touching faith in me. All right, let's get down to brass tacks. Baker's death? Are you sure that was an accident?"

"Absolutely no question. There were witnesses. He simply looked the wrong way and stepped into the path of the bus. The driver, I might add, is beyond reproach."

"All right, so what about the burglary at this Admiral Travers' house, the bug in the telephone?"

Ferguson nodded. "A smell of stinking fish there. All the hallmarks of an opportunistic housebreaking, but the bug says otherwise."

"Who would it be?"

"God knows, Dillon, but all my instincts tell me there's someone out there and they're up to no good."

"But what?" Dillon said. "That's the point."

"I'm sure you'll come up with an answer."

"So when do you want me to go out to the Virgins?"

"I'm not sure. Two or three days, we'll see." Ferguson eased a pillow behind his head.

"And where do I stay while I'm hanging around in London?" Dillon enquired.

"I'll arrange for you to stay with Admiral Travers in Lord North Street. For the moment, you can earn your keep by keeping an eye on the girl," Ferguson told him. "Now shut up, there's a good chap, I need a spot of shut-eye."

He folded his arms and closed his eyes. Dillon finished his Scotch and leaned back thinking about it.

Ferguson murmured, "Oh, Dillon, just one thing."

"And what would that be?"

"Dr. Wegner and that young fool Klaus Schmidt, the people you dealt with at Fehring? Well-intentioned amateurs, but the man you bumped into in Vienna who put you in touch with them, Farben? He was acting for me. I got him to set you up, then got someone who works for me to shop you to the Serbs."

"Believe it or not, Brigadier, but something of the sort had occurred to me. I presume the Stinger missiles were your idea?"

"Wanted to see you behind bars, you see," Ferguson said. "If I couldn't get you one way . . ." He shrugged. "Mind you, this present business has got nothing to do with it. Lucky for you the situation arose."

"Or you'd have left me to rot."

"Not really. They'd have shot you sooner or later."

"Ah, well, what does it matter now?" Dillon said. "You might say it's all come out in the wash when you think about it," and he closed his eyes and dozed himself.

At Lord North Street, just before six, it was still raining as Dillon sat at the kitchen table and watched Jenny Grant make the tea. He had only just been introduced, for Ferguson was closeted in the study with Travers.

She turned and smiled. "Would you like some toast or anything?"

"Not really. Would you mind if I smoked?"

"Not at all." She busied herself with the tea things. "You're Irish, but you sound different."

"North of Ireland," he said. "What you would call Ulster and others the six counties."

"IRA country?"

"That's right," he told her calmly.

She poured the tea. "And what exactly are you doing here, Mr. Dillon? Would I be correct in assuming the Brigadier wants you to keep an eye on me?"

"And why would you think that?"

She sat opposite and sipped some of her tea. "Because

you look like that kind of man."

"And how would you be knowing that sort of person, Miss Grant?"

"Jenny," she said, "and I used to know all sorts of men, Mr. Dillon, and they were usually the wrong kind." She brooded for a moment. "But Henry saved me from all that." She looked up and her eyes glistened. "And now he's gone."

"Another cup?" He reached for the pot. "And what do you do in St. John?"

She took a deep breath and tried hard. "I have a cafe and bar called Jenny's Place. You must visit some time."

"You know what?" Dillon smiled. "I might just take you up on that," and he drank some more of his tea.

In the study Travers was aghast. "Good heavens, Charles, IRA? I'm truly shocked."

"You can be shocked as much as you like, Garth, but I need the little bugger. I hate to admit it, but he's very, very good. I intend to send him out to St. John once I've got things sorted. In the meantime he can stay here and act as your minder, just in case anything untoward happens."

"All right," Travers said reluctantly.

"If the girl asks I've told him to tell her he's a diver I've brought in to help with this thing."

"Do you think she'll believe that? I find her rather a smart young woman."

"I don't see why not. He *is* a diver amongst other things." Ferguson got up. "By the way, you had a man from my department earlier who replaced the bug in your phone and gave you a cellular telephone, didn't he?"

"That's right."

Ferguson led the way out and they went in the kitchen, where Jenny and Dillon sat at the table. Ferguson said,

"Right, you two, I'm off. We'll all meet for dinner at eight. The River Room at the Savoy, I think." He turned to Dillon. "That suit you?"

Dillon said, "A jacket-and-tie job, that, and here's me with only the clothes I'm standing up in."

"All right, Dillon, you can go shopping tomorrow," Ferguson said wearily and turned to Travers. "Good thing you're as small as he is, Garth. You can fix him up with a blazer, I'm sure. See you later."

The front door banged behind him and Dillon smiled. "Always in a hurry, that man."

Travers said reluctantly, "All right, you'd better come with me and I'll show you where you're sleeping and find you something to wear."

He led the way out and Dillon winked at Jenny and followed him.

Not too far away the fake telephone engineer who had called himself Smith turned into an alley where an old van was parked and knocked on the rear door. It was opened by Johnson and Smith joined him inside. There were various items of recording equipment and a receiver.

"Anything?" Smith asked.

"Not a thing. It's been on all day. Housekeeper ordering groceries, asking for a repair man for the washing machine. The Admiral phoned the London Library to order a book and the Army and Navy club about a function next month. Bit of a bore, the whole thing. What about you?"

"I was watching the house a short while ago and Ferguson turned up."

"You sure?"

"Oh, yes, definitely him. The photos on the file Mr. Santiago has supplied are very good. He had a guy with him."

"Any ideas?"

"No. Small, very fair hair, black leather flying jacket. He stayed, Ferguson left."

"So what do we do now?"

"Leave the recorder on. I can do a sweep in the morning and listen to anything interesting. I'll watch the house while you take some time off. If they go out, I'll follow and speak to you on the car phone."

"Okay," Johnson said. "I'll catch up with you later."

They got out of the van, he locked it and they went their separate ways.

Ferguson hadn't arrived when the Admiral, Dillon and Jenny reached the Savoy and went to the River Room. The table had been ordered, however, and the headwaiter led them to it.

"I suppose we might as well have a drink," Travers said.

Dillon turned to the wine waiter. "Bottle of Krug, nonvintage." He smiled amiably at Travers. "I prefer the grape mix."

"Do you, indeed?" the Admiral said stiffly.

"Yes." Dillon offered Jenny a cigarette. She was wearing a simple white blouse and black skirt. "You're looking rather nice." His voice had changed, and for the moment he was the perfect English gentleman, public-school accent and all.

"Are you ever the same for five minutes together?" she asked.

"Jesus, and wouldn't that be a bore? Let's dance." He reached for her hand and led her to the floor.

"You know you're not looking too bad yourself," she said.

"Well the blazer fits, but I find the Navy tie a bit incongruous."

"Ah, I see it now, you don't like institutions?"

"Not totally true. The first time I came to the River Room, I belonged to a famous institution, the Royal Academy of Dramatic Art."

"You're kidding me?" she said.

"No, I was a student there for one year only and I was offered a job with the National Theatre. I played Lyngstrand in Ibsen's 'Lady From the Sea,' the one who was coughing his guts up all the time."

"And after that?"

"Oh, there were family commitments. I had to go home to Ireland."

"What a shame. What have you been doing lately?"

He told the truth for once. "I've been flying medical supplies into Yugoslavia."

"Oh, you're a pilot."

"Some of the time. I've been a lot of things. Butcher, baker, candlestick maker. Diver."

"A diver?" She showed her surprise. "Really? You're not having me on?"

"No, why should I?"

She leaned back as they circled the floor. "You know, I get a funny feeling about you."

"What do you mean?"

"Well, it may sound crazy, but if someone asked me to speculate about you, for some totally illogical reason I'd say you were a soldier."

Dillon's smile was slightly lopsided. "Now what gave me away?"

"I'm right then." She was delighted with herself. "You were once a soldier."

"I suppose you could put it that way."

The music stopped, he took her back to the table and

excused himself. "I'm just going to see what cigarettes they have in the bar."

As he went away, the Admiral said, "Look, my dear, no sense in getting too involved with him, you know, not your sort."

"Oh, don't be an old snob, Admiral." She lit a cigarette. "He seems perfectly nice to me. He's just been flying medical supplies into Yugoslavia and he used to be a soldier."

Travers snorted and came right out with it. "Soldier of the bloody IRA."

She frowned. "You can't be serious."

"Infamous character," Travers said. "Worse than Carlos. They've been after him for years all over the place. Only reason he's here is because Charles has done a deal with him. He's going to help out with this thing, go to St. John, find the submarine and so on. Apparently the damned man's also a diver."

"I can't believe it."

As Dillon came out of the bar, he met Ferguson arriving and they came down to the table together.

"You're looking well, my dear," Ferguson said to Jenny. "The coroner's inquest is at ten-thirty tomorrow, by the way. No need for you to go as Garth here made the formal identification."

"But I'd prefer to be there," she said.

"Very well, if that's what you'd like."

"How soon after that can we arrange cremation?"

"That *is* what you want?"

"His ashes, yes," she said calmly. "I'm not expecting a service. Henry was an atheist."

"Really." Ferguson shrugged. "Well, if you're happy to use our people, they could do it virtually straightaway."

"Tomorrow afternoon?"

"I suppose so."

"Good. If you would arrange that I'd be grateful. If you're ordering I'd like caviar to start, a steak medium rare and a salad on the side."

"Would you now?" Ferguson said.

"It's called celebrating life." She reached for Dillon's hand. "And I'd like to dance again." She smiled. "It's not often I get the chance to do the foxtrot with an IRA gunman."

There were no more than five or six people in the small oak-paneled court in Westminster the following morning. Jenny sat at the front bench with Travers and Ferguson, and Dillon stood at the back near the Court usher, once more in his flying jacket. There was a brief pause while one of the people sitting at the front approached the bench and received some sort of warrant from the Clerk of the Court. As he went out, Smith and Johnson came into the court and sat on a bench on the other side of the aisle from Dillon. They were both respectably dressed in jacket and tie, but one look was enough for Dillon. Twenty years of entirely the wrong kind of living had given him an instinct for such things.

The Clerk of the Court got things started. "Rise for her Majesty's Coroner."

The Coroner was old with very white hair and wore a gray suit. Jenny was surprised. She'd expected robes. He opened the file before him. "This is an unusual case and I have taken note of the facts placed before me and have decided that in consequence the presence of a jury is not necessary. Is Brigadier Charles Ferguson in court?"

Ferguson stood up. "Yes, sir."

"I see you have served a D notice in this matter on behalf of the Ministry of Defence and this court accepts that there must be reasons for doing so affecting National Security. I accept the order and will have it entered into these proceedings. I will also, at this point, make it clear to any member of the press present that it is an offense punishable by a term of imprisonment to report details of any case covered by a D notice."

"Thank you, sir." Ferguson sat down.

"As the witnesses' statements given to the police in this unfortunate matter seem perfectly straightforward, I only need official identification of the deceased to be able to close these proceedings."

The Clerk of the Court nodded to Travers, who got up and went to the stand. The Coroner glanced at his papers. "You are Rear Admiral Garth Travers?"

"I am, sir."

"And your relationship with the deceased?"

"A close friend of many years on vacation from St. John in the American Virgin Islands, staying with me at my house in Lord North Street."

"And you made the official identification?" Travers nodded. "Is Miss Jennifer Grant in court?" She stood awkwardly and he said, "I have a power of attorney here in your name. You wish to claim the body?"

"I do, sir."

"So be it and so ordered. My Clerk will issue the necessary warrant. You have the sympathy of the court, Miss Grant."

"Thank you."

As she sat, the Clerk called, "Rise for Her Majesty's Coroner."

They all did so and the Coroner went out. Travers turned to Jenny. "All right, my dear?"

"Fine," she said, but her face was pale.

"Let's go," he said. "Charles is just getting the warrant. He'll catch us up."

They passed Dillon and went out. Smith and Johnson

got up and filed out with the other people while Ferguson busied himself with the Clerk of the Court.

It was sunny outside and yet Jenny shivered slightly and drew her collar about her throat. "It's cold."

"You could probably do with a hot drink," Travers said, concerned.

Dillon was standing on the top step as Ferguson joined him. Smith and Johnson had paused a little distance away by the bus stop for Smith to take out a cigarette and Johnson was lighting it for him.

Dillon said to Ferguson, "Do you know those two?"

"Why, should I?" the Brigadier asked.

At that moment a bus stopped, Smith and Johnson and a couple of other people boarded it and it pulled away. "Brigadier, I've lasted all these years by trusting my instincts and they tell me we've got a couple of bad guys there. What were they doing at the inquest anyway?"

"Perhaps you're right, Dillon. On the other hand, there are many people who view Court proceedings of any sort as free entertainment."

"Is that a fact now?"

The Daimler drew in to the pavement at the bottom of the steps and Jack Lane got out and joined them. "Everything go off all right, sir?"

"Yes, Jack." Ferguson handed him the Court order. "Give that to old Cox. Tell him we'd like the cremation carried out this afternoon." He glanced at Jenny. "Three o'clock suit you?"

She nodded, paler than ever now. "No problem."

Ferguson turned to Lane. "You heard. There were a couple of men in Court, by the way. Dillon had his doubts about them."

"How could he tell?" Lane asked, ignoring the Irishman. "Were they wearing black hats?"

"Jesus, would you listen to the man?" Dillon said. "Such wit in him."

Lane scowled, took an envelope from his pocket and held it out to Ferguson. "As you ordered, sir."

"Give it to him then."

Lane pushed it into Dillon's hand. "A damn sight more than you deserve."

"What have we got here then?" Dillon started to open the envelope.

"You need clothes, don't you?" Ferguson said. "There's a charge card for you in there and a thousand pounds."

Dillon took the rather handsome piece of plastic out. It was an American Express Platinum Card in his own name. "Sweet Joseph and Mary, isn't this going a little over the top, even for you, Brigadier?"

"Don't let it go to your head. It's all part of a new persona I'm creating for you. You'll be told at the right time."

"Good," Dillon said. "Then I'll be on my way. I'll get spending."

"And don't forget a couple of suitcases, Dillon," Ferguson said. "You're going to need them. Lightweight clothing, it's hot out there at this time of year, and if it's not too much trouble, try and look like a gentleman."

"Wait for me," Jenny called and turned to the other two men. "I'll go with Dillon. Nothing else to do and it will help me kill time. I'll see you back at the house, Admiral."

She went down the steps and hurried after Dillon. "What do you think?" Travers asked.

"Oh, she has depths, that girl, she'll make out," Ferguson said. "Now let's get moving," and he led the way down to the car.

As the Daimler was driving along Whitehall toward the Ministry of Defence, the car phone sounded. Lane, sitting on the pull-down scat, his back to the chauffeur, answered, then glanced up at Ferguson, a hand over the receiver.

"The Deputy Director, Brigadier. He says he'd like an updating on how things are going. Wonders whether you could meet him and Sir Francis at Parliament. Afternoon tea on the Terrace."

"The cremation is at three," Ferguson said.

"You don't need to be there," Travers told him. "I'll see to it."

"But I'd like to be there," Ferguson said. "It's the civilized thing to do. The girl needs our support." He said to Lane, "Four-thirty to five. Best I can do."

Lane confirmed the appointment and Travers said, "Very decent of you, Charles."

"Me, decent?" Ferguson looked positively wicked. "I'll take Dillon along and introduce him. Just imagine, Sean Dillon, the Carlos of our times, on the Terrace of the Houses of Parliament. I can't wait to see Simon Carter's face," and he started to laugh helplessly.

Dillon and Jenny made for Harrods. "Try and look like a gentleman, that's what the man said," he reminded her. "What do you suggest?"

"A decent suit for general purposes, gray flannel perhaps and a blazer. A nice loose linen jacket and slacks, it really does get hot in St. John at this time of the year, really hot."

"I'm yours to command," he assured her.

They ended up in the bar upstairs with two suitcases filled with his purchases. "Strange having to buy an entire wardrobe," she said. "Socks, shirts, underwear. What on earth happened to you?"

"Let's say I had to leave where I was in a hurry." He

called over a waiter and ordered two glasses of champagne and smoked salmon sandwiches.

"You like your champagne," she said.

Dillon smiled. "As a great man once said, there are only two things that never let you down in this life. Champagne and scrambled eggs."

"That's ridiculous, scrambled eggs go off very quickly. Anyway, what about people? Can't you rely on them?"

"I never had much of a chance of finding out. My mother died giving birth to me and I was her first, so no brothers or sisters. Then I was an actor. Few friends there. Your average actor would shoot his dear old granny if he thought it would get him the part."

"You haven't mentioned your father. Is he still around?"

"No, he was killed back in seventy-one in Belfast. He got caught in the cross-fire of a firefight. Shot dead by a British army patrol."

"So you joined the IRA?"

"Something like that."

"Guns and bombs, you thought that would be an answer?"

"There was a great Irishman called Michael Collins who led the fight for Irish freedom back in the early twenties. His favorite saying was something Lenin once said: 'The purpose of terrorism is to terrorize, it's the only way a small country can hope to take on a great nation and have any chance of winning.' "

"There's got to be a better way," she said. "People are fundamentally decent. Take Henry. I was a tramp, Dillon, drugged up to my eyeballs and working the streets in Miami. Any man could have me as long as the price was right and then along came Henry Baker, a decent and kindly man. He saw me through the drug unit, helped me rehabilitate, took me to St. John to share his house, set me up in business."

She was close to tears. "And he never asked me for a thing, Dillon, never laid a hand on me. Isn't that the strangest thing?"

A life spent mainly on the move and one step ahead of trouble had left Dillon with little time for women. They were there on occasions to satisfy an urge, but no more than that and he'd never pretended otherwise, but now, sitting there opposite Jenny Grant, he felt a kind of warmth and sympathy that was new to him.

Jesus, Sean, don't go falling for her, now there's a good lad, he thought, but reached over and put a hand on one of hers. "It will pass, girl, dear, everything does, the one sure thing in this wicked old life. Now have a sandwich, it'll do you good."

The crematorium was in Hampstead, a red brick building, reasonably functional looking but surrounded by rather pleasant parkland. There were poplar trees, beds of roses and other flowers of every description. The Daimler arrived with Dillon sitting up front beside the chauffeur, and Ferguson, Travers and the girl in the rear. Old Mr. Cox was waiting for them at the top of the steps, discreetly dressed in black.

"As you've asked for no kind of service I've already had the coffin taken in," he said to Ferguson. "Presumably the young lady would like a final look?"

"Thank you," Jenny said.

She followed him, Travers with a hand on her arm, and Ferguson and Dillon brought up the rear. The chapel was very plain, a few rows of chairs, a lectern, a cross on the wall. The coffin stood on a velvet-draped dais pointing at a curtained section of the wall. Music played faintly from some hidden tape recorder, dreary anodyne stuff. It was all very depressing.

"Would you care to see the deceased again?" Mr. Cox asked Jenny.

"No, thank you. I just wanted to say goodbye. Let him go now."

She was totally dry-eyed as Cox pressed a button on a box in the wall and the coffin rolled forward, parting the curtains, and disappeared.

"What's through there?" she asked.

"The furnace room." Cox seemed embarrassed. "The ovens."

"When can I have the ashes?"

"Later this afternoon. What would your needs be in that direction? Of course some people prefer to strew the ashes in our beautiful garden, but we do have a columbarium where the urn may be displayed with a suitable plaque."

"No, I'll take them with me."

"That won't be possible at the moment. It takes time, I'm afraid."

Travers said, "Perhaps you could have the ashes delivered to my house in Lord North Street in a suitable receptacle." He was embarrassed.

Cox said, "Of course." He turned to Jenny. "I presume you'll be flying back to the Caribbean, Miss Grant? We do provide a suitable container."

"Thank you. Can we go now?" she asked Ferguson.

Travers and Jenny got into the Daimler and Dillon paused at the top of the steps. There was a car parked close to the entrance to the drive and Smith was standing beside it, looking across at them. Dillon recognized him instantly, but in the same moment, Smith got in the car and it shot away.

As Ferguson emerged from the chapel Dillon said, "One of those two men I saw at the inquest was standing over there a moment ago. Just driven away."

"Really? Did you get the number?"

"Didn't have a chance to see it, the angle the car was at. Blue Renault, I think. You don't seem too worried."

"Why should I be, I've got you, haven't I? Now get in the car, there's a good chap." As they drove away he patted Jenny's hand. "Are you all right, my dear?"

"Yes, I'm fine, don't worry."

"I've been thinking," Ferguson told her. "If Henry didn't tell you the exact location of the submarine, can you think of anyone else he might have spoken to?"

"No," she said firmly. "If he didn't tell me, then he didn't tell anyone."

"No other diver maybe, I mean, he must have friends who dive as well, or another diver who might be able to help."

"Well there's always Bob Carney," she said, "the diver I told you about. He knows the Virgin Isles like the back of his hand."

"So, if anybody could help it would most likely be he?" Ferguson asked.

"I suppose so, but I wouldn't count on it. There's a lot of water out there."

The Daimler turned into Lord North Street and stopped. Travers got out first and reached a hand to Jenny. Ferguson said, "Dillon and I have work to do. We'll see you later."

Dillon turned in surprise. "What's this?"

"I've an appointment to meet the Deputy Director of the Security Services, Simon Carter, and a Junior Minister called Sir Francis Pamer on the Terrace at the Houses of Parliament. I'm supposed to keep them informed of my plans and I thought it might be amusing to take you along. After all, Dillon, Simon Carter's been trying to get his hands on you for years."

"Holy Mother of God," Dillon said, "but you're a wicked man, Brigadier."

Ferguson picked up the car phone and dialed Lane at the Ministry of Defence. "Jack, American called Bob Carney, resident St. John, presently a diver. Everything you can get. The CIA should help."

He put the phone down and Dillon said, "And what are you up to now, you old fox?"

But Ferguson made no reply, simply folded his hands across his stomach and closed his eyes.

6

———

The House of Commons has sometimes been referred to as the most exclusive club in London, mainly because of the amenities which, together with the upper chamber, the House of Lords, include twenty-six restaurants and bars each providing subsidized food and drinks.

There is always a queue waiting to get in, supervised by policemen, composed not only of tourists, but of constituents with appointments to see their Members of Parliament and everyone has to take their turn, no matter who, which explained why Ferguson and Dillon waited in line, moving forward slowly.

"At least you look respectable," Ferguson said, taking in Dillon's double-breasted blazer and gray flannels.

"Thanks to your Amex card," Dillon told him. "They treated me like a millionaire in Harrods."

"Really?" Ferguson said dryly. "You do realize that's a Guard's Brigade tie you're wearing?"

"Sure and I didn't want to let you down, Brigadier. Wasn't the Grenadiers your regiment?"

"Cheeky bastard!" Ferguson said as he reached the security checkpoint.

It was manned not by the security guards usually found at

such places, but by very large policemen whose efficiency was in no doubt. Ferguson stated his business and produced his security card.

"Wonderful," Dillon said. "They all looked about seven feet tall, just like coppers used to do."

They came to the Central Lobby where people with an appointment to see their MP waited. It was extremely busy and Ferguson moved on, through a further corridor and down more stairs, finally leading the way out through an entrance on to the Terrace overlooking the Thames.

Once again, there were lots of people about, some with a glass in their hand enjoying a drink, Westminster Bridge to the left, the Embankment on the far side of the river. A row of tall, rather Victorian-looking lamps ran along the parapet. The synthetic carpetlike covering on the ground was green, but further along it changed to red, a distinct line marking the difference.

"Why the change in color?" Dillon asked.

"Everything in the Commons is green," Ferguson said. "The carpets, the leather of the chairs. Red for the House of Lords. That part of the Terrace up there is the Lords'."

"Jesus, but you English do love your class distinction, Brigadier."

As Dillon lit a cigarette with his Zippo, Ferguson said, "Here they are now. Behave yourself, there's a good chap."

"I'll do my best," Dillon said as Simon Carter and Sir Francis Pamer approached.

"There you are, Charles," Carter said. "We were looking for you."

"People all over the place," Pamer said. "Like a damned souk these days. Now what's happening, Brigadier? Where are we at with this business?"

"Well let's go and sit down and I'll tell you. Dillon here's going to handle things at the sharp end."

"All right," Pamer said. "What do you fancy, afternoon tea?"

"A drink would be more to my taste," Ferguson told him. "And I'm pressed for time."

Pamer led the way along to the Terrace bar and they found seats in the corner. He and Carter ordered gin and tonics, Ferguson Scotch. Dillon smiled with total charm at the waiter. "I'll have an Irish and water, Bushmills if you have it."

He had deliberately stressed his Ulster accent and Carter was frowning. "Dillon, did you say? I don't think we've met before."

"No," Dillon said amiably, "although not for want of trying on your part, Mr. Carter. Sean Dillon."

Carter's face was very pale now and he turned to Ferguson. "Is this some sort of practical joke?"

"Not that I'm aware of."

Carter shut up as the waiter brought the drinks and as soon as he had gone, continued. "Sean Dillon? Is he who I think he is?"

"As ever was," Dillon told him.

Carter ignored him. "And you'd bring a damned scoundrel like this, here to this particular place, Ferguson? A man that the Intelligence services have hunted for years."

"That may be," Ferguson said calmly. "But he's working for Group Four now, all taken care of under my authority, so let's get on with it, shall we?"

"Ferguson, you go too far." Carter was seething.

"Yes, I'm told that often, but to business. To give you a résumé of what's happened. There was a burglary at Lord North Street, which may or may not have been genuine. However, we did discover a bug in the telephone which could indicate some kind of opposition. Have you any agents working the case?" he asked Carter.

"Certainly not. I'd have told you."

"Interesting. When we were at the inquest on Baker this morning Dillon noticed two men who gave him pause for thought. He noticed one of them again later when we were at the crematorium."

Carter frowned. "But who could it be?"

"God knows, but it's another reason for having Dillon on the job. The girl still insists she doesn't know the site of the submarine."

"Do you believe her?" Pamer put in.

"I do," Dillon said. "She's not the sort to lie."

"And you would know, of course," Carter said acidly.

Dillon shrugged. "Why should she lie about it? What would be the point?"

"But she must know something," Pamer said. "At the very least she must have some sort of a clue."

"Who knows?" Ferguson said. "But at this stage of the game we must proceed on the assumption that she doesn't."

"So what happens next?" Carter demanded.

"Dillon will proceed to St. John and take it from there. The girl mentioned a diver, a man named Carney, Bob Carney, who was a close friend of Baker. Apparently he knows the area like the back of his hand. The girl can make a suitable introduction, persuade him to help."

"But there's no guarantee he can find the damned thing," Pamer said.

"We'll just have to see, won't we?" Ferguson looked at his watch. "We'll have to go."

He stood and led the way outside. They paused by the wall on the edge of the Terrace. Carter said, "So that's it then?"

"Yes," Ferguson told him. "Dillon and the girl will probably leave for St. John tomorrow or the day after."

"Well I can't say I like it."

"No one is asking you to." Ferguson nodded to Dillon. "Let's get moving."

He moved away and Dillon smiled at the two of them with all his considerable charm. "It's been a sincere sensation, but one thing, Mr. Carter." He leaned over the parapet and looked down at the brown water of the Thames. "Only fifteen feet, I'd say, maybe less when the tide's up. All that security at the front door and nothing here. I'd think about that if I were you."

"Two-knot current out there," Pamer said. "Not that I can swim myself. Never could. Should be enough to keep the wolves at bay."

Dillon walked away and Carter said, "It makes my skin crawl to think of that little swine walking around here, a free man. Ferguson must be crazy."

Pamer said, "Yes, I see your point, but what do you think about the girl? Do you believe her?"

"I'm not sure," Carter said. "And Dillon has a point. Why would she lie?"

"So we're no further forward?"

"I wouldn't say that. She knows the area, she knew Baker intimately, the kind of places he went to and so on. Even if she doesn't know the actual location she may be able to work it out with this Carney fellow to help her, the diver."

"And Dillon, of course."

"Yes, well, I prefer to forget about him and under the circumstances, what I could do with is another drink," and Carter turned and led the way into the bar.

At his suite in Paris Max Santiago listened patiently while Pamer gave him details of the meeting on the Terrace.

"Astonishing," he said when Pamer had finished. "If this Dillon is the kind of man you describe, he would be a formidable opponent."

"But what about the girl?"

"I don't know, Francis, we'll have to see. I'll be in touch."

He put the phone down momentarily, picked it up again and rang Smith in London and when he answered, told him exactly what he wanted him to do.

It was just after six and Dillon was in the study reading the evening paper by the fire when the doorbell sounded. He went and opened it and found old Mr. Cox standing there, a hearse parked at the curb. He was holding a cardboard box in his hands.

"Is Miss Grant at home?"

"Yes, I'll get her for you," Dillon told him.

"No need." Cox handed him the box. "The ashes. They're in a traveling urn inside. Give her my best respects."

He went down to the hearse and Dillon closed the door. The Admiral had gone out to an early evening function at his club, but Jenny was in the kitchen. Dillon called to her and she came out.

"What is it?"

He held up the box. "Mr. Cox just left this for you," and turned and went into the study and put it on the table. She stood beside him, looking at it, then gently opened the lid and took out what was inside. It wasn't really an urn, just a square box in dark, patterned metal with a clasp holding the lid in place. The brass plate said: Henry Baker 1929–1992.

She put it down on the table and slumped into a chair. "That's what it all comes down to at the final end of things, five pounds of gray ash in a metal box."

She broke then and started to cry in total anguish. Dillon put his hands on her shoulders for a moment only. "Just let

it come, it'll do you good. I'll make you a cup of coffee,"
and he turned and went along to the kitchen.

She sat there for a moment and it was as if she couldn't
breathe. She had to get out, needed air. She got up, went
into the hall, took the Admiral's old trenchcoat down from
the stand and pulled it on. When she opened the door it
had started to rain. She belted the coat and hurried along
the pavement and Smith, sitting in the van with Johnson,
saw her pass the entrance to the alley.

"Perfect," he said. "Let's get on with it," and he got out
and went after her, Johnson at his heels.

Dillon went along the hall to the study, the cup of coffee in
his hand, and was aware first of the silence. He went into
the study, put down the cup and went back to the hall.

"Jenny?" he called and then noticed that the door was
slightly ajar.

"For God's sake," he said, took down his flying jacket
and went out, putting it on. There was no sign of her, the
street deserted. He'd have to take a chance, turned left and
ran along the pavement toward Great Peter Street.

It was raining very hard now and he paused on the corner
for a moment, looking left and then right, and saw her at
the far end where the street met Millbank. She was waiting
for a gap in the traffic, saw her chance and darted across to
Victoria Tower Gardens by the river, and Dillon also saw
something else, Smith and Johnson crossing the road behind
her. At that distance, he didn't actually recognize them, but
it was enough. He swore savagely and started to run.

It was almost dark as Jenny crossed to the wall overlooking
the Thames. There was a lamp about every twenty feet,
rain slanting in a silver spray through a yellow light, and
a seagoing freighter moved downstream, its red and green

navigation lights plain. She took a few deep breaths to steady herself and felt better. It was at that moment she heard a movement behind her, turned and found Smith and Johnson standing there.

She knew she was in trouble at once. "What do you want?" she demanded and started to edge away.

"No need to panic, darling," Smith said. "A little conversation is all we need, a few answers."

She turned to run and Johnson was on her like a flash, pinning her arms and forcing her back against the wall. "Jenny, isn't it?" he asked and as she struggled desperately, he smiled. "I like that, do it some more."

"Leave off," Smith told him. "Can't you ever think of anything except what's in your pants?" Johnson eased away, but moved round to hold her from the rear and Smith said, "Now about this U-boat in the Virgin Islands. You don't really expect us to believe you don't know where it is?"

She tried to struggle and Johnson said, "Go on, answer the man or I'll give you a slapping."

A voice called, "Put her down. I mean, she doesn't know where you've been, does she? She might catch something."

Dillon's Zippo lighter flared as he lit the cigarette that dangled from the corner of his mouth. He walked forward and Smith went to meet him. "You want trouble, you've got it, you little squirt," and he swung a tremendous punch.

Dillon swayed to one side, reaching for the wrist, twisted it so that Smith cried out in agony, falling to one knee. Dillon's clenched fist swung down in a hammer blow of tremendous force across the extended arm, snapping the forearm. Smith cried out again, fell over on his side.

Johnson said, "You little bastard."

He threw Jenny to one side and took an automatic pistol from his left-hand raincoat pocket. Dillon moved in fast, blocking the arm to the side, so that the only shot Johnson got off went into the ground. At the same time the Irishman half-turned, throwing the other man across his extended leg, ramming his heel down so hard that he fractured two of Johnson's ribs.

Johnson writhed on the ground in agony and Dillon picked up the automatic. It was an old Italian Beretta, small caliber, somewhere close to a point-two-two.

"Woman's gun," Dillon said, "but it'll do the job." He crouched down beside Johnson. "Who do you work for, sonny?"

"Don't say a word," Smith called.

"Who said I was going to?" Johnson spat in Dillon's face. "Get fucked."

"Suit yourself."

Dillon rolled him over, put the muzzle of the gun against the back of his left knee and fired. Johnson gave a terrible cry and Dillon took a handful of his hair and pulled his head back.

"Do you want me to do the other one? I'll put you on sticks if you like."

"No," Johnson moaned. "We work for Santiago—Max Santiago."

"Really?" Dillon said. "And where would I find him?"

"He lives in Puerto Rico, but lately he's been in Paris."

"And you did the burglary at Lord North Street?"

"Yes."

"Good boy. See how easy it was?"

"You stupid bugger," Smith said to Johnson. "You've just dug your own grave."

Dillon tossed the Beretta over the wall into the Thames. "I'd say he's been very sensible. Westminster Hospital's not too far from here, first-class casualty department and free, even for animals like you, thanks to the National Health Service."

He turned and found Jenny staring at him in a daze and he took her arm. "Come on, love, let's go home."

As they walked away Smith called, "I'll get you for this, Dillon."

"No you won't," Dillon said. "You'll put it down to experience and hope that this Max Santiago feels the same way."

They emerged from the gardens and paused at the pavement edge, waiting for a gap in the traffic. Dillon said, "Are you all right?"

"My God!" she said wonderingly. "What kind of man are you, Sean Dillon, to do that?"

"They'd have done worse to you, my love."

He took her hand and ran with her across the road.

When they reached the house she went straight upstairs and Dillon went into the kitchen and put the kettle on, thinking about things as he waited for it to boil. Max Santiago? Progress indeed, something for Ferguson to get his teeth into there. He was aware of Jenny coming down the stairs and going into the study, made the coffee, put the cups on a tray. As he went to join her he realized she was on the phone.

"British Airways? What's the last flight to Paris tonight?" There was a pause. "Nine-thirty? Can you reserve me a seat? Grant—Jennifer Grant. Yes, I'll pick it up at reservations. Yes, Terminal Four, Heathrow."

She put the phone down and turned as Dillon entered. He put the tray on the desk. "Doing a runner are you?"

"I can't take it. I don't understand what's going on. Ferguson, you and now those men and that gun. I can't get it out of my mind. I was going away anyway, but I'm going to get out now while I can."

"To Paris?" he said. "I heard you on the phone."

"That's just a jumping-off point. There's someone I have to see, someone I want to take this to." She picked up the black metal box containing the ashes. "Henry's sister."

"Sister?" Dillon frowned.

"I'm probably about the only person left who knows he had one. There are special reasons for that so don't ask me and don't ask me where I'm going after Paris."

"I see."

She glanced at her watch. "Seven o'clock, Dillon, and the flight's at nine-thirty. I can make it, only don't tell Ferguson, not until I've gone. Help me, Dillon, please."

"Then don't waste time in talking about it," he said. "Go and get your bags now and I'll ring for a taxi."

"Will you, Dillon, honestly?"

"I'll go with you myself."

She turned and hurried out and Dillon sighed and said softly, "You daft bastard, what's getting into you?" and he picked up the phone.

It was very quiet in the waiting room of the small private nursing home in Farsley Street. Smith sat in an upright chair against the wall, his right forearm encased in plaster and held in a sling. The half hour after their encounter with Dillon had been a nightmare. They couldn't afford to go to a public hospital because that would have meant the police, so he'd had to go and get the van from the alley by Lord North Street from where he'd driven one-handed to Victoria Tower Gardens to retrieve Johnson. The trip to Farsley Street had been even worse. Dr. Shah emerged from the operating theater, a small, gray-haired Pakistani in green cap and gown, a mask hanging around his neck.

"How is he?" Smith asked.

"As well as can be expected with a split kneecap. He'll limp for the rest of his life."

"That fucking little Irish bastard," Smith said.

"You boys can never stay out of trouble, can you? Does Mr. Santiago know about it?"

"Why should he?" Smith was alarmed. "Nothing to do with him this one."

"I thought it might, that's all. He phoned me from Paris the other day on business so I knew he was around."

"No, not his bag this." Smith got up. "I'll get myself off home. I'll be in to see him tomorrow."

He went out of the glass front door. Shah watched him go, then walked past the reception desk, empty at that time of night, and went into his office. He always believed in covering himself. He picked up the phone and rang Santiago at the Ritz in Paris.

The traffic at that time in the evening was light and they were at Heathrow by eight o'clock. Jenny picked up her ticket at the reservation desk and went and booked in for the flight. She put her case through, but carried the traveling urn.

"Time for a drink?" Dillon suggested.

"Why not?"

She seemed in better spirits now and waited for him in the corner of the bar until he returned with an Irish whisky and a glass of white wine. "You're feeling better, I can tell," he said.

"It's good to be on the move again, to get away from it all. What will you tell Ferguson?"

"Nothing about you until the morning."

"You'll tell him I flew to Paris?"

"No point in not doing, he'd find that out in five minutes from a check on British Airways' passenger computer."

"That doesn't matter, I'll be well on my way by then. What about you?"

"St. John next stop. Tomorrow or the day after."

"See Bob Carney," she said. "Tell him I sent you, and introduce yourself to Billy and Mary Jones. They're running the cafe and bar for me while I'm away."

"What about you? When will you be back?"

"I don't honestly know. A few days, a week, I'll see how I feel. I'll look you up when I get back if you're still there."

"I don't know where I'll be staying."

"It's easy to find someone in St. John."

The flight was called and they finished their drinks, went down to the concourse and he accompanied her to the security entrance. "I'm sorry if I've made trouble for you with the Brigadier," she said.

"Entirely my pleasure," he assured her.

"You're quite a guy, Dillon." She kissed him on the cheek. "Frightening, mind you, but thank God you're on my side. I'll see you."

Dillon watched her go, then turned and made his way to the nearest row of telephones, took out a card with telephone numbers which Ferguson had given him and rang the Cavendish Square number. Kim answered the phone and informed him that the Brigadier was dining at the Garrick Club. Dillon thanked him, went out to the rank and took the first cab in the line.

"London," he said. "The Garrick Club. You know where that is?"

"Certainly, guv." The driver examined Dillon's open-necked shirt in the rear-view mirror. "Wasting your time there, guv, dressed like that. They won't let you in. Jacket-and-tie job. Members and their guests only."

"We'll have to see, won't we?" Dillon told him. "Just take me there."

• • •

When they reached the Garrick, the driver pulled in at the curb and turned. "Shall I wait, guv?"

"Why not? I'll be straight out again if what you say is true."

Dillon went up the steps and paused at the desk. The uniformed porter was civil enough. "Can I help you, sir?"

Dillon put on his finest public-school accent. "I'm looking for Brigadier Charles Ferguson. I was told he was dining here tonight. I need to see him most urgently."

"I'm afraid I can't allow you upstairs, sir. We do require a jacket and tie, but if you care to wait here I'll have a message sent to the Brigadier. What was the name, sir?"

"Dillon."

The porter picked up the telephone and spoke to someone. He put the phone down. "He'll be with you directly, sir."

Dillon moved forward into the hall, admiring the grand staircase, the oil paintings that covered the walls. After a while Ferguson appeared up there, looked over the rail at him and came down the stairs.

"What on earth do you want, Dillon? I'm halfway through my dinner."

"Oh, Jesus, Your Honor." Dillon stepped effortlessly into the Stage Irishman. "It's so good of you to see me, the grand man like yourself and this place so elegant."

The porter looked alarmed and Ferguson took Dillon by the arm and propelled him outside to the top of the steps. "Stop playing the fool, my steak will be quite ruined by now."

"Bad for you at your age, red meat." Dillon lit a cigarette, the Zippo flaring. "I've found out who the opposition is."

"Good God, who?"

"A name, that's all I have. Santiago—Max Santiago. He lives in Puerto Rico, but recently he's been in Paris. By the way, they also did the burglary."

"How did you find this out?"

"I had a run-in with our two friends from the coroner's court."

Ferguson nodded. "I see. I hope you didn't have to kill anyone?"

"Now would I do a thing like that? I'll leave it with you, Brigadier, I feel like an early night."

He went down the steps to the cab and got in. "I told you, guv," the cabby said.

"Oh, well," Dillon said. "You can't win them all. Take me to Lord North Street," and he leaned back and looked out at the London night scene.

Jack Lane, only recently divorced, lived alone in a flat in West End Lane on the edge of Hampstead. He was cooking a frozen pizza in his microwave oven when the phone rang and his heart sank.

"Jack? Ferguson here. Dillon had a run-in with those two suspicious characters who were at the coroner's court and the crematorium. They've been working for a Max Santiago, resident of Puerto Rico, recently in Paris."

"Is that all, sir?"

"It's enough. Get yourself down to the office. See if French Intelligence has anything on him, then try the CIA, the FBI, anybody you can think of. He must be on somebody's computer. Did you get anything on this Bob Carney fellow, the diver?"

"Yes, sir, an interesting man in more ways than one."

"Right, you can brief me in the morning, but get cracking on this Santiago thing now. Five hours earlier than us in the States, remember."

"I'll try to, sir."

Lane put the phone down with a groan, opened the microwave oven and looked with distaste at the pizza. What the hell, he'd nothing better to do and he could always pick up some fish and chips on the way to the Ministry.

At his flat, Smith was on his second large Scotch, his right forearm in plaster and held by a sling. He felt terrible and it was beginning to hurt a great deal. He was pouring another Scotch when the phone rang.

Santiago said, "Have you anything for me?"

"Not yet, Mr. Santiago." Smith searched wildly for something to say. "Maybe tomorrow."

"Shah has been on the phone. Johnson shot and you with a broken arm. 'Fucking little Irish bastard,' I believe that was the phrase you used. Presumably Dillon?"

"Well, yes, Mr. Santiago, we did have a run-in with him. We'd got the girl, see, and he managed to jump us. He had a gun."

"Did he really?" Santiago commented dryly. "And what did you say when he asked you who your employer was?"

Smith answered instinctively, "Not a bloody thing, it was Johnson who . . . "

He stopped dead and Santiago said, "Carry on, tell me the worst."

"All right, Mr. Santiago, the stupid bastard did give Dillon your name."

There was silence for a moment and then Santiago said, "I'm disappointed in you, my friend, most disappointed." The phone clicked and the line went dead.

Smith knew what that meant. More frightened than he had ever been in his life, he packed a suitcase one-handed, retrieved a thousand pounds mad money he kept in a sugar tin in the kitchen and left. Two minutes later he was behind

the wheel of the van and driving away one-handed. He had
an old girlfriend in Aberdeen who'd always had a weakness
for him. Scotland, that was the place to go. As far away
from Johnson as possible.

At the nursing home Shah sat behind his desk, the phone
to his ear. After a while he put it down, sighed heavily and
went out. He went into the small pharmacy at the side of
the operating theater, fitted a syringe together and filled it
from a phial he took from the medicine cupboard.

When he opened the door at the end of the corridor,
Johnson was sleeping, linked to a drip. Shah stood looking
down at him for a moment, then bared the left forearm
and inserted the needle. Johnson sucked in air very deeply
for about five times, then stopped altogether. Shah checked
for vital signs, found none and went out. He paused at the
reception desk, picked up the phone and dialed.

A voice said, "Deepdene Funeral Service. How may we
serve you?"

"Shah here. I have a disposal for you."

"Ready now?"

"Yes."

"We'll be there in half an hour."

"Thank you."

Shah replaced the receiver and went back to his office,
humming to himself.

It was almost eleven when Travers returned to Lord North
Street and found Dillon sitting in the study reading a book.
"Jennifer gone to bed?" Travers asked.

"More than an hour ago. She was very tired."

"Not surprising, been through a hell of a lot that girl.
Fancy a nightcap, Dillon? Can't offer you Irish, but a good
single malt perhaps?"

"Fine by me."

Travers poured it into two glasses, gave him one and sat opposite. "Cheers. What are you reading?"

"Epictetus." Dillon held the book up. "He was a Greek philosopher of the Stoic School."

"I know who he was, Dillon," Travers said patiently. "I'm just surprised that you do."

"He says here that a life not put to the test is not worth living. Would you agree to that, Admiral?"

"As long as it doesn't mean bombing the innocent in the name of some sacred cause or shooting people in the back, then I suppose I do."

"God forgive you, Admiral, but I never planted a bomb in the way you mean or shot anyone in the back in me life."

"God forgive me, indeed, Dillon, because for some obscure reason I'm inclined to believe you." Travers swallowed his whisky and got up. "Good night to you," he said and went out.

Things had gone better than Smith had expected and he soon had the hang of handling the wheel one-handed, just the fingers of his right hand touching the bottom of the wheel. The rain wasn't helping, of course, and beyond Watford he missed a turning for the motorway and found himself on a long dark road, no other vehicles in sight, and then headlights were switched on behind and a vehicle came up far too fast.

It started to overtake him, a large black truck, and Smith cursed, frightened to death, knowing what this was, and he frantically worked at the wheel. The truck swerved in, knocking him sideways, and with nowhere to go, the van spun off the road, smashed through a fence and turned over twice on its way down a seventy-foot bank. It came to a crumpled halt and Smith, still conscious as he lay on his side in the cab, could smell petrol as the fractured tank spilled its contents.

There was the noise of someone scrambling down the bank and footsteps approached. "Help me," Smith moaned, "I'm in here."

Someone struck a match. It was the last thing he remembered. One final moment of horror as it was flicked toward him through the darkness and the petrol fireballed.

7

In Paris at Charles de Gaulle Airport it was almost midnight by the time Jenny Grant had retrieved her suitcase and she walked out into the concourse quickly and found an Avis car rental desk.

"You're still open, thank goodness," she said as she got her passport and driving license out.

"But of course," the young woman on duty replied in English. "We always wait until the final arrival of the day, even when there is a delay. How long will you require the car for, mademoiselle?"

"Perhaps a week. I'm not certain, but I'll be returning here."

"That's fine." The girl busied herself with the paperwork and took a print from her charge card. "Follow me and I'll take you to the car."

Ten minutes later Jenny was driving out of the airport sitting behind the wheel of a Citroën saloon and headed west, Normandy the destination. The traveling urn was on the passenger seat beside her. She touched it briefly, then settled back to concentrate on her driving. She had a long way to go, would probably have to drive through the night, but that didn't matter because London and the terrible events of the last few days were behind her and she was free.

Dillon rose early, was in the kitchen cooking bacon and eggs at seven-thirty when Travers entered in his dressing gown.

"Smells good," the Admiral said. "Jenny about yet?"

"Well, to be honest with you, Admiral, she's not been about for some time." Dillon poured boiling water into a china teapot. "There you go, a nice cup of tea."

"Never mind that. What are you talking about?"

"Well, drink your tea like a good lad and I'll tell you. It began with her getting upset and going for a walk."

Dillon worked his way through his bacon and eggs while he related the events of the previous night. When he was finished the Admiral just sat there frowning. "You took too much on yourself, Dillon."

"She'd had enough, Admiral," Dillon told him. "It's as simple as that and I didn't see any reason to stop her."

"And she wouldn't tell you where she was going?"

"First stop Paris, that's all I know. After that, to some unknown destination to see Baker's sister. She's taking the ashes to her, that's obvious."

"Yes, I suppose so." Travers sighed wearily. "I'll have to tell Ferguson. He won't like it, won't like it one little bit."

"Well it's time he discovered what an unfair world it is," Dillon told him and opened the morning paper.

Travers sighed heavily again, gave up, went to his study and sat at the desk. Only then did he reluctantly reach for the phone.

It was just after nine when Jenny Grant braked to a halt outside the Convent of the Little Sisters of Pity in the village of Briac five miles outside Bayeux. She had driven through the night, was totally drained. Iron gates stood open, she drove inside and stopped in a graveled circular drive in front of the steps leading up to the door of the beautiful old building. A young novice, a white working smock over her robes, was raking the gravel.

Jenny got out holding the traveling urn. "I'd like to see the Mother Superior. It's most urgent. I've come a long way."

The young woman said in good English, "I believe she's in chapel, we'll see, shall we?"

She led the way through pleasant gardens to a small chapel, which stood separate from the main building. The door creaked when she opened it. It was a place of shadows, an image of the Virgin Mary floating in candlelight, and the smell of incense was overpowering. The young novice went and whispered to the nun who knelt in prayer at the altar rail, then returned.

"She'll be with you in a moment."

She went out and Jenny waited. After a while the Mother Superior crossed herself and stood up. She turned and came toward her, a tall woman in her fifties with a sweet, serene face. "I am the Mother Superior. How may I help you?"

"Sister Maria Baker?"

"That's right." She looked puzzled. "Do I know you, my dear?"

"I'm Jenny—Jenny Grant. Henry told me he'd spoken to you about me."

Sister Maria Baker smiled. "But of course, so you're Jenny." And then she looked concerned. "There's something wrong, I can tell. What is it?"

"Henry was killed in an accident in London the other day." Jenny held out the traveling urn. "I've brought you his ashes."

"Oh, my dear." There was pain on Sister Maria Baker's face and she crossed herself, then took the urn. "May he rest in peace. It was so kind of you to do this thing."

"Yes, but it wasn't just that. I don't know which way to turn. So many awful things have happened."

Jenny burst into tears and sat down in the nearest pew. Sister Maria Baker put a hand on her head. "What is it, my dear, tell me."

When Jenny was finished it seemed very quiet in the chapel. Sister Maria Baker said, "Mystery upon mystery here. Only one thing is certain. Henry's unfortunate discovery of that submarine is of critical importance to many people, but enough of that now."

"I know," Jenny said, "and I'll have to go back to St. John if only to help Sean Dillon. He's a bad man, sister, I know that, and yet so kind to me. Isn't that strange?"

"Not really, my dear." Sister Maria Baker drew her to her feet. "I suspect that Mr. Dillon is no longer so certain that what he longed for was right. But all that can wait. You need a few days of total rest, a time to reflect, and that's doctor's orders. I *am* a doctor, you know, we're a nursing order. Now let's find you a room," and they went out together, leaving the chapel to the quiet.

When Dillon and Travers were shown into the flat at Cavendish Square just before noon, Ferguson was sitting by the fire going over a file. Jack Lane was standing by the window looking out.

Dillon said, "God save all here."

Ferguson glanced up coldly. "Very amusing, Dillon."

"Well the correct reply is 'God save you kindly,' " Dillon said, "but we'll let it pass."

"What in the hell were you playing at?"

"She wanted to go, Brigadier, she'd had enough for the moment, it was as simple as that. The attack by those two apes in Victoria Tower Gardens finished her off."

"So you just decided to go along with her?"

"Not her, her needs, Brigadier." Dillon lit a cigarette. "She told me she wanted to see Baker's sister and begged me not to ask her where that would be. Said there were special reasons she didn't want to divulge."

"Would you be interested to know that Lane has run a check and can't find any mention of Baker having a sister?"

"Not at all. Jenny said she was probably the only person who knew he had one. Some dark family secret, perhaps."

"So, she flew to Paris and took off for God knows where?"

Lane cut in. "We did a check at Charles de Gaulle. She hired a car at the Avis desk."

"And after that, who the hell knows?" Ferguson was coldly angry.

Dillon said, "I told you, she'd had enough."

"But we need her, God dammit."

"She'll return to St. John when she's ready. In the meantime, we'll have to manage." Dillon shrugged. "You can't have everything in life, not even you."

Ferguson sat there glaring at him, thoroughly angry, then said, "At least we have some sort of a lead. Tell him, Jack."

Lane said, "Max Santiago. He's the driving force behind a hotel group in the States, home in Puerto Rico. Hotels in Florida, Vegas, various other places and a couple of casinos."

"Is that a fact?" Dillon said.

"Yes, my first break was with the FBI. Their highly illegal sensitive red information file. It's highly illegal because it lists people who can't be proved to have broken the law in any way."

"And why would Santiago be on that?"

"Suspicion of having contacts with the Colombian drug cartel."

"Really?" Dillon smiled. "The dog."

"It gets worse. Samson Cay Holding Company, registered in the U.S.A. and Switzerland, goes backwards through three other companies until you get to Santiago's name."

"Samson Cay?" Dillon leaned forward. "Now that is interesting. A direct link. But why?"

Lane said, "Santiago's sixty-three, old aristocratic family, born in Cuba, father a general and very involved with Batista. The family only got out by the skin of their teeth in nineteen fifty-nine when Castro took over. Given asylum in America and eventual citizenship, but according to the FBI file, the interesting thing is they had not much more than the clothes they stood up in."

"I see," Dillon said. "So how did good old Max develop a hotel chain that must be worth millions? The drug connection can't explain that. All that Colombian drug business is much more recent."

"The plain answer is nobody knows."

Travers had been sitting listening to all this, looking bewildered. "So what is the connection? To Samson Cay and U180, Martin Bormann, all that stuff?"

"Well, the FBI file took me to the CIA," Lane said. "They have him on their computer too, but for a different reason. Apparently Santiago's father was a great friend of General Franco in Spain, an absolutely rabid Fascist."

"Which could be the link with nineteen forty-five, the end of the war in Europe and Martin Bormann," Ferguson said.

Dillon nodded. "I see it now. The Kamaradenwerk, Action for Comrades."

"Could be." The Brigadier nodded. "More than likely. Just take one aspect. Santiago and his father reach America flat broke and yet mysteriously manage to get their hands on the very large funds necessary to go into business. We know for a fact that the Nazi Party salted away millions all over the world to enable their work to keep going." He shrugged. "All conjecture, but it makes sense."

"Except for one thing," Dillon said.

"And what's that?"

"How Santiago knew about Baker finding U180. I mean, how did he know about him coming to London, staying at Lord North Street with the Admiral, Jenny, me? He does seem singularly well-informed, Brigadier."

"I must say Dillon's got a point," Travers put in.

Ferguson said, "The point is well taken and we'll find the answer in time, but for the moment we'll just have to get on with it. You'll leave for the Caribbean tomorrow."

"Just as we planned?" Dillon said.

"Exactly. British Airways to Antigua, then onwards to St. John."

Dillon said, "Would you think it likely that Max Santiago will turn up there? He's had his fingers in everything else so far."

"We'll just have to see."

"As I said," Lane interrupted. "He has a home in Puerto Rico and that's very convenient for the Virgin Islands. Apparently he runs one of those multi-million-dollar motor yachts." He looked at his file. "It's called the *Maria Blanco*. Captain and a crew of six."

"If he turns up you'll just have to do the best you can," Ferguson said. "That's what you're going to be there for. You'll have your Platinum Card and traveler's checks for twenty-five thousand dollars. Your cover is quite simple. You're a wealthy Irishman."

"God save us, I didn't know there was such a thing."

"Don't be stupid, Dillon," Ferguson told him. "You're a wealthy Irishman with a company in Cork. General electronics, computers and so on. We've provided a nice touch for you. When you arrive in Antigua, there'll be a seaplane waiting. You *can* fly a seaplane, I presume?"

"I could fly a Jumbo if I had to, Brigadier, but then you knew that."

"So I did. What kind of plane did you say it was, Jack?"

"A Cessna 206, sir." Lane turned to Dillon. "Apparently it's got floats and wheels so you can land on sea or on land."

"I know the type," Dillon said. "I've flown planes like it."

"The center of things in St. John is a town called Cruz Bay," the Inspector carried on. "On occasions they've had a commercial seaplane service round there so there's a ramp in the harbor, facilities and so on."

Ferguson passed a folder across. "The documents department have done you proud. Two passports, Irish and British in your own name. Being born in Belfast, you're entitled to those. C.A.A. commercial pilot's license with a seaplane rating."

"They think of everything," Dillon said.

"You'll also find your tickets and traveler's checks in there. You'll be staying at Caneel Bay, one of the finest resorts in the world. Stayed there once myself some years ago. Paradise, Dillon, you're a lucky chap, paradise on a private peninsula not too far from Cruz Bay."

Dillon opened the file and leafed through some of the brochures. "Situated on its own private peninsula, seven beaches, three restaurants," he read aloud. "It sounds my kind of place."

"It's anyone's kind of place," Ferguson said. "The two best cottages are 7E and 7D. Ambassadors stay there, Dillon, film stars. I believe Kissinger was in 7E once. Also Harry Truman."

"I'm overwhelmed," Dillon said.

"It will all help with your image."

"One thing," Lane said. "It's an old tradition there that there are no telephones in the cottages. There are public telephones dotted around, but we've arranged for you to have a cellular portable phone. They'll give it to you when you check in."

Dillon nodded. "So I get there. Then what do I do?"

"That's really up to you," Ferguson said. "We hoped the girl would be there to assist, but thanks to your misplaced gallantry that isn't on for the moment. However, I would suggest you contact this diver she mentioned, this Bob Carney. He runs a firm called Paradise Watersports, based at Caneel Bay. There's a brochure there."

"Teaches tourists to dive," Lane said.

Dillon found the brochure and glanced through it. It was attractively set out with excellent underwater photos, but the most interesting one was of Captain Bob Carney himself seated at the wheel of a boat, good-looking, tanned and very fit.

"Jesus," Dillon said. "If you wanted an actor to play that fella you'd have trouble finding someone suitable at Central Casting."

Ferguson said, "An interesting man, this Carney chap. Tell him, Jack."

Lane opened another file.

"Born in Mississippi in nineteen forty-eight, but he spent most of his youth in Atlanta. Wife, Karye, a boy of eight, Walker, girl aged five named Wallis. He did a year at the University of Mississippi, then joined the Marines and went to Vietnam. Did two tours, in sixty-eight and sixty-nine."

"I always heard that was a bad time," Dillon said.

"Toward the end of his service he was with the 2nd Combined Action Group. He was wounded, received two Purple Hearts, the Vietnamese Cross of Valour and was recommended for a Bronze Star. That one got lost in channels."

"And afterwards he took to diving?"

"Not at first. He went to Georgia State University, courtesy of the Marine Corps, and did a bachelor's degree in Philosophy. Did a year in a graduate school in Oceanography."

"Is there anything else?"

Lane consulted the file. "He has a captain's ticket up to sixteen hundred tons, ran supply boats in the Mexican Gulf to the oil rigs, was a welder and diver in the oilfields. Went to St. John in seventy-nine." Lane closed the file.

"So there's your man," Ferguson said. "You've got to get him on our side, Dillon. Offer him anything, money no object, within reason, that is."

Dillon smiled. "I'm surprised at you, Brigadier. Money is never number one on the list to men like Carney."

"That's as may be." Ferguson got up. "That's it then, I'll see you again before you leave in the morning. What time is his plane, Jack?"

"Nine o'clock, sir, gets into Antigua just after two in the afternoon their time."

"Then I certainly won't see you." Ferguson sighed. "I suppose I must see you off in the right style. Bring him to the Garrick for dinner at seven-thirty, Garth, but now you must excuse me."

"He's all heart, isn't he?" Dillon said to the Admiral as they emerged onto the pavement.

"Never would have thought of describing him in quite

that way," Travers said and raised his umbrella at a passing cab.

It was perhaps an hour later that Ferguson met Simon Carter in the snug of a public house called the St. George not too far from the Ministry of Defence.

He ordered a gin and tonic. "Thought I'd better bring you up to date," he said. "There's a lot happened."

"Tell me," Carter said.

So Ferguson did, the attack on Jenny by Smith and Johnson, Santiago, Jenny's flight, everything. When he finished, Carter sat there thinking about it.

"The Santiago thing—that's very interesting. Your chap Lane may have a point, the Fascist angle, General Franco and all that."

"It would certainly fit, but Dillon's right. None of it explains how Santiago seems to be so well informed."

"So what do you intend to do about him?"

"Nothing I *can* do officially," Ferguson said. "He's an American citizen, a multi-millionaire businessman and in the eyes of the world, highly respected. I mean, that stuff on the FBI and CIA files is confidential."

"And there is the fact that we don't want to involve the Americans in this in any way," Carter pointed out.

"Heaven forbid, the last thing we want."

"So we're in Dillon's hands," the Deputy Director said.

"I know and I don't like it one little bit." Ferguson stood up. "You'll let Pamer know where we're at."

"Of course," Carter told him. "Perhaps this Carney chap, the diver you mentioned, can give Dillon a lead."

"I'll keep you posted," Ferguson said and went out.

In Paris, Santiago, who was going to a black-tie dinner at the American Embassy, was adjusting his tie in the mirror when the phone rang. It was Pamer, and Santiago listened while he brought him up to date.

"So they know your name, Max." Pamer was very agitated. "And all thanks to those damned men who were working for you."

"Forget them," Santiago said. "They're yesterday's news."

"What's that supposed to mean?"

"Don't be stupid, Francis, you're a big boy now. Try to act like one."

Pamer was horrified. "All right, Max, but what are we going to do?"

"They can't lay a finger on me, Francis, I'm an American citizen, and they won't want to include the American Government in this thing. In fact, Ferguson is acting quite illegally in sending Dillon to operate in another country's sovereign territory. The U-boat is in American waters, remember?"

"So what will you do?"

"I'll fly to Puerto Rico in the morning, then sail down to Samson Cay and operate from there. Dillon must stay at either the Hyatt or at Caneel Bay if he uses a hotel, and a simple phone call will confirm that. I suspect Caneel Bay if he wishes to cultivate the diver, this Carney."

"I suppose so."

"A pity about the girl. She'll turn up eventually though, and I still feel she could be the key to this thing. She could know more than she realizes."

"Let's hope so."

"For your sake particularly, I hope so too, Francis."

Dillon, suitably attired in his blazer and a Guards tie, followed Travers up the imposing stairway at the Garrick Club. "Jesus, they've got more portraits here than the National

Gallery," he said and followed Travers through to the bar where Ferguson waited.

"Ah, there you are," he said. "I'm one ahead of you. Thought we'd have a spot of champagne, Dillon, just to wish you bon voyage. You prefer Krug as I recall."

They sat in the corner and the barman brought the bottle over in an ice bucket and opened it. He filled three glasses and retired. Ferguson thanked him, then took an envelope from his pocket and passed it across. "Just in case things get rough, there's the name of a contact of mine in Charlotte Amalie, that's the main town in St. Thomas. What you might call a dealer in hardware."

"Hardware?" Travers looked bewildered. "What on earth would he need with hardware?"

Dillon put the envelope in his pocket. "You're a lovely fella, Admiral, and long may you stay that way."

Ferguson toasted Dillon. "Good luck, my friend, you're going to need it." He emptied his glass. "Now let's eat."

There was something in his eyes, something that said there was more to this, much more, had to be, Dillon told himself, but he got up obediently and followed Travers and the Brigadier out of the bar.

And at Briac at the Convent of the Little Sisters of Pity, Jenny sat alone in the rear pew of the chapel, resting her arms on the backrest of the pew in front of her, gazing at the flickering candlelight at the altar and brooding. The door creaked open and Sister Maria Baker entered.

"There you are. You should be in bed."

"I know, Sister, but I was restless and wanted to think about things."

Sister Maria Baker sat down beside her. "Such as?"

"Dillon for one thing. He's done many terrible things. He was a member of the IRA, for example, and when those two men attacked me last night . . . " She shivered. "He was so coldly savage, so ruthless, and yet to me he was kindness itself and so understanding."

"So?"

Jenny turned to her. "I'm not a good Christian. In fact, when Henry found me, I was a very great sinner, but I do want to understand God, I really do."

"So what's the problem?"

"Why does God allow violence and killing to take place at all? Why does he allow the violence in Dillon?"

"The simplest thing to answer, my child. What God does allow is free will. He gives us all a choice. You, me, and the Dillons of this world."

"I suppose so." Jenny sighed. "But I will have to go back to St. John and not just to help Dillon, but somehow for Henry too."

"Why do you feel so strongly?"

"Because Henry really didn't tell me where he discovered that U-boat, which means the secret must have died with him, and yet I have the oddest feeling that it didn't, that the information is back there in St. John, but I just can't think straight. It won't come, Sister."

She was distressed again and Sister Maria Baker took her hands. "That's enough, you need sleep. A few days' rest will work wonders. You'll remember then what you can't now, I promise you. Now let's have you in bed."

She took Jenny by the hand and led her out.

Ferguson's Daimler picked Dillon up at seven-thirty the following morning to take him to Gatwick and Travers insisted on accompanying him. The journey out of town at that time in the morning with all the heavy traffic going the other way was relatively quick, and Dillon was ready to go through passport control and security by eight-thirty.

"They've already called it, I see," Travers said.

"So it seems."

"Look here, Dillon," Travers said awkwardly. "We'll never see eye-to-eye, you and me, I mean the IRA and all that stuff, but I want to thank you for what you did for the girl. I liked her—liked her a lot."

"And so did I."

Travers shook Dillon's hand. "Take care, this Santiago sounds bad news."

"I'll try, Admiral."

"Another thing." Travers sounded more awkward than ever. "Charles Ferguson is a dear friend, but he's also the most devious old sod I've ever known in my life. Watch yourself in the clinches there too."

"I will, Admiral, I will," Dillon said, watched the Admiral walk away, then turned and went through.

A nice man, he thought as the Jumbo lifted off and climbed steadily, a decent man, but nobody's fool and he was right; there *was* more to all this than the surface of things, nothing was more certain than that, and Ferguson knew what it was. *Devious old sod.* An apt description.

"Ah, well, I can be just as devious," Dillon murmured and accepted the glass of champagne the stewardess offered.

8

The flight to Antigua took a little over eight hours thanks
to a tailwind, and they arrived just after two o'clock local
time. It was hot, really hot, very noticeable after London.
Dillon felt quite cheered and strode ahead of everybody else
toward the airport building, wearing black cord slacks and a
denim shirt, his black flying jacket over one shoulder. When
he reached the entrance a young black woman in a pale blue
uniform was standing there with a board bearing his name.

Dillon paused. "I'm Dillon."

She smiled. "I'm Judy, Mr. Dillon. I'll see you through
immigration and so on and then take you to your plane."

"You represent the handling agents?" he asked as they
walked through.

"That's right. I need to see your pilot's license and there
are a couple of forms to fill in for the aviation authority,
but we can do that while we're waiting for the luggage to
come through."

Twenty minutes later she was driving him out to the far side
of the runway in a courtesy bus, an engineer called Tony in
white overalls sitting beside her. The Cessna was parked
beside a number of private planes, slightly incongruous

160

because of its floats, with wheels protruding beneath.

"Shouldn't give you any problems," Tony said as he stowed Dillon's two suitcases. "Flies as sweet as a nut. Of course a lot of people are nervous about flying in the islands with a single engine, but the beauty about this baby is you can always come down in the water."

"Or something like that," Dillon said.

Tony laughed, reached into the cabin and pointed. "There's an air log listing all the islands and their airfields and charts. Our chief pilot has marked your course from here to Cruz Bay in St. John. Very straightforward. Around two hundred and fifty miles. Takes about an hour and a half." He glanced at his watch. "You should be there by four-thirty."

"It's American territory, but customs and immigration are expecting you. They'll be waiting at the ramp at Cruz Bay. When you're close enough, call in to St. Thomas and they'll let them know you're coming. Oh, and there will be a self-drive jeep waiting for you." Judy smiled. "I think that's about it."

"Thanks for everything." Dillon gave her that special smile of his with total charm and kissed her on the cheek. "Judy, you've been great." He shook Tony's hand. "Many thanks."

A moment later he was in the pilot's seat, closing the door. He strapped himself in, adjusted his earphones, then fired the engine and called the tower. There was a small plane landing and the tower told him to wait. They gave him the good word and he taxied to the end of the runway. There was a short pause, then the go signal and he boosted power, roared down the runway and pulled back the column at exactly the right moment, the Cessna climbing effortlessly out over the azure sea.

•　•　•

It was an hour later that Max Santiago flew into San Juan, where he was escorted through passport control and customs with a minimum of fuss by an airport official to where his chauffeur, Algaro, waited with the black Mercedes limousine.

"At your orders, Señor," he said in Spanish.

"Good to see you, Algaro," Santiago said. "Everything is arranged as I requested?"

"Oh yes, Señor. I've packed the usual clothes, took them down to the *Maria Blanco* myself this morning. Captain Serra is expecting you."

Algaro wasn't particularly large, five foot seven or eight, but immensely powerful, his hair cropped so short that he almost looked bald. A scar, running from the corner of the left eye to the mouth, combined to give him a sinister and threatening appearance in spite of the smart gray chauffeur's uniform he wore. He was totally devoted to Santiago, who had saved him from a life sentence for the stabbing to death of a young prostitute two years previously by the liberal dispensing of funds not only to lawyers but corrupt officials.

The luggage arrived at that moment and while the porters stowed it Santiago said, "Good, you needn't take me to the house. I'll go straight to the boat."

"As you say, Señor." They drove away, turned into the traffic of the main road and Algaro said, "Captain Serra said you asked for a couple of divers in the crew. It's taken care of."

"Excellent." Santiago picked up the local newspaper, which had been left on the seat for him, and opened it.

Algaro watched him in the mirror. "Is there a problem, Señor?"

Santiago laughed. "You're like an animal, Algaro, you always smell trouble."

"But that's what you employ me for, Señor."

"Quite right." Santiago folded the newspaper, selected a cigarette from an elegant gold case and lit it. "Yes, my friend, there is a problem, a problem called Dillon."

"May I know about him, Señor?"

"Why not? You'll probably have to, how shall I put it, take care of him for me, Algaro." Santiago smiled. "So listen carefully and learn all about him because this man is good, Algaro, very good indeed."

It was a perfect afternoon, the limitless blue sky with only the occasional cloud as Dillon drifted across the Caribbean at five thousand feet. It was pure pleasure, the sea constantly changing color below, green and blue, the occasional boat, the reefs and shoals clearly visible at that height.

He passed the islands of Nevis and St. Kitts, calling in to the local airport, moved on flying directly over the tiny Dutch island of Saba. He had a brisk tailwind and made good time, better than he had expected, found St. Croix on his port side on the horizon no more than an hour after leaving Antigua.

Soon after that, the main line of the Virgins lifted out of the heat haze to greet him, St. Thomas to port, the smaller bulk of St. John to starboard, Tortola beyond. He checked the chart and saw Peter Island below Tortola and east of St. John, Norman Island south of it, and south of there was Samson Cay.

Dillon called in to St. Thomas airport to notify them of his approach. The controller said, "Cleared for landing at Cruz Bay. Await customs and immigration officials there."

Dillon went down low, turning to starboard, found Samson Cay with no difficulty and crossed over at a thousand feet. There was a harbor dotted with yachts, a dock, cottages and a hotel block grouped around the beach amidst palm trees. The airstrip was to the north, no control tower, just an air sock on a pole. There were people lounging on the beach down there. Some stood up and waved. He waggled his wings and flew on, found Cruz Bay fifteen minutes later and drifted in for a perfect landing just outside the harbor.

He entered the harbor and found the ramp with little difficulty. There were several uniformed officials standing there and one or two other people, all black. He taxied forward, let the wheels down and ran up onto the ramp, killed the engine. One of the men in customs uniform held a couple of wedge-shaped blocks by a leather strap and he came and positioned them behind the wheels.

Dillon climbed out. "Lafayette, we are here."

Everyone laughed genially and the immigration people checked his passport, perfectly happy with the Irish one, while the customs men had a look at the luggage. Everything was sweetness and light and they all departed with mutual expressions of goodwill. As they walked away a young woman in uniform, rose pink this time, who had been waiting patiently at one side, came forward.

"I've got your jeep here as ordered, Mr. Dillon. If you could sign for me and show me your license, you can be on your way."

"That's very kind of you," Dillon said and carried the suitcases across and slung them on the backseat.

As he signed, she said, "I'm sorry we didn't have an automatic in at the moment. I could change it for you tomorrow. I've got one being returned."

"No, thanks, I prefer to be in charge myself." He smiled. "Can I drop you somewhere?"

"That's nice of you." She got in beside him and he drove away. About three hundred yards further on as he came to the road she said, "This is fine."

There was an extremely attractive looking development opposite. "What's that?" he asked.

"Mongoose Junction, our version of a shopping mall, but much nicer. There's also a super bar and a couple of great restaurants."

"I'll look it over sometime."

She got out. "Turn left, follow the main road. Caneel Bay's only a couple of miles out. There's a car park for residents. From there it's a short walk down to Reception."

"You've been very kind," Dillon told her and drove away.

The *Maria Blanco* had cost Santiago two million dollars and was his favorite toy. He preferred being on board to staying at his magnificent house above the city of San Juan, particularly since the death of his wife Maria from cancer ten years earlier. Dear Maria, his Maria Blanco, the one soft spot in his life. Of course, this was no ordinary boat, had every conceivable luxury, needed a captain and five or six crew members to man her.

Santiago sat at a table on the upper deck enjoying the sun and a cup of excellent coffee, Algaro standing behind him. The captain, Julian Serra, a burly, black-bearded man in uniform, sat opposite. He, like most of Santiago's employees, had been with him for years, had frequently taken part in activities of a highly questionable nature.

"So you see, my dear Serra, we have a problem on our hands here. The man Dillon will probably approach this diver, this Bob Carney, when he reaches St. John."

"Wrecks are notoriously difficult to find, Señor," Serra told him. "I've had experts tell me they've missed one by a few yards on occasions. It's not easy. There's a lot of sea out there."

"I agree," Santiago said. "I still think the girl must have some sort of an answer, but she may take her time returning. In the meantime, we'll surprise Mr. Dillon as much as possible." He smiled up at Algaro. "Think you can handle that, Algaro?"

"With pleasure, Señor," Algaro said.

"Good." Santiago turned back to Serra. "What about the crew?"

"Guerra, first mate. Solona and Mugica as usual, and I've brought in two men with good diving experience, Javier Noval and Vicente Pinto."

"And they're reliable?"

"Absolutely."

"And we're expected at Samson Cay?"

"Yes, Señor, I spoke to Prieto personally. You wish to stay there?"

"I think so. We could always drop anchor off Paradise Beach at Caneel, of course. I'll think about it." Santiago finished his coffee and stood up. "Right, let's get moving then."

Dillon took to Caneel from the moment he got there. He parked the jeep and, carrying his own bags, followed the obvious path. There was a magnificent restaurant on a bluff up above him, circular with open sides. Below it was the ruins of a sugar mill from the old plantation days. The vegetation was extremely lush, palm trees everywhere. He paused, noticing a gift shop on the left and set back. More important the smaller shop next to it said "Paradise Watersports," Carney's place. He remembered that from the brochure and went and had a look. As he would have expected, there were diving suits of various kinds on display, but the door was locked, so he carried on and came to the front desk lobby.

There were three or four people being dealt with at the desk before him so he dropped his bags and went back outside. There was a very large bar area, open at the sides, but under a huge barnlike roof, a vital necessity in a climate where instant heavy rain showers were common.

Beyond was Caneel Bay, he knew that from the brochure, boats of various kinds at anchor, a pleasant, palm-fringed beach beside another restaurant, people still taking their ease in the early evening sun, one or two windsurfers still out there. Dillon glanced at his watch. It was almost five-thirty and he started to turn away to go back to the front desk when he saw a boat coming in.

It was a 35-foot Sport Fisherman with a flying bridge, sleek and white, but what intrigued Dillon were the dozen or so airtanks stacked in their holders in the stern, and there were four people moving around on deck packing their gear into dive bags. Carney was on the flying bridge, handling the wheel, in jeans and bare feet, stripped to the waist, very tanned, the blond hair bleached by the sun. Dillon recognized him from the photo in the brochure.

The name of the boat was *Sea Raider,* he saw that as it got closer, moved to the end of the dock as Carney maneuvered it in. One of the dive students tossed a line, Dillon caught it and expertly tied up at the stern, then he moved along to the prow where the boat was bouncing against its fenders, reached over and got the other line. Dillon lit a cigarette, his Zippo flashing, and Carney killed the engines and came down the ladder. "Thanks," he called.

Dillon said, "My pleasure, Captain Carney," and he turned and walked away along the dock.

One of the receptionists from the front desk took him out to his cottage in a small courtesy bus. The grounds were an absolute delight, not only sweeping grassland and palm trees, but every kind of tropical plant imaginable.

"The entire peninsula is private," she said as they followed a narrow road. "We have seven beaches and, as you'll notice, most of the cottages are grouped around them."

"I've only seen two restaurants so far," he commented.

"Yes, Sugar Mill and Beach Terrace. There's a third at the end of the peninsula, Turtle Bay, that's more formal. You know, collar and tie and so on. It's wonderful for an evening drink. You look out over the Windward Passage to dozens of little islands, Carval Rock, Whistling Cay. Of course a lot further away you'll see Jost Van Dyke and Tortola, but they're in the British Virgins."

"It sounds idyllic," he said.

She braked in a turned circle beside a two-storied, flat-roofed building surrounded by trees and bushes of every description. "Here we are, Cottage Seven."

There were steps up to the upper level. "It isn't all one then?" Dillon asked.

She opened the door into a little vestibule. "People do sometimes take it all, but up here it's divided into two units. Seven D and Seven E."

The doors faced each other, she unlocked 7D and led the way in. There was a superb shower room, a bar area with a spare icebox. The bedroom-cum-sitting room was enormous and very pleasantly furnished with tiled floor and comfortable chairs and a sofa, and there were venetian blinds at the windows, two enormous fans turning in the ceiling.

"Is this all right?" she asked.

"I should say so." Dillon nodded at the enormous bed. "Jesus, but a man would have to be a sprinter to catch his wife in that thing."

She laughed and opened the double doors to the terrace

and led the way out. There was a large seating area and a narrow part round the corner that fronted the other windows. There was a grassy slope, trees and a small beach below, three or four large yachts of the ocean-going type at anchor some distance from shore.

"Paradise Beach," she said.

There was another beach way over to the right with a line of cottages behind it. "What's that?" he asked.

"Scott Beach and Turtle Bay is a little further on. You could walk there in fifteen minutes, although there *is* a courtesy bus service with stops dotted round the grounds."

There was a knock at the door, she went back inside and supervised the bellboy leaving the luggage. Dillon followed her. She turned. "I think that's everything."

"There was the question of a telephone," Dillon said. "You don't have them in the cottages, I understand."

"My, but I was forgetting that." She opened her carrying bag and took out a cellular telephone plus a spare battery and charger. She put it on the coffee table with a card. "Your number and instructions are there." She laughed. "Now I hope that really is everything."

Dillon opened the door for her. "You've been very kind."

"Oh, one more thing, our General Manager, Mr. Nicholson, asked me to apologize for not being here to greet you. He had business on St. Thomas."

"That's all right. I'm sure we'll catch up with each other later."

"I believe he's Irish too," she said and left.

Dillon opened the icebox under the bar unit, discovering every kind of drink one could imagine including two half-bottles of champagne. He opened one of them, poured a glass, then went out and stood on the terrace looking out over the water.

"Well, old son, this will do to take along," he said softly

and drank the champagne with conscious pleasure.

In the end, of course, the sparkle on the water was too seductive and he went inside, unpacked, hanging his clothes in the ample wardrobe space, then undressed and found some swimming trunks. A moment later he was hurrying down the grass bank to the little beach, which for the moment he had entirely to himself. The water was incredibly warm and very clear. He waded forward and started to swim, there was a sudden swirl over on his right, an enormous turtle surfaced, looked at him curiously, then moved sedately away.

Dillon laughed aloud for pure pleasure, then swam lazily out to sea in the direction of the moored yachts, turning after some fifty yards to swim back. Behind him, the *Maria Blanco* came round the point from Caneel Bay and dropped anchor about three hundred yards away.

Santiago had changed his mind about Samson Cay only after Captain Serra had brought him a message from the radio room. An enquiry by ship-to-shore telephone had confirmed that Dillon had arrived at Caneel Bay.

"He's booked into Cottage Seven," Serra said.

"Interesting," Santiago told him. "That's the best accommodation in the resort." He thought about it, tapping his fingers on the table, and made his decision. "I know it well, it overlooks Paradise Beach. We'll anchor there, Serra, for tonight at least."

"As you say, Señor."

Serra went back to the bridge and Algaro, who had been standing by the stern rail, poured Santiago another cup of coffee.

Santiago said, "I want you to go ashore tonight. Take someone with you. There's the Land-Rover Serra leaves permanently in the car park at Mongoose Junction. He'll give you the keys."

"What do you require me to do, Señor?"

"Call in at Caneel, see what Dillon is up to. If he goes out, follow him."

"Do I give him a problem?" Algaro asked hopefully.

"A small one, Algaro," Santiago smiled. "Nothing too strenuous."

"My pleasure, Señor," Algaro said and poured him another cup of coffee.

Dillon didn't feel like anything too formal, wore only a soft white cotton shirt and cream linen slacks, both by Armani, as he walked through the evening darkness toward Caneel Beach. He carried a small torch in one pocket provided by the management for help with the dark spots. It was such a glorious night that he didn't need it. The Terrace Restaurant was already doing a fair amount of business, but then Americans liked to dine early, he knew that. He went to the front desk, cashed a traveler's check for five hundred dollars, then tried the bar.

He had never cared for the usual Caribbean liking for rum punches and fruit drinks, settled for an old fashioned vodka martini cocktail, which the genial black waitress brought for him quite rapidly. A group of musicians were setting up their instruments on the small bandstand and way out across the sea he could see the lights of St. Thomas. It really was very pleasant, too easy to forget he had a job to do. He finished his drink, signed for it and went along to the restaurant, where he introduced himself to the head waiter and was seated.

The menu was tempting enough. He ordered grilled sea scallops, a Caesar salad, followed by Caribbean lobster tail. No Krug but a very acceptable half-bottle of Veuve Clicquot completed the picture.

He was finished by nine o'clock and wandered down to reception. Algaro was sitting in one of the leather armchairs looking at the *New York Times*. The girl on duty was the one who'd taken Dillon to the cottage.

She smiled. "Everything okay, Mr. Dillon?"

"Perfect. Tell me, do you know a bar called Jenny's Place?"

"I sure do. It's on the front, just past Mongoose Junction on your way into town."

"They stay open late I presume?"

"Usually till around two in the morning."

"Many thanks."

He moved away and walked along the dock, lighting a cigarette. Behind him Algaro went out and hurried along the car park by Sugar Mill, laughter drifting down from the people dining up there. He moved past the taxis waiting for customers to where the Land-Rover waited. Felipe Guerra, the *Maria Blanco*'s mate, sat behind the wheel.

Algaro got in beside him and Guerra said, "Did you find him?"

"I was within touching distance. He was asking about that bar, Jenny's Place. You know it? On the front in Cruz Bay."

"Sure."

"Let's take a look. From the sound of it he intends to pay the place a visit."

"Maybe we can make it interesting for him," Guerra said and drove away.

Dillon drove past Mongoose Junction, located Jenny's Place, then turned and went back to the Junction car park. He walked along the front of the harbor through the warm night, went up the steps, glanced up at the red neon sign and entered. The cafe side of things was busy, Mary Jones taking orders while two waitresses, one white, the other black, worked themselves into a frenzy as they attempted to serve everybody. The bar was busy also although Billy Jones seemed to be having no difficulty in managing on his own.

Dillon found a vacant stool at the end of the bar and waited until Billy was free to deal with him. "Irish whisky, whatever you've got, and water."

He noticed Bob Carney seated at the other end of the long bar, a beer in front of him, talking to a couple of men who looked like seamen. Carney was smiling and then as he turned to reach for his beer, became aware of Dillon's scrutiny and frowned.

Billy brought the whisky and Dillon said, "You're Billy Jones?"

The other man looked wary. "And who might you be?"

"Dillon's the name—Sean Dillon. I'm staying at Caneel. Jenny told me to look you up and say hello."

"Jenny did?" Billy frowned. "When you see Miss Jenny?"

"In London. I went to Henry Baker's cremation with her."

"You did?" Billy turned and called to his wife. "Woman, get over here." She finished taking an order, then joined them. "This is my wife, Mary. Tell her what you just told me."

"I was with Jenny in London." Dillon held out his hand. "Sean Dillon. I was at Baker's funeral, not that there was much doing. She said he was an atheist, so all we did was attend the crematorium."

Mary crossed herself. "God rest him now, but he did think that way. And Jenny, what about her? Where is she?"

"She was upset," Dillon said. "She told me Baker had a sister."

Mary frowned and looked at her husband. "We never knew that. Are you sure, mister?"

"Oh, yes, he had a sister living in France. Jenny wouldn't say where, simply flew off to Paris from London. Wanted to take his ashes to the sister."

"And when is she coming back?"

"All she said was she needed a few days to come to terms with the death and so on. As I happened to be coming out here she asked me to say hello."

"Well I thank you for that," Mary said. "We've been so worried!" A customer called from one of the tables. "I'll have to go. I'll see you later."

She hurried away and Billy grinned. "I'm needed too, but hang around, man, hang around."

He went to serve three clamouring customers and Dillon savoured his whisky and looked around the room. Algaro and Guerra were drinking beer in a corner booth. They were not looking at him, apparently engaged in conversation. Dillon's eyes barely paused, passed on, and yet he recognized him from the reception at Caneel, the cropped hair, the brutal face, the scar from eye to the mouth.

"Judas Iscariot come to life," Dillon murmured. "And what's your game, son?" for he had learned the hard way over many years never to believe in coincidence.

The two men Carney had been talking to had moved on and he was sitting alone now, the stool next to him vacant. Dillon finished his drink, moved along the bar through the crowd. "Do you mind if I join you?"

Carney's eyes were very blue in the tanned face. "Should I?"

"Dillon, Sean Dillon." Dillon eased on to the stool. "I'm staying at Caneel. Cottage Seven. Jenny Grant told me to look you up."

"You know Jenny?"

"I was just with her in London," Dillon said. "Her friend, Henry Baker, was killed in an accident over there."

"I heard about that."

"Jenny was over for the inquest and the funeral." Dillon nodded to Billy Jones, who came over. "I'll have another Irish. Give Captain Carney whatever he wants."

"I'll have a beer," Carney said. "Did Jenny bury him in London?"

"No," Dillon told him. "Cremation. He had a sister in France."

"I never knew that."

"Jenny told me few people did. It seems he preferred it that way. Said she wanted to take the ashes to her. Last I saw of her she was flying to Paris. Said she'd be back here in a few days."

Billy brought the whisky and the beer and Carney said, "So you're here on vacation?"

"That's right. I got in this evening."

"Would you be the guy who came in the Cessna floatplane?"

"Flew up from Antigua." Dillon nodded.

"On vacation?"

"Something like that." Dillon lit a cigarette. "The thing is I'm interested in doing a little diving, and Jenny suggested I speak to you. Said you were the best."

"That's nice of her."

"She said you taught Henry."

"That's true." Carney nodded. "Henry was a good diver, foolish, but still pretty good."

"Why do you say foolish?"

"It never pays to dive on your own, you should always have a buddy with you. Henry would never listen. He would just up and go whenever he felt like it, and that's no good when you're diving regularly. Accidents can happen no matter how well you plan things." Carney drank some more beer and looked Dillon full in the face. "But then I'd say you're the kind of man who knows that, Mr. Dillon."

He had the slow, easy accent of the American southerner as if everything he said was carefully considered.

Dillon said, "Well in the end it was an accident that killed him in London. He looked the wrong way and stepped off the pavement in front of a London bus. He was dead in a second."

Carney said calmly, "You know the old Arab saying? 'Everybody has an appointment in Samarra.' You miss Death in one place, he'll get you in another. At least for Henry it was quick."

"That's a remarkably philosophical attitude," Dillon told him.

Carney smiled. "I'm a remarkably philosophical fellow, Mr. Dillon. I did two tours in Vietnam. Everything has been a bonus since. So you want to do some diving?"

"That's right."

"You any good?"

"I manage," Dillon told him. "But I'm always willing to learn."

"Okay. I'll see you at the dock at Caneel at nine o'clock in the morning."

"I'll need some gear."

"No problem, I'll open the shop for you."

"Fine." Dillon swallowed his whisky. "I'll see you then." He hesitated. "Tell me something. You see the two guys in the booth in the far corner? I particularly mean the ugly one with the scar. Do you happen to know who they are?"

"Sure," Carney said. "They work on a big motor yacht from Puerto Rico that calls in here now and then. It's owned by a man called Santiago. It's usually based at Samson Cay, that's over on the British side of things. The younger guy is the mate, Guerra, the other is a real mean son of a bitch called Algaro."

"Why do you say that?"

"He half-killed a fisherman outside one of the bars here about nine months ago. He was lucky to get away without doing some prison time. They laid a real hefty fine on him, but his boss paid it, so I heard. He's the kind of guy to step around."

"I'll certainly remember that." Dillon got up. "Tomorrow then," and he walked out through the crowd.

Billy came down the bar. "You want another beer, Bob?"

"What I need is something to eat, my wife being away and all," Carney said. "What did you make of him?"

"Dillon? He said he was in London with Jenny. Happened to be coming down here and she told him to look us up."

"Well that sure was a hell of a coincidence." Carney reached for his glass and noticed Algaro and Guerra get up and leave. He almost got up and went after them, but what the hell, it wasn't his problem, whatever it was, and in any case, Dillon was perfectly capable of looking after himself, he'd never been more certain of anything in his life.

Dillon drove out of Cruz Bay, changing down to climb the steep hill up from the town, thinking about Carney. He'd liked him straightaway, a calm, quiet man of enormous inner strength, but then, remembering his background, that made sense.

He breasted the hill, remembering that in St. John you kept on the left-hand side of the road just like England, was suddenly aware of the headlights coming up behind him very fast. He expected to be overtaken, wasn't, and as the vehicle behind moved right in on his tail knew he was in trouble. He recognized it as a Land-Rover in his rearview mirror an instant before it bumped him, put his foot down hard and pulled away, driving so fast that he went straight past the turning to Caneel Bay.

The Land-Rover had the edge and suddenly it swerved out to the right-hand side of the road and moved alongside. He caught a brief glimpse of Algaro's face, illuminated in the light from the dashboard as he gripped the wheel, and then the Land-Rover swerved in and Dillon spun off the road into the brush, bounced down a shallow slope and came to a halt.

Dillon rolled out of the jeep and got behind a tree. The Land-Rover had stopped and there was silence for a moment. Suddenly a shotgun roared, pellets scything through the branches overhead.

There was silence and then laughter. A voice called, "Welcome to St. John, Mr. Dillon," and the Land-Rover drove away.

Dillon waited until the sound had faded into the night, then he got back into the jeep, engaged four-wheel drive, reversed up the slope onto the road and drove back toward the Caneel turning.

In London it was three-thirty in the morning when the phone rang at the side of Charles Ferguson's bed in his flat at Cavendish Square. He came awake on the instant and reached for it.

"Ferguson here."

Dillon stood on the terrace, a drink in one hand, the cellular telephone in the other. "It's me," he said, "ringing you from the tranquil Virgin Islands, only they're not so tranquil."

"For God's sake, Dillon, do you know what time it is?"

"Yes, time for a few questions and hopefully some answers. A couple of goons just tried to run me off the road, old son, and guess who they were? Crewmen off Santiago's yacht, the *Maria Blanco*. They also loosed off a shotgun in my direction."

Ferguson was immediately alert, sat up and tossed the bedclothes aside. "Are you certain?"

"Of course I am." Dillon was not particularly angry, but made it sound as if he were. "Listen, you devious old sod, I want to know what's going on. I've only been in the damned place a few hours and yet they know me by name. I'd say they were expecting me, as they're here too, and how could that be, Brigadier?"

"I don't know," Ferguson told him. "That's all I can say for the moment. You're settled in all right?"

"Brigadier, I have an insane desire to laugh," Dillon told him. "But yes, I'm settled in, the cottage is fine, the view sublime and I'm diving with Bob Carney in the morning."

"Good, get on with it, then, and watch yourself."

"Watch myself?" Dillon said. "Is that the best you can do?"

"Stop whining, Dillon," Ferguson told him. "This sort of thing's exactly why I chose you for the job. You're still in one piece, right?"

"Just about."

"There you are then. They're trying to put the frighteners on you, that's all."

"That's all, he says."

"Leave it with me. I'll be in touch."

Ferguson put the phone down, switching off the light, and lay there thinking about it. After a while he drifted into sleep again.

Dillon went to the small bar. There were tea and coffee bags there. He boiled the water and opted for a cup of tea, taking it out on the terrace, looking out into the bay where there were lights on some of the boats. More to things than met the eye, he was more convinced than ever, and he hadn't liked the shotgun. It made him feel naked. There was an answer to that of course, a visit to the address Ferguson had given him in St. Thomas, the hardware specialist. That could come in the afternoon after he'd dived with Carney.

The moment he and Guerra were back on board Algaro reported to Santiago. When he was finished Santiago said, "You did well."

Algaro said, "He won't do anything about it, will he, Señor, the police I mean?"

"Of course not, he doesn't want the authorities to know why he's here, that's the beauty of it. That U-boat is in American waters, so legally it should be reported to the Coast Guard, but that's the last thing Dillon and this Brigadier Ferguson he works for want."

Algaro said, "I see."

"Go to bed now," Santiago told him.

Algaro departed and Santiago went to the rail. He could see a light in Cottage Seven. At that moment it went out. "Sleep well, Mr. Dillon," he said softly, turned and went below.

9

It was nine o'clock the following morning when Ferguson arrived at Downing Street. He had to wait for only five minutes before an aide took him upstairs and showed him into the study where the Prime Minister was seated at his desk, signing one document after another.

He looked up. "Ah, there you are, Brigadier."

"You asked to see me, Prime Minister?"

"Yes, I've had the Deputy Director of the Security Services and Sir Francis on my back about this Virgin Islands affair. Is it true what they tell me, that you've taken on this man Dillon to handle things?"

"Yes," Ferguson said calmly.

"A man with his record? Can you tell me why?"

"Because he's right for the job, sir. Believe me, I find nothing admirable in Dillon's past. His work some years ago for the IRA is known to us although nothing has ever been proven against him. The same applies to his activities on the international scene. He's a gun for hire, Prime Minister. Even the Israelis have used him when it suited them."

"I can't say I like it. I think Carter has a point of view."

"I can pull him out if that is what you wish."

"But you'd rather not?"

181

"I think he's the man for this particular job. To be frank, it's a dirty one and it has already become apparent since we last spoke that there are people he will have to deal with who play very dirty indeed."

"I see." The Prime Minister sighed. "Very well, Brigadier, I leave it to your own good judgment, but do try and make your peace with Carter."

"I will, Prime Minister," Ferguson said and withdrew.

Jack Lane was waiting in the Daimler. As it drove away he said, "And what was that all about?"

Ferguson told him. "He's got a point, of course."

"You know how I feel, sir, I was always against it. I wouldn't trust Dillon an inch."

"Interesting thing about Dillon," Ferguson said. "One of the things he's always been known for is a kind of twisted sense of honor. If he gives his word he sticks to it and expects others to do the same."

"I find that hard to believe, sir."

"Yes, I suppose most people would."

Ferguson picked up the car phone and rang through to Simon Carter's office. He wasn't there, he was meeting with Pamer at the House of Commons.

"Get a message through to him now," Ferguson told Carter's secretary. "Tell him I need to see them both urgently. I'll meet them on the Terrace at the House in fifteen minutes." He replaced the phone. "You can come with me, Jack, you've never been on the Terrace, have you?"

"What's going on, sir?"

"Wait and see, Jack, wait and see."

Rain drifted across the Thames in a fine spray, clearing the Terrace of people. Except for a few who stood under the awnings, drink in hand, everyone else had taken to the bars and cafes. Ferguson stood by the wall holding a large golfer's umbrella his chauffeur had given him, Lane sheltering with him.

"Doesn't it fill you with a sense of majesty and awe, Jack, the Mother of Parliaments and all that sort of thing?" Ferguson asked.

"Not with rain pouring down my neck, sir."

"Ah, there you are." They turned and saw Carter and Pamer standing in the main entrance to the Terrace. Carter was carrying a black umbrella, which he put up, and he and Pamer joined them.

Ferguson said, "Isn't this cozy?"

"I'm not in the mood for your feeble attempts at humor, Ferguson, now what do you want?" Carter demanded.

"I've just been to see the P.M. I understand you've been complaining again, old boy? Didn't do you any good. He's told me to carry on and use my judgment."

Carter was furious, but he managed to control himself and glanced at Lane. "Who's this?"

"My present assistant, Detective Inspector Jack Lane. I've borrowed him from Special Branch."

"That's against regulations, you can't do it."

"That's as may be, but I'm not a deckhand on your ship. I run my own and, as my time is limited, let's get down to facts. Dillon arrived in St. John around five o'clock in the evening their time yesterday. He was attacked by two crew members of Santiago's boat, the *Maria Blanco,* who ran him off the road in his jeep and fired a shotgun at him."

"My God!" Pamer said in horror.

Carter frowned. "Is he all right?"

"Oh, yes, a rubber ball our Dillon, always bounces back. Personally I think they were trying it on, hassling him. Of course the interesting thing is how come they knew who he was and knew he was there?"

"Now look here," Pamer began, "I trust you're not suggesting any lack of security on our part?"

Carter said, "Shut up, Francis, he's got a valid point. This Santiago man is far too well informed." He turned to Ferguson. "What are you going to do about it?"

"Actually, I was thinking of taking a brief holiday," Ferguson told him. "You know, sun, sea and sand, swaying palms? They tell me the Virgins are lovely at this time of the year."

Carter nodded. "You'll stay in touch?"

"Of course, dear old boy." Ferguson smiled and turned to Lane. "Let's go, Jack, we've lots to do."

On the way back to the Ministry Ferguson told his chauffeur to pull in beside a mobile sandwich bar on Victoria Embankment. "This man does the best cup of tea in London, Jack."

The owner greeted him as an old friend. "Rotten day, Brigadier."

"It was worse on the Hook, Fred," the Brigadier said and walked with his cup of tea to the wall overlooking the Thames.

As Lane received his cup of tea he said to Fred, "What did he mean, the Hook?"

"That was a really bad place that was, worst position in the whole of Korea. So many dead bodies that every time you dug another trench, arms and legs came out."

"You knew the Brigadier then?"

"Knew him? I was a platoon sergeant when he was a second lieutenant. He won his first Military Cross carrying me on his back under fire." Fred grinned. "That's why I never charge for the tea."

Lane, impressed, joined Ferguson and leaned on the parapet under the umbrella. "You've got a fan there, sir."

"Fred? Old soldier's tales. Don't listen. I'm going to need the Learjet. Direct flight to St. Thomas should be possible."

"I believe the work on those new tanks the RAF did has extended the range to at least four thousand miles, sir."

"There you are then." Ferguson glanced at his watch. "Just after ten. I want that Learjet ready to leave Gatwick no later than one o'clock, Jack. Top priority. Allowing for the time difference, I could be in St. Thomas somewhere between five or six o'clock their time."

"Do you want me with you, sir?"

"No, you'll have to hold the fort."

"You'll need accommodation, sir. I'll see to that."

Ferguson shook his head. "I've reserved it at this Caneel place where I booked Dillon in."

"You mean you were expecting what happened to happen?"

"Something like that."

"Look, sir," said Lane in exasperation, "exactly what is going on?"

"When you find out, tell me, Jack." Ferguson emptied his cup, went and put it on the counter. "Thanks, Fred." He turned to Lane. "Come on, Jack, must get moving, lots to do before I leave," and he got into the rear of the Daimler.

Santiago was up early, even went for a swim in the sea, and was seated at the table in the stern enjoying his breakfast in the early morning sunshine when Algaro brought him the telephone.

"It's Sir Francis," he said.

"A wonderful morning here," Santiago said. "How's London?"

"Cold and wet. I'm just about to have a sandwich lunch and then spend the whole afternoon in interminable Committee meetings. Look, Max, Carter saw the Prime Minister and tried to put the boot into Ferguson because he was employing Dillon."

"I didn't imagine Carter to be quite so stupid. Ferguson still got his way of course?"

"Yes, the P.M. backed him to the hilt. More worrying, he asked for another meeting with me and Carter, and told us Dillon had been attacked on his first night in St. John. What on earth was that about?"

"My people were just leaning on him a little, Francis. After all, and as you made clear, he knows of my existence."

"Yes, but what Ferguson's now interested in is how *you* knew who Dillon was, the fact that he was arriving in St. John and so on. He said you were far too well informed, and Carter agreed with him."

"Did he make any suggestion as to how he thought I was getting my information?"

"No, but he did say he thought he'd join Dillon in St. John for a few days."

"Did he now? That should prove interesting. I look forward to meeting him."

Pamer said, genuine despair in his words, "God dammit, Max, they know of your involvement. How long before they know about mine?"

"You're not on the boards of any of the companies, Francis, and neither was your father. No mention of the name Pamer anywhere, and the great thing about this whole affair is that it is a private war. As I've already told you, Ferguson won't want the American authorities in on this. We're rather like two dogs squabbling over the same bone."

"I'm still worried," Pamer told him. "Is there anything else I can do?"

"Keep the information flowing, Francis, and keep your nerve. Nothing else you can do."

Santiago put the phone down and Algaro said, "More coffee, Señor?"

Santiago nodded. "Brigadier Ferguson is coming."

"Here to Caneel?" Algaro smiled. "And what would you like me to do about him, Señor?"

"Oh, I'll think of something," Santiago said and drank his coffee. "In the meantime, let's find out what our friend Dillon is up to this morning."

Guerra went round to Caneel Beach in an inflatable, taking one of the divers with him, a young man called Javier Noval. They wore swimming shorts, tee-shirts and dark glasses, just another couple of tourists. They pulled in amongst other small craft at the dock, Guerra killed the outboard motor and Noval tied up. At that moment Dillon appeared at the end of the dock. He wore a black tracksuit and carried a couple of towels.

"That's him," Guerra told Noval. "Get going. I'll stay out of the way in case he remembers me from last night."

Bob Carney was manhandling dive tanks from a trolley on to the deck of a small twenty-five-foot dive boat, turned and saw Dillon. He waved and went along the dock to join him, passing Noval, who stopped to light a cigarette close enough to listen to them.

Carney said, "You're going to need a few things. Let's go up to the dive shop."

They moved away. Noval waited and then followed.

There was a wide range of excellent equipment. Dillon chose a three-quarter-length suit of black and green in padded nylon, nothing too heavy, a mask, fins and gloves.

"Have you tried one of these?" Carney opened a box. "A Marathon dive computer. The wonder of the age. Automatic readings on your depth, elapsed time under water, safe time remaining. Even tells you how long you should wait to fly."

"That's for me," Dillon told him. "I always was lousy at mental arithmetic."

Carney itemized the bill. "I'll put this on your hotel account."

Dillon signed it. "So what have you got planned?"

"Oh, nothing too strenuous, you'll see." Carney smiled. "Let's get going," and he led the way out.

Noval dropped down into the inflatable. "The other man is called Carney. He owns the diving concession here. Paradise Watersports."

"So they are going diving?" Guerra asked.

"They must be. Dillon was in the shop with him buying equipment." He glanced up. "Here they come now."

Dillon and Carney passed above them and got into the dive boat. After a moment Carney fired the engine and Dillon cast off. The boat moved out of the bay, weaving its way through various craft anchored there.

Guerra said, "There's no name on that boat."

"*Privateer,* that's what it's called," Noval told him. "I asked one of the beach guards. You know, I've done most of my diving around Puerto Rico, but I've heard of this Carney. He's big stuff."

Guerra nodded. "Okay, we'd better get back and let Señor Santiago know what's happening."

Noval cast off, Guerra started the outboard, and they moved away.

The *Privateer* was doing a steady twenty knots, the sea not as calm as it could have been. Dillon held on tight and managed to light a cigarette one-handed.

"Are you prone to sea sickness?" Carney asked.

"Not that I know of," Dillon shouted above the roar of the engine.

"Good, because it's going to get worse before it gets better. We've not too far to go though."

Waves swept in, long and steep, the *Privateer* riding up over them and plunging down, and Dillon hung on, taking in the incredible scenery, the peaks of the islands all around. And then they were very close to a smaller island, turned in toward it and moved into the calmer waters of a bay.

"Congo Cay," Carney said. "A nice dive." He went round to the prow, dropped the anchor and came back. "Not much to tell you. Twenty-five to ninety feet. Very little current. There's a ridge maybe three hundred feet long. If you want to limit your depth you could stay on top of that."

"Sounds the kind of place you'd bring novices," Dillon said, pulling on the black and green diving suit.

"All the time," Carney told him calmly.

Dillon got into his gear quickly and fastened a weight belt round his waist. Carney had already clamped tanks to their inflatable jackets and helped Dillon ease into his while sitting on the side of the boat. Dillon pulled on his gloves.

Carney said, "See you at the anchor."

Dillon nodded, pulled down his mask, checked that the air was flowing freely through his mouthpiece and went over backwards into the sea. He swam under the keel of the boat until he saw the anchor line and followed it down, pausing only to swallow a couple of times, a technique aimed at equalizing the pressure in his ears when they became uncomfortable.

He reached the ridge, paused with a hand on the anchor and looked at Carney descending to join him through a massive school of silversides. At that moment, an extraordinary thing happened. A black tip reef shark about nine feet in

length shot out of the gloom scattering clouds of fish before
it, swerved around Carney, then disappeared over the ridge
as fast as it had come.

Carney made the okay sign with finger and thumb. Dillon
replied in kind and followed him as he led the way along
the reef. There were brilliant yellow tube sponges everywhere, and when they went over the edge there was lots
of orange sponge attached to the rock faces. The coral
outcroppings were multi-colored and very beautiful, and at
one point Carney paused, pointing, and Dillon saw a huge
eagle ray pass in the distance, wings flapping in slow
motion.

It was a very calm, very enjoyable dive, but no big deal,
and after about thirty minutes, Dillon realized they'd come
full circle because the anchor line was ahead of them.
He followed Carney up the line nice and slow, finally
swam under the keel and surfaced at the stern. Carney,
with practiced ease, was up over the stern pulling his gear
behind him. Dillon unstrapped his jacket, slipped out of it
and Carney reached down and pulled jacket and tank on
board. Dillon joined him a moment later.

Carney busied himself clipping fresh tanks to the jackets
and went and pulled in the anchor. Dillon put a towel over
his shoulders and lit a cigarette. "The reef shark," he said.
"Does that happen often?"

"Not really," Carney said.

"Enough to give some people a heart attack."

"I've been diving for years," Carney told him, "and I've
never found sharks a problem."

"Not even a great white?"

"How often would you see one of those? No, nurse
sharks in the main and they're no problem. Around here,
reef sharks now and then or lemon sharks. Sure, they could
be a problem, but hardly ever. We're big and they're big

and they just want to keep out of the way. Having said that, did you enjoy the dive?"

"It was fine." Dillon shrugged.

"Which means you'd like a little more excitement." Carney started the engine. "Okay, let's go for one of my big boy dives," and he gunned the engine and took the *Privateer* out into open water.

They actually passed at some distance *Maria Blanco* still at anchor off Paradise Beach, and Guerra was in the deckhouse, scanning the area with binoculars. He recognized the boat and told Captain Serra, who examined the chart and then took a book on dive sites in the Virgin Islands from a drawer in the chart table.

"Keep watching," he told Guerra and leafed through.

"They've anchored," Guerra told him, "and run up the dive flag."

"Carval Rock," Serra said. "That's where they're diving."

At that moment Algaro came in and held the door open for Santiago, who was wearing a blue blazer and a Captain's cap, a gold rim to the peak. "What's happening?"

"Carney and Dillon are diving out there, Señor." Serra indicated the spot and gave Santiago the binoculars.

Santiago could just see the two men moving in the stern of *Privateer*. He said, "That couldn't be the site, could it?"

"No way, Señor," Serra told him. "It's a difficult place to dive, but hundreds of dives are made there every year."

"Never mind," Santiago said. "Put the launch in the water. We'll go and have a look. We'll see what these two divers of yours, Noval and Pinto, can do."

"Very well, Señor, I'll get things moving," and Serra went out followed by Guerra.

Algaro said, "You wish me to come too, Señor?"

"Why not?" Santiago said. "Even if Dillon sees you it doesn't matter. He knows you exist."

The rock was magnificent, rising up out of a very turbulent sea, birds of every kind perched up there on the ridge, gulls descending in slow motion in the heavy wind.

"Carval Rock," Carney said. "This is rated an advanced dive. Descends to about eighty or so feet. There's the wreck of a Cessna over on the other side that crashed a few years back. There are some nice ravines, fissures, one or two short tunnels and wonderful rock and coral cliffs. The problem is the current. Caused by tidal movement through the Pillsbury Sound."

"How strong?" Dillon asked as he fastened his weight belt.

"One or two knots is fairly common. Above two knots is unswimmable." He looked over and shook his head. "And I'd say it's three knots today."

Dillon lifted his jacket and tank on to the thwart and put it on himself. "Sounds as if it could be interesting."

"Your funeral."

Carney got his own gear on and Dillon turned to lean over and wash out his mask and saw a white launch approaching. "We're going to have company."

Carney turned to look. "I doubt it. No dive master I know would take his people down in this current today, he'd go somewhere easier."

The swells were huge now, the *Privateer* bucking up and down on the anchor line. Dillon went over, paused to check his air supply and started down to what looked like a dense forest below. He paused on the bottom, waiting until Carney had reached him, beckoned and turned toward the rock. Dillon followed, amazed at the strength of the current pushing against him, was aware of a stream of white bubbles over to his left and saw an anchor descend.

On the launch, Santiago sat in the wheelhouse while Serra went to the prow and dropped the anchor. Algaro was helping Noval and Pinto into their diving equipment.

Serra said finally, "They are ready to go, Señor, what are your orders?"

"Tell them to just have a look around," Santiago said. "No trouble. Leave Carney and Dillon alone."

"As you say, Señor."

The two divers were sitting together on the port side. Serra nodded and together they went over backwards into the water.

Dillon followed Carney with increasing difficulty because of the strength of the current up across rock and coral, following a deep channel that led through to the other side of the rocks. The force was quite tremendous and Carney was down on his belly pulling himself through with gloved hands, reaching for one handhold after another, and Dillon went after him, the other man's fins just three or four feet in front of him.

There was a kind of threshold. Carney was motionless for a while and then passed through, and Dillon had the same problem, faced with a kind of wall of pressure. He clawed at the rocks with agonizing slowness, foot by foot, and suddenly was through and into another world.

The surface was fifty feet above him and as he surged forward, he found himself in the middle of a school of tarpon at least four feet in length. There were yellow tail snappers, horse-eyed jacks, bonita, king mackerel and barracuda, some of them five feet long.

Carney plunged down to the other side, the rock face falling below, and Dillon followed him. They closed together and Dillon was aware of the current as they turned and saw Noval and Pinto trying to come through the cut. Noval almost made it, then lost his grip and was pushed into Pinto and they disappeared back to the other side.

Carney moved on and Dillon followed, down to seventy-five feet, and the current took them now in a fierce three-knot riptide that bounced them along the front of the wall in an upright position. They were surrounded by clouds of silversides, flying through space, the ultimate dream, and Dillon had never felt so excited. It seemed to go on forever, and then the current slackened and Carney was using his fins now and climbing.

Dillon followed through a deep ravine that led into another, waterlike black glass, checked his computer and was surprised to find that they had been under for twenty-five minutes. They moved away from the rock itself now, only three or four feet above the forest of the seabed, and came to a line and anchor. Carney paused to examine it, then turned and shook his head, moving on toward the left, finally arriving at their own anchor. They went up slowly, leaving the line at fifteen feet and swimming to one side of the boat, surfacing at the keel.

Carney reached down to take Dillon's tank and the Irishman got a foot in the tiny ladder and pulled himself up and over the stern. He felt totally exhilarated, unzipped his diving suit and pulled it off as Carney stowed their tanks.

"Bloody marvelous."

Carney smiled. "It wasn't bad, was it?"

He turned and looked across at the launch which was anchored over on the port side, swinging on its anchor chain in the heavy sea. Dillon said, "I wonder what happened to the two divers we saw trying to get through the cut?"

"They couldn't make it, I guess, that was rough duty down there." The launch swung round, exposing the stern. "That's the *Maria Blanco*'s launch," Carney added.

"Is that a fact?"

Dillon dried himself slowly with a towel and stood at the rail looking across. He recognized Algaro at once, standing in the stern with Serra, and then Santiago came out of the wheelhouse.

"Who's the guy in the blazer and cap?" Dillon enquired.

Carney looked across. "That's Max Santiago, the owner. I've seen him in St. John a time or two."

Santiago was looking across at them and on impulse, Dillon raised an arm and waved. Santiago waved back and at that moment Noval and Pinto surfaced.

"Time to go home," Carney said and he went round to the prow and heaved in the anchor.

On the way back Dillon said, "The *Maria Blanco,* where would it anchor when it's here, Caneel Bay?"

"More likely to be off Paradise Beach."

"Could we take a look?"

Carney glanced at him, then looked away. "Why not? It's your charter."

Dillon got the water bottle from the icebox, drank about a pint, then passed it to Carney and lit a cigarette. Carney drank a little and passed it back.

"You've dived before, Mr. Dillon."

"And that's a fact," Dillon agreed.

They were close to Paradise now and Carney throttled back the engine and the *Privateer* passed between two of the oceangoing yachts that were moored there and came to the *Maria Blanco*. "There she is," he said.

There were a couple of crewmen working on deck, who looked up casually as they passed. "Jesus," Dillon said, that thing must have made a dent in Santiago's wallet. A couple of million, I'd say."

"And then some."

Carney went up to full power and made for Caneel Beach. Dillon lit another cigarette and leaned against the wall of the deckhouse. "Do you get many interesting wrecks in this area?"

"Some," Carney said. "There's the *Cartanser Senior* off Buck Island over to St. Thomas, an old freighter that's a popular dive, and the *General Rodgers*. The Coast Guard sank her to get rid of her."

"No, I was thinking of something more interesting than that," Dillon said. "I mean you know this area like the back of your hand. Would it be possible for there to be a wreck on some reef out there that you'd never come across?"

Carney slowed as they entered the bay. "Anything's possible, it's a big ocean."

"So there could be something out there just waiting to be discovered?"

The *Privateer* coasted in beside the dock. Dillon got the stern line, went over and tied up. He did the same with the other line as Carney cut the engine, went back on board and pulled on his track suit.

Carney leaned by the wheel looking at him. "Mr. Dillon, I don't know what goes on here. All I know for certain is you are one hell of a diver, and that I admire. What all this talk of wrecks means I don't know and don't want to as I'm inclined to the quiet life, but I will give you one piece of advice. Your interest in Max Santiago?"

"Oh, yes?" Dillon said, continuing to put his diving equipment in a net diving bag.

"It could be unhealthy. I've heard things about him that aren't good, plenty of people could tell you the same. The way he makes his money, for example."

"A hotel keeper as I heard it." Dillon smiled.

"There's other ways that involve small planes or a fast boat by night to Florida, but what the hell, you're a grown man." Carney moved out on deck. "You want to dive with me again?"

"You can count on it. I've got business in St. Thomas this afternoon. How would I get there?"

Carney pointed to the other side of the dock where a very large launch was just casting off. "That's the resort ferry. They run back and forth during the day, but I figure you missed this one."

"Damn!" Dillon said.

"Mr. Dillon, you arrived at Cruz Bay in your own floatplane, and the front desk, who keep me informed of such things, tell me you pay with an American Express Platinum Card."

"What can I say, you've got me," Dillon told him amicably.

"Water taxis are expensive, but not to a man of your means. The front desk will order you one."

"Thanks." Dillon crossed to the dock and paused. "Maybe I could buy you a drink tonight. Will you be at Jenny's Place?"

"Hell, I'm there every night at the moment," Carney said, "otherwise I'd starve. My wife and kids are away on vacation."

"I'll see you then," Dillon said and turned and walked away along the dock toward the front desk.

The water taxi had seats for a dozen passengers, but he had it to himself. The only crew was a woman in a peaked cap and denims, who sat at the wheel and made for St. Thomas at a considerable rate of knots. It was noisy and there wasn't much chance to speak, which suited Dillon. He sat there smoking and thinking about the way things had gone so far, Algaro, Max Santiago and the *Maria Blanco*.

He knew about Santiago, but Santiago knew about him, that was a fact and yet to be explained. There had almost been a touch of comradeship in the way Santiago had waved back at him at Carval Rock. Carney, he liked. In fact, everything about him he liked. For one thing, the American knew his business, but there was power there and real authority. An outstanding example of a quiet man it wouldn't pay to push.

"Here we go," the water taxi driver shouted over her shoulder, and Dillon glanced up and saw that they were moving in toward the waterfront of Charlotte Amalie.

It was quite a place and bustling with activity, two enormous cruise liners berthed on the far side of the harbor. The waterfront was lined with buildings in white and pastel colors, shops and restaurants of every description. It had been a Danish colony, he knew that, and the influence still showed in some of the architecture.

He followed a narrow alley called Drake's Passage that was lined with colorful shops offering everything from designer clothes to gold and jewelry, for this was a free port, and came out into Main Street. He consulted the address Ferguson had given him and crossed to where some taxis waited.

"Can you take me to Cane Street?" he asked the first driver.

"I wouldn't take your money, man," the driver told him amiably. "Just take the next turning through to Back Street. Cane is the third on the left."

Dillon thanked him and moved on. It was hot, very hot, people crowding the pavements, traffic moving slowly in the narrow streets, but Cane Street, when he came to it, was quiet and shaded. The house he wanted was at the far end, clapboard, painted white with a red corrugated iron roof. There was a tiny garden in front of it and steps leading up to a porch on which an ageing black man with gray hair sat on a swing seat reading a newspaper.

He looked up as Dillon approached. "And what can I do for you?"

"I'm looking for Earl Stacey," Dillon told him.

The man peered at him over the top of reading glasses. "You ain't gonna spoil my day with no bills, are you?"

"Ferguson told me to look you up," Dillon said, "Brigadier Charles Ferguson. My name is Dillon."

The other man smiled and removed his glasses. "I've been expecting you. Come right this way," and he pushed open the door and led the way into the house.

"I'm on my own since my wife died last year." Stacey opened a door, switched on a light and led the way down wooden steps to a cellar. There were wooden shelves up to the ceiling, pots of paint stacked there, cupboards below. He reached in and released some kind of catch and pulled it open like a door revealing another room. He switched on a light.

"Come into my parlor."

There was all kinds of weaponry, rifles, submachine guns, boxes of ammunition. "It looks like Christmas to me," Dillon told him.

"You just tell me what you want, man, and Ferguson picks up the tab, that was the arrangement."

"Rifle first," Dillon said. "Armalite perhaps. I like the folding stock."

"I can do better. I got an AK assault rifle here with a folding stock, fires automatic when you want, thirty-round magazine." He took the weapon from a stand and handed it over.

"Yes, this will do fine," Dillon told him. "I'll take it with two extra magazines. I need a handgun now, Walther PPK for preference, and a Carswell silencer. Two extra magazines for that as well."

"Can do."

Stacey opened a very large drawer under the bench which ran along one wall. Inside there was an assortment of handguns. He selected a Walther and passed it to Dillon for approval. "Anything else?"

There was a cheap-looking plastic holster with the butt of a pistol sticking out of it and Dillon was intrigued. "What's that?"

"It's an ace-in-the-hole." Stacey took it out. "That metal strip on the back is a magnet. Stick it underneath anywhere and as long as it's metal it'll hold fast. The gun don't look much, point-two-two Belgian, semi-automatic, seven-shot, but I've put hollow-nosed rounds in. They fragment bone."

"I'll take it," Dillon said. "One more thing. Would you happen to have any C4 explosive?"

"The kind salvage people use for underwater work?"

"Exactly."

"No, but I tell you what I do have, something just as good, Semtex. You heard of that stuff?"

"Oh, yes," Dillon said. "I think you could say I'm familiar with Semtex. One of Czechoslovakia's more successful products."

"The terrorist's favorite weapon." Stacey took a box down from the shelf. "The Palestinians, the IRA, all those cats use this stuff. You gonna use this underwater yourself?"

"Just to make a hole in a wreck."

"Then you need some detonation cord, a remote-control unit or I've got some chemical detonating pencils here. They work real good. You just break the cap. I got some timed for ten minutes and others for thirty." He pushed all the items together. "Is that it?"

"A night sight would be useful and a pair of binoculars."

"I can do them too." He opened another drawer. "There you go."

The night sight was small, but powerful, extending if needed like a telescope. The binoculars were by Zeiss and pocket size. "Excellent," Dillon said.

Stacey went and found an olive-green Army holdall, unzipped it, put the AK assault rifle in first and then the other things. He closed the zip, turned and led the way out, switching off the light and pushing the shelving back into place. Dillon followed him up the cellar stairs and out to the porch.

Stacey offered him the bag. "Mr. Dillon, I get the impression you intend to start World War Three."

"Maybe we can call a truce," Dillon said. "Who knows?"

"I wish you luck, my friend. I'll send my bill to Ferguson."

Stacey sat down, put on his reading glasses and picked up his newspaper, and Dillon walked out through the small garden and started back toward the waterfront.

He was walking along the side of the harbor to where the water taxis operated from when he saw that the Caneel ferry was in, a gangplank stretching down to the dock. The Captain was standing at the top as Dillon went up.

"You staying at Caneel, sir?"

"I certainly am."

"We'll be leaving soon. Just heard someone's on the way down from the airport."

Dillon went into the main cabin, put his bag on a seat and accepted a rum punch offered by one of the crew. He glanced out of the window and saw a large taxi bus draw up, a single passenger inside, went and sat down and drank some of his punch. One of the crew came in and put two suitcases in the corner, there was the sound of the gangplank being moved, the Captain went into the wheelhouse and started the engines. Dillon checked his watch. It was five-thirty. He put his plastic cup on the table, lit a cigarette and at the same time was aware of someone slumping down beside him.

"Fancy meeting you, dear boy," Charles Ferguson said. "Bloody hot, isn't it?"

10

Dillon had a quick swim off Paradise Beach, conscious that the *Maria Blanco* was still at anchor out there, then he went back up to the cottage, had a shower and changed into navy blue linen slacks and a short-sleeved white cotton shirt. He went out, crossed the vestibule and tapped on the door of 7E.

"Come," Ferguson called.

Dillon entered. The set-up was similar to his own, the bathroom marginally larger as was the other room. Ferguson, in gray flannel slacks and a white Turnbull and Asser shirt, stood in front of the mirror in the small dressing room easing the Guards tie into a neat Windsor knot at his neck.

"Ah, there you are," he said, took a double-breasted navy blue blazer and pulled it on. "How do I look, dear boy?"

"Like an advertisement for Gieves and Hawkes, the bloody English gentleman abroad."

"Just because you're Irish doesn't mean you have to feel inferior all the time," Ferguson told him. "Some very reasonable people were Irish, Dillon, my mother for instance, not to mention the Duke of Wellington."

"Who said that just because a man had been born in a stable didn't mean he was a horse," Dillon pointed out.

"Dear me, did he say that? Most unfortunate." Ferguson picked up a Panama hat and a Malacca cane with a silver handle.

"I never knew you needed a cane," Dillon said.

"Bought this during the Korean War. Strong as steel because it has a steel core weighted with lead at the tip. Oh, and here's a rather nice device."

He turned the silver handle to one side and pulled out a steel poniard about nine inches long.

"Very interesting," Dillon said.

"Yes, well we are in foreign parts. I call it my pig sticker." There was a click as Ferguson rammed the poniard home. "Now, are you going to offer me a quick drink before we go out or aren't you?"

Dillon had negotiated a supply of Krug from room service, had several half-bottles in one of the iceboxes. He filled two glasses and went out to Ferguson on the terrace, picking up the Zeiss field glasses on the way.

"That large white motor yacht out there is the *Maria Blanco*."

"Really?" Dillon passed him the Zeiss glasses and the Brigadier had a look. "A sort of minor floating palace I'd say."

"So it would appear."

Ferguson still held the glasses to his eyes. "As a young man I was a subaltern in the Korean War. One year of unmitigated hell. I did a tour of duty on a position called the Hook. Just like the First World War. Miles of trenches, barbed wire, mine fields and thousands of Chinese trying to get in. They used to watch us and we used to watch them. It was like a game, a particularly nasty game, which exploded into violence every so often." He sighed and lowered the glasses. "What on earth am I prattling on about, Dillon?"

"Oh, I'd say you're going the long way round to the pub to tell me that you suspect Santiago's watching too."

"Something like that. Tell me how far things have gone and don't leave anything out, not a single damn thing."

When Dillon was finished, he refilled the Brigadier's glass while Ferguson sat there thinking about it.

"What do you think the next move should be?" Dillon asked.

"Well, now you've gone and got yourself tooled up by Stacey I suppose you're eager for confrontation, a gunfight at the OK Corral?"

"I've taken precautions, that's all," Dillon said. "And I needed the Semtex to blast a way into the U-boat."

"If we find it," Ferguson said. "And not a murmur from the girl."

"She'll turn up eventually."

"And in the meantime?"

"I'd like to take things further with Carney. We really do need him on our side."

"I can see that, but it would be a question of how to approach him. Would a cash offer help?"

"Not really. If I'm right, Carney is the kind of man who'll only do a thing if he really wants to or if he thinks it right."

"Oh, dear." Ferguson sighed. "Heaven save me from the romantics of this world." He stood up and glanced at his watch. "Food, Dillon, that's what I need. Where shall we eat?"

"We could walk up to Turtle Bay Dining Room. That's more formal, I hear, but excellent. I've booked a table."

"Good, then let's get moving, and for heaven's sake put a jacket on. I don't want people to think I'm dining with a beachcomber."

Out in the gathering darkness of Caneel Bay, an inflatable from the *Maria Blanco* nosed in beside Carney's Sport Fisherman, *Sea Raider,* the only sound the muted throbbing of the outboard motor. Serra was at the helm and Algaro sat in the stern. As they bumped against the hull of *Sea Raider* he went up over the rail and into the wheelhouse, took a tiny electronic box from his pocket, reached under the instrument panel until he found metal and put it in place attached by its magnet.

A moment later he was back in the inflatable. "Now the small dive boat, *Privateer,*" he said and Serra turned and moved toward it.

Max Santiago, wearing a white linen suit, was sitting in Caneel Bay Bar sipping a mint julep when Algaro came in. He wore a black tee-shirt and a loose-fitting baggy suit in black linen that made him look rather sinister.

"Did everything go well?" Santiago asked.

"Absolutely. I've put a bug on both of Carney's dive boats. That means we can follow wherever he goes without being observed. Ferguson booked in just after six. I checked with the reservations desk. Dillon has booked a table for two up at Turtle Bay Dining Room."

"Good," Santiago said. "It might be amusing to join him."

Captain Serra entered at that moment. "Have you any further orders, Señor?"

"If Dillon does as he did last night, he may probably visit this bar, Jenny's Place," Santiago said. "I'll probably look in there myself."

"So I'll take the launch round to Cruz Bay, Señor, to pick you up from there?"

Santiago smiled. "I've had a better idea. Go back to the *Maria Blanco,* pick up some of the crew and take them into Cruz. They can have a drink on me later, let off a little steam if you follow me."

"Perfectly, Señor." Serra smiled and went out.

It was just after midnight at the Convent of the Little Sisters of Pity and Jenny Grant, who had gone to bed early, was restless and unable to sleep. She got up, found her cigarettes, lit one and went and sat on the padded windowseat and peered out into driving rain. She could see the light still on in the window of Sister Maria Baker's office, but then, she never seemed to stop working. Strange how Henry had always kept her very existence a secret. It was as if he'd been somehow ashamed of her, the religious thing. He'd never been able to handle that.

Jenny felt much better than when she had arrived, infinitely more rested and yet restless at the same time. She wondered what was happening in St. John and how Dillon was getting on. She'd liked Dillon, that was the simple truth, in spite of everything in his background of which she thoroughly disapproved. On the other hand, you could only speak as you found, and to her he had been good, kind, considerate and understanding.

She went back to bed, switched off the light and dozed and had a dream of the half-waking sort, the U-boat in dark waters and Henry diving deep. Dear Henry. Such an idiot to have been down there in the first place and somewhere dangerous, somewhere unusual, somewhere people didn't normally go. It had to be.

She came awake in the instant and spoke out loud in the darkness. "Oh, my God, of course, and so simple."

She got out of bed and went to the window. The light was still on in the Mother Superior's office. She dressed quickly in jeans and sweater and hurried across the court-yard through the rain and knocked on the door.

When she entered, she found Sister Maria Baker seated behind her desk working. She glanced up in surprise. "Why, Jenny, what is it? Can't you sleep?"

"I'll be leaving tomorrow, Sister, I just wanted to let you know. I'm going back to St. John."

"So soon, Jenny? But why?"

"The location of the U-boat that Henry found and that Dillon is looking for? I think I can find it for him. It just came to me as I was falling asleep."

Ferguson sat on the terrace at Turtle Bay and looked out to the Sir Francis Drake Channel, islands like black cutouts against the dark sky streaked with orange as the sun descended.

"Really is quite extraordinary," the Brigadier said as they sipped a fruit punch.

" 'Sunsets exquisitely dying,' that's what the poet said," Dillon murmured.

The cicadas chirped ceaselessly, night birds calling to each other. He got up and moved to the edge of the terrace and Ferguson said, "Good heavens, I didn't realize you had a literary bent, dear boy."

Dillon lit a cigarette, the Zippo flaring. He grinned. "To be frank with you I'm a bloody literary genius, Brigadier. I did Hamlet at the Royal Academy. I can still remem-ber most of the text." His voice changed suddenly into a remarkable impression of Marlon Brando. "I could have been somebody, I could have been a contender."

"Don't get maudlin on me at this stage in your life, Dillon, never pays to look back with regret because you can't change anything. And you've wasted too much time already on that damned cause of yours. I trust you realize that. Stay with the present. The main point which concerns me at the moment is how this wretched man Santiago comes to be so well informed."

"And wouldn't I like to know that myself?" Dillon said.

Santiago walked in through the arched gateway, Algaro at his shoulder. He looked around the terrace, saw Dillon and Ferguson and came over. "Mr. Dillon? Max Santiago."

"I know who you are, Señor," Dillon replied in excellent Spanish.

Santiago looked surprised. "I must congratulate you, Señor," he replied in the same language. "Such fluency in a foreigner is rare." He turned to Ferguson and added in English, "A pleasure to see you at Caneel Bay, Brigadier. Have a nice dinner, gentlemen," and he left followed by Algaro.

"He knew who you are and he knew you were here," Dillon said.

"So I noticed." Ferguson stood up. "Let's eat, I'm starving."

The service was good, the food excellent and Ferguson thoroughly enjoyed himself. They split a bottle of Louis Roederer Crystal Champagne and started with grilled sea scallops in a red pepper and saffron sauce, followed by a Caesar salad and then a pan-roasted pheasant. Ferguson, napkin tucked in his collar, devoured everything.

"To be honest, dear boy, I really prefer nursery food, but one must make an effort."

"An Englishman abroad again?" Dillon inquired.

"Ferguson, I need hardly point out, is the most Scots of Scottish names, Dillon, and as I told you, my mother was Irish."

"Yes, but Eton, Sandhurst and the Grenadier Guards got mixed up in that little lot somewhere."

Ferguson poured some more Crystal. "Lovely bottle. You can see right through it. Very unusual."

"Czar Nicholas designed it himself," Dillon told him. "Said he wanted to be able to see the champagne."

"Extraordinary. Never knew that."

"Didn't do him any good when the Bolsheviks murdered him."

"I'm glad you said murdered, Dillon, there's some hope for you still. What's friend Santiago doing?"

"Having dinner at the edge of the garden behind you. The ghoul with him, by the way, is called Algaro. He must be his minder. He's the one who ran me off the road and fired a shotgun."

"Oh, dear, we can't have that." Ferguson asked the waiter for tea instead of coffee. "What do you suggest our next move should be? Santiago is obviously pressing and intends we should know it."

"I think I need to speak to Carney. If anybody might have some ideas about where that U-boat is, it would be he."

"That's not only exquisitely grammatical, dear boy, it makes sense. Do you know where he might be?"

"Oh, yes."

"Excellent." Ferguson stood, picked up his Panama and Malacca cane. "Let's get moving then."

Dillon drove into the car park at Mongoose Junction and switched off. He took the holstered Belgian semi-automatic from his jacket pocket. "What on earth is that?" Ferguson demanded.

"An ace-in-the-hole. I'll leave it under the dashboard."

"Looks like a woman's gun to me."

"And like most women it gets the job done, Brigadier, so don't be sexist." Dillon clamped the holster under the dashboard. "Okay, let's go and see if we can find Carney."

They walked along the front from Mongoose Junction to Jenny's Place. It was about half-full when they went inside, Billy Jones working the bar, Mary and one waitress between them handling the dinner trade. There were only four tables taken and Carney sat at one.

Captain Serra and three of the crew from the *Maria Blanco* were at a booth table in the corner. Guerra, the mate, was one of them. Dillon recognized him from the first night, although the fact that Guerra said, "That's him," in Spanish and they all stopped talking was sufficient confirmation.

"Hello there." Mary Jones approached and Dillon smiled.

"We'll join Bob Carney. A bottle of champagne. Whatever you've got!"

"Two glasses." Ferguson raised his hat politely.

Mary took his arm, her teeth flashing in a delighted smile. "I like this man. Where did you find him? I love a gentleman."

Billy leaned over the bar. "You put him down, woman."

"It's not his fault," Dillon said. "He's a Brigadier. All that army training."

"A Brigadier General." Her eyes widened.

"Well, yes, that's true in your army," Ferguson said uncomfortably.

"Well, you go and join Bob Carney, honey. Mary's gonna take care of you right now."

Carney was just finishing an order of steak and french fries, a beer at his elbow, and looked up as they approached. "Mr. Dillon?" he said.

"This is a friend of mine, Brigadier Charles Ferguson," Dillon told him. "May we join you?"

Carney smiled. "I'm impressed, but I should warn you, Brigadier, all I made was corporal and that was in the Marines."

"Grenadier Guards," Ferguson told him, "hope you don't mind?"

"Hell, no, I guess we elite unit boys have got to stick together. Sit down." As they each pulled up a chair he went back to his steak and said to Dillon, "You ever in the army, Dillon?"

"Not exactly," Dillon told him.

"Hell, there's nothing exact about it, not that you hear about the Irish Army too much except that they seem to spend most of their time fighting for the United Nations in Beirut or Angola or someplace. Of course, there is the other lot, the IRA." He stopped cutting the last piece of steak for a moment, then carried on. "But no, that wouldn't be possible, would it, Dillon?"

He smiled and Ferguson said, "My dear chap, be reasonable, what on earth would the IRA be interested in here? What's more to the point, why would I be involved?"

"I don't know about that, Brigadier. What I do know is that Dillon here is a mystery to me and a mystery is like a crossword puzzle. I've just got to solve it."

Santiago came in followed by Algaro and the other four stood up. "We've got company," Dillon told Ferguson.

The Brigadier looked round. "Oh, dear," he said.

Bob Carney pushed his plate away. "Just to save you more questions, Santiago you know and that creep Algaro. The one with the beard is the captain of the *Maria Blanco*, Serra. The others will be crew."

Billy Jones brought a bottle of Pol Roget in a bucket, opened it for them, then went across to the booth to take Santiago's order. Dillon poured the champagne, raised his glass and spoke to Carney in Irish.

"Jesus," Carney said. "What in the hell are you saying, Dillon?"

"Irish, the language of kings. A very ancient toast. May the wind be always at your back. Appropriate for a ship's captain. I mean, you do have a master's ticket amongst other things?"

Carney frowned, then turned to Ferguson. "Let's see if I can put it together. He works for you?"

"In a manner of speaking."

At that moment, they heard a woman's voice say, "Please don't do that."

The waitress serving the drinks at Santiago's table was a small girl, rather pretty with her blonde hair in a plait bound up at the back. She was very young, very vulnerable. Algaro was running his hand over her buttocks and started to move down a leg.

"I hate to see that," Carney said and his face was hard.

Dillon said, "I couldn't agree more. To say he's in from the stable would be an insult to horses."

The girl pulled away, the crew laughing, and Santiago looked across, his eyes meeting Dillon's. He smiled, turned and whispered to Algaro, who nodded and got to his feet.

"Now let's keep our heads here," Ferguson said.

Algaro crossed to the bar and sat on a vacant stool. As the girl passed, he put an arm round her waist and whispered in her ear. She went red in the face, close to tears. "Leave me alone," she said and struggled to free herself.

Dillon glanced across. Santiago raised his glass and toasted him, a half-smile on his face, as Algaro slipped a hand up her skirt. Billy Jones was serving at the other end of the bar and he turned to see what was happening. Carney got to his feet, picked up his glass and walked to the bar. He put an arm around the girl's shoulders and eased her away, then he poured what was left of his beer into Algaro's crotch.

"Excuse me," he said, "I didn't see you there," and he turned and walked back to the table.

Everyone stopped talking and Dillon took the bottle from the ice bucket and refilled the Brigadier's glass. Algaro stood up and looked down at his trousers in disbelief. "Why, you little creep, I'm going to break your left arm for that."

He moved to the table fast, arms extended, and Carney turned, crouching to defend himself, but it was Dillon who struck first, reversed his grip on the champagne bottle and smashed it across the side of Algaro's skull not once but twice, the bottle splintering, champagne going everywhere. Algaro pulled himself up, hands on the edge of the table, and Dillon, still seated, kicked sideways at the kneecap. Algaro cried out and fell to one side. He lay there for a moment, then forced himself up on to one knee.

Dillon jumped up and raised a knee into the unprotected face. "You've never learned to lie down, have you?"

The other members of the crew of the *Maria Blanco* were on their feet, one of them picking up a chair, and Billy Jones came round the bar in a rush, a baseball bat in his hand. "Can it or I'll call the law. He asked for it, he got it. Just get him out of here."

They stopped dead, not so much because of Billy as Santiago, who said in Spanish, "No trouble. Just get him and leave."

Captain Serra nodded and Guerra, the mate, and Pinto went and helped Algaro to his feet. He appeared dazed, blood on his face, and they led him out followed by the others. Santiago stood up and raised his glass, emptied it and left.

Conversation resumed and Mary brought a brush and pan to sweep up the glass. Billy said to Dillon, "I couldn't get there fast enough. I thank you guys. How about another bottle of champagne on the house?"

"Include me out, Billy," Carney said. "Put the meal on my tab. I'm getting too old for this kind of excitement. I'm going home to bed." He stood up. "Brigadier, it's been interesting."

He started toward the door and Dillon called, "I'd like to dive in the morning. Does that suit you?"

"Nine-thirty," Carney told him. "Be at the dock," and he turned and went out.

His jeep was in the car park at Mongoose Junction. He walked along there, thinking about what had happened, was unlocking the door when a hand grabbed his shoulder and as he turned, Guerra punched him in the mouth.

"Now then you bastard, let's teach you some manners."

Serra stood a yard or two away supporting Algaro, Santiago beside them. Guerra and the other two crew members moved in fast. Carney ducked the first blow and punched the mate in the stomach, half-turning, giving Pinto a reverse elbow strike in the face and then they were all over him. They held him down, pinning his arms, and Algaro shuffled over.

"Now then," he said.

It was at that precise moment that Dillon and Ferguson, having taken a raincheck on the champagne, turned the corner. The Irishman went in on the run as Algaro raised a foot to stamp down on Carney's face, sent him staggering and punched the nearest man sideways in the jaw. Carney was already on his feet. Algaro was past it, but when Captain Serra moved in to help the other three it raised the odds and Dillon and Carney prepared to defend themselves, the jeep at their backs, arms raised, waiting. There was a sudden shot, the sound of it flat on the night air. Everyone stopped dead, turned and found Ferguson standing beside Dillon's jeep holding the Belgian semi-automatic in one hand.

"Now do let's stop playing silly buggers, shall we?" he said.

There was a pause and Santiago said in Spanish, "Back to the launch." The crew shuffled away unwillingly, Serra and Guerra supporting Algaro, who still looked dazed.

"Another time, Brigadier," Santiago said in English and followed them.

Carney wiped a little blood from his mouth with a hand-kerchief. "Would somebody kindly tell me what in the hell is going on?"

"Yes, we do need to talk, Captain Carney," Ferguson said briskly, "and sooner rather than later."

"Okay, I give in." Carney smiled bleakly. "Follow me and we'll go to my place. It's not too far away."

Carney said, "It's the damnedest thing I ever heard of."

"But you accept it's true?" Ferguson asked. "I have a copy of the translation of the diary in my briefcase at Caneel, which I'd be happy for you to see."

"The U-boat thing is perfectly possible," Carney said. "They were in these waters during World War Two, that's a known fact, and there are locals who'll tell you stories about how they used to come ashore by night." He shook his head. "Hitler in the Bunker, Martin Bormann—I've read all those books, and it is an interesting thought that if Bormann landed on Samson Cay and didn't go down with the boat, it would explain all those sightings of him in South America in the years since the war."

"Good," Dillon said. "So you accept the existence of U180, but where would it be?"

"Let me get a chart." Carney went out and came back with one which he unrolled. It was the Virgin Islands chart for St. Thomas up to Virgin Gorda. "There's Samson Cay south of Norman Island in the British Virgins. If that hurricane twisted, which they sometimes do, and came in from an easterly direction, the U-boat would definitely be driven somewhere toward the west and south from St. John."

"Ending where?" Ferguson said.

"It wouldn't be anywhere usual. By that I mean somewhere people dive, however regularly, and I'll tell you something else. It would have to be within one hundred feet."

"What makes you say that?" Dillon asked.

"Henry was a recreational diver, that means no decompression is necessary if you follow the tables. One hundred and thirty feet is absolute maximum for that kind of sport diving, and at that depth he could only afford ten minutes bottom time before going back up to the surface. To examine the submarine and find the diary." Carney shook his head. "It just wouldn't be possible, and Henry was sixty-three years of age. He knew his limitations."

"So what are you saying?"

"To discover the wreck, enter it, hunt around and find that diary." Carney shrugged. "I'd say thirty minutes bottom time, so his depth would likely be eighty feet or so. Now dive masters take tourists to that kind of depth all the time, that's why I mean the location has got to be quite out of the ordinary."

He frowned and Ferguson said, "You must have some idea."

"The morning Henry made his discovery must have been the day after the hurricane blew itself out. He'd gone out so early that he was coming back in at around nine-thirty when I was taking a dive party out. We crossed each other and we spoke."

"What did he say?" Dillon asked.

"I asked him where he'd been. He said French Cap. Told me it was like a millpond out there."

"Then that's it," Ferguson said. "Surely?"

Carney shook his head. "I use French Cap a lot. The water is particularly clear. It's a great dive. In fact I took my clients out there after meeting Henry that morning and he was right, it was like a millpond. The visibility is spectacular." He shook his head. "No, if it was there it would have been found before now."

"Can you think of anywhere else?"

Carney frowned. "There's always South Drop, that's even further."

"You dive there?" Ferguson asked.

"Occasionally. Trouble is if the sea's rough, it's a long and uncomfortable trip, but it could be the sort of place. A long ridge running to a hundred and seventy or so on one side and two thousand on the other."

"Could we take a look at these places?" Ferguson asked.

Carney shook his head and examined the chart again. "I don't know."

Ferguson said, "I'd pay you well, Captain Carney."

"It isn't that," Carney said. "Strictly speaking, this thing is in United States territorial waters."

"Just listen, please," Ferguson said. "We're not doing anything wicked here. There are some documents on U180, or so we believe, which could give my government cause for concern. All we want to do is recover them as quickly as possible and no harm done."

"And Santiago, where does he fit in?"

"He's obviously after the same thing," Ferguson said. "Why, I don't know at this time, but I will, I promise you."

"You go to the movies, Carney," Dillon said. "Santiago and his bunch are the bad guys. Blackhats."

"And I'm a good guy?" Carney laughed out loud. "Get the hell out of here and let me get some sleep. I'll see you at the dock at nine-thirty."

Santiago, standing in the stern of the *Maria Blanco,* looked toward Cottage Seven and the lights which had just come on in both sections.

"So they are back," he said to Serra, who stood beside him.

"Now that they've made contact with Carney they may make their move sometime tomorrow," Serra said.

"You'll be able to follow them in the launch whichever boat they are in, thanks to the bugs, at a discreet distance of course."

"Shall I take the divers?"

"If you like, but I doubt that anything will come of it. Carney doesn't know where U180 is, Serra, I'm convinced of that. They've asked him for suggestions, that's all. Take the dive-site handbook for this area with you. If they dive somewhere that's mentioned in the book, you may take it from me it's a waste of time." Santiago shook his head. "Frankly, I'm inclined to think that the girl has the answer. We'll just have to wait for her return. By the way, if we ever did find the U-boat and needed to blast a way in, could Noval and Pinto cope?"

"Most assuredly, Señor, we have supplies of C4 explosive on board and all the necessary detonating equipment."

"Excellent," Santiago said. "I wish you luck tomorrow then. Good night, Captain."

Serra walked away and Algaro slipped out of the dark. "Can I go with the launch in the morning?"

"Ah, revenge, is it?" Santiago laughed. "And why not? Enjoy it while you can, Algaro," and he laughed as he went down to the salon.

11

It was a beautiful morning when Dillon and Ferguson went down to the dock. *Sea Raider* was tied up, no sign of anyone around, and *Privateer* was moving out to sea with four people seated in the stern.

"Perhaps we got it wrong," Dillon observed.

"I doubt it," Ferguson said. "Not that sort of fellow."

At that moment Carney turned on to the end of the dock and came toward them pushing a trolley loaded with air tanks. "Morning," he called.

"Thought you'd left us," Dillon said, looking out toward *Privateer*.

"Hell, no, that's just one of my people taking some divers out to Little St. James. I thought we'd use *Sea Raider* today because we've a lot further to go." He turned to Ferguson. "You a good sailor, Brigadier?"

"My dear chap, I've just called in at the gift shop to obtain some seasickness pills of which I've taken not one but two."

He went on board and climbed the ladder to the flying bridge, where he sat in solitary splendor on one of the swivel seats while Dillon and Carney loaded the tanks. When they were finished Carney went up, joined Ferguson and switched on the engines. As they eased away from the dock, Dillon went into the deckhouse. He wasn't using his net dive bag, had put his diving gear into the olive-green army holdall Stacey had given him in St. Thomas. Underneath was the AK assault rifle, stock folded, and a thirty-round clip inserted ready for action plus an extra magazine. There was also his ace-in-the-hole Belgian semi-automatic which he'd retrieved from the jeep. As with all Sport Fishermen, there was a wheel in the deckhouse as well as on the flying bridge so the boat could be steered from there in rough weather. Dillon felt under the instrument panel until he encountered a metal surface and clamped the holster and gun in place.

He went up the ladder and joined the others. "What's our course?"

"Pretty well due south through Pillsbury Sound, then south-west to French Cap." Carney grinned at Ferguson, who swung from side to side as the boat started to lift over waves to the open sea. "You okay, Brigadier?"

"I'll let you know. I presume you would anticipate our friends from the *Maria Blanco* following?"

"I've been looking, but I haven't seen anything yet. There's certainly no sign of the *Maria Blanco* herself, but then they'd use the white launch we saw at Carval Rock. That's a good boat. Good for twenty-five or -six knots. I don't get much more than twenty out of this." He said to Dillon, "There's some glasses in the locker if you want to keep a weather eye open."

Dillon got them out, focused and checked astern. There were a number of yachts and a small vehicle ferry with trucks on board crossing from St. Thomas, but no launch. "Not a sign," he said.

"Now I find that strange," Ferguson observed.

"You worry too much, Brigadier," Carney told him. "Now

let's get out of here," and he pushed the throttle forward and took *Sea Raider* out to open water fast.

The launch was there, of course, but a good mile behind, Serra at the wheel, his eye occasionally going to the dark screen with the blob of light showing what was the *Sea Raider*. Algaro stood beside him and Noval and Pinto busied themselves with diving equipment in the stern. Algaro didn't look good. He had a black eye and his mouth was bruised and swollen.

"No chance of losing them?"

"No way," Serra said. "I'll show you." There was a steady and monotonous pinging sound coming from the screen. When he swung the wheel, turning to port, it raised its pitch, sounded frantic. "See, that tells us when we're off track." He turned back to starboard, straightening when he got the right sound again, checking the course reading.

"Good," Algaro said.

"How are you feeling?" Serra asked.

"Well, let's put it this way. I'll feel a whole lot better when I've sorted those bastards out," Algaro said, "particularly Dillon," and he turned and went and joined the others.

The water heaved in heavy, long swells as they drifted in to French Cap Cay. Dillon went to the prow to lower the anchor while Carney maneuvered the boat, leaning out under the blue awning of the flying bridge to give him instructions.

"There's what we call the Pinnacle under here," he said. "Its top is about forty-five feet down. That's what we're trying to catch the anchor on." After a while he nodded. "That's it," he called and cut the engines.

"What are we going to do?" Dillon asked as he zipped up his diving suit.

"Not much we can do," Carney told him as he fastened his weight belt. "It's around ninety-five feet at the most, ranging up to fifty. We can do a turn right round the rock base and general reef area. The visibility is incredible. You'll not find better anywhere. That's why I don't believe this is the right spot. That U-boat would have been spotted before now. By the way, I think you picked up my diving gloves by mistake yesterday and I've got yours." He rummaged in Dillon's holdall and found the rifle. "Dear God," he said, taking it out. "What's this?"

"Insurance," Dillon said as he pulled on his fins.

"An AK47 is considerably more than that." Carney unfolded the stock and checked it.

"I would remind you, Mr. Carney, that it was our friends who fired the first shot," Ferguson said. "You're familiar with that weapon?"

"I was in Vietnam, Brigadier. I've used one for real. They make a real ugly, distinctive sound. I never hope to hear one fired again."

Carney folded the stock, replaced the AK in the holdall and finished getting his diving gear on. He stepped awkwardly on to the diving platform at its rear and turned. "I'll see you down there," he said to Dillon, inserted his mouthpiece and tumbled backwards.

Serra watched them from about a quarter of a mile away through a pair of old binoculars. Noval and Pinto stood ready in their diving suits. Algaro said, "What are they doing?"

"They've anchored and Dillon and Carney have gone down. There's just the Brigadier on deck."

"What do you want us to do?" Noval asked.

"We'll go in very fast, but I won't anchor. We'll make it a drift dive, catch them by surprise, so be ready to go."

He pushed the launch up to twenty-five knots and as it surged forward, Noval and Pinto got the rest of their equipment on.

Carney hadn't exaggerated. There were all colors of coral, barrel and tube sponges, fish of every description, but it was the visibility that was so incredible, the water tinged with a deep blue stretching into a kind of infinity. There was a school of horse-eyed jacks overhead as Dillon followed Carney and a couple of manta rays flapped across the sandy slope to one side.

But Carney had also been right about the U-boat. No question that it could be on a site like this. Dillon followed him along the reef and the base of the rock until finally Carney turned and spread his arms. Dillon understood the gesture and swung round for the return to the boat and saw Noval and Pinto ahead of them and perhaps twenty feet higher. He and Carney hung suspended, watching them, and then the American gestured forward and led the way back to the anchor line. They paused there and looked up and saw the keel of the launch moving in a wide circle. Carney started up the line and Dillon followed him, finally surfacing at the stern.

"When did they arrive?" Dillon asked Ferguson as he shrugged off his jacket and tank.

"About ten minutes after you went down. Roared up at a hell of a speed, didn't put the anchor down, simply dropped two divers over the stern."

"We saw them." Dillon took his gear off and looked across at the launch. "There's Serra the captain and our old chum Algaro glowering away."

"They did a neat job of trailing us, I'll say that," Carney

said. "Anyway, let's get moving."

"Are we still going to try this South Drop Place?" Dillon asked.

"I'm game if you are. Haul up the anchor."

Noval and Pinto surfaced beside the launch and heaved themselves in as Dillon went into the prow and started to pull in the anchor, only it wouldn't come. "I'll start the engine and try a little movement," Carney said.

It made no difference and Dillon looked up. "Stuck fast."

"Okay." Carney nodded. "One of us will have to go down and pull it free."

"Well that's me obviously." Dillon picked up his jacket and tank. "We need you to handle the boat."

Ferguson said, "Have you got enough air left in that thing?"

Dillon checked. "Five hundred. That's ample."

"Your turn, Brigadier," Carney said. "Get in the prow and haul that anchor up the moment it's free and try not to give yourself a hernia."

"I'll do my best, dear boy."

"One thing, Dillon," Carney called. "You won't have the line to come up on and there's a one- to two-knot current so you'll most probably surface well away from the boat. Just inflate your jacket and I'll come and get you."

As Dillon went in off the stern Algaro said, "What's happening?"

"Probably the anchor got stuck," Noval said.

Dillon had, in fact, reached it at that precise moment. It was firmly wedged in a deep crevasse. Above him Carney was working the boat on minimum engine power, and as the line slackened Dillon pulled the anchor free. It dragged over coral for a moment, then started up. He tried to follow, was aware of the current pushing him to one side and didn't fight it, simply drifted up slowly and surfaced. He was perhaps fifty yards away from *Sea Raider* and inflated his jacket, lifted high on the heavy swell.

The Brigadier had just about got the anchor in and Noval was the first one to spot Dillon. "There he is."

"Wonderful." Algaro shouldered Serra aside and took over the wheel. "I'll show him."

He gunned the engine, the launch bore down on Dillon, who frantically swam to one side, just managing to avoid it. Carney cried out a warning, swinging *Sea Raider* round from the prow, Ferguson almost falling into the sea. Dillon had his left hand raised, holding up the tube that allowed him to expel the air from his buoyancy jacket. The launch swerved in again, brushing him to one side. Algaro, laughing like a maniac, the sound clear across the water, was turning in a wide circle to come in again.

The Brigadier had the AK out of the holdall, was wrestling with it when Carney came down the ladder, his hands sliding on the guard rails. "I know how those things work, you don't, Brigadier."

He put it on full automatic, fired a burst over the launch. Serra was wrestling with Algaro now and Noval and Pinto had hit the deck. Carney fired another careful burst that ripped up some decking in the prow. By that time Dillon had disappeared and Serra had taken over the wheel. He turned in a wide circle and took off at full speed.

Ferguson surveyed the area anxiously. "Has he gone?"

Dillon surfaced some little distance away and Carney put down the AK, went into the lower wheelhouse and took the boat toward him. Dillon came in at the stern and Carney hurried back to relieve him of his jacket and tank.

"Jesus, but that was lively," Dillon said when he reached the deck. "What happened?"

"Algaro decided to run you down," the Brigadier told him.

Dillon reached for a towel and saw the AK. "I thought I heard a little gunfire." He looked up at Carney. "You?"

"Hell, they made me mad," Carney said. "You still want to try South Drop?"

"Why not?" Ferguson looked at the dwindling launch. "I don't think they'll be bothering us again."

"Not likely." Carney pointed south. "Rain squall rolling in and that's good because I know where I'm going and they don't," and he went up the ladder to the flying bridge.

The launch slowed half a mile away and Serra raised the glasses to his eyes and watched *Sea Raider* disappear into the curtain of rain and mist. He checked the screen. "They're moving south."

"Where are they going? Any ideas?" Algaro asked.

Serra took the dive-site handbook from a shelf, opened it and checked the map. "That was French Cap. The only one marked here further out is called South Drop." He riffled through the pages. "Here we are. There's a ridge at about seventy feet, around a hundred and sixty or seventy on one side, then it just drops on the other, all the way to the bottom. Maybe two thousand."

"Could that be it?"

"I doubt it. The very fact that it's in the handbook means it's dived reasonably frequently."

Noval said, "The way it works is simple. Dive masters only bring clients this far out in good weather. Any other kind and the trip is too long and rough, people get sick." He shrugged. "So a place like South Drop wouldn't get dived as often, but Captain Serra is right. The fact that it's in the handbook at all makes it very unlikely the U-boat is there. Somebody would have spotted it years ago."

"And that's a professional's opinion," Serra said. "I think Señor Santiago is right. Carney doesn't know anything. He's just taking them to one or two far-out places for want of something better to do. Señor Santiago thinks the girl is our only chance, so it's a question of waiting for her return."

"I'd still like to teach those swine a lesson," Algaro told him.

"And get shot at again."

"That was an AK Carney was firing, I recognized the sound. He could have knocked us all off." Algaro shrugged. "He didn't and he won't now."

Pinto was reading the section on South Drop in the site guide. "It sounds a good dive," he said to Noval, "except for one thing. It says here that black tip reef sharks have been noted."

"Are they dangerous?" Algaro demanded.

"Depends on the situation. If they get stirred up the wrong way, they can be a real threat."

Algaro's smile was unholy. "Have we still got any of that filthy stuff left you had in the bucket when you were fishing from the launch yesterday?" he asked Noval.

"You mean the bait we were using?" Noval turned to Pinto. "Is there any left?"

Pinto moved to the stern, found a large plastic bucket and took the lid off. The smell was appalling. There were all kinds of cut-up fish in there, mingled with intestines, rotting meat and oil.

"I bet the sharks would like that," Algaro said. "That would bring them in from miles around."

Noval looked horrified. "It would drive them crazy."

"Good, then this is what we do." Algaro turned to Serra. "Once they've stopped, we close in through the rain nice and quietly. We're bound to home in on them with that electronic gadget, am I right?"

Serra looked troubled. "Yes, but . . . "

"I don't want to hear any buts. We wait, give them time to go down, then we go in very fast, dump this shit over the side and get the hell out of it." There was a smile of pure joy on his face. "With any kind of luck Dillon could lose a leg."

The *Sea Raider* was at anchor, lifting in a heavy, rolling swell. Ferguson sat in the deckhouse watching as the other two got ready. Carney opened the deck locker and took out a long tube with a handle at one end.

"Is that what they call an underwater spear gun?" Ferguson asked.

"No, it's a power gun." Carney opened a box of ammunition. "What we call a power-head. Some people use a shotgun cartridge. Me, I prefer a .45ACP. Slide it on the rear chamber here, close her up nice and tight. There's a firing pin in the base. When I jab it against the target, the cartridge is fired, the bullet goes through but the gases blast a hole the size of your hand."

"And good night, Vienna." Dillon pulled on his jacket and tank. "You're going fishing this time?"

"Not exactly. When I was out here last there were reef sharks about and one of them got kind of heavy. I'm just being careful."

Dillon went in first, falling back off the diving platform, swam to the line and went down very quickly. He turned at the anchor and saw Carney following, the power-head in his left hand. He hovered about fifteen feet above Dillon, beckoned and started along the ridge, pausing on the edge of the drop.

The water was gin clear and Dillon could see a long way, the cliff vanishing way below. Carney beckoned again and turned to cross the reef to the shallower side. There was

an eagle ray passing in slow motion in the far distance and
suddenly a reef shark crossed its path and passed not too
far from them. Carney turned, made a dismissive gesture
and Dillon followed him to the other side.

Ferguson, aware of the rain in the wind, moved into the
deckhouse, found the thermos flask that was full of hot
coffee and poured himself a cup. He seemed to hear something, a muted throbbing, moved to the stern and stood
there listening. There was a sudden roar as Serra pushed
his engine up to full speed. The launch broke from the
curtain of rain and cut across *Sea Raider*'s prow. Ferguson
swore, dropped the thermos flask and started for the AK in
the holdall in the deckhouse, aware of the men on the deck
of the launch, the bucket emptying into the water. By the
time he had the AK out they were gone, the sound of the
engine rapidly disappearing into the rain.

Dillon was aware of something overhead, glanced up and
saw the keel of the launch moving fast and then the bait
drifting down into the water. He hovered there, watching
as a barracuda went in like lightning, tearing at a piece
of meat.

He was aware of a tug at his ankle, glanced down and
saw Carney gesturing for him to descend. The American
was flat on the bottom when Dillon reached him, and
above them, there was a sudden turbulence in the water
and a shark went in like a torpedo. Dillon lay on his back
like Carney, looking up as another shark swerved in, jaws
open. And then, to his horror, a third flashed in overhead.
They seemed to be fighting amongst themselves and one
of them snapped at the barracuda, taking its entire body,
leaving only the head to float down.

Carney turned to Dillon, pointed across the ridge to the

anchor line, motioned to keep low and led the way. Dillon followed, aware of the fierce turbulence, glanced back and saw them circling each other now and most of the bait had gone. He kept right behind Carney and so low that his stomach scraped the bottom, only starting to rise as they reached the anchor.

Something knocked him to one side with tremendous force, he bounced around as one of the sharks brushed past. It turned and started in again and Carney, above him, a hand on the line, jabbed the power-head. There was an explosion, the shark twisted away, leaving a trail of blood.

The other two sharks circled it, then one went in, jaws open. Carney tugged at Dillon's arm and started up the line. About halfway up Dillon looked down. The third shark had joined in now, tearing at the wounded one, blood in the water like a cloud. Dillon didn't look back after that, surfaced at the dive platform beside Carney and hauled himself on board, tank and all.

He sat on deck, laughing shakily. "Does that happen often?"

"There's a first time for everything." Carney took his tank off. "Nobody tried to do that to me before." He turned to Ferguson. "Presumably that was the launch? I expect the bastard came in on low power, then went up to full speed at the last minute."

"That's it exactly. By the time I got to the AK they were away," Ferguson said.

Carney dried himself and put on a tee-shirt. "I'd sure like to know how they managed to follow us though, especially in this rain and mist."

He went and hauled in the anchor and Dillon said, "I should have told you, Brigadier, I have my ace-in-the-hole stowed under here. Maybe you could have got to it faster."

He ran his hand under the instrument panel to find it and his fingers brushed against the bug. He detached it and held it out to Ferguson in the palm of his hand. "Well, now," Ferguson said, "we're into electronic wizardry, are we?"

"What in the hell have you got there?" Carney demanded as he came round from the prow.

Dillon held it out. "Stuck under the instrument panel on a magnet. We've been bugged, my old son, no wonder they were able to keep track of us so easily. They probably did the same thing to *Privateer* in case we used that."

"But she stayed close inshore this morning."

"Exactly, otherwise they might have got confused."

Carney shook his head. "You know I'm really going to have to do something about these people," and he went up the ladder to the flying bridge.

On the way back to St. John there was a break in the weather, another rain squall sweeping across the water. The launch was well ahead of it, pulled in beside the *Maria Blanco*, and Serra and Algaro went up the ladder and found Santiago in the stern under the awning.

"You look pleased with yourself," he said to Algaro. "Have you been killing people again?"

"I hope so." Algaro related the morning's events.

When he finished, Santiago shook his head. "I doubt whether Dillon sustained any lasting damage, this Carney man knows his business too well." He sighed. "We're wasting our time. There's nothing to be done until the girl returns. We'll run over to Samson Cay, I'm tired of this place. How long will it take, Serra?"

"Two hours, Señor, maybe less. There's a squall out there off Pillsbury Sound, but it's only temporary."

"Good, we'll leave at once. Let Prieto know we're coming." Serra turned away and Santiago said, "Oh, and by the way, phone up one of your fishermen friends in Cruz Bay. I want to know the instant that girl turns up."

The squall was quite ferocious, driving rain before it in a heavy curtain, but having a curious smoothing effect on the surface of the sea. Carney switched off the engines and came down the ladder and joined Ferguson and Dillon in the deckhouse.

"Best to ride this out. It won't last long." He grinned. "Normally I wouldn't carry alcohol, but this being a private charter."

He opened the plastic icebox and came up with three cans of beer. "Accepted gratefully." Ferguson pulled the tab and drank some down. "God, but that's good."

"There are times when an ice-cold beer is the only thing," Carney said. "Once in Vietnam I was in a unit that got mortared real bad. In fact, I've still got fragments in both arms and legs too small to be worth fishing out. I sat on a box in the rain, eating a sandwich while a Corpsman stitched me up and he was out of morphine. I was so glad to be alive I didn't feel a thing. Then someone gave me a can of beer, warm beer, mind you."

"But nothing ever tasted as good?" Dillon said.

"Until the smoke cleared and I saw a guy sitting against a tree with both legs gone." Carney shook his head. "God, how I came to hate that war. After my time I went to Georgia State on the Marines. When Nixon came and the police turned up to beat up the antiwar demonstrators all us veterans wore white tee-shirts with our medals pinned to them to shame them."

He laughed and Ferguson said, "The Hook in Korea was just like that. More bodies than you could count, absolute hell, and you ended up wondering what you were doing there."

"Heidegger once said that for authentic living what is necessary is the resolute confrontation of death," Dillon told them.

Carney laughed harshly. "I know the works of Heidegger, I took a Bachelor of Philosophy degree at Georgia State and I'll tell you this. I bet Heidegger was seated at his desk in the study when he wrote that."

Ferguson laughed. "Well said."

"Anyway, Dillon, what do you know about it? Which was your war?" Carney asked.

Dillon said calmly, "I've been at war all my life." He stood up, lit a cigarette and went up the ladder to the flying bridge.

Carney said, "Hey, wait a minute, Brigadier, that discussion we had about the Irish army last night at Jenny's Place when I made a remark about the IRA? Is that what he is, one of those gunmen you read about?"

"That's what he used to be, though they like to call themselves soldiers of the Irish Republican Army. His father was killed accidentally in crossfire by British soldiers in Belfast when he was quite young so he joined the glorious cause."

"And now?"

"I get the impression that his sympathy for the glorious cause of the IRA has dwindled somewhat. Let's be polite and say he's become a kind of mercenary and leave it at that."

"I'd say that's a waste of a good man."

"It's his life," Ferguson said.

"I suppose so." Carney stood up. "Clearing now. We'd better go."

He went up the ladder to the flying bridge. Dillon didn't say a word, simply sat there in the swivel chair smoking, and Carney switched on the engines and took the *Sea Raider* in toward St. John.

• • •

It was perhaps ten minutes later that Carney realized that the motor yacht bearing down on them was the *Maria Blanco*. "Well, damn me," he said. "Our dear old friend Santiago. They must be moving on to Samson Cay."

Ferguson climbed the ladder to the flying bridge to join them and Carney took the *Sea Raider* in so close that they could see Santiago in the stern with Algaro.

Carney leaned over the rail and called, "Have a nice day," and Ferguson lifted his Panama.

Santiago raised his glass to them and said to Algaro, "What did I tell you, you fool. The sharks probably came off worst."

At that moment Serra came along from the radio room and handed him the portable phone. "A call from London, Señor, Sir Francis."

"Francis," Santiago said. "How are you?"

"I was wondering if you'd had any breakthrough yet?"

"No, but there's no need to worry, everything is under control."

"One thing has just occurred to me. Can't imagine why I didn't think of it before. The caretakers of the old hotel at Samson Cay during the war, they were a black couple from Tortola, May and Joseph Jackson. She died years ago, but he's still around. About seventy-two, I think. Last time I saw him he was running a taxi on the Cay."

"I see," Santiago said.

"I mean, he was there when my mother arrived and then Bormann, you take my point. Sorry, I should have thought of it before."

"You should, Francis, but never mind. I'll attend to it." Santiago put the phone down and turned to Algaro. "Another job for you, but there's no rush. I'm going for a lie down. Call me when we get in."

• • •

Later in the afternoon Dillon was lying on a sun lounger on the terrace when Ferguson appeared.

"I've just had a thought," the Brigadier said. "This millionaire's retreat at Samson Cay. Might be rather fun to have dinner there. Beard the lion in his den."

"Sounds good to me," Dillon said. "We could fly over if you like. There's the airstrip. I passed over it on my way here and that Cessna of mine can put down on land as well as water."

"Perhaps we can persuade Carney to join us? Ring the front desk on your cellular phone, get the number and ask for the general manager's name."

Which Dillon did, writing the details down quickly. "There you go, Carlos Prieto."

Within two minutes Ferguson was speaking to the gentleman. "Mr. Prieto? Brigadier Charles Ferguson here, I'm staying at Caneel. One of my friends has a floatplane here and we thought it might be rather fun to fly over this evening and join you for dinner. It's a dual-purpose plane. We could put down on your airstrip. There would be three of us."

"I regret, Brigadier, but dining facilities are reserved for our residents."

"What a shame, I'd so hate to disappoint Mr. Santiago."

There was a slight pause. "Mr. Santiago was expecting you?"

"Check with him, do."

"A moment, Brigadier." Prieto phoned the *Maria Blanco,* for Santiago always preferred to stay on board when at Samson Cay. "I'm sorry to disturb you, Señor, but does the name Ferguson mean anything to you?"

"Brigadier Charles Ferguson?"

"He is on the telephone from Caneel. He wishes to fly

over in a floatplane, three of them, for dinner."

Santiago laughed out loud. "Excellent, Prieto, marvelous, I wouldn't miss it for the world."

Prieto said, "We look forward to seeing you, Brigadier. At what time may we expect you?"

"Six-thirty or seven."

"Excellent."

Ferguson handed the cellular phone back to Dillon. "Get hold of Carney and tell him to meet us at Jenny's Place at six in his best bib and tucker. We'll have a cocktail and wing our way to Samson Cay. Should be a jolly evening," he said and went out.

12

It was seven o'clock in the evening when Jenny Grant reached Paris and Charles de Gaulle airport. She returned the hired car, went to the British Airways reservation desk and booked on the next flight to London. It was too late to connect with any flight to Antigua that day, but there was space the following morning on the nine A.M. flight from Gatwick arriving in Antigua just after two in the afternoon, and they even booked her on an onward flight to St. Thomas on one of the Liat inter-island service planes. With luck she would be in St. John by early evening.

She waited for her tickets, went and booked in for the London flight so that she could get rid of her luggage. She went to one of the bars and ordered a glass of wine. Best to stay overnight at Gatwick at one of the airport hotels. She felt good for the first time since she'd heard the news of Henry's death, excited as well, and couldn't wait to get back to St. John to see if she was right. She went and bought a phone card at one of the kiosks, found a telephone and rang Jenny's Place at Cruz Bay. It was Billy Jones who answered.

"Billy? It's me—Jenny."

"My goodness, Miss Jenny, where are you?"

"Paris. I'm at the airport. It's nearly seven-thirty in the evening here. I'm coming back tomorrow, Billy, by way of Antigua, then Liat up to St. Thomas. I'll see you around six."

"That's wonderful. Mary will be thrilled."

"Billy, has a man called Sean Dillon been in to see you? I told him to look you up."

"He sure has. He's been sailing around with Bob Carney, he and a Brigadier Ferguson. In fact, I just heard from Bob. He tells me they're meeting in here, the three of them, for a drink at six o'clock."

"Good. Give Dillon a message for me. Tell him I'm coming back because I think I might know where it is."

"Where what is?" Billy demanded.

"Never mind. Just you give him that message. It's very important."

She put the phone down, picked up her hand luggage and still full of excitement and elation, passed through security into the international lounge.

Ferguson and Dillon parked the jeep in the car park at Mongoose Junction and walked along to Jenny's Place. In blazer and Guards tie, the Panama at a suitable angle, the Brigadier looked extremely impressive. Dillon wore a navy blue silk suit, a white cotton shirt buttoned at the neck. When they entered Jenny's Place the bar was already half-full with the early evening trade. Bob Carney leaned on the bar wearing white linen slacks and a blue shirt, a blazer on the stool beside him.

He turned and whistled. "A regular fashion parade. Thank God I dressed."

"Well, we are meeting the Devil face to face, in a manner of speaking." Ferguson laid his Malacca cane on the bar. "Under the circumstances I think one should make an effort.

Champagne, innkeeper," he said to Billy.

"I thought that might be what you'd want. I got a bottle of Pol Roget on ice right here." Billy produced it from beneath the bar and thumbed out the cork. "Now the surprise I've been saving."

"And what's that?" Carney asked.

"Miss Jenny was on the phone from Paris, France. She's coming home. Should be here right about this time tomorrow."

"That's wonderful," Carney said.

Billy filled three glasses. "And she gave me a special message for you, Mr. Dillon."

"Oh, and what would that be?" Dillon inquired.

"She said it was important. She said to tell you she's coming back because she thinks she might know where it is. Does that make any kind of sense to you, because it sure as hell doesn't to me?"

"All the sense in the world." Ferguson raised his glass and toasted the others. "To women in general, gentlemen, and Jenny Grant in particular. Bloody marvelous." He emptied his glass. "Good, into battle," and he turned and led the way out.

Behind them, the bearded fisherman who had been sitting at the end of the bar listening, got up and left. He walked to a public phone just along the waterfront, took out the piece of paper Serra had given him and rang the *Maria Blanco*. Santiago was in his cabin getting ready for the evening when Serra hurried in carrying the phone.

"What on earth is it?" Santiago demanded.

"My informant in St. John. He just heard Dillon and his friends talking to Jones, the bartender at Jenny's Place. Apparently she was on the phone from Paris, will be in St. John tomorrow evening."

"Interesting," Santiago said.

"That's not all, Señor, she sent a message to Dillon to say she was coming back because she thinks she might know where it is."

Santiago's face was very pale and he snatched the phone. "Santiago here. Now repeat your story to me." He listened and finally said, "You've done well, my friend, you'll be taken care of. Continue to keep your eyes open."

He handed the portable phone to Serra. "You see, everything comes to he who waits," and he turned back to the mirror.

Ferguson, Dillon and Carney crossed from Mongoose and followed the trail to Lind Point toward the seaplane ramp. Ferguson said, "Rather convenient having a ramp here and so on."

"Actually we do have a regular seaplane service some of the time," Carney said. "When it's operating, you can fly to St. Thomas or St. Croix, even direct to San Juan on Puerto Rico."

They reached the Cessna and Dillon walked round checking it generally, then pulled the blocks away from the wheels. He opened the rear door. "Okay, my friends, in you go."

Ferguson went first, followed by Carney. Dillon opened the other door, climbed into the pilot's seat, slammed and locked the door behind him, strapping himself in. He released the brakes and the plane rolled down the ramp into the water and drifted outwards on the current.

Ferguson looked across the bay in the fading light. "Beautiful evening, but I've been thinking. We'll be flying back in darkness."

"No, it's a full moon tonight, Brigadier," Carney told him.

"I checked the weather forecast," Dillon added. "Clear, crisp night, perfect conditions. The flight shouldn't take more than fifteen minutes. Seat belts fastened, life jackets under the seat."

He switched on, the engine coughed into life, the propeller turned. He taxied out of harbor, checked to make sure there was no boat traffic and turned into the wind. They drifted up into the air and started to climb, leveling out at a thousand feet. They passed over part of the southern edge of St. John, then Reef Bay and finally Ram Head before striking out to sea toward Norman Island, Samson Cay perhaps four miles south of it. It was a flight totally without incident, and exactly fifteen minutes after leaving Cruz Bay he was making his first pass over the island. The *Maria Blanco* was lying in the harbor below, three hundred yards off-shore, and there were a number of yachts, still a few people on the beach in the fading light.

"A real rich folks' hideaway," Bob Carney said.

"Is that so?" Ferguson said, unimpressed. "Well I hope they do a decent meal, that's all I'm interested in."

Carlos Prieto came out of the entrance to reception and looked up as the Cessna passed overhead. There was an ancient Ford station wagon parked at the bottom of the steps, an ageing black man leaning against it.

Prieto said, "There they are, Joseph, get up to the airstrip and bring them in."

"Right away, sir." Joseph got behind the wheel and drove off.

As Prieto turned to go inside, Algaro emerged. "Ah, there you are, I've been looking for you. Do we have an old black somewhere around called Jackson, Joseph Jackson?"

"We certainly do. He was the driver of that station wagon

that just drove off. He's gone to the airstrip to pick up Brigadier Ferguson and the others. Do you need him for anything important?"

"It can wait," Algaro told him and went back inside.

Dillon put the Cessna down for a perfect landing, taxied toward the other end of the airstrip, turning into the wind, and switched off. "Not bad, Dillon," Ferguson told him. "You can fly a plane, I'll grant you that."

"You've no idea how good that makes me feel," Dillon said.

They all got out and Joseph Jackson came to meet them. "Car waiting right over here, gents. I'll take you down to the restaurant. Joseph's the name, Joseph Jackson. Anything you want, just let me know. I've been around this island longer than anybody."

"Indeed?" Ferguson said. "I don't suppose you were here in the War? I understand it was unoccupied?"

"That ain't so," Jackson said. "There was an old hotel here, belonged to an American family, the Herberts. The hotel was unoccupied during the War, but me and my wife, May, we came over from Tortola to look after things."

They had reached the station wagon and Ferguson said, "Herbert, you say, they were the owners?"

"Miss Herbert's father, he gave it to her as a wedding present, then she married a Mr. Vail." Jackson opened the rear door for Ferguson to get in. "Then she had a daughter."

Dillon sat beside Ferguson and Carney took the front seat beside Jackson. The old boy was obviously enjoying himself.

"So, Miss Herbert became Mrs. Vail, who had a daughter called Miss Vail?" Dillon said.

Jackson started the engine and cackled out loud. "Only

Miss Vail then became Lady Pamer, what do you think of that? A real English lady, just like the movies."

"Switch off that engine!" Ferguson ordered.

Jackson looked bewildered. "Did I say something?"

Bob Carney reached over and turned the key. Ferguson said, "Miss Vail became Lady Pamer, you're sure?"

"I knew her, didn't I? She came here at the end of the War with her baby, little Francis. That must have been in April forty-five."

There was a heavy silence. Dillon said, "Was anyone else here at the time?"

"German gent named Strasser. He just turned up one night. I think he got a fishing boat to drop him off from Tortola, but Lady Pamer, she was expecting him . . . "

"And Sir Joseph?"

"He came over from England in June. Mr. Strasser, he moved on. The Pamers left and went back to England after that. Sir Joseph, he used to come back, but that was years ago when the resort was first built."

"And Sir Francis Pamer?" Ferguson asked.

"Little Francis?" Jackson laughed. "He growed up real fine. I've seen him here many times. Can we go now, gents?"

"Of course," Ferguson said.

Jackson drove away, Dillon took out a cigarette and no one said a word until they reached the front entrance. Ferguson produced his wallet, extracted a ten-pound note and passed it to Jackson. "My thanks."

"And I thank you," Jackson told him. "I'll be ready for you gents when you want to go back."

The three of them paused at the bottom of the steps. Dillon said, "So now we know how Santiago comes to be so well informed."

"God in heaven," Ferguson said. "A Minister of the

Crown and one of the oldest families in England."

"A lot of those people thought Hitler had the right ideas during the nineteen-thirties," Dillon said. "It fits, Brigadier, it all fits. What about Carter?"

"The British Secret Service was unfortunate enough to employ dear old Kim Philby, Burgess, MacLean, all of whom also worked for the KGB and sold us down the river to Communism without a moment's hesitation. Since then, there was Blunt, rumours of a fifth man, a sixth." Ferguson sighed. "In spite of the fact that I don't care a jot for Simon Carter, I must tell you that I believe he's an old-fashioned patriot and honest as the day is long."

Carlos Prieto appeared at the top of the steps. "Brigadier Ferguson, what a pleasure. Señor Santiago is waiting for you in the bar. He's just come over from the *Maria Blanco*. He prefers to stay on board while he's here."

The lounge bar was busy with the rich and the good as one would expect in such a place. People tended to be older rather than younger, the men especially, mostly American, being rather obviously close to the end of their working lives. There was a preponderance of trousers in fake Scottish plaid swelling over ample bellies, white tuxedos.

"God save me," Dillon said, "I've never seen so many men who resembled dance-band leaders in their prime."

Ferguson laughed out loud and Santiago, who was seated in a booth by the bar, Algaro bending over him, turned to look at them. He stood up and reached out a hand urbanely. "My dear Brigadier Ferguson, such a pleasure."

"Señor Santiago," Ferguson said formally. "I've long looked forward to this meeting." He pointed briefly at Algaro with his Malacca cane. "But do we really have to have this creature present? I mean couldn't he go and feed the fish or something?"

Algaro looked as if he would have liked to kill him on the spot, but Santiago laughed out loud. "Poor Algaro, an acquired taste, I fear."

"The little devil." Dillon wagged a finger at Algaro. "Now go and chew a bone or something, there's a good boy."

Santiago turned and said to Algaro in Spanish, "Your turn will come, go and do as I have told you."

Algaro went out and Ferguson said, "So, here we are. What now?"

"A little champagne perhaps, a pleasant dinner?" Santiago waved to Prieto, who snapped his fingers at a waiter and escorted him with a bottle of Krug in an ice bucket. "One can be civilized, can't one?"

"Isn't that a fact?" Dillon checked the label. "Eighty-three. Not bad, Señor."

"I bow to your judgment." The waiter filled the glasses and Santiago raised his. "To you, Brigadier Ferguson, to the playing fields of Eton and the continued success of Group Four."

"You *are* well informed," the Brigadier said.

"And you, Captain Carney, what a truly remarkable fellow you are. War hero, sea captain, diver of legendary proportions. Who on earth could they get to play you in the movie?"

"I suppose I'd just have to do it myself," Carney told him.

"And Mr. Dillon. What can I say to a man whose only rival in his chosen profession has been Carlos."

"So you know all about us," Ferguson said. "Very impressive. You must need what's in that U-boat very badly indeed."

"Let's lay our cards on the table, Brigadier. You want what should still be in the captain's quarters, Bormann's briefcase containing his personal authorization from the Führer, the Blue Book and the Windsor Protocol."

There was a pause and it was Carney who said, "Interesting, you didn't call him Hitler, you said the Führer."

Santiago's face was hard. "A great man, a very great man who had a vision of the world as it should be, not as it has turned out."

"Really?" Ferguson commented. "I'd always understood that if you counted Jews, Gypsies, Russians and war dead from various countries, around twenty-five million people died to prove him wrong."

"We both want the same thing, you and I," Santiago said. "The contents of that case. You don't want them to fall into the wrong hands. The old scandal affecting so many people, the Duke of Windsor, putting the Royal Family in the eye of the storm again. The media would have a field day. As I say, we both want the same thing. I don't want all that to come out either."

"So the work continues," Ferguson said. "The Kamaraden? How many names are on that list, famous names, old names who have prospered since the War in industry and business, all on the back of Nazi money?"

"Jesus," Dillon said. "It makes the Mafia look like small beer."

"Come now," Santiago told him. "Is any of this important after all these years?"

"It sure as hell must be, either to you or close friends," Carney said, "otherwise why would you go to such trouble?"

"But it is important, Mr. Carney," Ferguson said. "That's the point. If the network continues over the years, if sons become involved, grandsons, people in higher places, politicians, for example." He drank some more champagne. "Imagine, as I say, just for example, having someone high in Government. How useful that would be and then, after so many years, the kind of scandal that could bring everything down around your ears."

Santiago waved for the waiter to pour more champagne. "I thought you might be sensible, but I see not. I don't need you, Brigadier, or you, Mr. Carney. I have my own divers."

"Finding it is not enough," Carney said. "You've got to get into that tin can and that requires expertise."

"I have divers, Mr. Carney, an ample supply of C4, is that the name of the explosive? I only employ people who know what they are doing." He smiled. "But this is not getting us anywhere." He stood up. "At least we can eat like civilized men. Please, gentlemen, join me."

The Ford station wagon slowed to a halt at the side of the air strip, Algaro sitting in the rear behind Joseph Jackson. "Is this where you wanted, mister?"

"I guess so," Algaro said. "Those people you brought in from the plane, what were they like?"

"Nice gentlemen," Jackson said.

"No, what I mean is, were they curious? Did they ask questions?"

Jackson began to feel uncomfortable. "What kind of questions you mean, mister?"

"Let's put it this way," Algaro told him. "They talked and you talked. Now what about?"

"Well the English gentleman, he was interested in the old days. I told him how I was caretaker here in the Herbert place during the big War with my wife."

"And what else did you tell him?"

"Nothing, mister, I swear." Jackson was frightened now.

Algaro put a hand on the back of his neck and squeezed. "Tell me, damn you!"

"It was nothing much, mister." Jackson struggled to get away. "About the Pamers."

"The Pamers?"

"Yes, Lady Pamer and how she came here at the end of the War."

"Tell me," Algaro said. "Tell me everything." He patted him on the side of the face. "It's all right, just tell the truth."

Which Jackson did and when he was finished, Algaro said, "There, that wasn't too bad, was it?"

He slid an arm across Jackson's throat, put his other hand on top of his head and twisted, breaking the neck so cleanly that the old man was dead in a second. He went round, opened the door and pulled the body out. He positioned it with the head just under the car by the rear wheel, took out a flick knife, sprung it and stabbed the point into the rear off-side tire so that it deflated. He got the tool kit out, raised the car on the hydraulic jack, whistling as he pumped it up.

Very quickly, he undid the bolts and removed the tire. He stood back and kicked at the jack and the rear of the station wagon lurched to one side and descended on Jackson. He took out the spare tire and laid it beside the other one, then walked across to the Cessna and stood looking at it for quite some time.

The meal was excellent. West Indian chicken wings with blue cheese, conch chowder followed by baked red snapper. No one opted for dessert and Santiago said, "Coffee?"

"I'd prefer tea," Dillon told him.

"How very Irish of you."

"All I could afford as a boy."

"I'll join you," Ferguson said and at that moment Algaro appeared in the doorway.

"You must excuse me, gentlemen." Santiago got up and

went and joined Algaro. "What is it?"

"I found out who the Jackson man was, the old fool driving that Ford taxi."

"So what happened?"

Algaro told him briefly and Santiago listened intently, watching as the waiter took tea and coffee to the table.

"But it means our friends now know that Sir Francis is involved in this business."

"It doesn't make any difference, Señor. We know the girl is returning tomorrow, we know she thinks she knows where the U-boat is. Who needs these people any more?"

"Algaro," Santiago said. "What have you done?"

As Santiago returned to the table, Ferguson finished his tea and stood up. "Excellent dinner, Santiago, but we really must be going."

"What a pity. It's been quite an experience."

"Hasn't it? By the way, a couple of presents for you." Ferguson took the two tracking bugs from his pocket and put them on the table. "Yours, I think. Give my regards to Sir Francis next time you're in touch, or I could give your regards to him."

"How well you put it," Santiago said and sat down.

They reached the front entrance to find Prieto standing at the top of the steps looking flustered. "I'm so sorry, gentlemen, but I've no idea what's happened to the taxi."

"It's of no consequence," Ferguson said. "We can walk there in five or six minutes. Good night to you. Excellent meal," and he went down the steps.

It was Carney who noticed the station wagon just as they reached the airstrip. "What's he doing over there?" he said and called, "Jackson?"

There was no reply. They walked across and saw the

body at once. Dillon got down on his knees and got as close as he could. He stood up, brushing his clothes. "He's been dead for some time."

"The poor bastard," Carney said. "The jack must have toppled over."

"A remarkable coincidence," Ferguson said.

"Exactly." Dillon nodded. "He tells us all about Francis Pamer and bingo, he's dead."

"Just a minute," Carney put in. "I mean, if Santiago knew about the old boy's existence, why leave it till now? I'd have thought he'd have got rid of him a lot earlier than this."

"But not if he didn't realize he existed," Ferguson said.

Dillon nodded. "Until somebody told him, somebody who's been feeding all the other information he needed."

"You mean, this guy Pamer?" Carney asked.

"Yes, isn't it perfectly dreadful," Ferguson said. "Just shows you you can't trust anyone these days. Now let's get out of here."

He and Carney got in the rear seats and strapped themselves in. Dillon got a torch from the map compartment and did an external inspection. He came back, climbed into the pilot's seat and closed the door. "Everything looks all right."

"I don't think he'll want to kill us yet," Ferguson said. "All the other little pranks have been aggravation, but he still needs us to hopefully lead him to that U-boat, so let's get moving, there's a good fellow, Dillon."

Dillon switched on, the engine roared into life, the propeller turned. He carefully checked the illuminated dials on the instrument panel. "Fuel, oil pressure." He recited the litany. "Looks good to me. Here we go."

He took the Cessna down the runway and lifted into the night, turning out to sea.

• • •

It was a magnificent night, stars glittering in the sky, the sea and the islands below bathed in the hard white light of the full moon. St. John loomed before them. They crossed Ram Head, moving along the southern coast, and it happened, the engine missed a beat, coughed and spluttered.

"What is it?" Ferguson demanded.

"I don't know," Dillon said and then checked the instruments and saw what had happened to the oil pressure.

"We've got problems," he said. "Get your life jackets on."

Carney got the Brigadier's out and helped him into it. "But surely the whole point of these things is that you don't have to crash, you can land on the sea," Ferguson said.

"That's the theory," Dillon told him and the engine died totally and the propeller stopped.

They were at nine hundred feet and he took the plane down in a steep dive. "Reef Bay dead ahead," Carney said.

"Right, now this is how it goes," Dillon told them. "If we're lucky, we'll simply glide down and land on the water. If the waves are too much we might start to tip, so bail out straightaway. How deep is it down there, Carney?"

"Around seven fathoms close in."

"Right, there's a third alternative, Brigadier, and that's going straight under."

"You've just made my night," Ferguson told him.

"If that happens, trust Carney, he'll see to you, but on no account waste time trying to open the door on your way down. It'll just stay closed until we've settled and enough water finds its way inside and equalizes the pressure."

"Thanks very much," Ferguson said.

"Right, here we go."

The surface of the bay was very close now and it didn't

look too rough. Dillon dropped the Cessna in for what seemed like a perfect landing and something went wrong straightaway. The plane lurched forward sluggishly, not handling at all, then tipped and plunged beneath the surface nose-down.

The water was like black glass, they were already totally submerged and descending, still plenty of air in the cabin, the lights gleaming on the instrument panel. Dillon felt the water rising up over his ankles and suddenly it was waist deep and the instrument panel lights went out.

"Christ almighty!" Ferguson cried.

Carney said, "I've unbuckled your belt. Be ready to go any second now."

The Cessna, still nose-down, touched at that moment a patch of clear sand at the bottom of the bay, lifted a little, then settled to one side, the tip of the port wing braced against a coral ridge. The rays of the full moon drifting down through the water created an astonishing amount of light and Dillon, looking out through the cockpit window as the water level reached his neck, was surprised at how far he could see.

He heard Carney say, "Big breath, Brigadier, I'm opening the door now. Just slide out through and we'll go up together."

Dillon took a deep breath himself and as the water passed over his head, opened his door, reached for the wing strut and pulled himself out. He turned, still hanging on the strut, saw Carney clutching at the Brigadier's sleeve, kicking away from the wing, and then they started up.

It was usually argued that if you went up too fast and didn't expel air slowly on the way there was a danger of rupturing the lungs, but in a situation like this there was no time for niceties and Dillon floated up, the rays of moonlight filtering down through the clear water, aware of Carney and the Brigadier to the left and above him. It all seemed to happen in slow motion, curiously dreamlike, and then he broke through to the surface and took a deep lungful of salt air.

Carney and Ferguson floated a few yards away. Dillon swam toward them. "Are you all right?"

"Dillon." Ferguson was gasping for breath. "I owe you dinner. I owe you both a dinner."

"I'll hold you to that," Dillon said. "You can take me to the Garrick again."

"Anywhere you want. Now do you think it's possible we could get the hell out of here?"

They turned and swam toward the beach, Carney and Dillon on either side of the older man. They staggered out of the water together and sat on the sand recovering.

Carney said, "There's a house not too far from here. I know the people well. They'll run us into town."

"And the plane?" Ferguson asked.

"There's a good salvage outfit in St. Thomas. I'll phone the boss at home tonight. They'll probably get over first thing in the morning. They've got a recovery boat with a crane that'll lift that baby straight off the bottom." He turned to Dillon. "What went wrong?"

"The oil pressure went haywire and that killed the engine."

"I must say your landing left much to be desired," Ferguson said and stood up wearily.

"It was a good landing," Dillon said. "Things only went sour at the very last moment and there has to be a reason for that. I mean, one thing going wrong is unfortunate, two is highly suspicious."

"It'll be interesting to see what those salvage people find," Carney commented.

As they started across the beach, Dillon said, "Remember when I was checking the plane back at Samson, Brigadier, and you said you didn't think he'd want to kill us yet?"

"So?" Ferguson said. "What's your point?"

"Well I think he just tried."

The man Carney knew at the house nearby got his truck out and ran them down to Mongoose, where they went their separate ways, Carney promising to handle the salvaging of the plane and to report back to them in the morning.

Back at the cottage at Caneel Dillon had a hot shower, standing under it for quite some time thinking about things. Finally, he poured himself a glass of champagne and went and stood on the terrace in the warm night.

He heard his door open and Ferguson came in. "Ah, there you are." He too wore a robe, but also had a towel around his neck. "I'll take a glass of that, dear boy, and also the phone. What time is it?"

"Just coming up to midnight."

"Five o'clock in the morning in London. Time to get up," and Ferguson dialed the number of Detective Inspector Jack Lane's flat.

Lane came awake with a groan, switched on the bedside lamp and picked up the phone. "Lane here."

"It's me, Jack," Ferguson told him. "Still in bed, are we?"

"For God's sake, sir, it's only five o'clock in the morning."

"What's that got to do with it? I've got work for you, Jack. I've discovered how our friend Santiago has managed to stay so well informed."

"Really, sir?" Lane was coming awake now.

"Would you believe Sir Francis Pamer?"

"Good God!" Lane flung the bedclothes to one side and sat up. "But why?"

Ferguson gave him a brief account of what had happened, culminating in old Joseph Jackson's revelations and the plane crash.

Lane said, "It's difficult to believe."

"Isn't it? Anyway, give the Pamer family the works, Jack. Where did old Sir Joseph's money come from, how does Sir Francis manage to live like a prince? Use all the usual sources."

"What about the Deputy Director, sir, do I inform him in any way?"

"Simon Carter?" Ferguson laughed out loud. "He'd go through the roof. It would be at least a week before he could bring himself to believe it."

"Very well, sir. I'll get moving on things right away."

Ferguson said, "So, that's taken care of."

"I've been thinking," Dillon said. "You were right when you said earlier that you didn't think Santiago was ready to kill us yet because he needed us. So, assuming the crash was no accident, I wonder what made him change his mind?"

"I've no idea, dear boy, but I'm sure we'll find out." Ferguson punched the numbers on the cellular phone again. "Ah, Samson Cay Resort? Mr. Prieto, if you please."

A moment later a voice said, "Prieto here."

"Charles Ferguson calling from Caneel. Wonderful evening, excellent meal. Do thank Mr. Santiago for me."

"But of course, Brigadier, it was kind of you to call."

Ferguson replaced the phone. "That will give the bastard pause for thought. Give me another drop of champagne, dear boy, then I'm off to my bed."

Dillon filled his glass. "Not before you tell me something."

Ferguson swallowed half the champagne. "And what would that be?"

"You knew you'd be coming to St. John from the beginning, booked your accommodation at the same time you booked mine and that was before I got here, before it became apparent that Santiago knew my name and who I was and why I was here."

"Which means what?"

Dillon said, "You knew Pamer was up to no good before I left London."

"True," Ferguson said. "I just didn't have any proof."

"But how did you know?"

"Process of elimination, dear boy. After all, who knew about the affair at all? Henry Baker, the girl, Admiral Travers, myself, Jack Lane, you, Dillon, the Prime Minister. Every one of you could be instantly discarded."

"Which only left Carter and Pamer."

"Sounds like an old-fashioned variety act, doesn't it? Carter, as I told you earlier and based on my past experience of the man, is totally honest."

"Which left the good Sir Francis?"

"Exactly and that seemed absurd. As I've said before, a baronet, one of England's oldest families, a Government Minister." He finished his champagne and put the glass down. "But then, as I think the great Sherlock Holmes once said, when you've exhausted all the possibilities, then the impossible must be the answer." He smiled. "Goodnight, dear boy, I'll see you in the morning."

13

The following morning Santiago went for a swim in the sea, then sat in the stern under the awnings, had coffee and toast and a few grapes while he thought about things. Algaro waited by the rail patiently, saying nothing.

"I wonder what went wrong," Santiago said. "After all, it would be unusual for you to make a mistake, Algaro."

"I know my business, I did what was necessary, Señor, believe me."

At that moment Captain Serra presented himself. "I've just had a call from my man in Cruz Bay, Señor. It appears the Cessna crashed in Reef Bay last night, that's on the south coast of St. John. It finished up forty feet down on the bottom. Ferguson, Carney and Dillon all survived.

"Damn them to hell!" Algaro said angrily.

"Soon enough." Santiago sat there, frowning.

Serra said, "Have you any order, Señor?"

"Yes." Santiago turned to Algaro. "After lunch, you take Guerra and go to St. John in the launch. The girl should arrive at around six in the evening."

"You wish us to bring her to you, Señor?"

"That won't be necessary. Just find out what she knows, I'm sure that's not beyond your capability."

Algaro's smile was quite evil. "At your orders, Señor," and he withdrew.

Serra waited patiently while Santiago poured more coffee. "How long will the launch take to make the run to Cruz Bay?" Santiago asked.

"Depending on the weather, two to two and a half hours, Señor."

"About the same time as the *Maria Blanco* would take?"

"Yes, Señor."

Santiago nodded. "I may want to return to our mooring at Paradise some time tonight. I'm not sure. It depends on events. In any case, get me Sir Francis in London."

It took twenty minutes for Serra to run Pamer to earth and he finally located him at a function at the Dorchester. He sounded rather irritated when he came to the phone. "Who is this? I hope it's important, I've got a speech to make."

"Oh, I'm sure you'll do marvelously, Francis."

There was a pause and Pamer said, "Oh, it's you, Max, how are things?"

"We succeeded in locating the old man you mentioned, Jackson. What a mind. Quite remarkable. Remembered everything about nineteen forty-five in sharpest detail."

"Oh, my God," said Pamer.

Santiago, who had never seen any point in not facing up to the facts of any situation, carried on, "Luckily for you, he had an accident when changing a wheel on his car and has gone to a better place."

"Please, Max, I don't want to know this."

"Don't be silly, Francis, this is hold-on-to-your-nerves time, particularly as the old boy told everything he knew to Ferguson before my man helped him on his way. Unfortunate that."

"Ferguson knows?" Pamer felt as if he were about to

choke and tore at his tie. "About my mother and father,
Samson Cay, Martin Bormann?"

"I'm afraid so."

"But what are we going to do?"

"Get rid of Ferguson obviously, Dillon as well, and Carney. The girl arrives this evening and my information is that
she knows where the U-boat is. She'll be of no further use
after that, of course."

"For God's sake, no," Pamer implored and suddenly
turned quite cold. "I've just thought of something. My
secretary asked me if there was anything wrong with my
financial affairs this morning. When I asked her why, she
told me she'd noticed a trace being run through the computer. I didn't think anything of it. I mean, when you're
a Minister, they keep these various checks going for your
own protection."

"Right," Santiago said. "Have the source checked at once
and report back to me."

He handed the phone to Serra. "You know, Serra," he
said, "it's a constant source of amazement to me, the frequency with which I become involved with stupid people."

When Ferguson, Dillon and Carney drove down to Reef
Bay in Carney's jeep, they could see the Cessna suspended
on the end of the crane at the stern of the salvage boat, clear
of the water. There were three men on deck in diving suits
and one in a peaked cap, denim shirt and jeans. Carney
whistled, the man turned, waved then, dropped into an
inflatable at the side of the boat, started the outboard and
aimed for shore.

He came up the beach holding Ferguson's Malacca cane,
and said to Carney, "This belong to somebody?"

Ferguson reached for it. "I'm deeply indebted to you.
Means a great deal to me."

Carney introduced them. "What's the verdict, or haven't you had time yet?"

"Hell, it's open and shut," the salvage captain said and turned to Dillon. "Bob tells me your oil pressure gauge went wild?"

"That's true."

"Not surprising. The filler cap was blown off. That kind of pressure is usually only generated when there's a substantial amount of water in the oil. As the engine heats up, the water turns to steam and there you go."

"Wouldn't you say it was kind of strange to have that much water in the oil?" Carney asked.

"Not for me to say. What is certain is some vandal or other intended you harm. Somebody went to work on the bottom of the floats with what looks like a fire axe, that's why your landing was fouled. The moment you hit the water, it poured into those floats." He shrugged. "The rest, you know. Anyway, we'll haul her back to St. Thomas. I'll arrange repairs and keep you posted." He shook his head. "You guys were real lucky," and he went back to the inflatable and returned to the salvage boat.

They sat in a booth at Jenny's Place and Mary Jones brought them chowder and hunks of French bread. Billy supplied the beer, ice-cold, and shook his head. "You gents must live right. I mean, you shouldn't be here."

He walked away and Dillon said, "So you were wrong, Brigadier, he did try to have us killed. Why?"

"Maybe it had something to do with what that old guy Jackson said," Carney put in.

"Yes, that would be part of it, but I'm still surprised," Ferguson said. "I still thought we had our uses."

"Well, we sure will have when Jenny gets in," Carney told him.

"Let's hope so." The Brigadier raised his arm. "Let's have some more beer, innkeeper, it really is quite excellent."

When Pamer called Santiago back it was six o'clock in the evening in London.

"It couldn't be worse," he said. "That computer trace has been authorized by Detective Inspector Lane, he's Ferguson's assistant at the moment, on temporary loan from Special Branch. It's a check on my family's financial background, Max, searching way back. I'm finished."

"Don't be a fool. Just stay cool. Just think of the time scale. If you consider when Ferguson found out about you, he can only have had time to speak to this Lane and tell him to start digging."

"But what if he's spoken to Simon Carter or the P.M.?"

"If he had, you'd know by now, and why should he? Ferguson's played this whole thing very close to his chest and that's the way he'll continue."

"But what about Lane?"

"I'll have him taken care of."

"For God's sake no," Pamer moaned. "I can't take any more killing."

"Do try to act like a man occasionally," Santiago said. "And you do have one consolation. Once we have the Bormann documents in our hands, the Windsor Protocol should prove a very useful tool to have in your possession, and there must be people whose fathers or grandfathers appear in the Blue Book who'd give anything to prevent that fact coming out." He laughed. "Don't worry, Francis, we'll have lots of fun with this one."

He replaced the phone, thought about it, then picked it up again and dialed another London number. He spoke in Spanish. "Santiago. I have a major elimination for you which must be carried out tonight. A Detective Inspector Jack Lane, Special Branch. I'm sure you can find the address." He handed the phone back to Algaro. "And now, my friend, I think it's time you and Guerra departed for St. John."

It was half-past five when Jenny came in on the ferry to Cruz Bay. It was only a few hundred yards along the front to Jenny's Place and when she went in there were already a few people at the bar, Billy Jones standing behind. He came round to meet her.

"Why, Miss Jenny, it's so good to see you."

"Is Mary here?"

"She sure is. In the kitchen getting things right for this evening. Just go through."

"I will in a moment. Did you speak to Dillon? Did you give him my message?"

"I did. He and that friend of his and Bob Carney have been as thick as thieves these past few days. I don't know what's going on, but something sure is."

"So Dillon and Brigadier Ferguson are still at Caneel?"

"They sure are. You want to get in touch with him?"

"As soon as possible."

"Well you know they don't have telephones in the cottages at Caneel, but Dillon has a cellular phone. He gave me the number." He went behind the bar, opened the cash register drawer and took out a piece of paper. "Here it is."

Mary came through the kitchen door at that moment and came to a dead halt. "Jenny, you're back." She kissed her on the cheek, then held her at arm's length. "You look terrible, honey, what you been doing?"

"Nothing much." Jenny gave her a tired smile. "Just driving halfway across France, then catching a plane to

London, another to Antigua, a third to St. Thomas. I've never felt so tired in my life."

"What you need is food, a hot bath and a night's sleep."

"That's a great idea, Mary, but I've things to do. A cup of coffee would be fine. Let me have it in the office, I want to make a telephone call."

Algaro and Guerra had obtained the address of the house at Gallows Point from the fisherman who was Captain Serra's contact in Cruz Bay. They had already paid the place a visit, although Algaro had decided against a forced entry at that time. They went back to the waterfront, watched the ferry come in from St. Thomas and the passengers disembark. Out of the twenty or so passengers only five were white and three of those were men. As the other woman was at least sixty, there was little doubt who the younger one with the suitcase was. They followed her at a discreet distance and saw her go up the steps to the cafe.

"What do we do now?" Guerra asked.

"Wait," Algaro told him. "She'll go to the house sooner or later."

Guerra shrugged, took out a cigarette and lit it and they went and sat on a bench.

Dillon was actually swimming off Paradise beach, had left the cellular phone with his towel on a recliner on the beach. He heard the phone and swam as fast as he could to the shore.

"Dillon here."

"It's Jenny."

"Where are you?"

"At the bar, I just got in. How have things been?"

"Well, let's say it's been lively and leave it at that. There were people waiting for me the moment I got here, Jenny, the wrong sort of people. There's a man called Santiago, who was responsible for the break-in at Lord North Street, and those two thugs who tried to jump you by the Thames. He's been hanging around here in a motor yacht called the *Maria Blanco* causing us as much trouble as possible."

"Why?"

"He wants Bormann's briefcase, it's as simple as that."

"But how did he know about the U-boat's existence?"

"There was a leak at the London end of things, someone connected with Intelligence. You were right about Bob Carney. Quite a guy, but he's not been able to come up with a solution. Do you really think you can help, Jenny?"

"It's just an idea, so simple that I'm afraid to tell you, so let's leave it until we meet." She glanced at her watch. "Six o'clock. I could do with a hot bath and all the trimmings. Let's say we'll meet here at seven-thirty, and bring Bob."

"Fine by me."

Dillon put the phone down, toweled himself dry, then he picked it up and tried Carney's house at Chocolate Hole. It was a while before he answered. "Dillon here."

"I was in the shower."

"We're in business, Jenny's just phoned me from the bar. She just got in."

"Has she told you where it is?"

"No, she's still being mysterious. She wants to see us at the bar at seven-thirty."

"I'll be there."

Dillon rang off, then hurried back up the slope to the cottage to report to Ferguson.

When Jenny came out of the office Mary was standing at the end of the bar talking to her husband. "You still look like a bad weekend, honey," she said.

"I know. I'm going to walk up to the house, have a

shower and put on some fresh clothes, then I'm coming back. I've arranged to meet Dillon, Brigadier Ferguson and Bob Carney at seven-thirty."

"You ain't walking anywhere, honey. Billy, you take her up in the jeep, check out the house. Make sure everything's in order, then bring her back when she's ready. I'll get young Annie from the kitchen to tend bar while you're gone."

"No need for that, Mary," Jenny told her.

"It's settled. Don't give me no argument, girl. Now on your way."

When Jenny emerged from the bar, Billy Jones was at her side carrying the suitcase. Algaro and Guerra followed them at a distance, saw them get in the jeep in the car park at Mongoose Junction and drive away.

"He's taking her up to the house, I bet you," Guerra said.

Algaro nodded. "We'll walk up, it's not far. He'll have left by the time we get there. We'll get her then."

Guerra said, "No sign of Dillon or the other two. That means she hasn't had a chance to speak to them yet."

"And maybe she never will," Algaro told him.

Guerra paused and licked his lips nervously. "Now look, I don't want to get in anything like that, not with any woman. That's bad luck."

"Shut your mouth and do as you're told," Algaro told him. "Now let's get moving."

At the Ministry of Defence, just before midnight, the light still shone from the windows of Ferguson's office overlooking Horse Guards Avenue. Jack Lane finished his preliminary reading of the first facts to emerge from the computer concerning the Pamer family and very interesting reading they made. But he'd done enough for one night. He put them in his briefcase, placed it in the secure drawer of his desk, got his raincoat, switched off the lights and left.

He came out of the Horse Guards Avenue entrance and walked along the pavement. The young man sitting behind the wheel of the stolen Jaguar on the opposite side of the road checked the photo on the seat beside him with a torch, just to make sure, then slipped it into a pocket. He wore glasses and a raincoat over a neat blue suit, looked totally ordinary.

He started the engine, watched Lane cross the road and start along Whitehall Court. Lane was tired and still thinking of the Pamer affair, glanced casually to the right, was aware of the Jaguar, but had plenty of time to cross the road. There was the sudden roar of the engine, he half-turned, too late, the Jaguar hit him with such force that he was flung violently to one side. Lane lay there, trying to push himself up, was aware that the Jaguar was reversing. The rear bumper fractured his skull, killing him instantly, and the car bumped over his body.

The young man got out and walked forward to check that the Inspector was dead. The street was quite empty, only the rain falling as he got back into the Jaguar, swerved around Lane's body and drove away. Five minutes later he dumped the Jaguar in a side street off the Strand and walked rapidly away.

At Gallows Point, Jenny had a long hot shower and washed her hair while downstairs Billy opened shutters to air the rooms, got a broom and swept the front porch. Algaro and Guerra watched from the bushes nearby.

"Damn him, why doesn't he go?" Algaro said.

"I don't know, but I wouldn't advise trying anything with that one," Guerra said. "They tell me he used to be heavyweight boxing champion of the Caribbean."

"I'm frightened to death," Algaro said.

After a while, Jenny came out on the porch and joined Billy. She wore white linen trousers, a short-sleeved blouse, looked fresh and relaxed.

"Now that's better," Billy said.

"Yes, I actually feel human again," she said. "We'll go back now, Billy."

They got in the jeep and drove away and the two men emerged onto the dirt road. "Now what?" Guerra demanded.

"No problem," Algaro said. "We'll get her later. For now, we'll go back to the bar," and they set off down the road.

It was almost dark when Bob Carney went into Jenny's Place and found her serving behind the bar with Billy. She came round and greeted him warmly with a kiss and drew him over to a booth.

"It's good to see you, Jenny." He put a hand on hers. "I was real sorry about Henry. I know what he meant to you."

"He was a good man, Bob, a decent, kind man."

"I saw him on that last morning," Carney told her, "coming in as I was leaving with a dive party. He must have gone out real early. I asked him where he'd been, and he told me French Cap." He shook his head. "Not true, Jenny. Dillon and I checked out French Cap, even had a look at South Drop."

"But they're sites people go to anyway, Bob. That U-boat couldn't have just sat there all those years without someone having seen it."

It was at that moment that Dillon and Ferguson entered. They saw Carney and Jenny at once and came over. Ferguson raised his Panama. "Miss Grant."

She held out a hand to Dillon, he took it for a moment and there was an awkwardness between them. "Did things work out all right?"

"Oh, yes, I saw Henry's sister. Sorry I was so mysterious. The truth is she's a nun, Little Sisters of Pity. In fact she's the Mother Superior."

"I never knew that," Carney said.

"No, Henry never talked about her, he was an atheist, you see. He felt she was burying herself away to no purpose. It led to a rift between them."

Billy came up at that moment. "Can I get you folks some drinks?"

"Later, Billy," she said. "We have business to discuss here."

He went away and Ferguson said, "Yes, we're all ears. Hopefully you're going to tell us the location of U180."

"Yes, Jenny." Bob Carney was excited now. "Where is it?"

"I don't know is the short answer," she said simply.

There was consternation on Ferguson's face. "You don't know? But I was led to believe you did."

Dillon put a restraining hand on the Brigadier's arm. "Give her a chance."

"Let me put it this way," Jenny said. "I think I might know where that information may be found, but it's so absurdly simple." She took a deep breath. "Oh, let's get on with it." She turned to Carney. "Bob, the *Rhoda* is still moored there in the harbor. Will you take us out there?"

"Sure, Jenny."

Carney stood up and Ferguson said, "The *Rhoda*?"

Carney explained. "Henry's boat, the one he was out in that day. Come on, let's go."

They went down the steps to the road and went along the waterfront to the dock, and Algaro and Guerra watched them descend to an inflatable. Carney sat in the stern, started the outboard and they moved out into the harbor.

"Now what?" Guerra asked.

"We'll just have to wait and see," Algaro replied.

Carney switched on the light in the deckhouse and they all crowded in. "Well, Miss Grant," Ferguson said. "We're all here, so what have you got to tell us?"

"It's just an idea." She turned to Carney. "Bob, what do a lot of divers do after a dive?"

"You mean, check their equipment . . . "

She broke in. "Something much more basic. What I'm thinking of is the details of the dive."

Carney said, "Of course."

"What on earth is she getting at?" Ferguson demanded.

"I think I see," Dillon said. "Just like pilots, many divers keep logs. They enter details of each dive they make. It's common practice."

"Henry was meticulous about it," she said. "Usually the first thing he did after getting back on board and drying himself. He usually kept it in here." She opened the small locker by the wheel, reached inside and found it at once. It had a red cover, Baker's name stamped on it in gold. She held it out to Dillon. "I'm afraid I might be wrong. You read it."

Dillon paused, then turned the pages and read the last one. "It says here he made an eighty- to ninety-foot dive at a place called Thunder Point."

"Thunder Point?" Carney said. "I'd never have thought it. No one would."

"His final entry reads: Horse-eyed jacks in quantity, yellow-tail snappers, angel and parrot fish and one type VII German Submarine, U180, on ledge on east face."

"Thank God," Jenny Grant said. "I was right."

There was a profound silence as Dillon closed the log and Ferguson said, "And now I really could do with that drink."

Algaro and Guerra watched them return. Algaro said, "She's told them something, I'm sure of it. You stay here and keep an eye on things while I go down to the public phone and report in."

Inside, they sat at the same booth and when Billy came over Ferguson said, "This time champagne is very definitely in order." He rubbed his hands. "Now we can really get down to brass tacks."

Dillon said to Carney, "You seemed surprised, I mean about the location, this Thunder Point. Why?"

"It's maybe twelve miles out. That's close to the edge of things. I've never dived there. No one dives there. It's the most dangerous reef in this part of the world. If the sea is at all rough, it's a hell of a haul to get there and when you do, the current is fierce, can take you every which way."

"How do you know this if you've never dived it?" Dillon asked.

"There was an old diver here a few years back, old Tom Poole. He's dead now. He dived it on his own years back. He told me he happened to be that far out by chance and realized it was calmer than usual. From what he said it's a bit like South Drop. A reef around seventy feet, about a hundred and eighty feet on one side and two thousand on the other. In spite of the weather being not too bad, the old boy nearly lost his life. He never tried again."

"Why didn't he see the U-boat?" Ferguson demanded.

"Maybe he just didn't get that far, maybe it's moved position since his time. The one thing we know for sure is it's there because Henry found it," Carney told him.

"I just wonder why he even attempted such a dive," Jenny said.

"You know what Henry was like," Carney told her. "Always diving on his own when he shouldn't, and that morning, after the hurricane, the sea was calmer than I've ever seen it. I figure he was just sailing out there for the pure joy of it, realized where he was and saw that conditions were exceptional. In those circumstances he would have dropped his hook on that reef and been over the side in no time at all."

"Well, according to Rear Admiral Travers," Dillon said, "and he talked extensively to Baker, Bormann was using the captain's cabin except that it wasn't really a cabin. It just had a curtain across. It's on the port side opposite the radio and sound room, that's in the forward part of the boat. The idea of having it there was so the captain had instant access to the control room."

"That seems reasonably straightforward to me," Carney said.

"Yes, but the only access from the control room is by the forward watertight hatch and Baker told Travers it was corroded to hell, really solid."

"Okay," Carney said, "so we'll have to blow it. C4 is the thing, the stuff Santiago was going on about when we were at Samson."

"I'm ahead of you there," Dillon told him. "I couldn't get hold of any C4, but I thought Semtex would be an acceptable substitute. I've also got chemical detonating pencils."

"Is there anything you forgot?" Carney asked ironically.

"I hope not."

"So when do we go?" Ferguson demanded.

Dillon said, "I'd say that's up to Carney here, he's the expert."

Carney nodded, slightly abstracted. "I'm thinking about

it." He nodded again. "The way I see it, we want to be in and out before Santiago even knows what's going on."

"That makes sense," Ferguson agreed.

"They can't track us any longer because we got rid of the bugs in both boats. We could capitalize on that by leaving around midnight, making the trip under cover of darkness. Dawn at five to five-thirty. We could go down at first light."

"Sounds good to me," Dillon said.

"Right, I left *Sea Raider* at Caneel Bay this evening so we'll leave from there. You'll need to pick up that Semtex you mentioned. Any extras we need I can get from the dive shop."

"But not right now," Ferguson told him. "Now we eat. All this excitement has given me quite an appetite."

It started to rain a little and Algaro and Guerra sheltered under a tree. "Mother of God, is this going to take all night?" Guerra demanded.

"It takes as long as is needed," Algaro told him.

Inside, they had dined well on Mary's best chowder and grilled snapper, were at the coffee stage when Dillon's cellular phone rang. He answered it, then handed it across to Ferguson. "It's for you. Somebody from Special Branch in London."

The Brigadier took the phone. "Ferguson here." He listened and suddenly turned very pale and his shoulders sagged. "Just a moment," he said wearily and got up. "Excuse me. I'll be back," and he went out.

"What in the hell is that all about?" Carney asked.

"Well, it's not good, whatever it is," Dillon said. Ferguson returned at that moment and sat down.

"Jack Lane, my assistant, is dead."

"Oh, no," Jenny said.

"Hit-and-run accident round about midnight. He'd been working late, you see. The police have found the car dumped in a side street off the Strand. Blood all over it. Stolen of course."

"Another remarkable coincidence," Dillon said. "You tell him to check up on Pamer and in no time he's lying dead in a London side street."

It was the first time he'd seen real anger in Ferguson's face. Something flared in the Brigadier's eyes. "That hadn't escaped me, Dillon. The bill will be paid in full, believe me."

He took a deep breath and stood up. "Right, let's get going. Are you coming with us, my dear?"

"I don't think so," Jenny told him. "That kind of boat ride is the last thing I need after what I've been through, but I'll come and see you off. I'll follow you in my jeep. You carry on, I'll catch you up, I just want a word with Mary."

She went into the kitchen and Dillon beckoned Billy to the end of the bar. "Do you think you and Mary could spend the night at Jenny's house?"

"You think there could be a problem?"

"We've had too many for comfort," Ferguson told him.

Dillon took the Belgian semi-automatic from his pocket. "Take this."

"That bad?" Billy inquired.

"That bad."

"Then this is better." Billy took a Colt .45 automatic from under the counter.

"Fine." Dillon slipped the Belgian semi-automatic back in his pocket. "Take care. We'll see you in the morning."

In the kitchen Mary was working hard at the stove. "What you doing now, girl?"

"I've got to go up to Caneel, Mary, Bob Carney is taking

the Brigadier and Mr. Dillon on a special dive. I want to see them off."

"You should be in bed."

"I know. I'll go soon."

She went out through the bar and hurried down the steps. Algaro said, "There she is. Let's get after her."

But Jenny started to run, catching Ferguson, Dillon and Carney at Mongoose Junction. Algaro and Guerra watched as their quarry got into her jeep, Carney at her side, and followed Dillon and Ferguson out of the car park.

"All right," Algaro said. "Let's get after them," and they ran toward their own vehicle.

At the cottage, Dillon got the olive-green army holdall, took everything out, the Semtex and fuses, the AK, and the Walther and its silencer. Ferguson came in as he was finishing, wearing cord slacks, suede desert boots and a heavy sweater.

"Are we going to war again?" he asked.

Dillon stowed everything back in the holdall. "I hope not. Carney and I are going to have enough on our plate just making the dive, but you know where everything is if you need it."

"You think you can pull it off?"

"We'll see." Dillon found his tracksuit top. "I'm sorry about Lane, Brigadier."

"So am I."

Ferguson looked bleak. "But our turn will come, Dillon, I promise you. Now let's get on with it."

As they made for the door, Dillon paused and opened the bar cupboard. He took out half a bottle of brandy and dropped it into the holdall. "Purely medicinal," he said and held the door open. "It's going to be bloody cold down there at that time of the morning."

• • •

Carney had brought the *Sea Raider* in to the end of the dock at Caneel. Jenny was sitting on a bench looking down at the boat as he checked the air tanks. A three-piece band was playing in the bar, music and laughter drifting over the water on the night air. Ferguson and Dillon walked along the front, passed the Beach Terrace Restaurant and came along the dock. Ferguson stepped on board and Dillon passed him the holdall.

He turned to Jenny. "Are you all right?"

"Fine," she said.

"Not long now," Dillon told her. "As some poet put it, 'all doubts resolved, all passion spent.'"

"And then what will you do?" she asked.

Dillon kissed her briefly on the cheek. "Jesus, girl, will you give a man a chance to draw breath?"

He took the Belgian semi-automatic out of his pocket. "Put that in your purse and don't tell me you don't know what to do with it. Just pull the slider, point and fire."

She took it reluctantly. "You think this is necessary?"

"You never can tell. Santiago has been ahead of us too many times. When you get back to the bar you'll find that Billy and Mary intend to spend the night with you."

"You think of everything, don't you?"

"I try to. It would take a good man to mess with Billy."

He stepped on board and Carney looked down at them from the flying bridge. "Cast off for us, Jenny."

He switched on the engines, she untied the stern line and handed it to Dillon, went and did the same with the other. The boat drifted out, then started to turn away.

"Take care, my dear," Ferguson called.

She raised an arm as *Sea Raider* moved out to sea. Dillon looked back at her, standing there under the light at the end of the dock, and then she turned and walked away.

• • •

She went past the bar and the shop, and started up the path
past the Sugar Mill Restaurant to the car park where the
taxis waited. Algaro and Guerra had watched the departure
from the shadows and now they followed her.

"What shall we do?" Guerra whispered.

"She's bound to go home sooner or later," Algaro said.
"The best place to deal with her, all nice and quiet and we
don't even need to follow her."

Jenny got into her jeep and started the engine and they
waited until she was driving away before moving toward
their own vehicle.

There were still a few people in the bar when she went in
and Mary was helping one of the waitresses to clear the
tables. She came to the end of the bar and Billy joined them.

"They got off all right then?" Billy asked.

"That's right."

"Are we going to be told what they're up to, Miss Jenny?
Everyone is sure acting mighty mysterious."

"Maybe one of these days, Billy, but not right now."

She yawned, feeling very tired, and Mary said, "Don't
you hold her up with any damn fool questions, she needs her
sleep." She turned to Jenny. "Mr. Dillon asked us to spend
the night with you and that's what we're going to do."

"All right," Jenny said. "I'll go on up to the house."

"Maybe you should wait for us, Miss Jenny," Billy told
her. "It will only take us five minutes to close."

She opened her purse and took out the Belgian semi-
automatic. "I've got this, Billy, and I know how to use it.
I'll be fine. I'll see you soon."

She'd parked the jeep right outside at the bottom of the
steps and she slid behind the wheel, turned on the engine

and drove away, so tired that for a moment she forgot to
switch on the lights. The streets were reasonably quiet now
as she drove out toward Gallows Point and she was at the
house in five minutes. She parked in the driveway, went up
the steps, found her key and unlocked the front door. She
switched on the porch light, then went in.

God, but she was tired, more tired than she had ever been,
and she mounted the stairs wearily, opened her bedroom
door and switched on the light. It was hot, very hot in spite
of the ceiling fan, and she crossed to the French windows
leading to the balcony and opened them. There were a few
heavy spots of rain and then a sudden rush, the kind of thing
that happened at night at that time of year. She stood there
for a moment enjoying the coolness, then turned and found
Algaro and Guerra standing just inside the room.

It was as if she was dreaming, but that terrible face told her
otherwise, the cropped hair, the scar from the eye to the
mouth. He laughed suddenly and said to Guerra in Spanish,
"This could prove interesting."

And Jenny, in spite of her tiredness, surprised even herself by darting forward and around them to the door, almost
made it, and it was Guerra who caught her right wrist and
swung her around. Algaro struck her heavily across the
face, then hurled her back on the bed. She tried to pull
the gun from her purse. He took it from her, turned her
on her face, pulling her left arm up, twisted and applied
some special kind of leverage. The pain was terrible and
she cried out.

"You like that, eh?" Algaro was enjoying himself and
tossed the gun across the room. "Let's try some more."

And this time, the pain was the worst thing she'd ever
known and she screamed at the top of her voice. He turned
her over, slapped her heavily again and took a flick knife

from his pocket. When he jumped the blade she saw that it was razor sharp. He grabbed a handful of her hair.

"Now I'm going to ask you some questions." He stroked the blade across her cheek and pricked it gently with the needle point so that blood came. "If you refuse to answer, I'll slit your nose and that's just for starters."

She was only human and terrified out of her mind. "Anything," she pleaded.

"Right. Where would we find the wreck of U180?"

"Thunder Point," she gasped.

"And where would that be?"

"It's on the chart. About ten or twelve miles south of St. John. That's all I know."

"Dillon, the Brigadier and Carney, we saw them leave from the dock at Caneel Bay. They've gone to Thunder Point to dive on the U-boat, is that right?" She hesitated and he slapped her again. "Is that right?"

"Yes," she said. "They're diving at first light."

He patted her face, closed the knife and turned to Guerra. "Lock the door."

Guerra seemed bewildered. "Why?"

"I said lock the door, idiot." Algaro walked past him and swung it shut, turning the key. He turned and his smile was the cruellest thing Jenny had ever seen in her life. "You did say you'd do anything?" and he started to take his jacket off.

She screamed again, totally hysterical now, jumped to her feet, turned and ran headlong through the open French windows on to the balcony in total panic, hit the railings and went over, plunging down through the heavy rain to the garden below.

Guerra knelt beside her in the rain and felt for a pulse. He shook his head. "She looks dead to me."

"Right, leave her there," Algaro said. "That way it looks like an accident. Now let's get out of here."

The sound of their jeep's engine faded into the night and Jenny lay there, rain falling on her face. It was only five minutes later that Billy and Mary Jones turned into the drive in their jeep and found her at once, lying half across a path, half on grass. "My God." Mary dropped to her knees and touched Jenny's face. "She's cold as ice."

"Looks like she fell from the balcony," Billy said.

At that moment Jenny groaned and moved her head slightly. Mary said, "Thank God, she's alive. You carry her inside and I'll phone for the doctor," and she ran up the steps into the house.

14

Algaro spoke to Santiago from a public telephone on the waterfront. Santiago listened intently to what he had to say. "So, the girl is dead? That's unfortunate."

"No sweat," Algaro told him. "Just an accident, that's how it will look. What happens now?"

"Stay where you are and phone me back in five minutes."

Santiago put the phone down and turned to Serra. "Thunder Point, about ten or twelve miles south of St. John."

"We'll have a look on the chart, Señor." Santiago followed him along to the bridge and Serra switched on the light over the chart table. "Ah, yes, here we are."

Santiago had a look, frowning slightly. "Dillon and company are on their way there now. They intend to dive at first light. Is there any way we could beat them to it if we left now?"

"I doubt it, Señor, and that's open sea out there. They'd see the *Maria Blanco* coming for miles."

"I take your point," Santiago said, "and, as we learned the other day, they're armed." He examined the chart again and nodded. "No, I think we'll let them do all the work for us. If they succeed, it will make them feel good. They'll sail back to St. John happy, maybe even slightly off-guard because they will think they have won the game."

"And then, Señor?"

"We'll descend on them when they return to Caneel, possibly at the cottage. We'll see."

"So, what are your orders?"

"We'll sail back to St. John and anchor off Paradise Beach again." The phone was ringing in the radio room. "That will be Algaro calling back," and Santiago went to answer it.

Algaro replaced the phone and turned to Guerra. "They intend to let those bastards get on with it and do all the work. We'll hit them when they get back."

"What, just you and me?"

"No, stupid, the *Maria Blanco* will be back off Paradise Beach in the morning. We'll rendezvous with her then. In the meantime, we'll go back to the launch and try to catch a little shut-eye."

Jenny's head, resting on the pillow, was turned to one side. She looked very pale, made no movement even as the doctor gave her an injection. Mary said, "What do you think, Doctor?"

He shook his head. "Not possible to make a proper diagnosis at this stage. The fact that she's not regained consciousness is not necessarily bad. No overt signs of broken bones, but hairline fractures are always possible. We'll see how she is in the morning. Hopefully she'll have regained consciousness by then." He shook his head. "That was a long fall. I'll have her transferred to St. Thomas Hospital. She can have a scan there. You'll stay with her tonight?"

"Me and Billy won't move an inch," Mary told him.

"Good." The doctor closed his bag. "The slightest change, call me."

Billy saw him out, then came back up to the bedroom. "Can I get you anything, honey?"

"No, you go and lie down, Billy, I'll just sit here with her," Mary said.

"As you say."

Billy went out and Mary put a chair by the bed, sat down and held Jenny's hand. "You'll be fine, baby," she said softly. "Just fine. Mary's here."

At three o'clock they ran into a heavy squall, rain driving in under the canopy over the flying bridge, stinging like bullets. Carney switched off the engine. "We'll be better off below for a while."

Dillon followed him down the ladder and they went into the deckhouse where Ferguson lay stretched out on one of the benches, his head propped up against the holdall. He yawned and sat up. "Is there a problem?"

Sea Raider swung to port, buffeted by the wind and rain. "Only a squall," Carney said. "It'll blow itself out in half an hour. I could do with a coffee break anyway."

"A splendid idea."

Dillon found the thermos and some mugs and Carney produced a plastic box containing ham and cheese sandwiches. They sat in companionable silence for a while eating them, the rain drumming against the roof.

"It's maybe time we discussed how we're going to do this thing," Carney said to Dillon. "For a no-decompression dive at eighty feet, we're good for forty minutes."

"So a second dive would be the problem?"

Ferguson said, "I don't understand the technicalities, would someone explain?"

"The air we breathe is part oxygen, part nitrogen," Carney told him. "When you dive, the pressure causes nitrogen to be absorbed by the body tissues. The deeper you go, the increase in pressure causes more nitrogen to be absorbed. If you're down too long or come up too quickly, it can form bubbles in your blood vessels and tissues, just like shaking a bottle of club soda. The end result is decompression sickness."

"And how can you avoid that?"

"First of all by limiting the time we're down there, particularly on the first dive. Second time around, we might need a safety stop at fifteen feet."

"And what does that entail?" Ferguson asked.

"We rise to that depth and just stay there for a while, decompressing slowly."

"How long for?"

"That depends."

Dillon lit a cigarette, the Zippo flaring in the gloom. "What we're really going to have to do is find that submarine fast."

"And lay the charge on the first dive down," Carney said.

"Baker did say it was lying on a ledge on the east face."

Carney nodded. "I figure that to be the big drop side so we won't waste time going anywhere else." He swallowed his coffee and got up. "If we had the luck, went straight down, got in the control room and laid that Semtex . . ." He grinned. "Hell, we could be in like Flynn and out and back up top in twenty minutes."

"That would make a big difference to the second dive," Dillon said.

"It surely would." The rain had stopped, the sea was calm again now and Carney glanced at his watch. "Time to get moving, gents," and he went back up the ladder to the flying bridge.

• • •

In London it was nine o'clock in the morning and Francis Pamer was just finishing a delicious breakfast of scrambled eggs and bacon which his housekeeper had prepared when the phone rang. He picked it up. "Pamer here."

"Simon Carter."

"Morning, Simon," Pamer said, "any word from Ferguson?"

"No, but something rather shocking which affects Ferguson has happened."

"What would that be?"

"You know his assistant, the one he borrowed from Special Branch, Detective Inspector Lane?"

Pamer almost choked on the piece of toast he was eating. "Yes, of course I do," he managed to say.

"Killed last night when he was leaving the Ministry of Defence around midnight. Hit and run. Stolen car apparently, which the police have recovered."

"How terrible."

"Thing is, Special Branch aren't too happy about it. It seems the preliminary medical report indicates that he was hit twice. Of course, that could simply mean the driver panicked and reversed or something. On the other hand, Lane sent a lot of men to prison. There must be many who bore him a grudge."

"I see," Pamer said. "So Special Branch are investigating?"

"Oh, yes, you know what the police are like when one of their own gets hit. Free for lunch, Francis?"

"Yes," Pamer said. "But it would have to be at the House. I'm taking part in the debate on the crisis in Croatia."

"That's all right. I'll see you on the Terrace at twelve-thirty."

Pamer put the phone down, his hand shaking, and looked at his watch. No sense in ringing Santiago now, it would be four in the morning over there. It would have to wait. He pushed his plate with the rest of his breakfast on it away from him, suddenly revolted, bile rising in his throat. The truth was he had never been so frightened in his life.

Way over toward the east the sun was rising as *Sea Raider* crept in toward Thunder Point, Carney checking the fathometer. "There it is," he said as he saw the yellow ridged lines on the black screen. "You get to the anchor," he told Dillon. "I'll have to do some maneuvering so you can hit that ridge at seventy feet."

There was a heavy swell, the boat, with the engines throttled back, just about holding her own. Dillon felt the anchor bite satisfactorily, called up to Carney on the flying bridge and the American switched off the engines.

Carney came down the ladder and looked over the side. "There's a rough old current running here. Could be three knots at least."

Ferguson said, "I must say the water seems exceptionally clear. I can see right down to the reef."

"That's because we're so far from the mainland," Carney said. "It means there is very little particulate matter in the water. In fact, it gives me an idea."

"What's that?" Dillon asked.

Carney took off his jeans and tee-shirt. "This water is so clear, I'm going to go trolling. That means I'll stay at less than ten feet, work my way across and locate the edge of the cliff. If I'm lucky and the water down there is as clear as it looks, I might manage to pinpoint the U-boat."

He zipped up his diving suit and Dillon helped him into his tank. "Do you want a line?"

Carney shook his head. "I don't think so."

He pulled on his mask, sat on the high thwart, waited for the swell to rise high and went over backwards. The water was so clear that they could mark his progress for a while.

"What's the point of all this?" Ferguson asked.

"Well, by staying at such a shallow depth, it will have no effect on the diving later. It could save time, and time is crucial on this one, Brigadier. If we use too much of it, we just wouldn't be able to dive again, perhaps for many hours."

Carney surfaced a hundred yards away and waved his arms. Ferguson got out the old binoculars and focused them. "He's beckoning."

Carney's voice echoed faintly. "Over here."

Dillon switched on the engines by the deckhouse wheel and throttled down. "Try and get the anchor up, Brigadier, I'll do my best to give you a bit of movement."

Ferguson went round to the prow and got to work, while Dillon tried to give him some slack. Finally, it worked, the Brigadier shouted in triumph and hauled in. Dillon throttled down and coasted toward Carney.

When they came alongside, the American called, "Drop the hook right here."

Ferguson complied, Dillon switched off the engine, Carney swam around to the dive platform, slipped off his jacket and climbed aboard.

"Clearest I've ever seen," he said. "We're right on the edge of the cliff. There's been a lot of coral damage recently, maybe because of the hurricane, but I swear I can see something sticking out over a ledge."

"You're sure?" Ferguson demanded.

"Hell, nothing's certain in this life, Brigadier, but if it is the U-boat, we can go straight down and be inside in a matter of minutes. Could make all the difference. Now let's see what you've got in the bag, Dillon."

Dillon produced the Semtex. "It'll work better if it's rolled into a rope and placed around the outer circle of the hatch."

"You would know, would you?" Carney asked.

"I've used the stuff before."

"Okay, let's have a look at those chemical detonating fuses." Dillon passed them to him and Carney examined them. "These are good. I've used them before. Ten- or thirty-minute delay. We'll use a ten."

Dillon was already into his diving suit and now he sliced a large section off the block of Semtex and first kneaded it, then rolled it between his hands into several long sausages. He put it into his dive bag with the detonating fuses.

"I'm ready when you are."

Carney helped him on with his gear, then handed him an underwater spot lamp. "I'll see you at the anchor and remember, Dillon, speed is everything, and be prepared for that current."

Dillon nodded and did what Carney had done, simply sat on the thwart, waited until the swell lifted and went in backwards.

The water was astonishingly clear and very blue, the ridge below covered with elkhorn coral and large basket sponges in muted shades of orange. As he waited at the anchor, a school of barracuda-like fish called sennet moved past him and when he looked up, there were a number of large jacks overhead.

The current was strong, so fierce that when he held on to the anchor chain his body was extended to one side. He glanced up again and Carney came down toward him, paused for a moment, already drifting sideways, and gestured. Dillon went after him, checking his dive computer, noting that he was at sixty-five feet, followed Carney over the edge of the cliff, looking down into the blue infinity below and saw, to the left, the great scar where the coral had broken away, the bulk of U180, the prow sticking out from the ledge.

They descended to the conning tower, held on to the top of the bridge rail, dropped down from the high gun platform to the ragged fifteen-foot gash in the hull below the conning tower. Dillon hovered as Carney went inside, checked his dive computer and saw that it was seven minutes since leaving *Sea Raider*. He switched his spot lamp on and went after the American.

It was dark and gloomy, a confusion of twisted metal in spite of the illumination from Carney's lamp. He was crouched beside the forward hatch, trying to turn the unlocking wheel with no success.

Dillon opened his dive bag, took out the Semtex and handed a coil to Carney. They worked together, Dillon taking the top of the hatch, Carney the bottom, pressing the plastic of the explosive in place until they had completed a full circle. They finished, Carney turned and held out a gloved hand. Dillon passed him two of the chemical detonating pencils. Carney paused, broke the first one and pushed it onto the Semtex at the top of the circular hatch. A small spiral of bubbles appeared at once. Carney did the same at the bottom of the circle with the other.

Dillon glanced at his computer. Seventeen minutes. Carney nodded and Dillon turned and went out through the rent, rose to the edge of the cliff, went straight to the anchor and started up the line, holding on with one hand, Carney just behind him. As they left the line at fifteen feet and moved under the keel of the stern, he checked the computer again. Twenty-one minutes. He broke through to the surface, slipped out of his jacket and climbed on to the diving platform.

"You found it?" Ferguson demanded.

"Just like Carney said," Dillon told him. "In like Flynn and out again. Twenty minutes, that's all. Just twenty bloody minutes."

Carney was changing the tanks for fresh ones. "Sweet Jesus, I've never seen such a sight. I've been diving twenty years or more and I've got to tell you, I've never seen anything to beat that."

Dillon lit a cigarette with his Zippo. "Santiago, eat your heart out."

"I'd like to take him down, weight him with lead and leave him inside," Carney said, "except it would be an insult to brave sailors who died down there."

The surface of the sea lifted, spray scattering, foam appeared, moved outwards in concentric circles over the swell. They stood at the rail watching until the activity dwindled.

Finally Carney said, "That's it. Let's get moving."

They got their diving gear on again. Dillon said, "What happens now? I mean, how long?"

"If we're lucky and we find what we want straightaway, then there's no problem. The whole forward part of the boat has been sealed all these years." Carney tightened his weight belt. "That should mean no silt, very little detritus. Human remains will have dissolved years ago except for a few bones. In other words, it should be relatively clear." He sat on the thwart and pulled on his fins. "If I think we should stop on the way back, I'll just signal and hang in there."

Dillon followed him down, aware of motion in the water, some sort of current like shockwaves that hadn't been there before. Carney hovered over the edge of the cliff and when Dillon joined him, he saw the problem at once. The force of the explosion had caused the U-boat to move, the stern had lifted, the prow, stretching out over that 2,000-feet drop, was already dipping.

They held on to the bridge rail beside the gun and Dillon could actually feel the boat move. He looked at Carney and the American shook his head. He was right, of course, another few feet higher at the stern and U180 would slide straight over into oblivion, and Dillon couldn't accept that.

He turned to go down, was aware of Carney's restraining hand, managed to pull free and jack-knifed, heading for the rent in the hull, pulling himself into the control room. Everything was stirring with the effects from the explosion, the movement of the boat. He switched on his spot lamp and moved forward and saw the great ragged hole where the hatch cover had been.

It was dark in there, far murkier than he had expected, again from the effects of the explosion. He shone his spotlight inside and as he pulled himself through was aware of a strange, eerie noise as if some living creature was groaning in pain, was aware of the boat moving, lurching a little. Too late to retreat now and his own stubbornness refused to let him.

The radio and sound room was on the right, the captain's quarters opposite to his left, no curtain left now, long since decayed over the years. There was a metal locker, a door hanging off, the skeleton of a bunk. He splayed the beam of the torch around and saw it lying in the corner, coated with filth, a metal briefcase with a handle, just like the one Baker had taken to London.

He ran a hand across it, silver gleamed dully, and then the floor tilted at an alarming angle and everything seemed to be moving. He bounced against the bulkhead, dropping the case, grabbed it again, turned and started through the hatch. His jacket snagged and he stopped dead, struggling frantically, aware of the boat tilting farther. And then Carney was in front of him, reaching through to release him.

The American turned and made for that gash in the hull and Dillon went after him, the whole boat tilting now, sliding, the strange, groaning noises, metal scraping across the edge, and Carney was through, drifting up, and Dillon rose to join him, hovering on the edge of the cliff, and as they turned to look down, the great whalelike shape of U180 slid over the edge and plunged into the void.

Carney made the okay sign, Dillon responded, then followed him across the ridge to the anchor line. He checked his computer. Another twenty minutes, which was fine, and he followed up the line slowly, but Carney was taking no chances. At fifteen feet he stopped and looked down. Dillon nodded, moved up beside him and raised the briefcase in his right hand. He could tell that Carney was smiling.

They stayed there for five minutes, then surfaced at the stern to find Ferguson leaning over anxiously. "Dear God. I thought the end of the world had come," he said.

They stowed the gear, made everything shipshape. Carney pulled on jeans and a tee-shirt, Dillon his tracksuit. Ferguson got the thermos, poured coffee and added brandy from the half-bottle.

"The whole bloody sea erupted," he said. "Never seen anything like it. Sort of boiled over. What happened?"

"She was lying on a ledge, Brigadier, you knew that," Carney said. "Already sticking right out, and the force of the explosion made her start to move."

"Good God!"

Carney drank some of the coffee. "Christ, that's good.

Anyway, this idiot here decided he was going to go inside anyway."

"Always suspected you were a fool, Dillon," Ferguson told him.

"I got the briefcase, didn't I? It was in the corner of the captain's quarters on the floor, and then the whole damn boat started to go, taking me with it because I got snagged trying to get back out of the hatch."

"What happened?"

"A mad, impetuous fool called Bob Carney who'd decided to follow me and pulled me through."

Carney went and looked over the side, still drinking his coffee. "A long, long way down. That's the last anyone will ever see of U180. It's as if she never existed."

"Oh, yes, she did," Ferguson said. "And we have this to prove it," and he held up the briefcase.

There wasn't much encrusting. Carney got a small wire brush from the tool kit and an old towel. The surface cleaned up surprisingly well, the Kriegsmarine insignia clearly etched into the right-hand corner. Carney unfastened the two clips and tried to raise the lid. It refused to move.

"Shall I force it, Brigadier?"

"Get on with it," Ferguson told him, his face pale with excitement.

Carney pushed a thin-bladed knife under the edge by the lock, exerted pressure. There was a cracking sound and the lid moved. At that moment it started to rain. Ferguson took the briefcase into the deckhouse, sat down with it on his knees and opened it.

The documents were in sealed envelopes. Ferguson opened the first one, took out a letter and unfolded it. He passed it to Dillon. "My German is a little rusty, you're the language expert."

Dillon read it aloud. "From the Leader and Chancellor of the State. Reichsleiter Martin Bormann is acting under my personal orders in a matter of the utmost importance to the State. He is answerable only to me. All personnel, military or civil, without distinction of rank, will assist him in any way he sees fit." Dillon handed it back. "It's signed Adolf Hitler."

"Really?" Ferguson folded it again and put it back in its envelope. "That would fetch a few thousand at auction at Christie's." He passed another, larger envelope over. "Try that."

Dillon opened it and took out a bulky file. He leafed through several pages. "This must be the Blue Book, alphabetical list of names, addresses, a paragraph under each, a sort of thumbnail sketch of the individual."

"See if Pamer is there."

Dillon checked quickly. "Yes, Major, Sir Joseph Pamer, Military Cross, Member of Parliament, Hatherley Court, Hampshire. There's an address in Mayfair. The remarks say he's an associate of Sir Oswald Mosley, politically sound and totally committed to the cause of National Socialism."

"Really?" Ferguson said dryly.

Dillon looked through several more pages and whistled softly. "Jesus, Brigadier, I know I'm just a little Irish peasant, but some of the names in here, you wouldn't believe. Some of England's finest. A few of America's also."

Ferguson took the file from him, glanced at a couple of pages, his face grave. "Who would have thought it?" He put the file back in its envelope and passed another. "Try that."

There were several documents inside and Dillon looked them over briefly. "These are details of numbered bank accounts in Switzerland, various South American countries and the United States." He handed them back. "Anything else?"

"Just this." Ferguson passed the envelope to him. "And we know what that must be, the Windsor Protocol."

Dillon took the letter out and unfolded it. It was written on paper of superb quality, almost like parchment, and was in English. He read it quickly, then passed it over. "Written at a villa in Estoril in Portugal in July 1940, addressed to Hitler and the signature at the bottom seems to be that of the Duke of Windsor."

"And what does it say?" Carney asked.

"Simple enough. The Duke says too many have already died on both sides, the war is pointless and should be ended as soon as possible. He agrees to take over the throne in the event of a successful German invasion."

"My God!" Carney said. "If that's genuine, it's dynamite."

"Exactly." Ferguson folded the letter and replaced it in its envelope. "If it *is* genuine. The Nazis were past masters at forgery." But his face was sad as he closed the case.

"Now what?" Carney asked.

"We return to St. John where Dillon and I will pack and make our way back to London. I have a Learjet awaiting my orders at St. Thomas." He held up the case and smiled bleakly. "The Prime Minister is a man who likes to hear bad news as quickly as possible."

The *Maria Blanco* had dropped anchor off Paradise Beach mid-morning and Algaro and Guerra, in the launch, had made contact at once. Santiago, sitting at his massive desk in the salon, listened as they went over the events of the previous night, then turned to Serra, who was standing beside him.

"Tell me about the situation as you see it, Captain."

"A long run out there, Señor, perhaps two and a half hours to come back because they'll be sailing into the wind all the way. I'd say they'll be back quite soon, probably just before noon."

"So what do we do, hit them tonight?" Algaro asked.

"No." Santiago shook his head. "I'd anticipate Ferguson making a move back to London as soon as possible. According to our information he has a Learjet on standby at St. Thomas airport." He shook his head. "No, we make our move on the instant."

"So what are your orders?" Algaro demanded.

"The simple approach is the best. You and Guerra will go ashore in one of the inflatables dressed as tourists. Leave the inflatable on Paradise below Cottage Seven, where Ferguson and Dillon are staying. Serra will give you each a walkie-talkie so you can keep in touch with each other and the ship. You, Algaro, will stay in the general vicinity of the cottage. Read a book on the beach, enjoy the sun, try to look normal if that's possible."

"And me, Señor?" Guerra asked.

"You go down to Caneel Beach and wait. When Carney's boat arrives, notify Algaro. Ferguson and Dillon must return to the cottage to change clothes and pack. That's when you strike. Once you have the Bormann briefcase, you return in the inflatable and we'll get out of here. Remember, the briefcase is distinctive. It's made of aluminium and is silver in appearance."

"Do we return to San Juan, Señor?" Serra asked.

"No." Santiago shook his head. "Samson Cay. I want time to consider my next move. The contents of that case will be more than interesting, Serra, they could give my life a whole new meaning." He opened a drawer at his right hand. There were a number of handguns in there. He selected a Browning Hi Power and pushed it across to Algaro. "Don't fail me."

"I won't," Algaro said. "If they have that briefcase, we'll get it for you."

"Oh, they'll have it all right." Santiago smiled. "I have every faith in our friend Dillon. His luck is good."

When *Sea Raider* moved in through all the moored yachts to the dock at Caneel Bay, the sun was high in the heavens. There were people wind-surfing out in the bay and the beach was crowded with sun worshippers. Guerra was one of them, sitting on a deck chair in flowered shirt and Bermuda shorts, dark glasses shading his eyes. He saw Dillon step on to the dock to tie up. He returned on board, then came back, the olive-green holdall in one hand. Ferguson followed him carrying the briefcase, Carney walking at his side.

Guerra pulled on a white floppy sunhat that, with the brim down, partially concealed his features, adjusted the dark glasses and moved off the beach along the front of the restaurant to where the path from the dock emerged. He reached it almost at the same time as the three men, and at that moment a young black receptionist hurried out of the front desk lobby.

"Oh, Captain Carney, I saw you coming in. There was an urgent message for you."

"And what was it?" Carney demanded.

"It was Billy Jones. He said to tell you Jenny Grant had an accident last night. Fell from a balcony at her house up at Gallows Point. She's there now. They're moving her over to St. Thomas Hospital real soon."

"My God!" Carney said and nodded to the girl. "That's okay, honey, I'll handle it."

"Another bloody accident," Dillon said bitterly and handed the holdall to Ferguson. "I'm going to see her."

"Yes, of course, dear boy," Ferguson replied. "I'll go back to the cottage, have a shower, get packed and so on."

"I'll see you later." Dillon turned to Carney. "Are you coming?"

"I sure as hell am," Carney told him, and they hurried off toward the car park together.

With the holdall in his right hand and the briefcase in his left, Ferguson set off, following the path that led past the cottages fronting Caneel Bay. Guerra paused in the shelter of some bushes and using the walkie-talkie called up Algaro, who, sitting on the beach at Paradise, answered at once.

"Yes, I hear you."

"Ferguson is on his way and alone. The others have gone to see the girl."

"They've what?" Algaro was thrown, but quickly pulled himself together. "All right, meet me on the downside of the cottage."

Guerra switched off and turned. He could see Ferguson a couple of hundred yards further on and hurried after him.

Ferguson put the briefcase on the bed, then pulled off his sweater. He should have felt exhilarated, he told himself looking down at the case, but then too much had happened. Joseph Jackson at Samson Cay, a poor old man who had never done anyone harm in his life, and Jack. He sighed, opened the door to the bar cupboard and found a whisky miniature. He poured it into a glass, added water and drank it slowly. Jack Lane, the best damn copper he had ever

worked with. And now Jenny Grant. Her accident so-called
was beyond coincidence. Santiago had much to answer for.
He took the briefcase from the bed and stood it at the
side of the small desk, checked that the front door was
locked, then went into the bathroom and turned on the
shower.

Guerra and Algaro went up the steps and entered the lobby.
Very gently, Guerra tried the door. He shook his head.
"Locked."

Algaro beckoned and led the way out, back down the
steps. It was very quiet, no one about, and the garden surrounding the cottage was very luxuriant, shielding a great
deal of it from view. Above their heads, a large terrace
jutted out, there was a path, some steps, a low wall, a
small tree beside it.

"Easy," Algaro said. "Stand on the wall, brace yourself
on the tree and I'll make a step up for you with my hands.
You can reach the terrace rail. I'll wait at the door." He
handed him the Browning. "Take this."

Guerra was on the terrace in a matter of seconds. The
venetian blinds were down at the windows, but he managed
to peer inside through narrow slats. There was no sign of
Ferguson. Very gently he tried the handle to the terrace
door which opened to his touch. He took out the Browning,
aware of the sound of the shower, glanced around the room,
saw no immediate sign of the briefcase and went to the
outside door and opened it.

Algaro moved in and took the Browning from him. "In
the shower, is he?"

"Yes, but I can't see the briefcase," Guerra whispered.

But Algaro did, moved quickly to the desk and picked it
up triumphantly. "This is it. Let's go."

As they turned to the door, Ferguson emerged from the bathroom tying the belt of a terry toweling robe. The dismay on his face was instant, but he didn't waste breath on words, simply flung himself at them. Algaro struck him across the side of the head with the barrel of the Browning and when Ferguson fell to one knee stamped him sideways into the wall.

"Come on!" Algaro cried to Guerra, pulled open the door and hurried down the steps.

Ferguson managed to get to his feet, dizzy, his head hurting like hell. He staggered across the room, got the terrace door open and went out in time to see Algaro and Guerra running down to the little beach at the bottom of the grass slope. They pushed the inflatable into the water, started the outboard and moved out from the shore. It was only then that Ferguson, looking up, realized that the *Maria Blanco* was anchored off there.

He never felt so impotent in his life, never so full of rage. He went into the bathroom, got a damp flannel for his head, found the field glasses and focused them on the yacht. He saw Algaro and Guerra go up the ladder and hurry along the stern to where Santiago sat under the awning, Captain Serra beside him. Algaro placed the briefcase on the table. Santiago placed his hands on it, then turned and spoke to Serra. The captain moved away and went on the bridge. A moment later, they started to haul up the anchor and the *Maria Blanco* began to move.

And then a strange thing happened. As if realizing he was being observed, Santiago raised the briefcase in one hand, waved with the other and went into the salon.

It was Billy who opened the front door to admit Dillon and Bob Carney at the house at Gallows Point. "I'm real glad to see you," he said.

"How is she?" Carney demanded.

"Not too good. Seems like she fell from the balcony outside her bedroom. When me and Mary found her, she was lying there in the rain."

"He wants her—the doctor—over to St. Thomas Hospital for a scan. They're coming to pick her up in an hour," Mary said.

"Can she speak?" Dillon asked as they went upstairs.

"Came to around an hour ago. It was you she asked for, Mr. Dillon."

"Did she tell you how it happened?"

"No. In fact, she ain't said much at all. Listen, I'll go and make coffee while you stay with her. Come on, Billy," she told her husband and they went out.

Carney said, "Her face is real bad."

"I know," Dillon said grimly, "and she didn't get that from any accident. If she'd fallen on her face from such a height it would have been smashed completely."

He took her hand and she opened her eyes. "Dillon?"

"That's right, Jenny."

"I'm sorry, Dillon, sorry I let you down."

"You didn't let us down, Jenny. We found the U-boat. Carney and I went down together."

"Sure, Jenny." Carney leaned over. "We blew a hole in her and we found Bormann's briefcase."

She didn't really know what she was saying, of course, but carried on. "I told him, Dillon, I told him you had gone to Thunder Point."

"Told who, Jenny?"

"The man with the scar, the big scar from his eye to his mouth."

"Algaro," Carney said.

She gripped Dillon's hand lightly. "He hurt me, Dillon, he really hurt me. Nobody ever hurt me like that," and she closed her eyes and drifted off again.

When Dillon turned, the rage on his face was a living thing. "He's a dead man walking, Algaro, I give you my word," and he brushed past Carney and went downstairs.

The front door was open, Billy sitting on the porch, and Mary was pouring coffee. "You gonna have some?"

"Just a quick one," Dillon said.

"How is she?"

"Drifted off again," Carney told her as he came out on the porch.

Dillon nodded to him and moved to the other end of the porch. "Let's examine the situation. It was probably round about midnight Algaro put the screws on Jenny and found out that we'd gone to Thunder Point."

"So?"

"No sign of the opposition turning up, either there or on the way back. Does Max Santiago seem the kind of man who'd just give up at this point?"

"No way," Carney said.

"I agree. I think it much more likely he decided to try and relieve us of Bormann's briefcase at the earliest opportunity."

"Exactly what I was thinking."

"Good." Dillon swallowed his black coffee and put the cup down. "Let's get back to Caneel fast. You check around the general area of Caneel Beach, the bar, the dock and I'll find Ferguson. We'll meet up in the bar later."

They went back to Mary and Billy. "You boys going?" Mary asked.

"Got to," Dillon said. "What about you?"

"Billy will run things down at the bar, but me, I'm going to St. Thomas with Jenny."

"Tell her I'll be in to see her," Dillon said. "Don't forget now," and he hurried down the steps followed by Carney.

• • •

When Dillon hammered on the door of 7E it was opened by Ferguson holding a flannel loaded with ice cubes to his head.

"What happened?" Dillon demanded.

"Algaro happened. I was in the shower and the door was locked. God knows how he got in, but I walked out of the bathroom and there he was with one of the other men. I did my best, Dillon, but the bastard had a Browning. Clouted me across the head."

"Let me see." Dillon examined it. "It could be worse."

"They had an inflatable on the beach and took off for *Maria Blanco*. It was anchored out there."

Dillon pulled up the venetian blinds in one of the windows. "Well it isn't now."

"I wonder where he's gone, back to San Juan perhaps." Ferguson scowled. "I saw him in the stern through those field glasses, saw Algaro give him the briefcase. He seemed to know I was watching. He raised the case in one hand and waved with the other." Ferguson scowled. "Cheeky bastard."

"I told Carney we'd see him in the bar," Dillon said. "Come on, we'd better go and break the bad news and decide what we're going to do."

In the darkest corner of the bar, Ferguson and Dillon shared a table. The Brigadier was enjoying a large Scotch tinkling with ice while Dillon had contented himself with Evian water and a cigarette. Carney came in quickly to join them and called to the waitress, "Just a cold beer."

"What happened?"

"I checked with a friend who was out fishing. They passed him heading south-east, which means they must be going to Samson Cay."

Dillon actually laughed. "Right, you bastard, I've got you now."

"What on earth do you mean?" Ferguson demanded.

"The *Maria Blanco* will be anchored off Samson tonight, and if you remember, the general manager, Prieto, told us that Santiago always stays on board when he's there. It's simple. We'll go in under cover of darkness and I'll get the briefcase back, if Carney will run us down there in *Sea Raider* of course."

"Try stopping me," Carney told him.

Ferguson shook his head. "You don't give up easily, do you, Dillon."

"I could never see the point." Dillon poured more Evian water and raised his glass.

15

It was toward evening as Dillon and Ferguson waited on the dock at Caneel Bay, sitting on the bench, the Irishman smoking a cigarette, the olive-green military holdall on the ground between them.

"I think that's him now," Ferguson said and pointed and Dillon saw *Sea Raider* coming in from the sea, slowly to negotiate the moored yachts. There were still people on the beach, some of them swimming in the evening sun, laughter drifting across the water.

Ferguson said, "From what I know of Santiago, I should think he'd be ready to repel boarders. Do you really think you can pull this off?"

"Anything's possible, Brigadier." Dillon shrugged. "You don't need to come, you know. I'd understand."

"I'll overlook the insult this time," Ferguson said coldly, "but don't ever say something like that to me again, Dillon."

Dillon smiled. "Cheer up, Brigadier. I've no intention of dying at a place called Samson Cay. After all, I've got a dinner at the Garrick Club to look forward to again with you."

He got up and moved to the edge of the dock as *Sea*

Raider drifted in. He waved up to Carney, jumped across the gap, got the fenders over, then threw a line to the Brigadier. Carney killed the engines and came down the ladder as they finished tying up.

"I've refuelled so everything's shipshape. We can leave any time you like."

Ferguson passed the holdall to Dillon and stepped across as Dillon took it into the deckhouse and put it on one of the benches.

At that moment the receptionist who'd given them the news about Jenny when they'd come in earlier came along the dock. "I've just taken a phone call from Mary Jones at St. Thomas Hospital, Mr. Dillon. She'd like for you to call her back."

Carney said, "I'll come with you."

The Brigadier nodded. "I'll wait here and keep my fingers crossed."

Dillon stepped over the side and turned along the dock, Carney at his side.

Mary said, "She's going to be fine, but a good job she had that scan. There's what they call a hairline fracture in the skull, but the specialist he say nothing that care and good treatment won't cure."

"Fine," Dillon said. "Don't forget to tell her I'll be in to see her."

Carney was leaning at the entrance of the telephone booth, his face anxious. "Hairline fracture of the skull," Dillon told him as he hung up. "But she's going to be okay."

"Well that's good," Carney said as they walked back to the dock.

"That's one way of putting it," Dillon said. "Another is that Santiago and Algaro have got a lot to answer for, not to mention that bastard Pamer."

Ferguson got up and came out of the deckhouse as they arrived. "Good news?"

"It could be worse," Dillon said and told him.

"Thank God!" Ferguson took a deep breath. "All right, I suppose we'd better get going."

Carney said, "Sure, but I'd like to know how we're going to handle this thing. Even in the dark, there's a limit to how close we can get in *Sea Raider* without being spotted."

"It seems to me the smart way would be an approach underwater," Dillon said. "Only there's no *we* about it, Carney. I once told you you were one of the good guys. Santiago and his people, they're the bad guys and that's what I am. I'm a bad guy, too. Ask the Brigadier, he'll tell you. That's why he hired me for this job in the first place. This is where I earn my keep and it's a one-man affair."

"Now look," Carney said. "I can hold up my end."

"I know that and you've got the medals to prove it. The Brigadier showed me your record, but Vietnam was different. You were stuck in a lousy war that wasn't really any of your business. I suppose you were just trying to stay alive."

"And I made it. I'm here, aren't I?"

"Remember when you and the Brigadier were swapping war stories about Vietnam and Korea and you asked me what I knew about war and I told you I'd been at war all my life?"

"So?"

"At an age when I should have been taking girls out to dances I was fighting the kind of war where the battlefield was rooftops and back alleys, leading British paratroopers a dance through the sewers of the Falls Road in Belfast, being chased by the SAS through South Armagh and they're the best."

"What are you trying to say to me?" Carney asked.

"That when I go over the rail of the *Maria Blanco* to recover that briefcase I'll kill anyone who tries to get in my way." Dillon shrugged. "Like I said, I can do that without a moment's hesitation because I'm a bad guy. I don't think you can, and thank God for it."

There was silence. Carney turned to Ferguson, who nodded. "He's right, I'm afraid."

"Okay," Carney said reluctantly. "This is the way it goes. I'll go as close to the *Maria Blanco* as we dare and drop anchor, then I'll take you the rest of the way in an inflatable." Dillon tried to speak and Carney cut him off. "No buts, that's the way it's going to be. I've got an inflatable moored out there on the buoy with *Privateer*. We'll pick it up on the way."

"All right," Dillon said. "Have it your way."

"And I come in, Dillon, if anything goes wrong, I come in."

"On horseback, bugles blowing?" Dillon laughed. "The South shall rise again? You people never could come to terms with losing the Civil War."

"There was no Civil War." Carney went up to the flying bridge. "You must be referring to the war for the independence of the Confederacy. Now let's get moving."

He switched on the engines, Dillon stepped over to the dock and untied the lines. A moment later and they were moving out into the bay.

The *Maria Blanco* was anchored in the bay at Samson Cay and Santiago sat in the salon, reading the documents in Bormann's briefcase for the third time. He'd never been so fascinated in his life. He examined the personal order from Hitler, the signature, then reread the Windsor Protocol. It was the Blue Book which was the most interesting though. All those names, Members of Parliament, Peers of the Realm, people at the highest levels of society who had supported, however secretly, the cause of National Socialism, but then it was hardly surprising. In the England of the great depression with something like four million people out of work, many would have looked at Germany and thought that Hitler had the right idea.

He got up, went to the bar and poured a glass of dry sherry, then returned to the desk, picked up the telephone and called the radio room. "Get me Sir Francis Pamer in London."

Pamer was sitting alone at the desk in his office at the House of Commons when the phone rang.

"Francis? Max here."

Pamer was immediately all attention. "Has anything happened?"

"You could say that. I've got it, Francis, right here on my desk, Bormann's briefcase, and Korvettenkapitän Paul Friemel was right. The Reichsleiter wasn't just shooting his mouth off while drunk. It's all here, Francis. Hitler's order to him, details of numbered bank accounts, the Windsor Protocol. Now there's an impressive-looking document. If they forged it, I can only say they did a good job."

"My God!" Pamer said.

"And the Blue Book, Francis, absolutely fascinating stuff. Such famous names and a neat little background paragraph for each. Here's an interesting one. I'll read it to you. Major, Sir Joseph Pamer, Military Cross, Member of Parliament, Hatherley Court, Hampshire, an associate of Sir Oswald Mosley, politically sound, totally committed to the cause of National Socialism."

"No." Pamer groaned and there was sudden sweat on his face. "I can't believe it."

"I wonder what your local Conservative Association would make of that? Still, all's well that ends well, as they say. A good thing I've got it and no one else."

"You'll destroy it of course?" Pamer said. "I mean, you'll destroy the whole bloody lot?"

"Leave it to me, Francis, I'll see to everything," Santiago said. "Just like I always do. I'll be in touch soon."

He put down the phone and started to laugh, was still laughing when Captain Serra came in. "Have you any orders, Señor?"

Santiago looked at his watch. It was just after seven. "Yes, I'll go ashore for a couple of hours and eat at the restaurant."

"Very well, Señor."

"And make sure the deck is patrolled tonight, Serra, just in case our friends decide to pay us a visit."

"I don't think we need worry, Señor, they'd have trouble getting close to us without being spotted, but we'll take every precaution."

"Good, make the launch ready, I'll be with you in a moment," and Santiago went into the bedroom, taking the briefcase with him.

Sea Raider crept to the west side of Samson Cay, round the point from the resort and the main anchorage. Carney switched off the engines, came down the ladder as Dillon went in to the prow and dropped the anchor.

"Shunt Bay they call this," Carney said. "I've been here before, a long time ago. Only four or five fathoms, clear sand bottom. You can't get down to it because of the cliffs so when guests want to swim here they bring them round from the resort by boat. We'll be safe here at this time of night."

Ferguson checked his watch. "Ten o'clock. What time will you go?"

"Maybe another hour. I'll see." Dillon went into the deckhouse, opened the holdall and took out the AK47 assault rifle and passed it to Ferguson. "Just in case."

"Let's hope not." Ferguson put it on the bench.

Dillon took the Walther from the holdall, checked it and put it in the dive bag with the Carswell silencer. Then he put in what was left of the Semtex and a couple of detonating fuses, the thirty-minute ones.

"You really are going to war," Ferguson said.

"You better believe it." Dillon slipped the night sight into the bag also.

Carney said, "I'll take you as close as I can in the inflatable, and hope to see you on the way back."

"Fine." Dillon smiled. "Break out the thermos, Brigadier, and we'll have some coffee and then it's action stations."

Santiago had enjoyed an excellent meal, starting with caviar, followed by grilled filet mignon with artichoke hearts, washed down by a bottle of Chateau Palmer 1966. Deliberate self-indulgence because he felt on top of the world. He liked things to go well and the Bormann affair had gone very well indeed. It was like a wonderful game. The information contained in the documents was so startling that the possibilities were endless.

He asked for a cigar, Cuban, of course, just like the old days before that madman Castro had ruined everything. Prieto brought him a Romeo and Julietta, trimmed the end and warmed it for him.

"The meal, it was satisfactory, Señor Santiago?"

"The meal, it was bloody marvelous, Prieto." Santiago patted him on the shoulder. "I'll see you tomorrow." He stood up, picked up the Bormann briefcase from the floor beside the table and walked to the door where Algaro was waiting. "We'll go back to the ship now, Algaro."

"As you say, Señor."

Santiago went down the steps and walked along the dock to the launch, savouring the night, the scent of his cigar. Yes, life could really be very good.

Carney took the inflatable round the point, the outboard motor throttled down, the noise of it a murmur in the night. There were yachts in the bay scattered here and there and a few smaller craft. *Maria Blanco,* anchored three hundred yards out, was by far the largest.

Carney killed the engine, took a couple of short wooden oars from the bottom of the boat and fitted them into the rowlocks. "Manpower the rest of the way," he said. "The way I see it and with those other boats around, I can get you maybe fifty yards away without being spotted."

"That's fine."

Dillon was already wearing his jacket and tank and a black nylon diving cowl Carney had found him. He took the Walther from his dive bag, screwed the Carswell silencer into place and slipped the weapon inside his jacket.

"You'd better pray you don't get a misfire," Carney said as he rowed. "Water does funny things to guns. I learned that in Vietnam in those damn paddy fields."

"No problem with a Walther, it's a Rolls-Royce," Dillon said.

They couldn't see each other, their faces a pale blur in the darkness. Carney said, "You actually enjoy this kind of thing?"

"I'm not too sure if enjoy is the right word exactly."

"I knew guys in Vietnam like that, Special Forces mainly. They kept drawing these hard assignments and then a strange thing happened. They ended up wanting more.

Couldn't get enough. Is that how you feel, Dillon?"

"There's a poem by Browning," Dillon told him. "Something about our interest being on the dangerous edge of things. When I was young and foolish in those early days with the IRA and the SAS chasing the hell out of me all over South Armagh, I also discovered a funny thing. I loved it more than anything I'd ever known. I lived more in a day, really lived, than in a year back in London."

"I understand that," Carney said. "It's like being on some sort of drug, but it can only end one way. On your back in the gutter in some Belfast street."

"Oh, you've no need to worry about that," Dillon told him. "Those days are over. I'll never go back to that."

Carney paused, sniffing. "I think I can smell cigar smoke."

They floated there in the darkness and the launch emerged on the other side of a couple of yachts and moved to the bottom of the *Maria Blanco*'s steel stairway under the light. Serra was on deck looking over. Guerra hurried down to take the line and tied up and Santiago went up to the deck followed by Algaro.

"Looks like he's carrying the briefcase with him," Carney said.

Dillon got the night sight from his dive bag and focused it. "You're right. He's probably afraid to let it out of his sight."

"What now?" Carney said.

"We'll hang on for a little while, give them a chance to settle down."

Santiago and Serra descended from the bridge to the main deck. Guerra and Solona stood at the bottom of the ladder, each armed with an M16 rifle. Algaro stood by the rail.

"Two hours on and four off. We'll rotate during the night and we'll leave the security lights on."

"That seems more than adequate. We might as well turn in now," Santiago said. "Good night, Captain."

He went along to the salon and Algaro followed him. "Do you need me any more tonight, Señor?"

"I don't think so, Algaro, you can go to bed."

Algaro withdrew, Santiago put the briefcase on the desk, then he took off his jacket and went and poured a cognac. He returned to the desk, sat down and leaned back, sipping his cognac and just looking at the briefcase. Finally, as he knew he would, he opened it and started to go through the documents again.

Dillon focused the night sight. He picked out Solona in the shadows by a lifeboat in the prow. Guerra, in the stern, had made no attempt to hide, sat on one of the chairs under the awning smoking a cigarette, his rifle on the table.

Dillon handed Carney the night sight. "All yours. I'm on my way."

He dropped back over the side of the inflatable, descended to ten feet and approached the ship. He surfaced at the stern of the launch, which was tied up at the bottom of the steel stairway. Suddenly, Solona appeared up above on the platform. Dillon eased under the water, aware of footsteps descending. Solona paused halfway down and lit a cigarette, the match flaring in cupped hands. Dillon surfaced gently at the stern of the launch, took the Walther from inside his jacket and extended his arm.

"Over here," he whispered in Spanish.

Solona glanced up, the match still flaring, and the silenced Walther coughed as Dillon shot him between the eyes. Solona fell back and to one side, slid over the rail and dropped ten feet into the water.

It didn't make too much of a splash, but Guerra noticed it and got to his feet. "Hey, Solona, is that you?"

"Yes," Dillon called softly in Spanish. "No problem."

He could hear Guerra walking along the deck above, went under and swam to the anchor. He opened his jacket, unzipped his diving suit and forced the Walther inside. Then he slipped out of the jacket and tank, clipped them to the anchor line and hauled himself up the chain, sliding in through the port.

Algaro, lying on his bunk, was only wearing a pair of boxer shorts because of the oppressive heat. For that reason, he had the porthole open and heard Guerra calling to Solona; he also heard Dillon's reply. He frowned, went to the porthole and listened.

Guerra called softly again, "Where are you, Solona?"

Algaro picked up the revolver on his bedside locker and went out.

Guerra called again, "Where are you, Solona?" and moved to the forward deck, the M16 ready.

"Over here, *amigo*," Dillon said and as Guerra turned, shot him twice in the heart, driving him back against the bulkhead.

Dillon went forward cautiously, leaned over to check that he was dead. There was no sound behind, for Algaro was bare-footed, but Dillon was suddenly aware of the barrel of the revolver against his neck.

"Now then, you bastard, I've got you." Algaro reached over and took the Walther. "So, a real professional's weapon? I like that. In fact I like it so much I'm going to keep it." He tossed the revolver over the rail into the sea. "Now turn round. I'm going to give you two in the belly so you take a long time."

Bob Carney, watching events through the night sight, had seen Algaro's approach, had never been so frustrated in his life at his inability to do something about it, was never totally certain what happened afterwards because everything moved so fast.

Dillon turned, his left arm sweeping Algaro's right to the side, the Walther discharging into the deck. Dillon closed with him. "If you're going to do it, do it, don't talk about it." They struggled for a moment, feeling each other's strength. "Why don't you call for help?"

"Because I'll kill you myself with my own hands," Algaro told him through clenched teeth. "For my own pleasure."

"You're good at beating up girls, aren't you?" Dillon said. "How are you with a man?"

Algaro twisted round, exerting all his strength, and pushed Dillon back against the rail at the prow. It was his last mistake, for Dillon let himself go straight over, taking Algaro with him, and the sea was Dillon's territory, not his.

Algaro dropped the Walther as they went under the water and started to struggle and Dillon held on, pulling him down, aware of the anchor chain against his back. He grabbed for it with one hand and got a forearm across Algaro's throat. At first he struggled very hard indeed, feet kicking, but quickly weakened. Finally, he was still. Dillon, his own lungs nearly bursting, reached one-handed and unbuckled his weight belt. He passed it around Algaro's neck and fastened the buckle again, binding him to the anchor chain.

He surfaced, taking in great lungfuls of air. It occurred to him then that Carney would be watching events through the night sight and he turned and raised an arm, then hauled himself back up the anchor chain.

He kept to the shadows, moving along the deck until he came to the main salon. He glanced in a porthole and saw Santiago sitting at the desk, the briefcase open, reading.

Dillon crouched down, thinking about it, then made his decision. He took what was left of the Semtex from his dive bag, inserted the two thirty-minute detonator fuses, went and dropped it down one of the engine room air vents, then returned and peered through the porthole again.

Santiago was sitting at the desk, but now he replaced the documents in his briefcase, closed it, yawned and got up and went into the bedroom. Dillon didn't hesitate. He moved into the companionway, opened the salon door and darted across to the desk, and as he picked up the briefcase, Santiago came back into the room.

The cry that erupted from his mouth was like a howl of anguish. "No!" he cried and Dillon turned and ran for the door. Santiago got the desk drawer open, grabbed a Smith & Wesson and fired blindly.

Dillon was already into the companionway and making for the deck. By now, the ship was aroused and Serra appeared from his cabin at the rear of the bridge, a gun in his hand.

"What's going on?" he demanded.

"Stop him!" Santiago cried. "It's Dillon."

Dillon didn't hesitate, but kept to the shadows, running to the stern and jumped over the rail. He went under as deep as he could, but the case made things awkward. He surfaced, aware that they were firing at him, and struck out for the darkness as fast as possible. In the end, it was Carney who saved him, roaring out of the night and tossing him a line.

"Hang on and let's get the hell out of here," he called, boosted speed and took them away into the friendly dark.

Serra said, "Guerra's dead, his body is still here, but no sign of Solona and Algaro."

"Never mind that," Santiago told him. "Dillon and Carney didn't come all the way in that inflatable from St. John.

Carney's Sport Fisherman must be nearby."

"True," Serra said, "and they'll up anchor and start back straightaway."

"And the moment they move, you'll see them on your radar, right? I mean, there's no other boat moving out to sea from Samson Cay tonight."

"True, Señor."

"Then get the anchor up."

Serra pressed the bridge button for the electric hoist. The motor started to whine. Santiago said, "What now?"

The three remaining members of the crew, Pinto, Noval and Mugica, were down on the forward deck and Serra leaned over the bridge rail. "The anchor line is jamming. Check it."

Mugica leaned over the prow, then turned. "It's Algaro. He's tied to the chain."

Santiago and Serra went down the ladder and hurried to the prow and looked over. Algaro hung there from the anchor chain, the weight belt around his throat. "Mother of God!" Santiago said. "Pull him up, damn you!" He turned to Serra. "Now let's get moving."

"Don't worry, Señor," Serra told him. "We're faster than they are. There's no way they can get back to St. John without us overtaking them," and he turned to the ladder and went up to the bridge as Noval and Mugica hauled Algaro's body in through the chain port.

At Shunt Bay, Ferguson leaned anxiously over the stern of *Sea Raider* as the inflatable coasted in out of the darkness.

"What happened?" he demanded.

Dillon passed the Bormann briefcase up to him. "That's what happened. Now let's get out of here."

He stepped on to the diving platform and Carney passed him the inflatable line and Dillon tied it securely, then went to the deckhouse and worked his way round to the prow and started to pull in the anchor. It came free of the sandy bottom with no difficulty. Behind him, Carney had already gone up to the flying bridge and was starting the engines.

Ferguson joined him. "How did it go?"

"He doesn't take prisoners, I'll say that for him," Carney said. "But let's get out of here. We don't have any kind of time to hang about."

Sea Raider plowed forward into the night, the wind freshening four to five. Ferguson sat in the swivel chair and Dillon leaned against the rail beside Carney.

"They're faster than we are, you know that," Carney said. "And he's going to keep coming."

"I know," Dillon told him. "He doesn't like to lose."

"Well, I sure as hell can't go any faster, we're doing twenty-two knots and that's tops."

It was Ferguson who saw the *Maria Blanco* first. "There's a light back there, I'm sure there is."

Carney glanced round. "That's them all right, couldn't be anyone else."

Dillon raised the night sight.

"Yes, it's the *Maria Blanco*."

"He's got good radar on that thing, must have," Carney said. "No way I can lose him."

"Oh, yes there is," Dillon said. "Just keep going."

Serra, on the bridge of the *Maria Blanco,* held a pair of night glasses to his eyes. "Got it," he said and passed the glasses to Santiago.

Santiago focused them and saw the outline of *Sea Raider*. "Right, you bastards." He leaned over the bridge rail and looked down at Mugica, Noval and Pinto, who all waited on the forward deck, holding M16 rifles. "We've seen them. Get yourselves ready."

Serra increased speed, the *Maria Blanco* raced forward over the waves and Santiago raised the glasses again, saw the outline of *Sea Raider* and smiled. "Now, Dillon, now," he murmured.

The explosion, when it came, was instantaneous, tearing the bottom out of the ship. What happened was so catastrophic that neither Santiago, Captain Serra nor the three remaining crew members had time to take it in as their world disintegrated and the *Maria Blanco* lifted, then plunged beneath the waves.

On the flying bridge of *Sea Raider* what they saw first was a brilliant flash of orange fire and then, a second or two later, the explosion boomed across the water. And then the fire disappeared, extinguished, only darkness remaining. Bob Carney killed the engine instantly.

It was very quiet. Ferguson said, "A long way down."

Dillon looked back through the night sight. "U180 went further." He put the night sight in the locker under the instrument panel. "He did say they were carrying explosives, remember?"

Carney said, "We should go back, perhaps there are survivors."

"You really think so after that?" Dillon said gently. "St. John's that way."

Carney switched on the engines, and as they plowed forward into the night Dillon went down the ladder to the deckhouse. He took off his diving suit, pulled on his tracksuit, found a pack of cigarettes, went to the rail.

Ferguson came down the ladder and joined him. "My God!" he said softly.

"I don't think he had much to do with it, Brigadier," Dillon said and he lit a cigarette, the Zippo flaring.

It was just after ten the following morning when a nurse showed the three of them into the private room at the St. Thomas Hospital. Dillon was wearing the black cord slacks, the denim shirt and the black flying jacket he'd arrived in on the first day, Ferguson supremely elegant as usual in his Panama, blazer and Guards tie. Jenny was propped up against pillows, her head swathed in white bandages.

Mary, sitting beside her, knitting, got up. "I'll leave you to it, but don't you gentlemen overtire her."

She went out and Jenny managed a weak smile. "My three musketeers."

"Now that's kind of fanciful." Bob Carney took her hand. "How are you?"

"I don't feel I'm here half the time."

"That will pass, my dear," Ferguson said. "I've had a word with the Superintendent. Anything you want, any treatment you need, you get. It's all taken care of."

"Thank you, Brigadier."

She turned to Dillon, looked up at him without speaking. Bob Carney said, "I'll be back, honey, you take care."

He turned to Ferguson, who nodded, and they went out.

Dillon sat on the bed and took her hand. "You look terrible."

"I know. How are you?"

"I'm fine."

"How did it all go?"

"We've got the Bormann briefcase. The Brigadier has his Learjet waiting at the airport. We're taking it back to London."

"The way you put it, you make it sound as if it was easy."

"It could have been worse. Don't go on about it, Jenny, there's no point. Santiago and his friends, that animal, Algaro, they'll never bother you again."

"Can you be certain of that?"

"As a coffin lid closing," he said bleakly.

There was a kind of pain on her face. She closed her eyes briefly, opened them again. "People don't really change, do they?"

"I am what I am, Jenny," he said simply. "But then you knew that."

"Will I see you again?"

"I don't think that's likely." He kissed her hand, got up, went to the door and opened it.

"Dillon," she called.

He turned. "Yes, Jenny?"

"God bless and take care of yourself."

The door closed softly, she closed her eyes and drifted into sleep.

They allowed Carney to walk out across the tarmac to the Lear with them, a porter pushing a trolley with the luggage. One of the two pilots met them and helped the porter stow the luggage while Dillon, Ferguson and Carney stood at the bottom of the steps.

The Brigadier held up the briefcase. "Thanks for this, Captain Carney. If you ever need help or I can do you a good turn." He shook hands. "Take care, my friend," and he went up the steps.

Carney said, "What happens now, in London, I mean?"

"That's up to the Prime Minister," Dillon said. "Depends what he wants to do with those documents."

"It was a long time ago," Carney said.

"A legitimate point of view."

Carney hesitated, then said, "This Pamer guy, what about him?"

"I hadn't really thought about it," Dillon said calmly.

"Oh, yes you have." Carney shook his head. "God help you, Dillon, because you'll never change," and he turned and walked away across the tarmac.

Dillon joined Ferguson inside and strapped himself in. "A good man that," Ferguson said.

Dillon nodded. "The best."

The second pilot pulled up the steps and closed the door, went and joined his colleague in the cockpit. After a while, the engines fired and they moved forward. A few moments later, they were climbing high and out over the sea.

Ferguson looked out. "St. John over there."

"Yes," Dillon said.

Ferguson sighed. "I suppose we should discuss what happens when we get back."

"Not now, Brigadier." Dillon closed his eyes. "I'm tired. Let's leave it till later."

The house at Chocolate Hole had never seemed so empty when Bob Carney entered it. He walked slightly aimlessly from room to room, then went in the kitchen and got a beer from the icebox. As he went to the living room the phone rang.

It was his wife, Karye. "Hi, honey, how are you?"

"I'm fine, just fine. How about the kids?"

"Oh, lively as usual. They miss you. This is an impulse call. We're at a gas station near Orlando. I just stopped to fill up."

"I'm sure looking forward to you coming back."

"It won't be long now," she said. "I know it's been lonely for you. Anything interesting happened?"

A slow smile spread across Carney's face and he took a deep breath. "Not that I can think of. Same old routine."

"Bye, honey, I'll have to go."

He put the phone down, drank some of his beer, went out on the porch. It was a fine, clear afternoon and he could see the islands on the other side of Pillsbury Sound and beyond. A long way, but not as far as Max Santiago had gone.

16

It was just before six o'clock the following evening in Ferguson's office at the Ministry of Defence and Simon Carter sat on the other side of the desk, white-faced and shaken as Ferguson finished talking.

"So what's to be done about the good Sir Francis?" Ferguson asked. "A Minister of the Crown, behaving not only dishonourably but in what can only be described as a criminal way."

Dillon, standing by the window in a blue Burberry trenchcoat, lit a cigarette and Carter said, "Does *he* have to be here?"

"Nobody knows more of this affair than Dillon, can't keep him out of it now."

Carter picked up the Blue Book file, hesitated, then put it down and unfolded the Windsor Protocol to read it again. "I can't believe this is genuine."

"Perhaps not, but the rest of it is." Ferguson reached across for the documents, replaced them in the briefcase and closed it. "The Prime Minister will see us at Downing Street at eight. Naturally I haven't invited Sir Francis. I'll meet you there."

Carter got up. "Very well."

He went to the door, was reaching for the handle when Ferguson said, "Oh, and Carter."

"Yes?"

"Don't do anything stupid like phoning Pamer. I'd stay well clear of this if I were you."

Carter's face sagged, he turned wearily and went out.

It was ten minutes later and Sir Francis Pamer was clearing his desk at the House of Commons before leaving for the evening when his phone rang. "Pamer here," he said.

"Charles Ferguson."

"Ah, you're back, Brigadier," Pamer said warily.

"We need to meet," Ferguson told him.

"Quite impossible tonight, I have a most important function, dinner with the Lord Mayor of London. Can't miss that."

"Max Santiago is dead," Ferguson said, "and I have here, on my desk, the Bormann briefcase. The Blue Book makes very interesting reading. Your father is featured prominently on page eighteen."

"Oh, dear God!" Pamer slumped down on his chair.

"I wouldn't speak to Simon Carter about this if I were you," Ferguson said. "That wouldn't really be to your advantage."

"Of course not, anything you say." Pamer hesitated. "You haven't spoken to the Prime Minister then?"

"No, I thought it best to see you first."

"I'm very grateful, Brigadier, I'm sure we can work something out."

"You know Charing Cross Pier?"

"Of course."

"One of the river boats, the *Queen of Denmark,* leaves there at six forty-five. I'll meet you on board. You'll need an umbrella, by the way, it's raining rather hard."

• • •

Ferguson put down the phone and turned to Dillon, who was still standing by the window. "That's it then."

"How did he sound?" Dillon asked.

"Terrified." Ferguson got up, went to the old-fashioned hall stand he kept in the corner and took down his overcoat, the type known to Guards officers as a British warm, and pulled it on. "But then, he would be, poor sod."

"Don't expect me to have any sympathy for him." Dillon picked up the briefcase from the desk. "Come on, let's get on with it," and he opened the door and led the way out.

When Pamer arrived at Charing Cross Pier the fog was so thick that he could hardly see across the Thames. He bought his ticket from a steward at the head of the gangplank. The *Queen of Denmark* was scheduled to call in at Westminster Pier and eventually Cadogan Pier at Chelsea Embankment. A popular run on a fine summer evening, but on a night like this, there were few passengers.

Pamer had a look in the lower saloon where there were half-a-dozen passengers and a companionway to the upper saloon where he encountered only two ageing ladies talking to each other in whispers. He opened a glass door and went outside, and looked down. There was someone standing at the rail in the stern holding an umbrella over his head. He went back inside, descended the companionway and went out on deck, opening his umbrella against the driving rain.

"That you, Ferguson?"

He went forward hesitantly, his hand on the butt of the pistol in his right-hand raincoat pocket. It was a very rare weapon from the exclusive collection of World War Two handguns his father had left him, a Volka specially designed for use by the Hungarian Secret Service and as silenced as a pistol could be. He'd kept it in his desk at the

Commons for years. The *Queen of Denmark* was moving away from the pier now and starting her passage upriver. Fog swirled up from the surface of the water, the light from the saloon above was yellow and sickly. There were no rear windows to the lower saloon. They were alone in their own private space.

Ferguson turned from the rail. "Ah, there you are." He held up the briefcase. "Well, there it is. The Prime Minister's having a look at eight o'clock."

"Please, Ferguson," Pamer pleaded. "Don't do this to me. It's not my fault that my father was a Fascist."

"Quite right. It's also not your fault that your father's immense fortune in post-war years came from his association with the Nazi movement, the Kamaradenwerk. I can even excuse as simply weakness of character the way you've been happy over the years to accept a large, continuing income from Samson Cay Holdings, mostly money produced by Max Santiago's more dubious enterprises. The drug business, for example."

"Now look here," Pamer began.

"Don't bother to deny it. I'd asked Jack Lane to investigate your family's financial background, not realizing I was sentencing him to death, of course. He'd really made progress before he was killed, or should I say murdered? I found his findings in his desk earlier today."

"It wasn't my fault, any of it," Pamer said wildly. "All my father and his bloody love affair with Hitler. I had my family name to think of, Ferguson, my position in the Government."

"Oh, yes," Ferguson conceded. "Rather selfish of you, but understandable. What I can't forgive is the fact that you acted as Santiago's lap dog from the very beginning, fed him every piece of information you could. You sold me out, you sold out Dillon, putting us in danger of our very lives. It was your actions that resulted in Jennifer Grant being attacked twice, once in London where God knows what would have happened if Dillon hadn't intervened. The second time in St. John, where she was severely injured and almost died. She's in a hospital now."

"I knew none of this, I swear."

"Oh, everything was arranged by Santiago, I grant you that. What I'm talking about is responsibility. On Samson Cay, a poor old man called Joseph Jackson who gave me my first clue to the truth behind the whole affair, the man who was caretaker at the old Herbert Hotel in 1945, was brutally murdered just after talking to me. Now that was obviously the work of Santiago's people, but how did he know of the existence of the old man in the first place? Because you told him."

"You can't prove that, you can't prove any of it."

"True, just as I can't prove exactly what happened to Jack Lane, but I'll make an educated guess. Those were computer printouts I found in his desk. That means he was doing a computer sweep on your family affairs. I presume one of your staff noticed. Normally, you wouldn't have been concerned, it happens to Crown Ministers all the time, but in the light of recent events, you panicked, feared the worst, and phoned Santiago, who took care of it for you." Ferguson sighed. "I often think the direct dialing system a curse. In the old days it would have taken the international operator at least four hours to connect you to a place like the Virgins. These days all you do is punch a rather long series of numbers."

Pamer took a deep breath and squared his shoulders. "As regards my family's business interests, that was my father's affair, not mine. I'll plead ignorance if you persist with this thing. I know the law, Ferguson, and you seem to have forgotten that I was a working barrister for a short while."

"Actually I had," Ferguson said.

"Santiago being dead, the only thing you have left is my father's inclusion in the Blue Book. Hardly my fault." He seemed to have recovered his nerve. "You can't prove a thing. I'll tough it out, Ferguson."

Ferguson turned and looked at the river. "As I said, I could understand your panic, an ancient name tarnished, your political career threatened, but the attacks on that girl, the death of that old man, the cold-blooded murder of Inspector Lane—on those charges you are every bit as culpable as the men who carried them out."

"Prove it," Pamer said, clutching his umbrella in both hands.

"Goodbye, Sir Francis," Charles Ferguson said and turned and walked away.

Pamer was trembling, and he'd totally forgotten about the Volka in his pocket. Too late now for any wild ideas like relieving Ferguson of the briefcase at gunpoint. He took a deep breath and coughed as the fog bit at the back of his throat. He fumbled for his cigarette case, got one to his mouth and tried to find his lighter.

There was the softest of footfalls and Dillon's Zippo flared. "There you go."

Pamer's eyes widened in fear. "Dillon, what do you want?"

"A word only." Dillon put his right arm around Pamer's shoulders under the umbrella and drew him against the stern rail. "The first time I met you and Simon Carter on the Terrace at the House of Commons I made a joke about security and the river and you said you couldn't swim. Is that true?"

"Well, yes." Pamer's eyes widened as he understood. He pulled the Volka from his raincoat pocket, but Dillon, in close, swept the arm wide. The weapon gave a muted cough, the bullet thudded into the bulkhead.

The Irishman grabbed for the right wrist, slamming it on the rail so that Pamer cried out and dropped the pistol in the river.

"Thanks, old son," Dillon said. "You've just made it easier for me."

He swung Pamer round and pushed hard between the shoulder blades so that he sagged across the stern rail, reached down, grabbed him by the ankles and heaved him over. The umbrella floated upside down, Pamer surfaced, raised an arm. There was a strangled cry as he went under again and the fog swirled across the surface of the Thames, covering everything.

Five minutes later the *Queen of Denmark* pulled in at Westminster Pier next to the bridge. Ferguson was first down the gangway and waited under a tree for Dillon to join him. "Taken care of?"

"I think you could say that," Dillon told him.

"Good. I've got my appointment at Downing Street now. I can walk there from here. I'll see you at my flat in Cavendish Square, let you know what happened."

Dillon watched him go, then moved away himself in the opposite direction, fading into the fog and rain.

Ferguson was admitted to Downing Street some fifteen minutes early for his appointment. Someone took his coat and umbrella and one of the Prime Minister's aides came down the stairs at that moment. "Ah, there you are, Brigadier."

"A trifle early, I fear."

"No problem. The Prime Minister would welcome the opportunity to consider the material in question himself. Is that it?"

"Yes." Ferguson handed him the briefcase.

"Please make yourself comfortable. I'm sure he won't keep you long."

Ferguson took a seat in the hall, feeling rather cold. He shivered and the porter by the door said, "No central heating, Brigadier. The workmen moved in today to install the new security systems."

"Ah, so they've finally started?"

"Yes, but it's bleeding cold of an evening. We had to light a fire in the Prime Minister's study. First time in years."

"Is that so?"

A few moments later there was a knock at the door, the porter opened it and admitted Carter. "Brigadier," Carter said formally.

The porter took his coat and umbrella and at that moment, the aide reappeared. "Please come this way, gentlemen."

The Prime Minister sat at his desk, the briefcase open at one side. He was reading through the Blue Book and glanced up briefly. "Sit down, gentlemen, I'll be with you directly."

The fire burned brightly in the grate of the Victorian fireplace. It was very quiet, only sudden flurries of rain hammering against the window.

Finally, the Prime Minister sat back and looked at them. "Some of the names on this Blue Book list are really quite incredible. Sir Joseph Pamer, for example, on page eighteen. I presume this is why you didn't ask Sir Francis to join us, Brigadier?"

"I felt his presence would be inappropriate in the circumstances, Prime Minister, and Sir Francis agreed."

Carter turned and glanced at him sharply. The Prime Minister said, "You have informed him of his father's presence in the Blue Book then?"

"Yes, sir, I have."

"I appreciate Sir Francis's delicacy in the matter. On the other hand, the fact that his father was a Fascist all those years ago is hardly his fault. We don't visit the sins of the fathers on the children." The Prime Minister glanced at the Blue Book again, then looked up. "Unless you have anything else to tell me, Brigadier?" There was a strange set look on his face, as if he was somehow challenging Ferguson.

Carter glanced at Ferguson puzzled, his face pale, and Ferguson said firmly, "No, Prime Minister."

"Good. Now we come to the Windsor Protocol." The Prime Minister unfolded it. "Do you gentlemen consider this to be genuine?"

"One can't be certain," Carter said. "The Nazis did produce some remarkable forgeries during the War, there is no doubt about that."

"It is a known fact that the Duke hoped for a speedy end to the War," Ferguson said. "This is in no way to suggest that he was disloyal, but he deeply regretted the loss of life on both sides and wanted it to end."

"Be that as it may, the tabloid press would have a field day with this and the effect on the Royal Family would be catastrophic, and I wouldn't want that," the Prime Minister said. "You've brought me the original of Korvettenkapitän Friemel's diary as I asked and the translation. Are these all the copies?"

"Everything," Ferguson assured him.

"Good." The Prime Minister piled the documents together, got up and went to the fire. He put the Windsor Protocol on top of the blazing coals first. "An old story, gentlemen, a long time ago."

The Protocol flared, curled into ash. He followed it with the Hitler Order, the bank lists, the Blue Book and finally Paul Friemel's diary.

He turned. "It never happened, gentlemen, not any of it."

Carter stood up and managed a feeble smile. "A wise decision, Prime Minister."

"Having said that, it would appear this business of using the services of the man Dillon worked out, Brigadier?"

"We only reached a successful conclusion because of Dillon's efforts, sir."

The Prime Minister came round the desk to shake hands and smiled. "I'm sure it's an interesting story. You must tell me sometime, Brigadier, but for now, you must excuse me."

By some mystery, the door opened smoothly behind them and the aide appeared to usher them out.

In the hall the porter helped them on with their coats. "A satisfactory conclusion all round, I'd say," Carter remarked.

"You think so, do you?" Ferguson said.

The porter opened the door and at that moment, the aide hurried in from the rear office. "A moment, gentlemen, we've just had a most distressing call from the River Police. They recovered the body of Sir Francis Pamer from the Thames a short time ago. I'm about to inform the Prime Minister."

Carter was struck dumb and Ferguson said, "Very sad. Thank you for letting us know," and he stepped out past the policeman on the step, put up his umbrella and started to walk along Downing Street to Whitehall.

He walked very fast, was almost at the security gates before Carter caught up with him and grabbed his arm. "What was it you said to him, Ferguson, I want to know."

"I gave him all the facts," Ferguson said. "You are aware of the part he played from the beginning in this affair. I reminded him of that. I can only imagine he decided to do the decent thing."

"Very convenient."

"Yes, isn't it." They were on the pavement of Whitehall now. "Do you want to share a cab?"

"Damn you to hell, Ferguson!" Simon Carter told him and walked away.

Ferguson stood there for a moment, rain bouncing from his umbrella, and a black cab swerved into the curb. The driver peered out, a cap down over his eyes and asked in perfect cockney, "You want a cab, guvnor?"

"Thank you." Ferguson climbed in and the cab pulled away.

Dillon removed his cap and smiled at Ferguson in the rearview mirror. "How did it go?"

Ferguson said, "Did you steal this thing?"

"No, it belongs to a good friend of mine."

"London-Irish, no doubt?"

"Of course. Actually it's not registered as a working cab, but as everyone assumes it is, it's great for parking. Now what about the Prime Minister?"

"He put everything on the fire, said it was an old story, was even charitable about Francis Pamer."

"Did you put him straight there?"

"I couldn't see the point."

"And how did Carter take it?"

"Rather badly. Just as we were leaving, the Prime Minister's office received a report from the River Police. They recovered Pamer's body."

"And Carter thinks he did it because of pressure from you?"

"I don't know what he thinks, or care. The only thing I worry about is Carter's competence. He dislikes me so much that it clouded his judgment. For example, he was so taken up with the mention of Sir Joseph Pamer in the

Blue Book on page eighteen that he missed the gentleman on page fifty-one."

"And who would that be?"

"An army sergeant from the First World War, badly wounded on the Somme, no pension, out of work in the twenties and understandably angry with the Establishment, another associate of Sir Oswald Mosley, who entered politics and became General Secretary of a major trade union. He died about ten years ago."

"And who are we talking about?"

"The Prime Minister's uncle on his mother's side."

"Mother of God!" Dillon said. "And you think he knew, the Prime Minister I mean?"

"That I knew? Oh, yes." Ferguson nodded. "But as he said, an old story and the evidence has just gone up in smoke anyway. Which is why I can afford to tell you, Dillon. After all your efforts in this affair I think you're entitled to know."

"Very convenient, I must say," Dillon observed.

"No, the Prime Minister was right, we can't visit the sins of the fathers on the children. Pamer was different. Where are we going, by the way?"

"Your place, I suppose," Dillon said.

Ferguson opened the window a little and let the rain blow in. "I've been thinking, Dillon, my department's under severe pressure at the moment. Besides the usual things we've got the Yugoslavian business and all this Neo-Nazi stuff in Berlin and East Germany. Losing Jack Lane leaves me in rather a hole."

"I see," Dillon said.

Ferguson leaned forward. "Right up your street, the sort of thing I have in mind. Think about it, Dillon."

Dillon swung the wheel, did a U-turn and started back the other way.

Ferguson was flung back in his seat. "What are you doing, for God's sake?"

Dillon smiled in the rearview mirror. "You did mention dinner at the Garrick Club, didn't you?"

If you enjoyed *Thunder Point* . . .

. . . then don't miss . . .

SHEBA

Available in paperback
from Berkley Publishing
in January.

*Here is a sample of this exciting
book of World War II intrigue* . . .

In 24 B.C. the Roman General, Aelius Gallus, tried to conquer Southern Arabia and succeeded only in losing most of his army in the awesome region known as the Empty Quarter, the Rubh Al Khali. Amongst the survivors was a Greek adventurer named Alexias, Centurion in the Tenth Legion, who walked out of the desert carrying with him a secret of the ancient world as astonishing as King Solomon's Mines, a secret that was lost for two thousand years. Until . . .

MARCH 1939

——————◆——————

BERLIN

As rain drifted across Berlin in a great curtain on the final evening of March a black Mercedes limousine moved along Wilhelmstrasse toward the new Reich Chancellery which had only opened in January. Hitler had given them a year to complete the project. His orders had been obeyed with two weeks to spare. Admiral Wilhelm Canaris, Chief of Military Intelligence, the Abwehr, leaned forward and wound down the window so that he could obtain a better view.

He shook his head. "Incredible. Do you realize, Hans, that the frontage on Voss-Strasse alone is a quarter of a mile long?"

The young man who sat next to him was his aide, a Luftwaffe Captain named Hans Miller. He had an Iron Cross Second and First Class and was handsome enough until he turned his head and the dreadful burn scar was visible on his right cheek and there was a walking stick on the floor at his feet, the unfortunate result of his having been shot down by an American volunteer pilot while flying with the German Condor Legion in the Spanish Civil War.

"With all those pillars, Herr Admiral, the marble, it's more like some marvel of the Ancient World."

"Instead of a symbol of the new order?" Canaris shrugged and wound up the window. "Everything passes, Hans, even the Third Reich, although our beloved Führer has given us a thousand years." He took a cigarette from his case and Miller gave him a light, as always slightly alarmed at the mocking tone of the older man's voice.

"As you say, Herr Admiral."

"Yes, it's a bizarre thought, isn't it? One day people could be wandering around what's left of the Chancellery—tourists—just like they inspect the ruins of the Temple of Luxor in Egypt saying, 'I wonder what they were like?' "

Miller was thoroughly uncomfortable now as the Mercedes drove through the gilded gates into a court of honor and moved toward the steps leading up to the massive entrance. "If the Herr Admiral could give me an idea of why we've been called."

"I haven't the slightest notion and it's me he wants to see, not you, Hans. I simply want you on hand if anything unusual turns up."

"Shall I wait in the car?" Miller asked as they pulled up at the bottom of the steps.

"No, you can wait in reception. Much more comfortable and you'll be able to feast on the new art forms of the Third Reich. Vulgar, but sustaining."

The Kriegsmarine Petty Officer who was his driver ran around to open the door. Canaris got out and waited courteously for Miller who had considerably more difficulty. His left leg was false from the knee down, but once on his feet he moved quite well with the aid of his stick, and they went up the steps together.

The S.S. guards were troops of the Leibstandarte Adolf Hitler and wore black dress uniform and full white leather harness. They saluted smartly as Canaris and Miller passed inside. The hall was truly remarkable with mosaic floor, doors seventeen feet high and great eagles carrying swastikas in their claws. A young Hauptsturmführer in dress uniform sat at a gold desk, two orderlies standing behind. He jumped to his feet.

"Herr Admiral. The Führer has asked for you twice."

"My dear Hoffer, I didn't get his summons until half an hour ago," Canaris said. "Not that that will do me any good. This is my aide, Captain Miller. Look after him for me."

"Of course, Herr Admiral." Hoffer nodded to one of the orderlies. "Take the Herr Admiral to the Führer's reception suite."

The orderly set off at a sharp pace and Canaris went after him. Hoffer came around the desk and said to Miller, "Spain?"

"Yes." Miller tapped his false foot. "I could still fly, but they won't let me."

"What a pity," Hoffer said and led him over to the seating area. "You'll miss the big show."

"You think it will come?" Miller asked, easing himself down and taking out his cigarette case.

"Don't you? And by the way, no smoking. Führer's express order."

"Damn!" Miller said, for his pain was constant and cigarettes helped.

"Sorry," Hoffer said sympathetically. "But coffee we do have and it's the best."

He turned, went to his desk and picked up the phone.

When the guard opened the enormous door to Hitler's study, Canaris was surprised at the number of people in the room. There were the three Commanders in Chief, Goering for the Luftwaffe, Brauchitsch for the Army and Raeder for the Kriegsmarine. There was Himmler, von Ribbentrop, generals like Jodl, Keitel and Halder. There was a heavy silence and heads turned as Canaris entered.

"Now that the Admiral has deigned to join us we can begin," Hitler said. "And I will be brief. As you know, the British today gave the Poles an unconditional guarantee of their full support in the event of war."

Goering said, "Will the French follow, my Führer?"

"Undoubtedly," Hitler told him, "but they will do nothing when it comes to the crunch."

"You mean invade Poland?" Halder, who was Chief of Staff at OKW, said. "What about the Russians?"

"They won't interfere. Let us say there are negotiations in hand and leave it at that. So, gentlemen, my will is fixed in this matter. You will prepare Case White, the invasion of Poland on September the first."

There were shocked gasps. "But my Führer, that only gives us six months," Colonel General von Brauchitsch protested.

"Ample time," Hitler told him. "If there are those who disagree, speak now." There was a profound silence. "Good, then get to work gentlemen. You may all leave except for you, Herr Admiral."

They all filed out and Canaris stood there waiting while Hitler looked out of the window at the rain. Finally he turned. "The British and the French will declare war, but they won't do anything. Do you agree?"

"Absolutely," Canaris said.

"We smash Poland, wrap things up in a few weeks. Once it's done what is the point of the British and French continuing? They'll sue for peace."

"And if not?"

Hitler shrugged. "Then I'll have Case Yellow implemented. We'll invade Belgium, Holland, France and drive the English into the sea. They'll come to their senses then. After all, they are not our natural enemies."

"I agree," Canaris said.

"Having said that, it occurs to me that I should demonstrate to our English friends as soon as possible that I *do* mean business."

Canaris cleared his throat. "Exactly what do you have in mind, my Führer?"

Hitler gestured toward the huge map of the world that hung on the far wall. "Come over here, Herr Admiral, and let me show you."

When Canaris returned to the reception hall at the Chancellery an hour later, Hoffer was seated behind his desk with the two orderlies. There was no sign of Miller. The S.S. Captain stood up and came to greet him.

"Herr Admiral."

"My aide?" Canaris asked.

"Hauptman Miller was badly in need of a smoke. He went back to your car."

"My thanks," Canaris said. "I'll find my own way."

He went out of the huge doors and stood at the top of the steps buttoning his greatcoat, looking out at the rain. He went down the steps, having the rear door of the limousine open before his driver realized what was happening, and climbed in beside Miller.

"My office," he called to the driver, then closed the glass partition.

Miller started to stub out his cigarette as they drove away and Canaris sat back. "Never mind. Just give me one of those things. I need it."

Miller got his cigarette case out and offered a light. "Is everything all right, Herr Admiral? I saw them all leave. I was worried."

"The Führer, Hans, gave us his personal order to invade Poland on September the first."

"My God," Miller said. "Case White."

"Exactly. He has been negotiating with the Russians who will do a deal, if you follow me. They'll let us get on with it in return for a slice of eastern Poland."

"And the British?"

"Oh, they'll declare war and I'm sure the French will go along. The Führer, however, is convinced they will do nothing on the Western Front and for once I agree. They'll sit there while we wrap up Poland and his feeling is that once it's an accomplished fact, we can all get around the negotiating table and get back to the status quo. Britain, as he informed us, is not our natural enemy."

"Do you agree, Herr Admiral?"

"He's right enough there, but the British are a stubborn lot, Hans, and Chamberlain is not popular. Since Munich his own people despise him." Canaris stubbed out his cigarette. "If there was a change at the top, Churchill for example." He shrugged. "Who knows?"

"And what would we do?"

"Implement Case Yellow. Invade the Low Countries and France and drive whatever army the British had brought across the channel into the sea."

There was a pause before Miller said, "Could this be done?"

"I think so, Hans, as long as the Americans don't interfere. Under the Führer's inspired leadership we have re-occupied the Rhineland, absorbed Austria and Czechoslovakia plus one or two bits and pieces. I have no doubt we'll win in Poland."

"But afterward, Herr Admiral? The French, the British?"

"Ah, well now we come down to why the Führer kept me back when everyone else left."

"A special project, Herr Admiral?"

"You could say that. He wants us to blow up the Suez Canal on the first of September, the day we invade Poland."

Miller, in the act of snapping his cigarette case open said, "Good God!"

Canaris took the case from him and helped himself. "He got the idea from this Colonel Rommel who commanded the Führer's escort battalion for the occupation of the Sudetenland. He thinks highly of Colonel Rommel, and with reason, and there is a certain mad logic to the idea. I mean, the Suez Canal is the direct link to the British Empire. Cut it, and all shipping to India, the Far East and Australia would have to go by way of Africa and the Cape of Good Hope. The military implications speak for themselves."

"But, Herr Admiral, how on earth would we get men and equipment into the area?"

Canaris shook his head. "No, Hans, you've got it wrong. We're not talking direct military action here, we're talking sabotage. The Führer wants us, the Abwehr, to blow up the Suez Canal on the day we invade Poland. Put the damn thing out of action. Close it down so fully that it would take a year or so to open it again."

"What a coup. It would shock the world," Miller said.

"More to the point, it would shock the British to the core and make them realize we mean business. At least that's the way our beloved Führer sees it." Canaris sighed. "Of course, how the hell we are to accomplish this is another matter, but we'll have to come up with something, at least on paper, and that's where you come in, Hans."

"I see, Herr Admiral."

The limousine pulled in to the curb outside the Abwehr offices at 74–76 Tirpitz Ufer. The Petty Officer hurried around to open the door for Canaris, and Miller scrambled out after him. The young Luftwaffe Officer was frowning slightly.

Canaris said. "Are you all right?"

"Fine, Herr Admiral. It's just that there's something stirring at the back of my mind, something that could suit our purposes."

"Really?" Canaris smiled and led the way up the steps, pausing at the door. "Well that is good news, but sooner rather than later, Hans, remember that," and he led the way inside.

It was perhaps an hour later and Canaris was seated at his desk working his way through a mass of papers, his two favorite dachshunds asleep in their basket in the corner when there was a knock at the door and Miller entered with a file in one hand and a rolled-up map under his arm. He limped forward, leaning on his stick.

"Could I have a word, Herr Admiral, on this Suez Canal venture?"

Canaris sat back. "So soon, Hans?"

"As I said, there was something at the back of my mind and when I got to my office I remembered. A report I received last month from a Professor of Archaeology here at the University, Professor Otto Ritter. He's recently returned from Southern Arabia. Intends to go back there soon. He needs additional funding."

"And what has this to do with us?" Canaris asked.

"As the Herr Admiral knows, all German citizens working abroad have to make a report to us here at Abwehr Headquarters of anything of an unusual nature that they may have come across."

"So?"

"Allow me, Herr Admiral." Miller went across to the map board on the far wall, unrolled the map under his

arm and pinned it in place. It showed Egypt and the Suez
Canal, the whole of Southern Arabia, the Red Sea and the
Gulf of Aden. "As you can see, Herr Admiral, the British
in Aden, the Yemen and then various Arab states along
the Gulf of Aden and the Indian Ocean, Dhofar and the
Oman."

"Well?" Canaris asked, examining the map.

"You will notice Dahrein, a port on the Gulf Coast. This
is where Ritter was working from. It belongs to Spain.
Rather like Goa on the Indian coast. The Spaniards have
been there for four hundred years."

"I can imagine what the place is like," Canaris said.

"North across the border with Saudi Arabia is the Rub'
Al Khali, the Empty Quarter, one of the most awesome
deserts on earth."

"And this is where Ritter was operating?"

"Yes, Herr Admiral."

"But what on earth was he doing?"

"There are remains of many ancient civilizations in the
area, inscriptions and graffiti on the rocks. Ritter is an
expert on ancient languages. He uses a rubber and latex
solution to take impressions which are brought back here
to the University."

"And what has this to do with the Suez Canal, Hans?"

"Bear with me, Herr Admiral. The area around there
called Saba has long been associated with the Queen of
Sheba."

"My God," Canaris said and returned to his desk. "Now
it's the Bible." He took a cigarette from a silver box. "I
always understood that except for the biblical reference
there has never been actual proof that she existed."

"Oh, she does exist, I can assure you," Miller said.
"There was a cult of the Arabian goddess, Asthar, their
equivalent of Venus. In legend, the Queen of Sheba was

high priestess of that cult and built a temple out there in the Empty Quarter."

"In legend," Canaris said.

"Ritter has found the ruins of it, Herr Admiral. Naturally he kept his discovery quiet. Such an event would rival the discovery of Tutankhamen's tomb in the Valley of the Kings. Archaeologists would descend from all over the world. As I said, he returned to Berlin for funding, but made a full description of his find in his report to Abwehr."

Canaris frowned. "But where is this leading?"

"This place is unknown, Herr Admiral, hidden out there in the desert. Used for supplies, an aircraft, it could provide a base for a strike against the canal."

Canaris got up and went to the map. He examined it and turned. "A thousand miles at least from that area to the Suez Canal."

"More like twelve hundred, Herr Admiral, but I'm sure I could find a way."

Canaris smiled. "You usually can, Hans. All right, bring Ritter to see me."

"When, Herr Admiral?"

"Why now, of course, tonight. I intend to sleep in the office anyway."

He returned to his papers and Miller went out.

Professor Otto Ritter was a small, balding man with a wizened face tanned to the shade of old leather by constant exposure to the desert sun. When Miller ushered him into the office to meet Canaris, Ritter smiled nervously, exposing gold-capped teeth.

Canaris said, "That will do, Hans." Miller went out and Canaris lit a cigarette. "So, Professor, a remarkable find. Tell me about it."

Muller stood there like a nervous schoolboy. "I was lucky, Herr Admiral. I've been working in the Shabwa area for some time and one night an old Bedouin staggered into my camp dying of thirst and fever. I nursed him back to life."

"I see."

"They're a strange people. Can't bear to be in debt so he repaid me by telling me where Sheba's temple was."

"Payment indeed. Tell me about it."

"I first saw it as an outcrop of reddish stone, out there in the vastness of the Empty Quarter. The Herr Admiral must understand that there are sand dunes out there that are hundreds of feet high."

"Remarkable."

"As I got closer we entered a gorge. I had two Bedouin with me as guards. We had journeyed by camel. There was a flat plain, very hard-baked, then a gorge, a broad avenue of pillars."

"And the temple? Tell me about that."

Which Ritter did, talking for a good half-hour while Canaris listened intently. Finally the Admiral nodded. "Fascinating. Captain Miller tells me you made an excellent report to Abwehr?"

"I hope I know my duty, Herr Admiral, I'm a party member."

"Indeed," Canaris observed dryly. "Then you will no doubt be pleased to return to this place with suitable funding and do what you are told to do. This is a project the Führer himself is interested in."

Muller drew himself up. "At your orders, Herr Admiral."

"Good." Canaris pressed a button on his desk. "We'll keep you informed."

Miller entered. "Herr Admiral?"

"Wait outside, Professor," Canaris said and waited until Ritter had gone out. "He seems harmless enough, but I still have my doubts, Hans. If you used this place as a base it would require a flight of say twelve hundred miles to the Canal and what real damage could one bomber do? In fact, do we have a plane that could make the flight?"

"I've already had a thought," Miller said, "but I'd like to explore it further before sharing it with you."

Canaris frowned. "Is this serious business, Hans?"

"I believe it could be, Herr Admiral."

"So be it." Canaris nodded. "I don't need to tell you to squeeze Ritter dry, details of this Dahrein place, how the Spanish run it and so on. At least they're on our side which could be useful."

"I'll see to it, sir."

"At your soonest, Hans. A feasibility study. I'll give you three days."